YVGENIE

Also by C.J. Cherryh

RUSALKA
CHERNEVOG

YVGENIE

C. J. CHERRYH

A DEL REY BOOK

BALLANTINE BOOKS · NEW YORK

A Del Rey Book
Published by Ballantine Books

Copyright © 1991 by C. J. Cherryh

All rights reserved under International and Pan-American Copyright Conventions. Published in the United States by Ballantine Books, a division of Random House, Inc., New York, and simultaneously in Canada by Random House of Canada Limited, Toronto.

Cherryh, C. J.
Yvgenie / C.J. Cherryh. — 1st ed.
p.   cm.
"A Del Rey book."
ISBN 0-345-36784-7
I. Title.
PS3553.H358Y9   1991   91-91909
813'.54—dc20   CIP

Manufactured in the United States of America

First Edition: November 1991

10 9 8 7 6 5 4 3 2 1

YVGENIE

1

The white owl flirted a wing past Ilyana's fingertips, a little breath of cold, a flurry of wing beats above the river and a long, sweeping glide back to the shore.

The boy, mist and shadow, waved his arm and sent Owl another course back toward her. She had met the boy when she was small, when first she had wandered alone in the woods, in the days when leshys still visited them. A fey, sad little boy had turned up sitting on an old log, and scowled at her when she came near—but curious, she had felt that from the first moment she had seen him; and a little girl who had no other child to play with had not minded the scowl. She had been very clever in her approach: she had shown him the smooth stones she had found, had let him see the jay's feather and the snakeskin she had picked up beside the stream—how could he resist? He had examined her discoveries, he had said not a word, but he had scowled a little less, and then she had shown him how she made leaf boats, like the real boat her father sailed on the river, except her father's had a great white sail.

The boy had put out his hand to catch her leaf boats. But they sailed right through.

He had come every day for a while. Then he had stopped coming, she had feared forever, and she had been desolate. But he had reappeared the next spring, and every year since, daily at the edge of summer, and fading away as the sun grew warmer.

He never spoke. He could not speak, for all she knew. He would only nod or shake his head to her questions, but they understood each other. And every year he grew older, right along with her.

To this day she had never seen another child, and she never expected to see one but him. She had heard about great Kiev, of course, and farms downriver, and she had heard of Vojvoda, the other side of the woods, where there were other children—but somehow there had always been dangers and there were very good reasons, so her parents assured her, that she should live safe in the woods, never visiting towns and cities. This might be so. She had no way to tell.

But her friend was her secret, her secret of secrets, that she had never told anyone, not even when she was small and foolish. Every springtime she looked for him, and every summer brought regret when he went away.

The springtime they both were twelve, he had brought Owl with him. Owl had looked at her with pale, mad eyes, ruffled up, immediately turned his back, and refused for all that visit to face her except over his shoulder.

It had been three years now—they were both, perhaps, fifteen. Owl still held his distance. Her friend mimed things to her with long, quick fingers: notice of the river, a sign to his face and toward her, a smile and a glance that could steal a heart. Owl glided up to perch as a sullen wisp against a tree trunk, and her friend shrugged, smiled shyly and offered his hand to her instead, touching her skin with the cool, faint sensation of his fingers. Ilyana, his lips said soundlessly, and he glanced down and closed his hand, as if he could no more be sure where her fingers were than she could feel his: that was as close as they could come to touching. She could gaze up into his eyes, this close, but it was still the edge of daylight, and if she did not imagine very, very hard, she could see the trees and the riverside behind them. His hand about hers felt only faintly chill.

He had grown so much taller. And he looked at her with such solemnity—the way she looked at him perhaps, with all the effort it took to see her, and all the bittersweet anticipation of so short a time he could stay. He had Owl; she had Babi and Patches and all, but he always seemed lonelier than she was—being, as she was almost certain, dead.

Perhaps he had died in late spring: perhaps that was why he haunted the woods in this one short season. He might have lived near here once. Or fallen off a boat, in the days when ordinary boats had used to come this high on the river. She was afraid to ask her parents, who were very quick to guess her secrets. She was equally afraid to ask him, although he could answer her questions with nods or shakes of his head: ghosts were often ghosts, so her uncle's tales advised her, because they had never realized that they were dead. In that case a careless word might send him away forever.

So she balanced now between the truth her eyes told her and the imagination of a touch beneath her chin, and his face near hers. Easier to feel that touch if she shut her eyes: and when she did so he dropped a shivery cool kiss on her cheek. That was nice.

On her lips, then. She opened her eyes wide and stepped back, not sure whether that had been a joke or not—to kiss her the way her father kissed her mother.

Not a joke, she thought, by the earnest look on his face. She felt—not shivery—but warm, and shaky in the knees, and short of breath—which might be a spell or a wish. She had no clear thought in her head for a moment, a very dangerous condition, her mother and her uncle would agree.

But her friend had meant no harm, she was sure. She was halfway sure that kiss had been—very sweet, if she had not been so startled.

And now that she thought along that line, perhaps it was only another change with time—like Owl's arrival. Like flowers blooming. Like the changes that had made her more and more aware of spring, and of the foxes' games, and the birds' dances and their seasonal obsession with twigs and straws. She knew what nature was; and she apprehended a very profound change in her thoughts this spring. Like a second birthday, this annual meeting, that she had waited for and waited for and sought by evening shadow, reckoning moon-phases and the rising of summer stars. This year she had plaited blue ribbons in her hair. She had worn—not her best frock for him: she was too secretive and clever for that—but a favorite one, with her own embroidery of lilies, while he appeared this year in much plainer clothing, leaner about the face and broader in the shoulders, as much a young man suddenly as she felt herself becoming a young woman. She apprehended that kiss suddenly as very much what was between her mother and her father—

And she did not think it wrong. She thought, now that she

did think of it, that this year was a very reasonable time he do that—unbearable if, after so many years of growing together, he should never have begun to love her, or if in a spring with all the woods gone giddy and wild, she should have had no feeling for him at all.

Danger, her heart said, and, here friendship could end, here it might go on, but forever changed—and what if he liked it and I didn't? Was it really pleasant, just then?

One wanted to know. One could try again. But where did one go from there?

To where the foxes went? She had no such plans. She had made no wishes one way or the other. She only thought—If I *were* to love, of course it would be him. There's no one else. There never could be.

She backed further away—it seemed safest, under the circumstances.

He held out his hands.

"I don't think we should," she whispered. She honestly had no idea what the next step could be except the one that she *knew* her mother would disapprove. "Why don't we go for a walk? Come up by the stable. Patches has grown so—"

He went on smiling at her and held out one hand, indicating the river shore with the other—no, he did not want to go up near the house; and he might be right: it was a good way to get caught. So she walked with him into the deeper shade, where it was easier to see each other.

Oh, so many details of his face were changed: she stood there only staring at him a breath or two before she felt uneasy and looked away to the water, which was far less an attraction. "Patches has grown, of course," she said, in a voice higher than she intended, and went on to tick off on her fingers the things that had happened since last year. "The fox kit went wild. We had a nest of mice this spring, and mother said if I let them loose near the house she'd wish me lost in the woods."

A chill touch came on her shoulder. She let it rest there, because if she turned around now, they would be facing each other much too closely. She said, "Don't do that. You make me nervous."

He took his hand away. So she did glance back at him, finding him still closer than she thought safe, holding his hand just a little way from touching her, as if to say he wanted to, but he would not if she forbade it.

His face was so much more grown-up—except the eyes, which regarded her with the familiar anxiousness to be understood: he shook his head at her, meaning, she hoped, that he was sorry he had scared her; and he signed to her that he wanted her to walk with him further along the shore.

That seemed far safer than looking into his eyes at this range. So she walked with him, while Owl glided along ahead of them, sometimes so milky white she could see the barring on his wings, sometimes nothing but gossamer in a shaft of evening sun.

They discovered curious branches the river had washed up, they found shells, they found dens of this and that creature that lived on this shore—all these things had used to occupy their walks. But such diversions seemed trivial now. She picked up a water-smoothed shell to show him, but it was an excuse for distraction, a chance to discover whether her hands were shaking.

She said, "You're not wishing me, are you?"

He put a hand on his heart, sank down on his heels and reached out to stir the foam at the water edge with his fingers. Froth moved: that was all the strength he had in the living world. Perhaps that was what he was trying to tell her—that he could not really touch her.

He could never really touch her.

And she did want him—not now, but someday, perhaps this year, perhaps the next or the next, at some time her thoughts and her heart agreed.

She caught some faint impression from him then. Listening to his thoughts was like seeing him by sunlight: the eyes saw and the ears heard so many substantial things it was hard to concentrate on one's imagination. His thoughts were like that: she had heard his as rarely as she had seen him by bright day, and beneath the murmur of the river and the sighing of the reeds and the leaves it seemed she could even hear his voice, saying something about the dark and waiting.

"I can almost hear you," she whispered.

He stood up, face to face with her. His lips moved—she thrust the river sound to the back of her mind and listened for

7

him. She said, ever so quietly herself, "I'm afraid to ask you questions. I might ask a wrong one. If I asked the wrong one mightn't I send you away?"

He shook his head.

"No question can hurt you?"

He touched his heart. He gestured toward her, inviting her to go on.

A thousand questions leaped up. She said, breathlessly, "Is it safe to ask what you are?"

That made him laugh. She thought, Foolish question. Of course. He's a ghost.

She asked, "Is it safe to ask why you come here?"

Another gesture from heart to her, to his eyes.

Flattering, but her father gave answers like that to her mother when he wanted his own way. She made herself coldly sensible like her mother, and asked, "But why here? Why here instead of the woods lately? Do you have anything special to do with this place?"

He reached and touched beneath her chin, said words too faint to hear.

He laid a finger on her lips, then, and a chill came on them and on her heart. She whispered, "So you can't answer everything."

The way he gazed into her eyes made her think about the kiss he had given her, and sent a shiver through her knees. She wished please not, not yet, she was hardly sure about the last one. She thought it had been nice. She just wanted to think a while about the next one.

He went on looking at her. She said, "I don't even know your name."

His lips moved. She heard ". . . your friend, Ilyana,"—which was what she wanted to hear, and all she wanted to hear, until she could get her feelings and her thinking straightened out. She was shaky—not scared, just—shaky all over.

While birds courted like crazy things through the branches of the trees.

He gestured upward. "Look at them," she heard.

She did look, and on the way down from looking up found herself looking straight into his eyes. She thought, But what comes of that is baby birds. And with a ghost?

8

She thought, or he said—she was not sure—

"—I'd never do you harm, Ilyana. I'd die first."

She said, aloud, before she thought, "You *are* dead."

That might have banished him then and there, if it were mere ignorance holding him to the earth. He had made her that reckless, that inconsiderate of her actions. But he said, ever so faintly to her ears: "You're why I come here, so long as I have the strength. I swear to you, I've never broken the rules."

"*What* rules?"

She thought, for no reason, of leshys, tall as trees and very like them. She thought of a ring of thorns, a stone, and golden leaves.

He said, "Don't betray me, Ilyana. Don't tell anyone. And never ask for my heart. I'd so quickly give it to you. Owl's such a hardhearted bird."

"You're a wizard!"

"Oh, yes." His voice came much more strongly now. And she had never been sure of the color of his eyes or his hair, but they seemed dusky now, and a faint flush colored his face against the shadow of the brush. "I was. And you are. Maybe it was your wish all along that brought me. Or mine. I fear I'm no more than a wish—my own, for life; and yours—perhaps for company. And mine again now—for you. Do you understand rusalki? Do you know now?—Please don't run."

It had crossed her mind. So did staying for questions, since it was still her friend gazing so closely into her eyes. "Rusalki are drowned girls—"

"And I'm not." Gentle laughter, a downward glance of still-boyish eyes, a look up again, under her lashes. "Neither drowned nor a girl. Nor particularly angry at my fate. So it can't be sailors that I court, nor travelers in the woods; it's only you, Ilyana. And forgive me—I've borrowed a little of your strength; but only enough to speak to you with my own voice. I won't take more than that, I swear to you."

"Oh, god."

"Please." He caught at her hand to stay her and from that chill touch a tingling ran through her bones. "I'm the one in danger now. I'm the one your thought can banish. I beg you don't. I beg you listen to me."

"God." Everything was tottering, her one friendship in all

her life gone first confusing and threatening, and imminently fatal, if rusalka was truly what he was.

"Nothing spiteful," he answered her thoughts, "nothing selfish—well, perhaps a little. I promise you, I'd never harm you. I'll do anything you want."

"Then tell me what I ask you."

"I have no choice."

"What do you want from me?"

"The things that only you can give."

"Riddles!" It was a danger with magical things, who might be bound to answer in riddles—on all the places where a trap might lurk.

He said, "There was a vodyanoi once, who lived along this stream."

"I know about him. His name is Hwiuur. My parents and my uncle warned me." Worse and worse thoughts: the old snake had never been in his den so long as she had lived. "What's he to do with you?"

"A threat to you. That's one thing. He's come back." His voice grew fainter. "I daren't borrow more from you. I can't stay longer. Believe me, Ilyana—"

"Don't wish at me! I won't believe you if you do things like that!"

"You're growing up, Ilyana. If I've any magic left, I wish it to come in this season, while I'm with you. I don't want you to be alone, Ilyana, and without me, you would be—alone—"

"Alone for what? I'm always alone! I've no *friend* but you!"

His voice was fading. He said, hardly audible, "I can't explain now. Don't fail me . . . tomorrow . . ."

"Ilyana!" faintly came from beyond the trees. Her mother was calling her. The twilight even out on the river was deeper than she had thought—god, it was nearly dark. And her friend mimed that she should go, now.

"Back in the morning!" she said, and ran.

"Ilyana!"

Her mother wanted her home, now, immediately, and when one's mother was a wizard, there could be no question of it— not wise to delay, not now, no thought of why, only obedience: I'm coming, she wanted her mother to know. Yes, mother, quick as I can, mother—

Unfair, unfair to wait all year for these few days—

—and have always to come home at dark, when he's most here—

She reached the safe ground of the ferry landing, beside the boat and cast a look back down the shore. She saw him lift his hand, then, slim figure made of mist, and saw Owl glide to a perch on his fist.

Then they both were gone.

She turned and ran up the path to the hedge, and struggled through the gap into the sunset yard where her house stood, rustic and weathered, across from her uncle Sasha's house on the hill. She pounded up the slanted wooden walk-up to the wide porch, opened the door—carefully: she had learned that lesson most distressfully—and slipped inside.

Her mother had her pale blond braids up under a kerchief, her sleeves rolled up, a stirring-spoon in hand, and a look on her face that said dinner was well toward done and a certain daughter was going to do all the dishes tonight by herself.

"Sorry," Ilyana said in a small voice. "Shall I bring up the dishwater?"

"Bring your father in while you're about it! God! 'Just out to the horses, dear . . .' As good invite the horses in for dinner!" A wave of the spoon. "Out, out, nobody cares when dinner's ready, as well throw everything together in a pot and boil it to mush, no one notices."

"Yes, mother."

"And ring the bell while you're about it! Your uncle's probably given up on dinner by now."

"Yes, mother!" She snatched up the bucket on her way out the door, rang the bell on the porch and ran down the walk-up and around the corner of the house to the rain barrel, within sight of the garden and the bathhouse, and the stable fence. Black Volkhi and spotted Missy and her filly Patches were having their supper, while Babi sat on the gate post, looking like a fat black cat at the moment (though he was not) while her father seemed to be fixing the gate latch.

"Mother wants us," she called out, and her father called back, "She wants her radishes, too, mouseling. Your filly's figured out the gate."

She wished Patches not to think about the gate and her

11

mother's green garden, all too close to the stable. Last week it had been the laundry, drying on the line. And she had had to do it all over again, by herself.

"I've wished her not to," she said in her own defense.

"Wishes don't seem to get between horses and gardens," her father said, and hammered a peg in. "There. That might work a fortnight."

She dipped the bucket into the rain barrel and poured for the washbasin on its stand next the barrel. Her father came and washed his face and arms, and, watching him, she thought (her mind was full of thoughts this evening, tumbling one over the other like foxes) how her friend's hands were slender like that.

"I'll carry it," he said, when he had thrown out the dirty water onto the ground and she had filled the pail to the top again. "Watch out, you'll get mud on your feet. Your mother's floors—"

It was always mother's floors. Even if it was *their* house. She swept her skirts out of the way to watch her boots and the puddles, and matched strides with his long legs as far as the front of the house, panting as she went.

"Where have you been running from?" he asked her, and her heart fairly turned inside out with guilt.

"Oh," she said, hating that feeling, ashamed because he could not really tell if she lied—and yet she chose the lies she told him more carefully than any of the truths she told her mother: "I was walking. My eyes got used to the dark. I had no idea it was so late."

"You weren't down by the river, were you?"

Oh, god, she hated lying to him. "No."

"Your mother worries, you know."

"Mother always worries."

"It's going to be clear tomorrow, weather's holding—why don't we gather up your uncle and go riding tomorrow?"

Babi skipped along at her feet, enthusiastic about riding or about supper, difficult to tell. And she had wanted to go, oh, she would have *died* to go a handful of days ago, but her father had had the garden to do and the stable roof to mend and uncle Sasha had been at his books and *then* it had rained for three days—so *now* her father asked.

She said, miserably, "No. I can't."

"Can't, is it? What appointment have you got that's so pressing?"

"I don't help mother enough." It was lame. It was the only thing she could think of on the spur of the moment. She said, all in a rush, face burning. "I'd better set the table," and rushed ahead of him and around the corner and up to the porch.

Pyetr Kochevikov considered his daughter's departing flurry of pale blue skirts and flying blond braids with a certain impression of having misheard something, somewhere, several days gone: Father, *please* may I take Patches out, *please* may I go riding, *nothing* will happen to us, *please*, father—

Likely nothing would have happened if he had let her go out alone, but the thought of a young rider, even wizardly gifted, on a very scarcely ridden young horse, made him a little anxious about turning her loose on her own, the rider in question being his own flesh and blood—

Himself, Pyetr Ilitch Kochevikov, who had not been reputed for sanity or sense in his youth: he *knew* the things she might do, he had them listed one and each. Eveshka's heritage had not been at fault when they had found Ilyana standing on the bathhouse roof ("So I can see the clouds!") or the time she had ridden Volkhi off into the woods ("I wasn't lost! He was!") or the year she had wanted a horse of her own *so* much that two grown-up wizards' spells had gone awry and old Missy the carter's horse had turned up in foal to high-spirited Volkhi. They had heard nothing else but "When can I ride her?" from the time the filly's feet had hit the ground; and, this being the long-awaited season for that—

I don't help mother enough?

Damn!

Sasha came through the front gate and walked up to him. Sasha peered off in the direction he had been staring, off toward the woods and nowhere, and said, "What were you staring at?"

"Nothing."

"With the bucket?"

He had forgotten he was holding it. He changed hands—the rope was cutting into his fingers—and said, seriously: "Sasha, something's going on with my daughter."

13

"What?"

"I don't know."

"Why do you think that?"

"Well, god, if I knew that, then I'd know, wouldn't I?"

Sometimes Pyetr made outstanding sense. Sometimes he did not. On this occasion, it surely meant that Eveshka's distress had gotten to him—with an upset daughter who was certainly the finish on matters. Pyetr might have known better what to do with a son, Sasha thought, climbing up to the porch at Pyetr's heels: Pyetr had had experience enough in the streets of Vojvoda to keep himself well ahead of any single fifteen-year-old boy, possibly even two of them; and he might have been very solemn and very strict and persuaded Eveshka to give way to his opinions more often with a son; while a daughter seemed the god's own judgment on Pyetr the gambler's son, who had been familiar with more of Vojvoda's bedrooms than (Sasha was sure) Pyetr had ever, ever confessed to him, let alone his wife; and god forbid Pyetr should explain such escapades to his daughter.

Pyetr had a wizard wife, Pyetr had a daughter fifteen-going-on-forever, it still seemed so few years; but those years had set their mark on Pyetr: made him content, true; happier, Pyetr swore, than ever in his misspent life. So where had Pyetr gotten those lines along his brow, that in the right angle of the sunlight, one could just this year begin to notice?

But one did not wish things to be different. A wizard got his wishes, that was exactly the trouble: his wishes came true, many of them not quite in the way the wizard in question intended; and if a young wizard learned nothing else as he grew older, it was that he was lucky to have *gotten* older—past all those youthful years when wishes seemed safer and more possible than they ever would seem again, when a youngster had no second thoughts nor deeper thoughts than I need and I want and I will.

They had brought the girl safely this far. She had done no harm, nor would want harm to living creature, so far as they could see: if anyone threatened Pyetr, perhaps—indeed, perhaps. But Pyetr's safety with a wizard child was what had most worried them; and child she was ceasing to be, most clearly so of late.

"About time," Eveshka said as they came trailing in to a supper already on the table. "There, dear, in the corner." —This to Pyetr, with the bucket. "God, your boots."

"I'll take them off," Pyetr said, leaned on the wall by the door and began to do that.

"No, no, your soup's getting cold, you'll get your hands dirty, god, sit down—"

Sasha sat. It seemed only prudent. Eveshka was constantly moving in the kitchen, busy about things he did not think quite needed urgent attention with supper at hand, although he would confess that the quality of housekeeping in his small cottage could bear a little of that zeal. He had admittedly grown careless, lost in his books: Eveshka accused him frequently on that account. Pyetr said they should go riding and Eveshka said he should tidy up the shelves—but somehow the shelves never did get dusted and Missy grew fat on apples and too much honeyed grain—which, to be sure, Missy deserved: she had seen things quite terrible for a horse, and Missy should have apples and Volkhi's company and the filly's forever and laze in the sun and get fat, for his opinion of priorities in the world—

Get out of those damned books, Pyetr would say. Smell the wind, for the god's sake! And Pyetr would take Volkhi over some jump that made his heart stop, and made him wish—

Wish warmheartedly and with tears in his eyes today for all the world to be right, with Pyetr, with Eveshka, with the daughter who, thank the god, was only half-wizard. He could not tell why such melancholy had afflicted him this afternoon. It came of having a heart, perhaps—which his teacher and late master had said could never be.

He loved them all: they were family to him, who had had not a single relative worth revisiting. Eveshka absolutely insisted he come down from the hill for supper every evening— swearing he would starve, else. The truth, he was well sure, was that she could not bear looking at his kitchen, or eating his cooking, and truth was, too, he had half-forgotten how to cook in the last near score of years, when once he had been quite good at it. His hearth was always out, he absolutely could not hold a fire—

And this house was always warm with light and voices.

"Wonderful," he said, smelling the soup.

Eveshka was pleased. "Wonderful," Pyetr echoed dutifully, and sat down at the table, seeming lost in thinking.

Daughters did that to a man, too, Sasha decided: it was probably a very good thing for him to live as isolate and as peacefully as he did, devoted to his studies and well away from women's business and household work. He had his work with the leshys, which was important, and which took him sometimes afield—less so, lately, true; but he had his books and his studies, which were extremely important, and he had Pyetr and his family right down the hill for the evenings, which, with Eveshka's preoccupation with tidiness battling the chaos a child made in the household, turned out to be just about the right distance.

He settled comfortably at the table, he had his supper set in front of him as the vodka jug rose from the corner and walked across the floor—a sight that would have surely created consternation in The Cockerel's taproom back in Vojvoda—where honest citizens would have sworn the jug was bewitched. It happened that it was. But that was not the cause that moved it: the cause lay in two small manlike paws and two bowed legs, and a Yard-thing who believed he had a perfect right to the kitchen and the vodka. Babi waddled over with the jug, expecting his drink and his supper, in that order, and Sasha obligingly took it, unstopped it and poured for the waiting mouth.

Generously. The evening felt chancy, the day had, the whole month had, come to think of it, and a well-disposed Babi was a potent protection.

It was the season for rains and storms. Maybe that was the feeling in the air lately. Maybe that was why Eveshka felt so constantly on edge, and why Ilyana had seemed that way to him this evening.

But no one mentioned problems at the table, thank the god: it was Pass the bowl, have some bread, don't mind if I do, until Pyetr said: "I think Sasha and I might go for a ride tomorrow."

"It might rain," Eveshka said.

"Have you asked it to?"

"Rains do happen without us."

"Well, then, wish it not. The horses need the stretch."

"People elsewhere might—"

"Want the rain," Pyetr sighed. Pyetr knew that well enough. But something happened, *someone* very close at hand

16

wished, one could feel a sudden small change in Things As They Were. Of wizards at this table there were three—not counting Babi, who was tugging at his trouser-leg, hoping for more vodka.

Pyetr filled his own cup and spilled some for Babi and some for the domovoi who lived in the cellar. There was immediately a happier feeling in the house.

Perhaps after all it had been the domovoi putting in his bid for attention, seldom as the bearish old creature woke. Certainly the timbers creaked and snapped in the way of a House-thing settling back to sleep, and there was none of that groaning that betokened a serious disturbance.

Sasha had another slice of bread—from grain not of their growing: Pyetr traded flour for it downriver, with simples and cures they made and be-wished. From that source they had butter likewise. Honey, the forest bees gave them. Fish they had from the river—Pyetr could not abide hunting, less so the longer they lived here, and he never could; but fish never left their young orphans by one's fireside all winter, to spoil one's appetite for hare or wildfowl—the god knew, they had even had a wounded swan one year, ungrateful creature, which had had a vicious habit of chasing people, even the one who fed it. It had knocked Ilyana down, Ilyana being all of seven, and they had flinched and worried for days about lightning bolts.

It comforted all of them that the swan had survived its indiscretion to fly free that autumn. They had even forgiven the swan—and praised Ilyana's youthful self-restraint, telling her how marvelously wise she was . . . god, he had forgotten all of that.

They had spent so much worry on her, a wizard-child being the handful she could be, and he wondered (but did not, of course, *want* to know) whether Ilyana truly understood their concern. The little girl who had not killed the swan, the little girl who loved her father, truly loved him, would never do Pyetr harm. Perhaps they might have relied on that more than they had and confused the child less—but that was all hindsight.

Maybe it was time now to tell Ilyana more than they had— the rest of the story about her grandfather Uulamets and the raven, about—

But the time for that was not his to choose. He only set it in mind that he should speak to Eveshka and Pyetr about it very soon now. He thought, Pyetr and I understood about living with people, but Eveshka never learned, here in the woods, alone with a demanding, worried father, and a mother—god, best not even think about Draga, not after dark.

—So how can Eveshka help but make mistakes, never having seen a mother with a child? And how can she help but worry?

Not mentioning that Pyetr had had no father to speak of, no father worth speaking of, at least, no one to teach him how to bring up a child—and not speaking of his own parents. A wizard-child's parents were very much in jeopardy. He was an orphan; and he had never told Ilyana that plain fact, either.

Terrible thoughts to share supper with—and surely unwarranted, where Ilyana was concerned. They had seen her refrain from the swan. The danger she posed was not as likely to Pyetr as to anyone who might threaten him—or who she might mistakenly believe threatened him. They were too hard on the girl, he decided that once and for all: the mouseling was coming to that age he remembered well, when all the books and the rules in the world (and he had certainly a good number of them) could not provide all the why-not's to keep wizardry from being a very dangerous thing.

Time, he thought, while Pyetr and Eveshka discussed radishes and the thinning of birch trees, time perhaps that they give the child an idea of the world outside the woods, perhaps take her downriver and show her how farmer-folk lived. Perhaps that would be the appropriate beginning of explanations—showing her those things she could not at this age understand . . . how ordinary folk did not discuss weather-making over turnip soup, or whether the thinning of birches on the river shore should be theirs or the leshys' choice.

He was not sure that he himself could understand ordinary folk, and he had grown up among them and even passed for ordinary in some degree. He knew the ways of the world outside, he knew the thoughts, he had seen most everything a boy could possibly see, working as The Cockerel's stableboy and as scullion in a tavern kitchen. The god only knew, what with Eveshka's shielding the child from this and from that, how much the girl did understand of men and women and their doings.

Certainly more about consequences by now than she had when she had circumvented the wishes of two very canny wizards and given Missy and Volkhi a most unplanned-for offspring. I want a horse! had given way to carrying water and grain for three and not two, and a great deal of mucking-out, especially in winters.

Not mentioning sitting up with Missy one thundery, rainy night, with three grown-ups trying to explain delicately to an anxious twelve-year-old it was not good to wish things to go faster. If a girl had to learn about the world, he supposed that there were worse teachers than old Missy.

High time, certainly, to trust the girl a bit—perhaps even to take her down as far as Anatoly's, maybe even Zmievka, where there were young folk near her own age. Time to risk, even, the chance of young romance: not likely that any lad in Zmievka could catch Ilyana's eye, or pass her father's scrutiny, let alone Eveshka's. But he had to talk to Pyetr about that, too, tomorrow, if he—

"So what have you been up to all day?" Pyetr asked him.

"Oh, reading." Perhaps he had dropped a stitch or two. He thought Pyetr might have asked him something before that.

"So do you *want* to go out tomorrow?"

He most wanted a little more time to his books right now. He had been following a particularly knotty thought the last several days; but he also saw himself getting as stodgy and housebound as master Uulamets had been, and decided that his sudden perception of the mouseling this evening just might be his wizardry forestalling the very problems he had been working on for fifteen years. Perhaps it was really, imminently, absolutely tomorrow, time to say something to Pyetr, and see whether Pyetr could reason with Eveshka about the child.

"Yes," he said, blinking present company into his thoughts. "Yes, that might be a very good idea."

Silly thing to say. Pyetr looked at him curiously across the table and said, "All right."

Eveshka's hair-brushing sent crackles through the air. It was wonderful hair, pale gold, so long she had to catch it up in handfuls to deal with it. Eveshka wished the tangles out of it, Pyetr was sure: he had never seen anyone go so hard at so much hair with so little breakage; but all the same he took the brush from her, picked up a heavy weight of it and applied gentler strokes to the task, at which Eveshka sighed and shut her eyes. She habitually smelled of violets and lavender and herbs from the kitchen. Tonight rosemary and wood smoke figured in, too, which, with the smell of her hair and the face the bronze mirror cast back to him, could make even a sensible long-wedded man forget that he had begun this evening tired and out of sorts. He bent and kissed her on the top of her head, kissed her on the temple, too.

At which she suddenly leapt up and hugged him fiercely, protesting she was sorry she had been so short today, the bread had gone wrong—

"The bread was fine," he said.

"I *wanted* it to be," she said. He understood how she loathed doing that. She used her magic as little as she could—and seldom on trifles. She was far too magical to throw her wishes around on petty problems, even if those were precisely the safest kind of wishes to make: that kind of solution to failures, they were all agreed, set a bad example for their daughter, teaching her too much wizardry and too little ordinary resourcefulness.

Eveshka said, resting her head against him: "When are you going down to Anatoly's?"

"Oh, I don't know, the weather's holding. Maybe—maybe three, four days, why not? Are we ready?"

In other years, she had been quick with an account of things she wanted, a few special things she would hope (but never wished) he might bargain for. In other springtimes the kitchen had been cluttered with little pots of salve and herbs she had put away during the winter, the trading goods they had to offer. But the season had crept up on her, perhaps: there was no sign of the packing baskets and herb-pots yet, and somehow, perhaps for that reason, he had not gotten around to thinking about going downriver either: everything seemed to be running late this year.

"I'll sail whenever you want me to," he said, to please her. "We can hold out on the flour another month, can't we? There's grain left—if you're not ready. Or do you want to come along this year, pack up Ilyana and sail with me? Sasha wouldn't mind. He's been suggesting it for years."

"I'll think about it," she murmured against his shoulder.

"You're not sick or anything?" Wizards never got sick, so far as he knew, never showed their age, never suffered a good many things ordinary folk did; but there were other ailments. There was worry, for one; there was solitude and seriousness and responsibility of a kind ordinary folk seldom thought about—a constant reckoning of consequences which he understood somewhat how to do from the outside of magic, but not—

Not from the inner cautions his wife had constantly to observe, or the fact that she had been dead for a hundred years—and then married a ne'er-do-well scoundrel, who could never quite understand her fears or truly advise her in wizardly crises.

Perhaps he was missing something now. He was not sure. He was not even sure her mood was not something entirely simple, having nothing to do with wizards. He had believed he understood women tolerably well in Vojvoda, at least the sort of women he had had most to do with—bored, rich wives and bored tavern-keepers' daughters who yearned alike after some risk in their lives, some sense of notice from someone. Neither, of course, could possibly explain his wife—whose temper could raise storms and whose good sense could fill a boat's sail with wind or turn a tsar's attention from a very foolish husband.

But whatever else Eveshka was, she was also a wife, and her husband might have been no wiser than certain other foolish husbands whose mistakes had, in his greener days, been all to his advantage.

"No," she sighed. "Not sick. I'm just worried about the weather."

"It's been fine."

"It might turn."

Sometimes with Eveshka one had the most distinct feeling one was not talking about the words one was using.

"Is there something in particular?" he asked her.

"You should go," she said. "You should, yes. Maybe even take that trip you've been talking about."

"Back to Kiev? Are you tired of me, perhaps?"

Silence for a few moments. "Never tired of you, don't be foolish."

"Is something the matter with Ilyana?"

"No."

"You know, none of you are making sense today."

"What, 'none of us?' "

"I asked her to go riding, thought we'd give young Patches a little time on the trail. I've heard nothing else for a month. And now she has to help you in the kitchen tomorrow. Are you two having a fight?"

Eveshka stood back and looked at him, hands on hips. "I didn't say a thing about the kitchen. Did *she* say that?"

"She didn't."

"Did she say anything about my scolding her?"

"Not a thing. Just that she ought to help you more. What's this about trips to Kiev?"

Eveshka frowned and walked away from him, arms folded. The lamplight hazed her in gold, head bowed, back turned, thinking about things he did not understand and she never explained. Ever.

"Well, I'm not going to Kiev," he told her. "I've been there. The tsarevitch is a greedy lout with no sense of humor. Why should I improve him? As good pay a visit to Vojvoda, where I *know* they have a rope ready."

No answer. He waited. He sighed. He went over to the laundry basket in the corner, took off his shirt and tossed it in.

Eveshka turned to him and said, "I don't know that anything is the matter. It's just—"

"It's just that every time there's a difficulty with my daughter, *I'm* packed off to the god knows where. She's fifteen, 'Veshka, she'd never harm a hair of my head, and it's not as if she throws tantrums these days. If there's something going on I don't know about, tell me."

"I dreamed of an owl last night."

Silly thing to say. But not so silly, if one remembered. "It's that time of year," he said. "I think of him, too. That's not so—"

She laid her fingers on her lips, made a little wave of her hand, and an ordinary man knew to stop there, with a wizard on the brink of thoughts she did not want to sleep with.

"Come to bed," he urged her. "There's no damned owl. If it were a swan you'd dreamed of, *then* I'd worry."

He won a laugh from her. "God," she said. "That dreadful creature."

"A narrow escape," he said. "It or me, I swear to you. Thank the god it flew. Ilyana could have attached herself to it."

"There could be worse places for hearts, all the same."

"The world's full of them. Every town's full of them. But she's in no danger of them riding in the woods, 'Veshka, and she's doing very well. Let her be a child this summer. Winter's time enough for lessons. Don't scold her. And don't make her stay in the house tomorrow."

Eveshka's brows drew together. "Don't scold her! Pyetr, I never scolded her."

"You do ask a lot of her."

"With reason!"

"She's a child, 'Veshka. She doesn't think of things in advance. Children don't. Even I remember that. She should enjoy herself, not be thinking of work all the time. Encourage her to go."

"A wizard-child can't grow up like a weed. She can't go through life doing whatever pleases her and only what pleases her. There's *discipline*, Pyetr. That's life and death to her and everyone in her reach. If she's feeling guilty about worrying me today, good! Let her have thoughts like that!"

"The swan lived."

"Not thanks to her doing the first thing that jumps into her head. Ask Sasha how dangerous she can be. Ask him what became of *his* parents."

"Not fair, 'Veshka."

"You're never here when—"

"Not by my choice!"

"I don't enjoy being always the one to tell her no, Pyetr. I know you can't do it—but what I *don't* like is you always being the one to give her the sweets after we've had a discussion. You're always the one with the presents, you're *always* the one who'll give her what she wants, and make me look like a—"

"That's not true, 'Veshka!"

Eveshka walked away from him, arms folded, collecting her composure. He knew to wait in such instances, dammit, no matter his own temper was touched. He said, unable to hold it: "*I'm never here when she needs me, either.* I didn't choose that. You never gave me a choice in it; and maybe it had to be, once, but there's no longer a reason for my sailing off down the river in crises, 'Veshka. She's outgrown any reason there ever was. She's a sweet, well-dispositioned little girl, wizard or not."

She looked at him and retorted, "I wish—"

And stopped herself, turned away with the back of her hand across her mouth.

Restraining herself from what, he had no idea. Nor dared ask right now. And maybe not tomorrow. That was always the problem.

It was a very fine cottage they had built on the hill, snug in snowfalls and springtime melt, safe and solid and at least as straight as the bathhouse roof—none of them were carpenters.

But it could be a very lonely house, at night, Sasha thought, taking the candle to his desk to save lighting another—parsimony his aunt would have approved, but Pyetr would not. Why break your neck in the dark? Pyetr would chide him, Pyetr's approach to most things being both extravagant and eminently practical.

And for all he could figure, he had no idea now whether the advice he meant to give Pyetr was on the mark or not; or whether tomorrow might not be the best day for it. Eveshka was clearly not in the best of moods tonight, for her to have sent out the call she had when the girl was late to supper.

Eveshka feared—feared the good god only knew what, precisely: that Ilyana, who had wizard blood from her and from two grandparents, might turn uncontrollable, *might* attract magic to her that no child could handle.

Possibly. Ilyana's ability was considerable and he had no real understanding himself how to govern her, except love and a great deal of listening—reasoning that if anyone had cared or asked him what his thoughts were when he had been her age, if anyone had ever offered seriously to listen to him before Pyetr had, and to advise him before master Uulamets had, then perhaps a great many things might have been different. Listening before advising the child seemed to him to be the best course.

And wishing tranquility in these woods: that too—they wished very little change, here on their river shore, far from the demands of ordinary folk or the possibility of visitors. They shared the land, they shared suppers, they shared their lives, when wizards as a rule gave up their hearts and lived with lone-liness. Certainly that had been the case with master Uulamets, Eveshka's father, and certainly it would have been the case with them, except for Pyetr—who was at all points the peace in the household, the center of all the friendship and the love they shared, husband, father, and friend—

Somehow he could never make Pyetr understand that, or make him realize how desolate their lives might have been with-out him. Thanks to Pyetr he had more than his books and his house, he had a place to go in the evenings where one could sit by the fire and talk. He had friends and a child to watch grow up, as good as one of his own—he had made Ilyana toys when she was small, he had whittled dolls out of wood and painted them with dyes; and carved a quite remarkable horse, with straw for a mane and yarn for a tail. But she had suddenly grown too old for toy horses, too old for toys, that was precisely the trouble he saw coming: there seemed so much difference between this year and last. The toys languished, though loved, in Ilyana's room, the dyes grew faint—the dolls had had the life hugged out of them years ago and the horse's mane was a disgrace he had offered to mend, but Ilyana would none of that, thank you, Patches was her horse and no one would change him.

Now Patches was a real horse. Soon enough Ilyana might ride the woods with a freedom a wizard-child could enjoy, with no fear of bandits, with the not inconsiderable blessing of the leshys, whose names she knew, one of whom had held her in his vast, twiggy arms when she was an infant—old Misighi had, on his first visit after she was born, smelled her over, regarded her with a vast, moss-green eye, and declared she looked to him like a baby mouse. So mouseling she had become; and their mouseling would go where she would in the world, ultimately— to whatever woodland fastness the leshys held now, or to the edge of fields where ordinary folk lived, or within sight of Kiev— the god knew. Since they could not be with her every step to guide her actions, it was the quality of her choices they had to assure.

Certainly a young wizard would make a few mistakes along the way. The vodka jug was one of his. So were the wishes that had brought Volkhi to them, and Missy; and the god only knew what calamity their flight might have caused in Vojvoda. He still did not know, nor wish to know, exactly what had set them free.

And generally, as tonight as he opened his book and began to write, in a house that had neither domovoi nor dvorovoi, nor any feeling of home—

Generally he did not think at all about Vojvoda, or his family. He most of all of them did not want his life to change—and he had to be careful of that, appended as he was to Pyetr's household.

Odd uncle Sasha. Sasha the maker of toys, for the last child he might ever see. He thought, If I'd stayed in Vojvoda, if I'd married, if it had really ever been a choice to be ordinary—

He wondered what had become of the aunt and uncle who had brought him up. He wondered—

But he sternly forbade himself such thoughts. The god only knew what disasters they could lead to, and as for what had become of his relatives in Vojvoda, who his cousin Mikhail had married, or whether he had a horde of younger cousins by now— it was as good as in the moon, that life, and never that close, any hope of an ordinary family, not for Sasha Misurov. He had the finest any man could dream of, and that should certainly be enough—

Even if the house was dark and lonely at night, and even if it made sounds that had nothing to do with a domovoi, and everything to do with emptiness.

It was so hard not to think—but one dared not, dared not dream or think at all under this roof, with her mother on the other side of the wall. Ilyana lay abed under coverlets her mother had sewn, furiously concentrated on the patterns of the lamplight on the wooden ceiling. God, the nights she had counted the joints, the pegs, the knotholes, and discovered the animal shapes in the wood of this room—while she tried not to listen to the words that strayed out of her parents' bedroom or to wonder what they were arguing about or why her name figured in it.

Most of all she dared not think of the pattern that reminded her of Owl—nor recall her friend waiting on the moonlit river shore.

But it seemed—it seemed something very like his presence

brushed the edges of her mind tonight, so vivid a touch she could imagine him standing at her bedside.

—But that can't happen. He can't come into the house. He daren't come here. It's only my imagination.

A ghost would have to belong here, to get inside, isn't that the rule? And surely he doesn't; and surely the domovoi would never let him in without so much as a sound—

Rusalki can kill you just by wanting to.

So he doesn't need to get into my bedroom if he did mean any harm, and it's stupid to be afraid of him. If he's a ghost he's been one since I first knew him, he's no different than he ever was, and if I don't stop thinking about him right now, mother's going to hear me.

Something still seemed to lurk in the shadows by the wardrobe, and of a sudden—

Babi turned up as a weight on her feet, eyes slitted, chin on manlike paws.

When her heart settled, then she dared sleep.

2

✠ ✠ ✠ ✠ "Get her out of the house," Sasha said to Pyetr as they were riding through the woods, while birds sang like lunatics in the cool dawn. "That's my opinion, whatever Eveshka says. Take her downriver with you. You don't spend enough time with her."

Pyetr thought instantly of crises developing on that trip, weather, meetings with people ashore, some of them ill-mannered or merely fools. "God, Eveshka would never have that."

"Eveshka's far too strict with the girl. Yesterday evening every truant from here to Kiev must have run home to his mother—instantly. Thieves and burglars in all the Russias must have mended their ways. Our mouse had reason to be upset."

An ordinary man could not hear such storms. But he could certainly see and feel their effects in people he loved.

"I've talked with 'Veshka."

"And she said?"

"Owls."

"Owls."

"She dreamed about one. She said an ordinary man—no, that's not fair—" The plain truth was that he did not remember exactly what he had said to 'Veshka or she had said to him last night: when they argued, he tended to forget exactly what he had said and what he had thought to himself; but when a man was arguing with a wizard, saying and thinking were very little different anyway. "It's that season, that's all. One can't help but remember—"

Sasha said: "She's certainly on edge. I can feel it in her."

28

An ordinary man also had to accept that his best friend knew more about his wife than he did, and constantly heard things from her that went past him. "So what can I do about it?"

"Warn her. Advise her. She listens to you."

"What do I know? At least 'Veshka had a father to look to. Mine was no good example. And your uncle Fedya was certainly no substitute."

"Master Uulamets was a lot of things; but he wasn't wise with his daughter—or with his wife."

"How can I advise her? How can I reason with her? I'm just an ordinary man. I don't understand. I can't hear, I can't see."

"Tell me, what would you have done if your father had decided you shouldn't be on the streets, and locked you in The Doe's basement?"

Appalling thought. "I'd have—"

"Of course you would."

First chance he got, up the chimney, or out the door. He would never have abided captivity. Never.

Sasha said, "If Eveshka's worried about her own nature in the girl, think about your own."

What gives you the right? he had asked his father, every time Ilya Kochevikov had made a desultory attempt at reining him in. Where were you when I needed you?

"I really think you ought to take her with you this next trip south," Sasha said. "Maybe to Anatoly's place. There might even be some young lad to think about."

Some young lad. His heart went thump. "God, give her something else to worry about while we're about it! She's got enough to deal with!"

"She's fifteen, Pyetr. She's never seen ordinary folk."

"What for the god's sake do you think I am?"

"You're everything she knows of the world outside this woods, but you're not as ordinary as you think. She needs some sense of other people, a whole variety of people. When she wishes, she needs to have some vision of what and who she might be touching."

"Her mother's never been out of this woods. Her grandfather never—"

"Yes, and it never helped them. It would be very hard for

Eveshka to go, this late. She wouldn't know how to see things. She wouldn't have any patience with the Fedyas and the 'Mitris of the world."

"They'd be cinders."

"Not as readily as you might think. But Eveshka certainly does have a way of finding the dark in the world. And your daughter doesn't, yet. Your daughter just might look past people like 'Mitri and see, for instance, old Ivan Ivanovitch, or some nice young farmer lad."

"She'd have no idea how to deal with boys."

"So tell her."

"Tell her what?"

"Whatever fathers tell their daughters. Tell her what you'd have told yourself when you were that age. Tell her what *you* needed to know."

"God, I wouldn't say that to her!"

"Forgive me." Sasha was distinctly blushing. "But someone should."

"She's still a child!"

"Not in all points. What were you thinking about when you were fifteen?"

"A drunken father. Money. Staying alive."

"And?"

A succession of female faces came to him, some of them nameless so far as he was concerned, one of them three times his age. Riotous living. Being drunk, on the rooftree of The Doe.

"She's a girl!" he said aloud, and then thought that that was all the more reason for worry.

"She's still your daughter."

Sasha knew Ilyana better than he did, too, Pyetr was sure. It was love for him that had made Sasha and Eveshka pack him off to far places whenever Ilyana had had some problem, for his safety, Eveshka had always said, and so had Sasha, whose parents had both burned to death the day his father had beaten a very frightened young wizard once too often. Lightnings might gather (literally) over the cottage. But bolts had never hit the house, and it had been a long time since Ilyana's last real tantrum. Perhaps their magic had won the day, or perhaps Ilyana had just grown old enough to think before she wished.

"My daughter, yes, but, god, Sasha, I can't talk to her about young men—"

"Should 'Veshka?"

"Sasha, I don't know my daughter that well. I've missed so much of her life—sometimes it seems it's all the important parts. You're more her father than I am. *You* talk to her."

"God, no!"

"Sasha, I'd botch it. I'd scare her half to death."

"Don't ever say that. Absolutely she'd listen to you. She tells me how very special her father is."

"Has she got the right fellow?"

"Don't joke. Not about that. You're the sun and the moon to her. She loves you more than anyone alive."

"She has no idea who I am. Or what I was. Or what I did or might have done."

"I think she knows very well what you are. And you should remember one other important thing."

"What, for the god's sake?"

"That I was about her age when I took up with you. *That's* what fifteen is."

It was true, god, it was true, he had let the years creep up on him with no understanding how they added up: he had hardly figured his wife out yet.

But Sasha had indeed set out into the world at about that age—carrying a half-dead fool through the woods, sustaining his life on wishes and a handful of berries; a fifteen-year-old had fought ghosts and wizards for his sake before all was done—not to mention that Eveshka had eluded her father and gotten herself killed, hardly a year older than fifteen: *that* disaster, they had certainly been thinking of—and denying with every wish of their hearts.

"She's growing up," Sasha said. "Whatever we've done hitherto, she's arrived quite naturally now at making choices of her own, choices that we won't always know about—nor should we. The child's due her day. She's smothered her magic so far—we've all encouraged that. But Eveshka smothers hers for more reasons than mothering: she refuses to let it out any longer. She thinks if she says nothing but no, a child is going to choose the same course and renounce magic. Maybe. But I certainly

wouldn't bet on it; besides which, in doing that, she's not showing the child how to be responsible for her wishes—and Ilyana
hasn't had the experience I'd had, nor the experience her mother
had had by her age, either. Let me tell you, you may have missed
a few scary moments, Pyetr, but for the next few years, you may
be the most important influence in her life. She worships you."

"God."

"Don't put on a face like that. I'm very serious. Your
wishes—if you can think of it that way—have as much power
now with the mouseling as mine or Eveshka's will hereafter.
She's had our teaching. She's had every piece of advice from us
she can stand or understand. She's had two very different teachers, in magic. But more and more now our mouse is going to
choose her own way, test her own ideas, put her fingers into the
fire to see if it's hot. Didn't we both?"

That rang true. But he had never stopped at burned fingers.

"She's your daughter," Sasha said. "In that much you already *know* the things she might do."

"God, no wonder Eveshka's worried."

Her friend had not been there in the morning, when it had been
easy to slip away. She had waited and she had waited by the
river shore, and finally given up and walked the long way around,
up the bank and into the woods the long circuit behind uncle's
cottage, all so her mother would not see her coming from the
riverside.

In the afternoon she wrote in her book, in which every wizard, her mother swore, had to keep faithfully all his wishes, all
his reasons, and all the possible things those wishes could touch.

Never lie to the book, her mother had told her: I'll never
read it without your leave. That's a promise, Ilyana.

She did not trust that promise. Her mother might have told
her so, but her mother might just as easily change her mind,
when her mother was so unsettled as she had been lately—and
while she had never caught her mother sneaking a look at her
book, her mother was not that easy to catch. That her mother
seemed to work magic very seldom might only mean that she
very rarely let anyone know she was doing it.

So Ilyana wrote small stupid things in the book, like: I should help mother more; I shouldn't upset her—instead of the thoughts that were really on her mind, such as: What if he's harmful? What if he came and hurt my family? Could I possibly be mistaken about him?

But then she thought—I've known him all my life. Surely I'd have understood by now whether he's good or bad, and he's never hurt anything. If he's a rusalka or anything of the kind, it can't be true that all of them kill things. The leshys haven't been here for years—but uncle sees them. He walks with them in the woods. They would surely have warned us. Babi at least would have objected.

She filled a desultory quarter of a page with dull, dutiful considerations of why her mother had to be strict with her. She thought that that would placate her mother if her mother was secretly reading her book.

Her mother was grinding herbs today, making the medicines for downriver, and when Ilyana finished her notes, she ground and measured and mixed until her arms ached, while her mother lectured her on why one should never use magic for housework, and told her how a wizard had to lead a thoroughly disciplined life. Her mother was very much on discipline, and Ilyana earnestly tried to listen, hoping for something new that would make the other things make sense—or only to hear something in a new way, as her uncle was wont to say, if her growing up were truly getting somewhere of a sudden.

But there was nothing but the same old lecture. Her mother said, for the hundredth time at least, "You don't want to fall into careless habits. Magic can't be a substitute for good work. Or ingenuity. Or caution. You can't want everything perfect. You *make* it perfect. Patience and discipline."

It did not seem to her that her mother's patience was all that long; and as for discipline, it all seemed to be hers in this house.

But she most earnestly tried not to think that.

In the late afternoon her father came riding in with uncle Sasha, and she felt cheated, because being out on the trail all day on Patches would have been ever so much nicer than grinding herbs. And she had not found her friend in the morning—about which she was *not* thinking, so she went back in the house and pounded herbs with a mallet until her mother came inside and complained about the racket.

"Honestly," her mother said, "if you wanted to ride you should have gone riding. Temper is not what I want to see from you. Not under this roof, not elsewhere. God, Ilyana, what ever is the matter with you lately?"

"Nothing," she said. And avoided looking at her mother.

"Ilyana," her mother said, "all your father has to do is love you. And I'm always the one who has to scold you. It's my responsibility. I have to talk to you in ways you understand. I'm trying to do better with you than I had when I was a child. Don't sulk. It's not becoming."

"I'm not sulking."

"I know a sulk, young woman. Don't lie, either."

"Yes, mother." She wanted to pound the board to splinters. But she would never get out of the house today if she did that. "I try." Dammit, she was going to cry. She wanted not to do that, and that helped, and it stopped. "I'm tired. My arms ache."

Her mother came over to her, patted her on the shoulder and said, "Ilyana, listen to me. Be wise. Be sensible. That's all I want you to do."

"Yes, mother."

Her mother sighed and brought a jar for the spice to go in. "Let's clean this up," she said. "Time we started supper. There'll be yesterday's bread. Running a house doesn't happen while you walk in the woods, Ilyana. There's wood to be cut, there's a garden to be weeded, there's bread to be baked—the god knows your uncle Sasha is a dear, but he doesn't *run* a house, he lives in one. He lets the clutter pile up because *he* knows where everything is—but with three of us in this one I assure you we rapidly wouldn't. There's always work, if you're at loose ends. You're getting to be a young woman, and this house being as much yours as ours, I'd think you'd start showing some initiative in taking care of it—dear, *don't* let that get on the floor."

"I'm sorry!"

"You have your father's temper. You sound exactly like him."

"Well, at least my father yells about *things*, he doesn't yell at *people*! I wish you'd—"

"Think what you're doing, dammit! God!"

They were yelling. And her mother was right, she *had* wished at her mother, like a fool.

"I'm sorry," she said. "I'm *sorry*, mother—god, you're driving me crazy!"

"Maybe you'd better listen to advice! And don't swear, young miss! It's dangerous!"

"I listen! I listen! But nobody ever listens to *me*!"

"Just—" Her mother put a hand to her brow and shook her head. "Just go outdoors for a while."

Her mother wanted her quiet, her mother *wanted* her to do as she was told before they got to wishing back and forth at each other, and most of all her mother wanted her to be happier than she had been in her life—surely her mother had not meant her to hear that last. Her mother wanted her out of the kitchen now, this moment, her mother was trying not to think things that scared her—

"Get out!"

Ilyana threw down the towel and fled the house as fast as her feet could carry her, not thinking, no, of anything but getting down the walk-up to the yard—

She stopped against the garden fence and caught her breath.

"Ilyana?" her father called out to her, from the stable.

She did not want to talk to her father right now, she did not want to talk to anyone: she was still trembling from that exchange inside, even if her mother had not wanted it to happen—

Only her mother thought it perfectly all right to wish at her and did not at all like it coming back, the same as her mother would cuff her ears when she had been too little to reason with and wish her No! so strongly she still felt the terror of it.

"Ilyana?" Her father had ducked through the stableyard fence. He was going to ask her what had happened; and hug her and make her safe again, but she had no desire to draw him into the quarrel or start a fight between her parents. —Mustn't wish at your father, no, Ilyana, it's not nice, it's not fair, he doesn't know you're doing it, and he can't wish back, Ilyana—

Her father's arms came around her. Her father said, "What's the matter, mouseling? God, you're shaking."

"I'm all right," she said, "I'm all right. It's just mother."

"What happened?"

It was impossible to talk about it. She waved an ineffectual hand and shook her head. Her father hugged her tighter, smoothed her hair, told her her mother loved her—and that made her heart ache. Probably it was true, only they hurt each other all the time, because her mother wanted her to do everything *she* wanted, and never wanted to listen to anyone else's reasons, refusing to regard anything she had to say as important, or in the least sensible.

"Poor mouseling." Her father lifted her chin and wiped her eyes with his thumb. "I'll talk to her. All right?"

"She thinks I have no sense at all. She thinks I'm lazy. She thinks I don't try."

More tears, which a wish stopped. She did not want to upset her father. Nothing was *his* fault, and he had argued with her mother last night as much as he could. Her mother ran everyone's lives, except uncle Sasha's. Uncle Sasha had had the good sense to move out and build a house up on the hill while she was still a baby.

And when her mother had had enough of her she had used to march her up the hill. Stay with your uncle, her mother would say. See if he puts up with you.

Her mother might make her sweets and show her cooking and teach her the names of flowers: those were the good things. But her mother did not like her off by herself, her mother did not want her doing anything exciting like clambering around on the boat down at the old ferry landing, or imagining she was sailing to Kiev, or doing anything, it seemed, but kitchen work and cleaning and writing in her book.

Which she was *sure* her mother read.

Her father said, "I really think you should have gone with us today. Baby mouse, your mother's not a bad woman. But she's a very serious woman. She takes responsibility for so very much—"

"I wish she'd just have fun sometimes."

"So do I, baby mouse. So do I."

"It's not fair."

"A lot of things happened to your mother, things she wouldn't want for you—things that have made her afraid all her life, and she tries too hard to make sure you're safe from them. You know that Sasha's not really your uncle. . . ."

She nodded. They had told her that. Maybe it was supposed to matter to her, but it never did, it never would. She had no uncle *but* Sasha, nor wanted any, and it made no difference she wanted to think about. Sasha had been a friend of her father's in Vojvoda. That was where her father and Sasha had both come from. But that was all they ever told her.

So what did it matter at all—if her mother never let her out of the house? Certainly she was not going to Vojvoda, ever, so long as her mother had anything to do with it.

Her father put his arm around her shoulders and walked with her along the garden fence, past the old tree that dwarfed the house. "Sasha and I met when he was about your age. He wasn't even sure he was a wizard then—he only suspected he might be, but he'd had no one to teach him, and he spent everything he had being careful. Which he was doing quite well at, for a boy who didn't have a mother or a father to teach him."

That was a lonely thought. "Was he all by himself?"

"Better if he had been. His uncle and aunt were scoundrels, both of them. And your uncle was a very good lad, not to turn them into toads—"

"You can't turn anybody into a toad. You might make them think like a toad."

"Well, he didn't do that either. —And I wouldn't put toads beyond your reach, mouse. You're stronger than you know you are. That's one reason your mother is so set on you holding your temper. She knows if you made a really bad choice she might not be able to stop you. You see what I'm saying? You'd hate to make me a toad by accident, wouldn't you? You'd much rather intend it."

"That's not funny, father."

"—Or remember the night the filly came and you wanted to hurry things?"

She did remember. She still could not comprehend why it would have hurt, but she did know now her wish had been too general and too risky, and her mother had rebuffed it so hard it hurt—haste, she understood: her mother had hugged her fiercely after, and said she was sorry, but she should never wish into situations she did not completely understand.

Which seemed to be the whole world, in her mother's considered opinion.

Nobody was happy with her. She was not happy with herself. She walked with her father's arm about her, kicking at last year's weed stalks, that tugged spitefully at her hem.

Her father said: "I think you should talk to your uncle Sasha. Mind, I don't know a thing about wizardry—but he says, and your grandfather used to say, that there's nothing in the world stronger than a wizard-child's wishes—thank the god, your uncle would say, babies just want to be fed and held. A toy or two. It's not till you start to grow up that your wishes get to involve other people, really to involve them, in ways that mean one of two people getting his own way in things that can break your heart. Then things truly get complicated. Don't they?"

"I just don't know why she won't listen to me."

"Maybe because she's not that much older than you are. Your wants are a lot like hers, and it's harder and harder to argue with you."

Not much more grown than her. That made no sense. "She's a *lot* older than I am. At least fifteen years!"

"Oh, but the difference between where you are and where she is grows less and less every year—a lot of difference when you were a baby, fifteen years ago. But the years grow a young child up faster than they grow any of us old, does that make sense? It doesn't seem yesterday that your uncle was your age. And hardly yesterday again since I was fifteen, doing things I assure you nobody's mother would approve. But I, mouse, I was just an ordinary boy, not a wizard who can leave just a little smoking spot where our house was. Your mother can do that, first thunderstorm that comes along. So can you, if you ever wanted to—you could do it without ever realizing you'd done it, so naturally your mother's a little anxious about tantrums."

The idea was strange. But her father always made her feel safer and wiser, just by being by her—for one thing because he never wished at her, would not, could not, it made no difference: the fact was he did not, and all the world else did. Her father always made sense to her, in ways even uncle Sasha did not, and her mother almost never.

"I can see that," she conceded.

He gave her a hug and a kiss, and they walked as far as the edge of the trees, where the old road had used to go through the woods. He stopped there, set his hands on her shoulders, looked at her very seriously and said,

"Your mother did something very terrible once. She didn't mean to. She never intended what happened. And don't let her know I even told you that much: someday you will know, but for now just take my word for it—it was bad and it went worse and worse before anyone could help her. It's because she's so very strong that she got in trouble. And she loves you very much and she can't explain to you."

"*Why* can't she explain?" What her father was saying offered for the first time in her whole life to make sense of her mother— but he shook his head and said, maddeningly:

"Some mistakes you have to be grown-up to make, or to understand; and you're getting there fast, mouse, but you're not there yet. Just, when you think your mother's holding you or watching you far too closely for your peace of mind, remember that she sees you as so much like her—she was sixteen when this thing happened, understand? And you're fifteen and your mother's dreadfully scared."

It traded mysteries for another mystery. And maybe she could want her father to tell her everything he knew and even make him do it, but it was more than wrong. There were secrets grown-ups kept: that was the rule she had learned, and if a nosy girl got into them she could look to have everyone she loved unhappy with her, maybe forever and ever.

Though some things were awfully hard not to want, when they were almost in her hands.

"Are you wishing me?" her father asked her.

She shook her head, shook it harder, and tried, in the way her uncle had taught her when she was troubled, to think about running water—

But that made her think about the river; and about Owl.

"I'm trying not to," she said, and put her arms about her father's neck and hugged him with all her might. "I love you."

Her father hugged her back, and said, "I love you too, mouse. Be good. All right?"

When her father said that it was easy to be good.

For at least as long as she could keep from thinking.

Pyetr's step echoed on the walk-up. A not at all happy Pyetr, Eveshka supposed, and tried to think simply about the herbs she was grinding and how she was going to try a little more rosemary in the stew this evening.

Pyetr opened the door and took his cap off, came over and put his arms around her and kissed her—which she was sure had everything to do with her daughter storming out of the house.

She said, in advance of complaints, "I know Ilyana's upset. I'm upset. We're both upset."

"Hush," he said, and hugged her and rested his chin against her head. "Hush, 'Veshka, it's all right."

She had not even known she was tired until then. Her shoulders ached. "She's just being difficult."

"She doesn't understand why you worry."

"I wasn't scolding her, I was talking to her. She's in a mood, that's all. There's nothing you can do with her."

"She's just fine, 'Veshka, the storm's over. No lightning. She's just confused why you were fighting."

"I'll tell you why we were fighting! She's so sure she knows everything in the world and of course we couldn't *possibly* understand her, since we don't agree with her! She's the first one in all the world to want her own damned way!"

"Hush."

"I'm not a child, Pyetr, don't coddle me. I *know* what she's going through."

"May I say, 'Veshka, please don't get angry at me—"

"It's not a good time, Pyetr. Today isn't a good time."

"Listen anyway. I trust you. What happened to you when you were sixteen wasn't all your fault. Your father made no few mistakes himself, bringing you up. You couldn't go to him. You couldn't trust him. He made that bed for himself and he regretted it all his life. Don't let him teach Ilyana. Hear me?"

She felt cold all over. And sixteen again. And scared, except for Pyetr's arms keeping her safe. The house timbers groaned: the domovoi in the cellar felt that chill.

"He's gone," she said. "There's nothing left of him, except what he passed to Sasha. Ask him."

"Except his lessons. Except his wishing you. And he did do that, 'Veshka."

"I don't do it with Ilyana!" She pulled away and stood squarely on her feet. "Dammit, Pyetr, I *don't* wish at her and I don't read her my father's lessons—I'm trying to tell her instead of letting her find things out the hard way, the way I did, and she's not listening."

"She wants very much to please you. She doesn't know how."

"Oh, damn, if she doesn't know how! She can try showing up for supper before it's on the table, she can try—"

" 'Veshka. 'Veshka." Pyetr held up his hands and looked upset with her. "Your *father* wanted his house kept, wanted his meals on time, wanted you to say Yes, papa, and Of course, papa, and Anything you *want*, papa. He wanted a damn doll in pretty braids, I saw it. He wanted you right where he could see you, because you looked like your *mother*, 'Veshka, and he was scared to death you were going to turn into her some night before you were grown if he couldn't turn you into his ideal of a young girl!"

"Pyetr, someone has to do the housework, or it doesn't get done, I don't wish the broom to dance around the room or wish the bucket up and down the hill—"

"It's more important to go riding, 'Veshka."

"Oh? 'It's more important to go riding?' And what, when you get home and supper isn't waiting? It's Where's my supper, 'Veshka? Are you sick, 'Veshka? I'm sorry about your *floor*, 'Veshka!"

He bit his lip, ducked his head a little. "I *am* sorry about the floor."

"But *I* mop it. And my *daughter* goes riding in the woods. My *daughter* can't remember to come home at dark, never mind I've done all the cooking—"

"A bargain. I'll mop the floor. You and Ilyana go riding."

"Oh, god, you'd mop the floor. You'd have water—"

"Now!" he said, holding up his finger. "Now, 'Veshka, *there's* a problem we should talk about."

"What problem?"

He threw up his hands, hit his cap on his leg, walked a small circle back again. "Dear wife, let somebody do something *right* for you."

"I'm not having water dripping into my cellar, all over my shelves—"

"Are you calling me a fool?"

"I don't want my shelves soaked in mop-water!"

"Am I a fool? Is Ilyana a fool? Is Sasha? God, I've waited years for this one, 'Veshka! And I *want* you to answer me. No squirming out of it."

"You're not a fool."

"Then will you let me mop the damn floor?"

"If my cellar floods—"

"If *our* cellar floods, dear wife, I'll bail it. I might even fix a rim around the trap so the water doesn't drip straight through. Some things a little carpentry solves better than magic."

Pyetr had not a smidge of magic, none, he swore it. But he certainly had an uncanny way of getting things he wanted out of two or three wizards of her acquaintance, and the wizards in question could wonder for days exactly what had happened to them and why they felt so good afterward.

"Bargain?" he said.

It was very certainly magical. She hugged him tight and felt a tingle from her head to her feet, which she had felt the first time she had laid eyes on him.

Her father was talking to her mother, with what good result Ilyana was dubious; but the air felt clearer, at least, and uncle Sasha had gone up the hill to sit on his porch with his book and his inkpot, so long as the light lasted: she could see him from the garden fence, where the berry vine made part of the hedge— almost ripe, she decided, coincidentally, and plucked an early dark one and popped it into her mouth, for a sweet, single taste.

She felt better, over all: and she put away everything her father had said in a place to consider later, on a day when she had not been so angry at her mother. At least she was not angry now. She did not think her mother was angry at her any longer either, and all in all she felt more cheerful, never mind she had given up the ride she had coaxed her father for since the weather had warmed, no matter she had done it because she had thought her friend might be down by the river this morning.

She pulled another berry which somehow was not as sweet as the first, and thought (she could not help it) that this year had gotten off to a bad start. Nothing she did seemed right. Her friend turned out—

Turned out both handsomer and more scary than she wanted to think about near the house, so she slipped through the garden fence and down the old road toward the woods.

Not directly or by any straight path toward the river, no, not right past the house this time, with mother always worrying about her drowning—

I don't wish to drown, mother! she was wont to declare, in her father's way of speaking. I swear to you, I absolutely wish *not* to drown, and I'm perfectly safe down on the dock, god!

Her mother had not been amused, or convinced.

Her mother, direly: Vodyaniye don't ask you to fall in. They'll come ashore after you.

Well, *I* haven't seen him, she had said to that. And her mother: Wish him asleep. Don't think about him.

All her life, don't think about this, don't think about that—

Now she was afraid to think about her friend, because she knew that a mother who was scared she was going to fall into the river and drown would have a great deal to say about rusalki, and have very definite wishes about the only company besides her parents and her uncle she had ever had or hoped to have— without even asking whether he had ever hurt her, or, the god forbid, listening to her explain she had known him all her life—

He was not a rusalka who was going to drink up her life or do harm to the woods. The leshys would never let anything wicked come into the woods, her parents had said that—though her father had said, once, that the leshys did not see good and bad the same way wizards did, that a nest of baby birds and a little girl were all the same in their sight, and that she should be careful in the deepest woods—where there were wild leshys who had no memory of debts to any of the two-footed kind, and who defended the woods with their ability to deceive and to cast true spells—because they *were* magical.

Which meant they would never let her friend come here if he harmed anything—if ghosts were truly magical creatures, or if wizardly ghosts were, and if the leshys could do anything to prevent him.

That was a question. That was, as her uncle would say, a very good question. She had no idea what the limits of the leshys might be: she remembered them visiting the hillside when she was small—like walking trees in a very faint dream. Her parents said the oldest had once held her in his arms and first called her mouse. Her uncle said they were shy creatures, and shyer as time passed—but she had always trusted in them to keep harm away. She had no idea, now she thought of it, what the limits of a ghost might be against the Forest-things she had believed in so implicitly, or whether rusalka could even describe a young man, who said—

Said (though he had never spoken before) that he had not died by drowning.

She was well along the path to the river shore, in the shivery kind of fear he had begun to make in her, when she thought, Maybe he won't be there this time either. Maybe I broke some rule, finding out what kind of ghost he really is. Ghosts are supposed to follow rules. Maybe he can't come back now. —Or maybe mother wished something to banish him forever. Maybe I'll never see him again!

She hurried along, batting brush aside, through thickets that caught at her skirts, in an afternoon that, in the thick of the woods, seemed much farther along toward twilight than she had realized. There was shadow enough now to see a ghost, with the sun far below the trees, and the shade was deepening by the moment.

The path let out on the river well beyond the old ferry dock, at the place she had last seen him. She took the steep slope with now and again a catch at a leafy branch, right down to the marshy edge of the water, where rushes grew—careful there: she had no desire to come home to supper with wet feet.

She looked up and down the shore, even looked up into the trees, in the thought of spotting Owl, who often came before him.

No more than this morning. She sighed; and felt a little chill down her back.

"Hello," he said.

She turned on her heel and looked directly at his chest—up, quickly, into pale, misty-lashed eyes.

"Where were *you* this morning?" Fright made her entirely too sharp with him.

"Near. Near you last night, too, but you've so many guards." He touched her cheek with icy fingers, and put chill arms around her. "Ilyana."

—

Babi turned up in the kitchen, looking for tidbits in advance of supper. From the yard, Pyetr's saw ripped away at a board for the cellar trap, and from high on the hill, came an impression that Sasha was busy with his book: Eveshka listened no more deeply than that into other people's business, no matter her daughter's opinion.

In the same virtue she did not wonder where her daughter was, late as it was getting. Pyetr was right. There was no cause for alarm and she did not wish to know, or worry, or do any other thing that a rebellious young girl might construe as spying.

But after Babi had had his bits from the kitchen counter, and she said, "Babi, where's Ilyana?"—*then* was time to worry, because Babi dropped his head onto small manlike paws, and made a despairing sound quite unlike Babi.

God, she did *not* like that.

So she went outside and called out to Pyetr over the noise of the saw: "Where's Ilyana?"

Pyetr stopped, straightened with a stretch of his back and wiped his brow. "I don't know. Down by the stable." He looked over his shoulder to see. But there was no Ilyana.

She had a worse and worse feeling. She looked up the hill toward Sasha's house, and saw Sasha get up from a seat on his porch and look—

Toward the river.

She had a dreadful impression then, of danger, of—

"Pyetr!" she cried, and ran down the walk-up, across the yard, through the hedge and headlong down the slope to the ferry dock—

Past the gray, weathered boat, then, with a stitch in her side, off the dry boards of the dock and down the overgrown shoreline, fending her way through reeds and a thin screen of young birches.

Ilyana was standing there, wrapped in mist, two lovers, one mortal, one—

"Ilyana!" Eveshka flung up an arm to ward off the white owl that instantly flew at her. It whisked away, shredding on insubstantial winds.

"Mother!" Ilyana gasped, thank the god she could cry out—while the ghost, the very familiar ghost, turned to face her with a familiar lift of the chin.

Young. Oh, yes, he would be that, here, with Ilyana. She remembered him that way, remembered him in the house, in her father's time.

"You damned dog!" she cried. "Wasn't I enough? Get out of here! Don't you *dare* touch my daughter!"

The whole world swirled and moved, and stopped, ringing with her mother's voice. Ilyana blinked, still dazed, still tingling to a touch unlike anything she had ever felt, a magic so intoxicating that for a moment yet she had no breath in her body.

Her mother screamed, "You sneaking *bastard*, get away from her!"

And her friend said faintly, "Eveshka, listen to me. . . . Please listen."

"Get *out* of here! *Out*, do you hear me? You've no right here! You've no claim on me and none on my daughter, Kavi Chernevog!"

"He wasn't *doing* anything!" Ilyana found breath to say, and ran and caught her mother's arm. The look her mother threw her was cold as ice, a rage that did not belong on her mother's face—

And oh, god, her father was here with the axe in his hand, at the same moment uncle Sasha slid down the bank through the sapling birches, all out of breath, with leaves snarled in his hair.

Her mother seized her arm so hard it bruised, shouting, "Go *away!*" at her friend. "Never come back, never!"

She wished her mother not to say that, and her mother wished at her with a force that made her dizzy.

Her uncle grabbed her and embraced her, and with an angry force she never imagined her gentle uncle had: "Get out of here, Chernevog, go back! You've no right here."

Her friend lifted his wrist and collected Owl, who assembled himself out of misty pieces. He looked at her then with a dreadful sadness and said, so faintly a breeze could have drowned his voice, "Ilyana, don't forget me, don't forget—"

Forget him?

She could not. She never would. Her friend and Owl were fading. Her uncle surrendered her to her father, but she did not want to go to him: he had the axe in one hand. She had never been scared of her father before: he had never carried a weapon in her sight, not the sword that hung among the coats next the door, not so much as a stick the time he had chased the bear out of the yard. Her father caught her face painfully in his hand and made her look him in the eyes. "Are you all right?" he demanded of her. "Ilyana?"

She tried to say she was. She stammered something like that, and tried to protest, "He never hurt me—" but no one was listening to her. Her father let her go and she ran up the shore—

Stopped, then, because her mother *wanted* her to stop, but her uncle said, "She's all right, she's just going to the house. Let her go."

Then she *could* run, up the slope and up through the hole in the hedge and across the yard to the rail of the walk-up before she ever stopped to catch her breath.

There was magic going on behind her. She felt it strangling her, her mother and her uncle were wishing, oh, god, wishing her friend back into his grave—and wishing Owl to the place he had died, somewhere far separate from him.

"Stop it!" she cried. "Stop it, stop it, *stop it!*"

There was silence after that, and a heaviness in the air. It was her they wished at now, wanting her quiet, and wanting her to know—

She wanted *not* to know. She wanted them to leave her alone. She shoved herself away from the rail, walking she had no notion where until she saw the stableyard fence ahead of her, and all the horses standing with their heads up and their nostrils working, staring toward the river.

They were afraid. So was she. Babi was in the yard with them, growling as she ducked through the rails—but not at her: Babi would never hurt her. She came up to her filly, patted a rock-hard shoulder, put her arms about a rigid neck, and Patches tossed her head and snorted, beginning to shiver.

She was shivering, too, now. This yard was the only safe place in the world, the only place she could keep danger out of, the only place with creatures she trusted and hearts she knew were honest.

She did not want to face her parents right now, she did not want to see uncle Sasha with anger on his face, or meet her father's look when he had hurt her: she could still feel the strength of his fingers when he had stared right into her eyes, as if—

As if she had done something horrible and wicked and it would show in her face forever, that she had let her friend kiss her and put his hands on her and make her feel—

So dizzy, so terribly dizzy and cold and warm and magical she wanted to hold on to that feeling. She wanted that moment back, if only to find out what it was. She wished—

—wished he were alive and they could have run away together into the woods so this never would have happened: her mother would not have called his name, her *mother* would not have said:

Wasn't I enough? . . .

She buried her face against Patches' mane and leaned on her solid shoulder, wanting to stay there against that warmth and not to think, but the thought kept coming back.

Wasn't I enough?

He was the mistake mother made, he was what father was talking about—mother knew him. Mother was in love with him, mother was with him before—

Before she met my father.

Eveshka, he had called her mother, in the tone only her father ever used. Sasha had come to this house with her father, and *Sasha* had known her friend on sight.

Worse and worse. Oh, god, all she ever wanted was someone to love and take care of the way her mother had someone, and for a handful of moments she had had that someone, until it turned out everyone in the world knew him, and her own mother had been with him when he was alive.

Now she understood her father being angry, and why he had bruised her face—but, but, god, they need not have sent Owl apart from him: that was somehow the worst thing they could do to him.

She did not cry often, but she cried now, mopping tears with Patches' mane, while Patches made those strange soft sounds that meant there was something going on that Patches did not like. Babi was in a shape that seemed all shoulders and teeth, growling, facing the yard or the river where her parents and Sasha were. She was not sure whether they could feel the anger she felt—

But it was over now; they were coming back up from the river. She looked past Patches' jaw and saw them pass the hedge and cross the yard to the walk-up, *felt* her mother catch sight of her and turn her way with angry intent, but Sasha caught her arm and stopped her. Her father was still carrying the axe when he went behind them up the walk-up, and she had no idea what he was going to do with it inside the house, but Babi went on growling and the horses kept smelling the wind and making nervous sudden shifts.

Looking at the river, she thought. They were definitely looking toward the river, which might mean they had done something down there that the horses and Babi had somehow felt, some truly dreadful magic.

She wanted her mother not to be angry at her, she wanted her father not to be, wanted uncle Sasha—

Her uncle's magic spoke to her heart, then, saying, It's not your fault, mouse. Don't wish at your father. Please. He's really upset, but he's all right, if you just don't wish at him right now.

She tried, oh, god, she tried not to. She did not blame him for being mad, she did not blame her mother, not truly, please.

She felt her uncle's presence like a comforting touch on the shoulder, heard her uncle whisper all the way from the house, Your mother loves you. No one's angry now. Your mother's just awfully upset and trying not to be, if you'll just be calm right now, can you do that, mousekin?

Yes, she promised him the way she had promised for her uncle before, when she was little and had tantrums.

Only this one was not her fault. It was not fair for them to be mad at her, it was not fair for them to have taken Owl away, it was not fair of them to think that what they were thinking had happened between them—

Even if it was true what they had been doing together, and even if it was true that she had felt dizzy and that he could have killed her. But he wouldn't have, she wanted them all to know that. We didn't—he wouldn't—

49

Her uncle said, I believe you, mousekin. He wasn't all bad when he was alive. And what you were doing—

She refused to hear him. Usually she could not shut uncle out. But this time she could. This time she made him shut up and leave her alone, and told him he would have to come after her and talk out loud, the way her father insisted reasonable people ought to do with each other, not wish thoughts into each other's heads or meddle in other people's embarrassment.

Oh, god, mother did *that* with him, too, when he wasn't dead. And father knows it.

The storm inside the house was ebbing. The one outside might be, but Ilyana had built a defense like a wall, and shut herself inside it. "I'd better talk to her," Sasha said, not sure Pyetr and Eveshka even heard him—Eveshka was sitting on the bench in front of the fire, Pyetr holding her hands tightly in his. But Pyetr, with more spare concentration than a wizard could afford, glanced over his shoulder and said, "God, do. She's scared, she's just scared, Sasha, she had no idea."

Whether Pyetr believed that or whether he was saying it to placate Eveshka, the god only knew: Sasha hoped it was the case. And beyond a doubt Pyetr would be out there himself, except he was the only one of them who could reason with Eveshka, the only one Eveshka might listen to, the way she was listening to Pyetr now, trusting Pyetr, trusting *them* to protect her daughter—

Which might be Eveshka's distracted urging to him, for all he knew. If it was, her breach of attention was dangerous, and he was going, now, anything to keep the peace.

So he slipped quickly out the door and soft-footed it down the walk-up and around the corner toward the stable. Ilyana was still standing with her arms about the filly's neck and Ilyana did not wish him to stop. That was a hopeful sign. But he felt—

Felt exposed to a presence at his back, something—

—familiarly dangerous. Babi had bristled up into his most fearsome shape, the horses clearly smelled something disturbing, and of a sudden he knew what it was.

Snake. Vodyanoi.

He spun about to face the river and said aloud, "Hwiuur,

you damnable sneak, go back to sleep! There's nothing here for you. Go away!"

The feeling immediately slid away like a serpent into water.

But another presence slipped up behind him. Ilyana's magic came *around* him. He had felt her tantrums, he had stilled her wild panics, but this was not anger, or fear, or *with* him—it *encompassed* him, it aimed *his* wishes at the danger—

It scared him more than the presence in the river did: he wanted her to know that on no uncertain terms.

She stopped at once, thank the god. He turned, saw her face and felt as if he had slapped her—

"No, mouse," he called out loudly enough for her to hear across the yard. "You're no more mouse—not when you wish like that. But be careful! You don't know everything yet!"

"I know more than I wanted to know!" she shouted, with tears in her voice, and that strength was there again, like a wall excluding him. "My mother was in love with him! Whose daughter *am* I, anyway?"

God. "You're Pyetr's!" he shouted back. "You're most undeniably Pyetr's, I swear to you that's so! Chernevog was in no condition to father a child when *you* began, and there was never any doubt whose you are."

"Could there have been? Why should I believe you? *Everyone's* lied to me!"

"Not so!" He walked as far as the stableyard gate and leaned his arms on the topmost rail, at comfortable speaking distance. "Ilyana, love, maybe we didn't tell you everything, but no one lied to you. We just kept the truth back too long."

"What truth?"

Wary young fish—suspecting a hook in what he offered. He had taught her that caution. They all had. So he used no words. He handed her his heart without warning, prepared for pain.

There was. She seemed confused, and let go the filly's mane and looked him in the eyes, something that was his looking right back at him, defensive and waiting.

She surely realized then what he had done. She had no notion yet what she could do with it, but she knew the moment he thought of it, that she could do him terrible harm, and he wanted her to know, with that, how implicitly he trusted her.

"That's what you should do," he told her, quietly, "before

you ever contemplate certain kinds of magic: put your heart somewhere absolutely safe before you make any sudden decision, mousekin. I have very little feeling now, except my own interest. You have all of that. All I have left is a heartless, self-interested reason for standing here. *I* want you well for my own sake. The part that can think of others—you have at the moment. You know me now, don't you? You know I wouldn't lie to you."

She did. And she wanted his heart back in him, because she was afraid of it—which was enough: it came back with pain, with anger, with a dread of grown-up hearts holding grown-up secrets. And very much of loneliness. That one chord rang through them both, that the loneliness was too long, and too much.

"Oh, mouse," he said, ducked through the rails and caught her in his arms, fever-warm and soggy as the much smaller girl who had cried on his shoulder for far smaller tragedies.

No truth for a while, not until she wanted it. Right now she only wanted both of them not to hurt, which was as kind and as dangerous a wish as a wizard had ever made for him.

"Hush, stop," he said against her ear. "You know you shouldn't wish changes on us. Not hurting can equally well mean dead."

"I wish—"

"Hush! I wish you good things, and life, mousekin, and, yes, it's very hard. I know."

"It's not fair!"

"Maybe it isn't. But the stronger you are, and you're very strong, mousekin, the more it's true. You can hurt someone so easily, with the best and kindest intentions. I've never been as lucky as your mother is, to have found someone like your father is for her—I don't know if there *is* anyone else in the world like him. There can't be many ordinary folk who could put up with us."

"It *hurts*, uncle."

"I know it does. Which is why, mousekin, other wizards give up their hearts—bestow them somewhere they can't be hurt, because caring and power together eventually will hurt you: and most of all corrupt your judgment. You see someone suffering and you want so much to do something about it that you might

52

forget your good sense, and do something harmful to innocent people you simply forgot to include in your idea. It's the rule about rainstorms. There's only so much rain to go around."

"So maybe they're drowning, elsewhere! Maybe watering our garden would help them— You don't know! You can't ever know! So we should never wish anything? Is that it?"

"You don't know the what of things unless you use your head, mouseling, and you don't know the true why of things unless you also use your heart. Try to keep both, even if it hurts right now, even if things seem too hard for you."

"They are!"

"No. No, you're stronger than that. And you'd better be strong today, mouse. It's time for me to tell you some things."

"What, that I'm going to be alone all my life?"

"The way I am? Yes. Possibly you will be. But you don't know what will happen next month, certainly not next year. No one I know can foretell that, and I come as close to doing it as anyone. We're deeply sorry we scared you. We're sorry we didn't warn you—but we never foresaw this, we absolutely didn't foresee it—though maybe we should have. Our wizardry failed us. If it's not our fault, certainly it's not yours."

A series of little breaths, a quiet sob, and she leaned her head against him. "Uncle, I think I love him. I don't even know."

"I know, I know. I wouldn't doubt—he was an extraordinary man."

"Man?" She pushed back against his chest. Tear-wet eyes looked up at him, wide and shocked.

"He's well over a hundred. So's your mother, mousekin. Your father's less than half that. And I'm the youngest, except for you. Your mother died when she was sixteen—"

"My mother's not my *mother*?"

"Oh, 'Veshka's very much your mother, mouse. But she did die. And Chernevog had something to do with that. He killed her."

The mouse opened her mouth and looked suddenly as if she might pass out. Quick as thinking, he grabbed her and made her sit down on the bottom rail of the gate, right where she was, and he knelt in the stableyard dust, pressing her chilled hands in his.

"It might be romantic to say what you're feeling right now

is shock, mousekin, but the fact is, it's also what comes of dealing with rusalki. He's very dangerous. Very attractive. The way Babi guards stableyards and vodyaniye live in water—attraction is a rusalka's nature. And they *feel* very good. —Are you going to faint?"

She made a little gasp, getting her breath, and shook her head bravely.

"That's my girl. You'll be all right." His heart said stop now, stop telling the child what had to hurt her. But cold good sense said keep going as long as he had her whole attention: it might not come again, not in her whole life, or his. "Your mother drowned on that shore. A vodyanoi carried her body to a cave north of here—yes, *that* vodyanoi, the one I chastised a moment ago—stay with me, now, mousekin! Chernevog murdered her and her bones lay in that cave under an old willow's roots a hundred years before your father found them. Do you know why the trees in the yard are the oldest trees about? Why all this woods is, as forests go, quite young? Your mother killed this woods, your mother damned near killed your father—not mentioning a number of innocent people she did kill, men, women, and children: she drew the life right out of them. Ask your mother about rusalki, little mouse. No one knows more than she does about *that* kind of ghost. She *was* one."

She looked at him as if she were sleepwalking, eyes wide, tear-tracks drying on her cheeks. Her hands were like ice, unresponsive to his.

"She's not dead," she said, hardly a sound at all. "My mother's not dead—"

"Your grandfather is. *That* was what it cost to get her back."

Eyes blinked. Like a wince. He *felt* that: it had not been her mother she had been thinking of when she had whispered an instant ago, Not dead. . . . And that: What it cost . . . had killed her last hope. Dead. Dead beyond recovery.

"Yes, he is, mouse. Don't even imagine that kind of exchange. Wizards are hard to kill. We're very hard to kill and by what I've seen, we're very hard to convince we're dead. But I saw him die. There's no doubt of it."

"Can't you let him have Owl back?"

"Mouse, he's *dead*. Owl's *dead*. They have no place in this world. Where they're buried, *if* they're buried, shouldn't matter to them. Owl held his heart once. That kind of creature's as tenacious as any wizard. Like your grandfather and his one-eyed raven. They're gone. Wherever they are, they don't belong here, and if you *are* in love with Kavi Chernevog, then believe this: what he has right now is not life, it's a hell I saw your mother go through. She *loved* your father—and in spite of her absolute best intentions, she would have killed him, she would have killed him just as surely as rain falls and fire burns. If you do love Chernevog and if, god help you both, he loves you—there's only one hope for him, and that's for you yourself to banish him from this earth."

"No!"

"Mouseling, that's not kind to him. That's the most selfish thing you can do. And if he kills you, you understand, you won't be the last he'll get. You listen to me: *listen!* Your grandfather and your grandmother and your mother were all wizards. That *never* should have happened. Your mother is, so to say, *twice-born*: her mother and her father both were wizards; and you're thank the *god* Pyetr's daughter and not mine and not Cherne-vog's, or I don't know what you'd have been, do you understand me? Wizard-blood is far, *far* better diluted: you already have it in too large a measure to handle easily, and we've done every-thing we could to see you grow up without killing your father or calling up something no young wizard would know how to deal with. That's still a danger. You have a very good heart, and hurt as you surely are, if I've taught you anything, you'll hold back what you *can* do about what's happened and think instead about what you *ought* to do. If we haven't taught you that—then we're *all* of us in trouble."

Her hands gave a little twitch in his, but that was all. They remained limp and cold. Finally she looked into his eyes, really looked at him, as if she were searching for something, and said, ever so faintly, "Do you really love me, uncle? Do any of you really love me?"

"With all our hearts, mouseling. No wizard *has* to have a child. No wizard can have one against her will. You were the most terrible risk your mother could take. And we had to get your father away from you, both of us, when your temper made you dangerous. He'd have held you, god, yes, Pyetr's held you while your mother and I just held our breaths. People do love

you. You don't have to want us to. And I doubt you had to want
Kavi Chernevog to, either. Someday when it hurts less I'll tell
you about him."

"Tell me now."

"No, mousekin. There's too much that's dark in that story,
that you don't need to hear today. But there's a lot that's not
dark at all, and I'll tell you both parts when I do."

"I can't wish him away until I know, can I? —Because you're
telling me to do something I'm not sure of; and magic won't
work when I doubt. Will it?"

She had him on that one, fair and hard. But there *was* too
much of that story to tell here, perched on a rail in the stableyard, and with Eveshka as upset as she was.

"First we'd better make sure your mother's all right."

"She didn't have to be so cruel. I don't feel the least bit sorry
for her."

"You don't know what she felt, either—finding him with
you, in that particular place? Part of that was pain, child. Part
of that was remembering; and part of that was the shock of
learning he wasn't as peacefully dead as she thought he was.
Chernevog went through hell in his life. I assure you, he's going
through it now. And your mother more than saw it—she felt it.
It wasn't just her child she wanted to save. It was *him*."

She was listening, she was listening very hard now. The color
was back in her face. Her hands were no longer lifeless. They
were clenched in his.

"Your mother," Sasha told her, "is one of the bravest people
I know, and she has a kinder heart than you could imagine. But
she would never give you her heart the way I just did—not to a
child. And that's true in several senses. She doesn't want you to
know her. She specifically wants you *not* to know her until
you're grown. And even then—she may doubt it's good for you."

"Why?" There was indignation in that question. And pain.

He said, "Because she's afraid you'll think too much about
her mistakes, and maybe, by thinking about them, fall into
them."

"How can I avoid them if no one tells me what they are?
Kavi Chernevog was her big mistake, wasn't he? And she never
told me, no one ever told me except my father, the other day—

and he didn't tell me what that mistake was! How am I to know anything?"

He laid a finger on her forehead. "With that, mouseling. With your own intelligence. There aren't any right answers to certain questions. There are best answers. But if you've left anything unconsidered in what you do, that's the thing that will most surely haunt your sleep at night. Do you understand me?"

Very softly, after a moment of looking into his eyes: "Yes, uncle."

"Good," he said, and stood up and pulled her to her feet. "Good for all of us."

3

The whole house felt charged with lightnings, which called to mind what her father had said about mother and thunderstorms. Ilyana made herself very quiet, coming through the door with uncle Sasha, and found her mother sitting on the bench in front of the hearth, her father sitting on the floor next to her. Her father's worried glance tried to warn her; but she knew. She knew. She kept all but the most shallow, immediate thoughts out of her head, and carefully bent and kissed her mother on the side of the face.

Her mother suddenly reached and caught her skirt. She panicked, then remembered uncle Sasha was there to protect her and made no effort to escape, while her mother hugged her so hard it hurt.

She knew she ought to feel sorry for her mother. She knew she should think about her mother's unhappiness, but she could not, right now. She found only pity enough to do the dutiful thing and put her arms about her mother's shoulders. Her mother's hair still had tiny twigs caught in it, the braids were coming undone; she had lost the kerchief somewhere, and torn her sleeve, and scratched her cheek on some branch, as it looked: she had run down to the bank, her mother actually must have run, when she could hardly remember her mother running in her life—

Which was one of the problems with her mother, dammit, and it did not make her feel any sorrier for her, it made her feel nothing but angrier, if she let herself think about it, and she did not want to do that. She said, quietly, smoothing her mother's hair, wishing her thoughts to herself.

"Mother, I'm upset. I'm thinking about it." Without her intending it, it turned out to be a recitation, word for word her mother's own example to her what to say when things got out of hand; she decided her mother's exact words could hardly upset her, since her mother did not approve the things she thought on her own. She tried not to want her mother to let her go, she tried not to want anything, which with nothing right, was hard. So she just wanted all of them to feel better, instead, and for her father not to be upset. After a moment her mother let her go, took hold of her hands and looked up at her with eyelashes damp and tear trails on her face.

"Ilyana. Child—"

(I'm not, mother, not as much as you think.)

"—I didn't aim at you."

Her mother was holding out for an answer. Ilyana said, as steadily as she could, "Uncle explained that." She thought maybe she could get the breath and the wit to go on and explain things of her own, how long she had known her friend, how he had never hurt her, but she could not get it out in time.

"He's not safe, Ilyana. He's not what you saw."

"I know. Uncle said he was a hundred years old. At least. He said you—"—died, she almost said, but that was not something to talk about with her mother upset as she was. She meant to say: Mother, he grew up with me—

But her mother squeezed her hands till the bones ground together and said, "Ilyana, don't ever call him back. Do you hear me? You *don't* know him. He's not anything you can possibly understand right now."

She thought, You don't think I understand anything. But I do, mother. Things like getting half the truth. And lies.

Like things you shouldn't have done.

Father has to be upset with her. With him. With me. God, what can he think, seeing me with this same man—

Who's not really fifteen years old at all.

Of a sudden she could not bear to face any of them, could not think how to get free of her mother's hold: she just said, "Let me go. Please let me go—" and thought she was going to be sick at her stomach.

Her mother wished not, her *mother* was wanting to know

what she was thinking, and she jerked her hands from her mother's and backed away, hitting the table so it screeched behind her. The whole house creaked, the domovoi complaining.

Her father grabbed her and hugged her so hard she could scarcely breathe. She said, "I'm sorry, papa," the word she had used for him when she was small; and stopped thinking and let him hold her until she was dizzy.

"Pyetr." Uncle's voice. Uncle's touch lighted on her shoulder, and her father let her go. "Pyetr, let me take her up the hill tonight. I think it will be better."

Like a baby, she thought, sent up the hill to stay in uncle's house till her tantrum stopped. She drew herself free and lifted her chin, as grown-up as she knew how to be, "No, no, I don't need to, it's all right. I'm sorry. I'd like my supper. Then I'd like just to be quiet a while."

Her mother touched her shoulder, said, "I'll get your supper. Sit down, dear. Sit down."

She did not know how she could face her father across the table. She winced as her mother wished something, but it was not at her.

Her father smoothed the hair at her temple, and said, in a voice so shaken it hurt to hear, "Mouse, I knew him. We were enemies and we weren't, and you saw him the way he was when your mother met him."

"Every year since—" Now it came out. She caught her breath, thinking, God, I shouldn't have said anything, I don't want to talk about that—

Her mother said, "Ilyana—every year—since when?"

Damn it, she was *eavesdropping*, her mother was probably passing everything to her father and her uncle, every private thought she had.

She wanted not to talk to them. She wanted to faint away and not deal with any of it.

And she did.

"Mouse?" Pyetr asked. She looked so pale, and so sad, and so frighteningly still against the pillows, in the lamplight of her bedroom.

Sasha said, at his side: "Wake up, mousekin. It's all right.

We won't talk about it. Your mother's bringing some supper for you."

She had just become a weight in Pyetr's arms, just gone out of a sudden; and scared him so he was still shaking, scared 'Veshka, too, he understood. Sasha was the calm one, Sasha still was: "Wake up," Sasha said; and without any fuss at all, Ilyana's eyelids fluttered and she began to wake up.

A little confused at being in bed, maybe. "You fainted, mouse-kin. You scared me."

"I'm sorry," she said, hushed, as if breath were still very short. "I'm really sorry, papa."

"Ilyana, it's not your fault. Nothing's your fault. I'm not even mad at Chernevog. I was as close to a friend as he had in the world."

Maybe she did not quite believe that exaggeration. But it confused her. A great many things surely confused her—and confusion might multiply wishes, but it subtracted effectiveness.

"We'll talk about it," he said. "Later. Are you going to be all right?"

"Yes," she said. "Yes. I'm fine."

"A fib, but I'll take it for a promise. *Don't* do that to me again."

"I'm—"

"—sorry. You've been talking to your uncle. Sorry's his word. Don't be sorry: you don't have to apologize to anyone. There's not a thing in the world you've done wrong, except I wish you'd told us a long time ago what was going on."

"Mother would have said don't."

He understood that. Eveshka said 'don't' to anything chancy. He was not in the habit of telling Eveshka when he had decided to risk his neck, either.

Your daughter, Sasha had said.

He said, "I got drunk once, jumped a fence that scared the hell out of me. Risked my horse's neck, not mentioning mine. It didn't scare me at the time, of course. But to this day I have nightmares about that fence coming at me."

"What's that to do with—?"

"Just that's who your papa is. A fool, sometimes. And prone to rush into things. But your papa didn't have anybody worrying about him. He never had anybody who gave a damn whether he survived. Mouse, you do have. Break your neck and you're going to make all of us very unhappy. But not with you. Do you understand what I'm saying?"

Maybe he shocked her, telling her things like that. It was the speech Sasha had talked about this morning, not the one he would give his daughter: the one someone should have given him—if anyone *had* cared whether he lived or died, before Sasha had begun to.

She said, faintly, "I didn't think it was dangerous. I still don't. He never, ever hurt me."

"I believe you," he said, on an uneasy stomach. "I almost believe his intentions. But I don't believe he can hold to them." He remembered Eveshka's touch—then, in those days when it was both dizzying and deadly. He knew the compulsion—on both sides; and thinking of his daughter trapped in it, his daughter locked in an embrace like that— "It's like vodka, mouse. It corrupts your judgment about the next cupful. Or the next wish and the one that patches it. You could die like that and not care. I know what you're not telling me. You don't have to tell me what it feels like. I've *felt* it."

Stop, he heard her say in his head; and Sasha laid a hand on his shoulder.

"Mousekin," Sasha said. "I know. It's all right. Rest. I'll stay here in the front room tonight. I'll be here. I'll bring you your supper in bed. All right?"

"All right," she said. And Sasha got him out the door.

Distress hit him then, like a weight in his chest: Eveshka's heart settled against his and he stood there, unable to move, scarcely able to breathe, the pain was so acute. Eveshka was finishing Ilyana's supper tray. She laid a napkin on it and gave it to Sasha to take into the room, all quite easy, quite calm. He realized that he was in the way: he opened the door for Sasha and shut it after him.

"How is she?" Eveshka's voice asked him; but her heart had already found that answer and the anxiousness smothered, if suffocated him.

"She's doing a lot better," he said, struggling for calm. "Eveshka, listen to me, you've got to give her more rein. A lot more, not less. *Trust* her."

He felt her panic arguing with his—he remembered things a man did not want to remember about his wife: and remembered things about himself, the young fool who had gotten himself skewered by a jealous husband, ensnared by a rusalka and damned near killed by Chernevog—before he had carried Chernevog's heart a while himself: he knew Chernevog, by that, the way he knew his wife, the way he knew Sasha, and all the pieces of their lives came together in him, or refused to go together at all—

He forced them to meet, dammit, one with the other, in his own opinions of what to do: trust Ilyana, he thought; and he thought unawares of Ilyana and Chernevog; and dying, and killing, and a watery cave that figured in their nightmares. He propped himself against the fireside stones, breaking a bit of kindling in his hands, snap, snap, snap, thicker and thicker pieces, until he could not break them any longer, then did break them once more. There was blood on his hands, then.

"God, you fool," Eveshka whispered. Her heart struggled to escape his. She wanted her daughter to herself, she gave no credence to his unwizardly opinions that were blind to the dangers reaching out for them, out of magic, out of that unnameable *place* magic used—

He said, leaning there, sucking a bloody knuckle, "You've made a mistake, wife. You understand me. Beat the horse—and she'll kill you, sooner or later. Don't do it with my daughter."

He was not talking to the heart lodged next to his, he was talking to a wizard, doubly and triply born—who found his daughter a cipher, and hurt his daughter because *she* let her nightmares override her good sense—

"A mistake," he said, "that's still able to be fixed. But not by doing the same thing your father did to you. Don't hedge her about with rules, 'Veshka. Chernevog will be back, I don't know when, but he'll be back: I doubt you drove him that far. This isn't something that's solved and panic won't help."

"The vodyanoi is awake," Eveshka said quietly, turning her back on him. "Sasha drove him off. More than that may have slipped its peg with what happened out there."

Glistening black coils, sleek as oil; cold, and mud, and bones. She was making him remember. He was dizzy for a moment, and the wife who feared anything unplanned came face to face with the boy who had walked The Doe's rooftree drunk, on a dare—that boy and the hard young man who had done it thereafter on bets—for money, because in Vojvoda, you had to have money or you fell further than that . . .

Eveshka did not understand that place. But she knew fighting for what she wanted, and she knew fighting to stay alive.

"What's a rusalka," he asked her, in that one point of understanding, "but a wish so strong it drinks the life out of anything it wants? How close will you hold Ilyana? Or me? If it's *that* again, 'Veshka—then, *dammit*, stay to me. Don't do it to our daughter!"

There was anger in front of him, then, terrible anger inside him. And fear. Her heart wanted free of obligations. It wanted—

But her heart had no magic to fight with. Neither did he.

The anger in front of him did. The anger could do anything it wanted. It would be a fool to do any of those things to a man who had her heart, and they both knew that—but that heart began to go this way and that in panic at the thought of it.

He said, " 'Veshka, is the word 'wrong' so damned difficult? Take it *back*, 'Veshka, I know it hurts, dammit—but I don't like what I'm seeing."

She looked at him coldly. She walked away and picked up a basket from the stack in the corner, and put it on the table.

Packing, then.

"What does that mean?" he asked.

"It means you can do what you like with her. Maybe you can do better."

Her heart was saying something else. It was feeling betrayal and terror and wanting fools it loved to do exactly what it thought safe.

She wanted him to do what she said, wanted not to hurt him any further, and wanted out of here before she killed him—because she was drowning in confusion—

And when she could not breathe, she would grab anything and anyone that could give that next breath to her—she would do it again and again, the way she had done, to live, her way—

He held on, he shut his eyes to shut it out, but the panic was not coming from the outside, it was inside him, a panic that must not get to his daughter—he could not let it get to her—

She said, a living voice, "I'm taking the boat. It's stocked, isn't it?"

He nodded, in the moment's sanity her cold voice made. He left the fireside, managed to reach the kitchen table and sit down, with the sudden thought that there had been no sound from Ilyana or Sasha. Sasha must be taking care of her, Sasha must be trying to get hold of the situation—

He leaned his head on his hands, tasted blood and realized he had bitten his lip. He did it then deliberately, pain to stop him thinking, pain like sunlight to distract a man's eyes from ghosts.

He heard her steps echo in the bedroom and eventually come back again; he heard her pass behind him to the door, getting her cloak. It was not like the first years of their marriage, when she would bolt and run—heart and all. He did not know now if she meant to take her heart back when she left or whether she might leave him like this, because what she was now was safe, and clearheaded, and cared for nothing more than itself. Perhaps she had no choice. Or she found no reason now to suffer with ordinary folk.

She said, the part of her that had no heart: "I'll call for it—when I can."

"Sasha?" he murmured, hoping Sasha could hear him—wondering if Sasha was all right. If Ilyana was. If Eveshka was not about to kill all of them along with her heart, a coldly reasoned self-murder—against the nightmare she had feared all these years—

"No," she said aloud. He heard the door open, felt a gust of cool night air against his left side.

He thought, he could not help himself: Chernevog wasn't worse than this. God, what has she become?

"Too strong," his wife's voice said from the door. "Too powerful to deal with magic."

Pain surpassed pain. He slumped onto his folded arms, wanting her to go, put distance between them; but he heard her walk back, while the whole house groaned in pain, felt her shadow against the wind as she bent over him. Her lips brushed his temple and he began to fall then, a long helpless slide into dark.

He thought she said, while he was spinning and falling: "I have to do this, Pyetr. I have to. Or we'll all of us die."

—

"I don't know what the hell she meant." His hands were still shaking at breakfast, but the heart next his was quiet, thank the god. Thank the god Ilyana was still sleeping—or thank Sasha, he thought, who was responsible for the breakfast and maybe for his sanity. "I'm not even sure she said it. It's what I remember."

Sasha sank slowly onto the other bench and stared at him.

"Have some tea." Pyetr picked up the pot. It was the cracked teacup Sasha had this morning; and the magical patch from Uulamets' time still held. So not everything had fallen apart, though his pouring splashed tea on the tabletop and the pot rattled as he set it down.

"She's on the river somewhere south of here," Sasha said, "she's taken the boat. I think the vodyanoi's gone after her."

"Oh, god, fine! What more?"

"Worry about the vodyanoi. It's even possible she's called it. I can't tell."

"Good god, Sasha—"

"She's very well this morning. She's watching the sun rise, listening to the water—she's improved a great deal since last night."

A memory came back, with a brief shortness of breath. "I was scared to death she had gone at you. I couldn't hear you."

"She told me hold Ilyana asleep and not to interfere." Sasha was a little pale himself this morning, and unshaven as yet—razors did not seem a good idea, considering the amount of tea on the table. "I couldn't, was the plain fact: I had to trust her. If we'd gone at it—"

Sasha did not need to finish. He had *felt* it. He did not want to remember that this morning. Sasha must have hauled him off to bed last night. And had breakfast on the table when he waked.

"Are *you* all right?" he asked Sasha.

"Considering. How are you feeling?"

"Better for the tea and the breakfast. What in hell are we going to do?" *That* question unsettled Eveshka's quiescent presence. He wondered if she had meant last night that she was not going to get better and she was not coming back, and that scared him.

Sasha said, "I don't know, to both questions."

"Don't listen to me like that. She doesn't like it."

"She can be patient under the circumstances." Sasha did something: he felt calmer of a sudden, numb in a certain spot. "She's right, I think, about how long she can keep this up."

"Keep *what* up, for the god's sake?"

"Easy, easy. —Using magic. Using magic is what she can't keep doing, considering her state of mind. I'm terribly afraid something's loose."

"What do you mean, 'loose?' "

"The vodyanoi, maybe, but he's not an instigator. He likes to think he is."

'Veshka's heart struggled to express itself, then calmed again, angry, now.

"She doesn't like that idea," he said.

"I think she knows it, though. The business with Cherne-vog—there are no coincidences in magic. No great ones, at least. Chernevog's condition certainly isn't coincidence. Anything that's ever been associated is always associated."

"What are you saying, he's linked to her? Is—" The heart in him disturbed his own. —Is she fading? he wondered. Is *that* what's going on—that she's going back to—

"—rusalka-form?" Sasha caught up his thought. "I don't think that's it. I certainly hope not. Calm. Easy. We'll solve this."

"I'd like to know how!" He was not sure now whose panic it was. He fought a shiver, bit an already bitten spot on his lip. "Sasha, she's not doing well."

"She's doing very well indeed." Sasha's voice laid calm down like a blanket. "She knows exactly what she's doing and she's asking us to keep the mouse from foolishness. It's what we knew could happen. I just never thought—never thought of Chernevog himself as an unsettled matter. But of course he was. It's the things you don't think about—and there may be a reason you're not thinking about them—that make a way to you. Silences can be the most dangerous spots."

"Something made us forget him? *He* made us forget him?"

"He was very strong; he was very—cheated of his life. His appearance in that place certainly isn't all that unreasonable."

"You think *he's* the cause? Or is something behind him?"

"I'm not sure," Sasha said, and Eveshka's heart shuddered in him, wanting—

"Certainly it's not Eveshka at fault," Sasha added in that same deathly hush. "If anything, this business came at her first—not a hundred years ago: I mean now, maybe with the mouse's birth, maybe in something that happened when she was with her mother."

Another shiver. Yes, he thought. And the shiver came through him, a twitch of his arms. "It might have been."

"She believes in magic as a thing with intent. She believes there's some—power behind the Yard-things and the Forest-things that doesn't like us, or at least, isn't like us. I don't think so, not—truly. I think it's something else, something far less alive, certainly less aware. Maybe she recognized some danger I didn't, maybe she sensed some gap in our defenses I didn't—I don't know. But I do think she's been fighting this back for longer than we know, without consciously knowing she was fighting anything specific, if you want my guess."

"This—what 'this?' "

"This slippage. This sliding into magic. I don't know whether she's fighting the danger or whether she *is* the danger."

Cold silence lay next his heart. He could not tell whether it was agreement: he tried not to think about it. He leaned his chin on his hand and listened to Sasha saying:

"—If she did any one thing wrong, it was sealing herself off alone with the problem and not explaining—if it was actually awareness. If it was going on, I didn't feel it going on. Or I didn't feel *what* was going on. But maybe Ilyana did: she used to have a bad habit of eavesdropping; I suppose all children must, before they understand it's wrong—but if the mouse got too close to her mother, I understand now why 'Veshka would have shut her out. Ilyana wouldn't. Ilyana wouldn't have any way to understand it: Ilyana started fighting her, and Ilyana still doesn't understand. That's our greatest danger. Our mouseling's been hurt, very badly hurt, and she's so young—"

Fear and hurt. Pyetr studiously found the teacup of overwhelming interest, picked it up and took a sip. The tea was cold. "What you're saying is that 'Veshka's the chink in our armor."

"In many senses, yes. 'Veshka's standoffishness from her

daughter—she sees it as protective, holding questions off till the mouse is old enough. I feel she's not chosen the best way—but 'Veshka—Honestly, 'Veshka can't feel at ease with the child; can't let go. Perhaps it's a limit she's decided for herself; but if it is—it's still real; and *I* can't answer the mouse's questions, not the deep ones that 'Veshka's rebuffs have created. I can say it—but the hurt's still there. Which may mean it's all on you. You're the one point—the one person in this world who can possibly hold all our hearts."

He shuddered, so badly his hand overset the cup and banged into the plate. He got a breath, rescued the cup before it reached the edge. "I'm sorry. I'm not doing so well this morning."

"You're doing very well. Steady. In one sense you already hold them. There's not one of us would see you come to harm. In that sense you're the most protected man in all the Russias. In another you know very well that you're another vulnerable point."

"A fool with a sword—"

"At close range, before any of us could protect you, yes— some fool with a sword could put it in our hearts. Literally."

"He'd truly be a fool. I don't think I'd want to see what would happen to him."

Sasha moved back from the table, sudden scrape of wood on wood. He said: "Abandon that thought. Please."

Sasha was not one to panic. Equally frightening, the rise of panic he felt inside.

"Nice weather," he said, with a break in his voice. It was often good to discuss the weather, when wizards were upset. "Looks like the sun's shining."

"The sun's in danger," Sasha said.

God, craziness. It was enough to make his skin crawl.

Sasha said, "That's better." A deep breath. "I think we'd better wake Ilyana."

"I'm not so sure. I'm not so sure you're doing that well, friend. And what in hell's going on with my wife?"

"She's wished—" Sasha stopped for another breath, and there was such fear in Sasha's expression his heart went cold. "She's left me to make the decision with Ilyana. She says I'm the only one—and *she's* the unstable point—I don't know how she knows that. —Eveshka, dammit—"

She was gone. She wanted him to know in parting—he heard her speaking clear as clear—

I love you, Pyetr. I can't come home till things are changed.

Come to me if there's no other hope. But Sasha will be gone then, and your life and your soul will be in danger.

Most of all, don't rely on Ilyana. Don't. You don't imagine what she can do to you.

Warn Sasha—

What? he wanted to ask her. Warn Sasha of *what*?

But her heart had left him by then.

Waking up was like any morning at first, with the birds under the eaves, and all, but that was only for a breath or two.

Then Ilyana realized that something was weighing down her bed on one side and she remembered—

Her father was sitting on the edge of her bed. Her father looked tired and sad, and he brushed her hair away from her face and asked:

"How are you, Ilyana?"

He almost never called her name unless she was in trouble; no one did, except her mother; but she was in trouble with her mother so often she could never tell what her mother meant.

She was certainly in trouble with her mother now. Mother and father had had a terrible fight, so bad uncle had had to hold her—

She did not even remember going to sleep. But her father was all right this morning. That was the important thing. She was glad he was all right.

She could not tell about her mother. Her mother was being very quiet this morning. That probably meant she was mad.

And her friend was gone. Her mother had banished him. Maybe forever.

A tear rolled down her face, just spilt, without her even thinking about it.

Damn.

She wanted not to cry. That stopped the tears, but it did not cure the feeling that lay cold as a stone in the middle of her chest.

"Ilyana?"

"Mother's mad, isn't she? I'm sorry."

"I'm glad you're sorry, mouse." He touched her under her chin. "Fact is—I want you to be very calm now and don't wish anything—"

That always meant something terrible. She wanted him to say it—fast and plain.

"Your mother's left, mouse. She's gone out on the river."

"There's a vodyanoi!"

"I know it. She knows it. But the greater danger's here."

"Me." Things were her fault, they were always her fault, dammit!

"Mouse, I want you to think as kindly toward her as you can. And be very honest with me—*please* be honest. Do you promise?"

"I didn't *do* anything!"

Her father patted her hand. "It's all right."

"What are you saying, that *I* made her leave?" Her father was mad at her. Her father was treating her the way her mother did when no one cared what was right, her father had his opinion, and that was her mother's doing, dammit, no telling what her mother had told him except it was Ilyana's fault, everything was always Ilyana's fault—her mother arranged it that way.

Another tear spilled, plop, down her cheek.

"Don't cry," her father wished her. But *her* wishing had to stop it. He gathered her up, covers and all, and held her and rocked her, while she laid her head on his shoulder dry-eyed and thought how she wanted—

No. She mustn't think bad thoughts. Mustn't want people hurt.

Even her mother, for trying to take her father away from her for good, and for pulling a tantrum and making him blame her, when it was all her mother's fault.

Her mother never wanted anybody to like her, her mother never, ever wanted her to have anybody, and if she had not fought back and if it were not for uncle Sasha, her mother would have made her father mad at her forever and driven him away. As it was, she was just miserable, and upset, and she wanted—

—wanted her friend back.

Mouse, her uncle reprimanded her. *No!*

Uncle Sasha believed she was wrong. Everyone did. All the time.

Even when she loved them. Her mother took everything she ever wanted away from her and nobody was ever on her side. She had no idea why her mother wanted her to be alone or why everyone thought she was a fool or why they always protected her mother.

Her uncle said, inside her head, Mousekin, don't think like that. Absolutely we're listening to you. But you have been wrong a couple of times in your life. Haven't you?

She had to admit yes, but she still refused to believe it this time. She told her uncle: I've been seeing my friend every spring, every spring since I was little. And he's never hurt me. I don't know why he would now.

She embarrassed her uncle. She caught something about her being grown-up now and grown-up girls being an entirely different question with a rusalka.

If men can be rusalki: that thought came through the confusion, too. Her uncle was not entirely sure that was possible.

So maybe *you're* wrong about what he is. So there, uncle. Who's not listening, now?

That was impertinent, her mother would say. That would get her sent to her room if her mother were here. Which her mother was not, this morning. And she was already *in* her room, with her father stroking her hair and saying:

"Dear mouse, don't give me trouble, please don't give me trouble today. Your mother's gone away so you'll have some rest and quiet. And we'll talk about it, if you like—"

If I don't like, too . . .

"But mostly, right now, mouse, I just want you to dry your eyes and come have breakfast and let's not worry about it."

He can only come here a few days more. And then it's another year. And I can't even talk to him—

Not wise, her uncle said.

Leave me alone! she wished him.

Bu she did not completely mean that. She really did not completely mean that.

"Breakfast?" her father asked.

She nodded against his shoulder. And wished her uncle not to be mad at her, which he was kind enough to tolerate.

"I'll make breakfast," Sasha insisted; and Pyetr decided to help—

Cleverly, he thought, because Ilyana needed something to take her mind off the situation—and two men trying to find essentials in her mother's carefully arranged shelves had her up off the bench in short order, had her protecting her mother's things; and perhaps, a devious man could surmise, beginning to want her mother back when it came to overdone cakes for breakfast, because two men who very well understood campfire cooking were not going to put off breakfast-making on a child who had not been well, no, absolutely not. They could make breakfast, they had done it before.

And of course they would clean up.

Babi sulked about the cakes. Babi still had extras and got tipsy on vodka. And the batter spilled across the hearth would *eventually* clean away, even though it had cooked on, between the stones, where no mop could reach it.

The domovoi complained, too, about the smoke.

And Ilyana sat at table with her chin on her hands and watched, back and forth, back and forth like a cat.

"You're trying to make me want her back," Ilyana said.

"It wouldn't be nice to spy on your father," Pyetr said.

She said, chin on fist now, frowning, "I didn't." And winced and shut her eyes as pottery clattered. "Uncle—"

"It didn't break," Sasha said.

"Mother's going to blame me. She always does."

"Nothing's broken," Pyetr said. "And your mother won't blame you. I take all responsibility. Why don't you run down to the stable and bridle up the horses?"

"I don't want to ride."

"No? What do you want to do today?"

"I don't know."

"Well, why don't we ride until you do?"

"I think I'd better write some things down."

"That might be a good idea," Sasha said.

"I don't think so," Pyetr said. "God, she's had enough of

magic. She's a *child*, for the god's sake. That's what's wrong: too much taking care of. She should skin a knee or something a little less damned *dire*, can't she?"

"Don't fight," Ilyana said; a wish; even he heard it. Ilyana had her lips clamped as if something else was going to escape.

"We're not fighting. Your uncle and I used to discuss things before—" He almost said, Before I married your mother. Which was true. He said instead, "We're friends. It doesn't mean you don't like somebody if you yell."

"I know," she said, with exactly her mother's frown.

It was not fair to Eveshka, either. He remembered the pain. He remembered—

She said, sullenly, "I'll go riding if you want."

"I'm not going to make you do anything, mouse. That's the point, isn't it? Your mother's just very fragile. Maybe she always will be. But she doesn't want you to grow up like her. She wants you—"

'Wants' was not a good word. He knew that after all these years, dammit, he knew better.

The mouse bit her lip. "I don't know what she wants. It changes. All the time."

"What would *you* like to do? That's the point. Go do it."

"You wouldn't like what I'd do."

He saw that expression in the mirror when he was shaving. On a bad day. He tilted his head and gave her one that matched it.

"Mouse, if you're a fool, I'm going to be very upset. There's a vodyanoi to consider now, in your slipping about the woods with secrets—he *doesn't* stay to the water. And let me tell you something about Chernevog."

"I don't want to hear!"

That stung. And he forgot what he was going to say.

Sasha said, "She's distressed, she didn't intend that."

"What about him?" the mouse asked, very quietly. And it came back to him what he had been going to say—that a man Chernevog's age had no business with a fifteen-year-old girl.

But he did not think, on second thought, and she would understand that.

Instead he said, "If you should see him—tell him *I'll* talk to him. Alone."

She looked upset with that idea, and not only, perhaps, for fear of what he might say to Chernevog in that exchange. Maybe she was thinking about the danger he could be in—knowing what Chernevog was. That was what he hoped she would see, at least.

She said, cautiously, "What would you say to him?"

"I'd ask him what he wants. I owe him my life, mouse. But I don't owe him yours. And I'd *pay* mine to keep you safe."

Something wizardous went on—so strong he felt his skin crawl.

She said, "Don't talk like that!"

"It's every bit true, mouse."

She jumped up from the bench and ran for her room. In a moment, through the open door, he saw her sit down on her bed with her book in her lap.

Not sun. Books.

He shook his head.

Sasha said quietly, "You scared her. That's good. She's thinking—very noisily right now. I can't avoid hearing."

"Don't tell me. I don't want to deal with her that way."

"She's making wishes to protect the house, she's making wishes for all of us to be wise—even her mother. Winding them around like yarn. That's the way she's thinking of it. Don't push her to do anything, even to enjoy herself. That's the real point, isn't it? Let her think."

The mouse came out with inkstains on her fingers and reddened eyes. Tears as well as ink on that page, Sasha thought, and put his own pen away and folded his book. She had done all that crying without disturbing the house—in any sense. No small feat.

"A very good mouse," he said. "I didn't even hear you."

"Where's my father?"

"Trimming horses' feet. Or weeding the garden. One or the other."

The mouse came very quietly and sat down opposite him at the kitchen table. "Uncle, what made me so mad was—nobody even asked if he'd done anything wrong. Nobody *ever* asks my opinion."

"You mean no one asked you this time. 'Ever' is quite a large word."

"It feels like 'ever.' "

"I'm distracting you. Yes. We were upset. I'll tell you, Chernevog was a very strong wizard. And one could suppose he's old enough to know better than what he's doing: we didn't have to explain to him why we were upset—he knew that when he came here. But I do agree with you: you weren't consulted. It had to scare you; it certainly scared me—I knew Chernevog. If he'd wanted a fight, it could have been bad down there—very bad."

She had not tried to say anything. He left a silence for her to think about that. Finally she said:

"I think I'll go help my father. Is Babi with him?"

"Last I saw."

She started for the door, turned around again with a lift of her chin. "Have you been talking to my mother?"

He shook his head. "No. But she's all right, I'm sure."

"There's a vodyanoi out there. She should be careful."

"She can handle the old Snake. No question."

A very good sign, he thought, watching her go out the door. And the inevitable afterthought, considering the blond braids and that outline against the sun: God, she looks like her mother.

Old Snake had not a chance if he crossed Eveshka right now, no more than Kavi Chernevog had had when, clinging to a scrap of life, he had drifted toward the only friends he had had in the world. And found Ilyana.

No. Not Chernevog as he had died. The boy who loved Owl had found Ilyana; and Ilyana had found someone to play with. And to love.

God help both of them, he thought, sick at heart.

But that was not the worst thing about the affair. The worst thing, the thing that haunted Eveshka and that haunted him and Pyetr, too, so far as Pyetr's understanding went—was that fifteen years ago they had patched something very wrong in the world; things once associated were always associated—and if there was a way for it to get back into the world it was through Kavi Chernevog or it was through Eveshka—

Or, likeliest of all, Ilyana. .

It proved one thing, that they had not been safe all these

years: things had begun going wrong very naturally, very quietly, from the very time they had left that place upriver, where Chernevog had died.

Baby mouse, Misighi had called her, lichenous, patch-hided old Misighi, no little crazed from the death of the previous forest. They had been so relieved when Misighi had found no harm in Ilyana as an infant, when he had cradled her in his gnarled arms, smelled her over and said, in that rumbling voice of his— new growth.

But after that, Misighi had not come to the house. A few leshys had. A very few. And he had asked why, in his wanderings in the woods—asked Wiun, for one, who was a little mad himself.

Wiun had said—A new wind, young wizard. A new wind will come.

And more and more rarely they would be there, leaving their backward tracks on the riverside. Sometimes the orphans of some storm would turn up near his porch, or on it, sometimes a nest of birds—a young squirrel.

But none lately. None last winter. The woods had a lonelier, crueler feeling this spring.

He had written it in his book, and worried about it, and worried that perhaps Pyetr's going to Kiev had been a mistake, coming home again with, perhaps, too much of the outside clinging about him—too much of tsars and tsarevitches and the noise of marketplaces and the smell of smoke. Pyetr declared he would not go to Kiev again: and suddenly that statement seemed ominous—as if all along their suppositions had been wrong, their fears misplaced: Pyetr could never have been in danger from Ilyana among the leshys. They would have kept him safe from harm—by means a man might not like; but he would have been safe.

Instead they had sent him south—and the leshys had ceased to visit them. They had made a choice of some kind, without knowing they were choosing.

God. Why didn't we see it? Why did we ever think of it as waiting? Everything was going on around us. Misighi, Misighi, do you hear me, old friend?

Where did the years go? We thought it was your time being

so long—but we're the one's who've slept too long. Come back and see the mouse now, Misighi. She's grown so. And she's not wicked, she never was. You knew that when you held her.

But what's in Chernevog's heart? What does he want, but life he can't have again, Misighi? Have you known about him, all this time, and not said?

All those times we met through the years—and you never once mentioned him? Or couldn't you? Or couldn't I once have suspected he wouldn't die?

At least there was a sort of peace in the day—even if her filly managed to figure out the gate again, and got into her mother's garden. Ilyana even found herself laughing—and laughing and laughing with tears in her eyes as Patches raced around and around the yard with a carrot-stem in her mouth, while her uncle and her father and Babi chased after her. Uncle could have wished Patches back into the stableyard, she could have done it herself except she was laughing so hard, but uncle and father and Babi were all enjoying themselves, certainly Patches was, and meanwhile Missy escaped out the gate that uncle was trying to get Patches into and trotted straight for the garden.

She could not chase horses anymore. She was laughing so hard she was bent double, and finally, as they were about to get Patches in, her father yelled at her to get the gate. She managed to do that, then sat down on the bottom rail, holding the gate shut with her arm, and gasped and wiped her eyes, thinking that somehow something had just broken loose inside, and it might have been pain and it might have been laughter. Maybe it was both, because it could not be funny enough to make her stomach hurt.

Her father and Sasha were both out of breath from laughing and running and the Missy-chase was going slower and slower, until Missy was just trotting around the yard ahead of them.

Her father finally waved at Sasha, saying, between gasps, "For the god's sake, wish her *in*."

Missy arrived, Ilyana got up and opened the gate and shut it behind her, and leaned on it.

Her father tousled her bangs. All three of them leaned panting on the gate.

Her father gasped, "God, why don't we go riding now?"

And that set them all off again.

She had never laughed so much in her life. She felt better. And feeling better after what had happened felt like betraying her friend—but she could at least feel guilty now, instead of scared and mad. She did not, truly *did* not want to die. She wanted the rest of her life, now, because it seemed there were things to learn—

Like finding out her father and her uncle could laugh like that. It was wonderful and it was scary—completely beyond uncle's power to stop it, and beyond hers, which she had always understood was terribly dangerous for wizards—

But it *was* funny, dammit, and surely laughing like that could never be wrong.

That was what the house felt like without her mother. She saw for the first time in her life what her mother's presence did, and what her mother's shape was in the house—a sad and frightening shape, that right now had no house to be in tonight.

She asked her uncle, while they were smoothing horse tracks out of her mother's garden, "Is my mother really all right?"

"Why should you think not, mouse?"

"Can you tell her something from me?"

"All right."

"Tell her I'm not mad at her anymore. I don't want her to come back yet. And I can't talk to her right now. But tell her I—" Want her to be happy? Was that bad to wish? "Tell her—no, ask her . . . if she wouldn't please want herself to be happier."

Her uncle looked at her as if that surprised him, but not that much. "That's very kind of you, mouse."

"I wish—god, I can't *stop* myself today!"

"That's all right. You're old enough to let loose a few wishes—you're old enough to use your father's axe, too, if you'll get him to teach you how."

Her uncle meant that wishes were like that axe, a very dangerous thing to use badly. She thought about her mother and said, "I think my mother is so scared. What of?"

"There's a thing, mouse—I'm not even sure it's a thing: maybe it's just the place magic comes from—that she dealt with once, in a way she shouldn't have. She still knows how to reach

79

into that place. If she ever loses her good sense, she might get scared enough to do that; and if she did—she could become what your grandmother was. That's enough to give anyone nightmares. Your mother killed people. I think she could forget that— if she didn't know she could do it again and that she could *want* to do it again."

"She can want *not* to do it again!"

"Oh, she does. She does. But she can't believe it. The fact is, mouse, once you've used that kind of magic, it starts using you. It's like drinking too much vodka. Only you don't get silly. You get dangerous. I'll tell you something—I've done it. I've done it very briefly, and in a very minor way, and *I* got away from it as fast as I could. Your mother—"

People always stopped in the middle of important things. She wanted the rest of it, she *needed* the rest of it now, dammit!

"I'll tell you, mouse, I couldn't tell you when you were small, because little children are very apt to try exactly what you tell them not to: they're curious, they test things, and they don't understand that consequences are real. But this is the most important Don't there is in the world: Don't ever use any magic but your own. Don't borrow; absolutely don't borrow magic. For one thing, it makes you drunk and it spoils your judgment. For another thing, the creatures that will offer it to you are all harmful. Every one of them. The good ones, like Babi, won't let you. Babi would show you his teeth if you even thought about it. Does that tell you something, or doesn't it?"

She nodded, sobered.

Her uncle said, leaning on his hoe, "All the ones that will lend their magic seem connected to something—in that place Babi goes to when he isn't here. Maybe there's more than one place. But whatever it is, it's not like here. And if you go borrowing magic—it's like pulling on a little string that turns out to be tied to a snake, but the snake's got his head in deep water, and he's holding on to something else, something that's pulling back very strongly, do you understand me? That's what it feels like."

A little shiver went over her skin. Her uncle went on:

"A rusalka's not quite that. A rusalka borrows life: the same kind of mistake: it only happens to kill people. But a wizard wishes nothing outside of nature; while a sorcerer when he uses magic borrows something I can't even put a name to, maybe something alive: your mother thinks it is. I'm less sure of that, but I do believe it's at least self-interested; and as far as any of us understand, it doesn't seem to have any law or limits the sorcerer doesn't give it. Pretty soon he can't remember what he's changed and he's not thinking how things are connected—he can fix things, right? Pretty soon it's making the decisions, or the total of his wishes are—and he's not. That's a feeling you don't ever want to have, mouse, not ever in your life. Once you've gone over that brink every choice you make to stop yourself is an uphill climb. Every fear you have and every knotty problem you face, it's so easy to remember the quick solution and to forget the mess it got you into. You lose your wisdom. You lose your sense. Thank the god I could step back again to safe ground. Your mother went so deep in that it's very easy for her to slip back: your mother fights on that slanting ground all alone, for the rest of her life. No other wizard can get into her heart and help her. I've tried."

"She's hurting my father!"

"Your father loves her without her wanting him to, and in spite of everything, it's his decision. Yes, she hurts him. And she knows it. She even tried to send him to Kiev, so he'd forget about her. Foolish thought. He got himself in trouble. He nearly got himself hanged—your father can be a very reckless man when he's at loose ends, and the plain fact was, he didn't care about his own safety when he was apart from your mother and you. He was desperately unhappy, he got into a dice game with some people, and he drank too much. And I'll tell you the rest of it when you're old enough not to wish the tsarevitch to break out in hives, or worse. Your mother did enough to him."

Her parents had dimensions she had had no idea of. They had done things she had no conception of. There had been a whole world going on she had not seen while she was growing up. Of course she remembered the year her father had gone to Kiev. But she had thought that was because she had had a really awful tantrum and her mother had just told him to go further away than usual.

It was the time she had decided once for all she had better grow up and stop having tantrums, because she had figured out that every time she had one her mother sent her father away.

And she hated him being gone. Uncle was better company than mother was, but she wanted—

God, she had never figured out how much she had been wanting her father back—after her mother and uncle wished him out—exactly the kind of wickedness she had been about to accuse her mother of doing. She wanted her uncle to know she had just figured that out, and that she was truly, truly embarrassed.

"Children do that sort of thing," her uncle said. "Grown-ups have to think very carefully what their wants do to other people. You're very definitely growing up, mouse. Some people never do get that grown-up."

—But I've got to think what else I've been wanting from people—

—like for my parents to love me and my mother to stop yelling at me. But my mother and my uncle can wish me to mind my own business. Wishing at my father . . . that's really unfair.

Her uncle said, "The test for whether it's right to want something of someone, mouse, is not whether you think it won't hurt them, and not even whether you think it's for their own good—but whether you'd want them wishing it about you. You figured that out very well a moment ago. But don't worry about wanting your parents to love you or your father to stay— although I do think you ought to watch that, and remember that it's a lot better to let go and trust someone you love to do the right thing on his own."

That was what she had been trying to say. Her uncle found it for her. She said, "My mother doesn't trust me. She won't let me out of her sight. And I'm not a baby anymore."

"Your mother had almost learned to trust herself when you came along. And knowing you were magical, and loving you and your father, both, she's grown more and more afraid of a little girl she might have wanted—at some time—far too much and at far too great a risk to things as they were. You were a change, a really major change, the sort every wizard's afraid of. Once she had your father and once she had you, she wasn't on her own anymore. She couldn't assure herself you could take care of yourself the way your father can—because of course a child can't. And that's precisely where you can help your mother: she's been looking out for you through some very scary years—and now she has to learn to trust your judgment."

"Should I wish her that?"

"Wish, yes—and *do*, mouse. Doing is of equal importance. What, besides your friend, upset your mother when she saw you on the river shore?"

"I don't know." A lecture was coming. Her uncle could be so kind talking to her; and then he could frown and scold her. She hated this part.

"You weren't supposed to be down by the river. Personally, I don't think it's a reasonable prohibition—but she made it; and you'd slipped down there in secret, and you were doing something your mother didn't know about. Maybe she *had* told herself she could trust you, and what she saw shook her so badly—"

"I *don't* think I was doing anything wrong!"

"That's because you're making choices for yourself, a lot of which don't go wrong, and in your own best judgment, you didn't think this one would. You're not a baby who'll fall off the porch anymore and I don't honestly fault you for making a decision. Nor even for making the decision not to tell us. It may, for one thing, have been *his* wanting you not to tell—"

She had not even suspected that. God!

"—But really, outside of the danger he is to you, the hurt he's dealt your mother is very real and very serious. He didn't tell you all the truth about your mother, and about what he did. Possibly he remembers only up to a point—possibly he has his own interests. She is your mother, and your father loves her, and I think you can figure out from here what you ought to do. Can't you, mouse?"

"That's a dirty trick, uncle. No, I don't know what to do!"

"It certainly is. And I don't either, except that you've figured out now that getting your mother to trust your judgment is a very important point, because hers in his case is very complicated—but I'm not going to wish you into it. You don't become grown-up at midday on your birthday. It's not a day, it's a progression of days, and it never quite stops—*I'm* still growing up. Your mother is. So's your father. But there is, step by step, a point that your mother should trust your judgment on grownup matters, the same way she watched you and gradually decided you wouldn't fall off the porch if she let you play there on your own."

"She had to let me try, didn't she?"

"And hasn't she? And can't she make mistakes? You're in grown-up things now, mouse. In whatever way you reckon him, Chernevog is an encounter far more dangerous than falling off the porch—and you weren't where you were supposed to be. You scared your mother out of her good sense—and she slipped. Do you understand that?"

It made a kind of sense. She was not sure she agreed about being wrong. She was not sure her uncle had even said she was wrong.

But if she tried to explain that to her mother, her mother would start wishing at her and she would forget all her own good sense and wish at her right back.

She was not sure whose fault that would be, but it was certainly what would happen; and she decidedly did not want that.

So it was better to fix her mother's bean rows, since she could not fix things with her mother. She *might* go down to the river this evening to see if her friend was back, maybe with her uncle knowing about it and giving her permission—

But her friend might not come then. He might believe she had turned against him if she did not come back or if she told her uncle. And in spite of everything her uncle said, her friend—Kavi—would be reasonable, if only she could find him and talk to him quietly without people getting upset and without her uncle or her mother wishing at him.

If her friend was Kavi Chernevog (and he had not, confronted, denied it) then he was not fifteen years old. And if he was who they thought—and if he had done all these nameless dreadful things and killed her mother—still, her mother was alive; and Kavi had not been a thoroughly bad person: she did not get that impression, not even from her father, who had been as upset with him as she had ever seen her father upset with anyone—her father had called himself the only friend Kavi had ever had . . . and would her father be a friend to anyone wicked? No. Absolutely not.

So Kavi was not absolutely wicked. Nor quite a murderer, nor quite hateful to her mother—something had happened, maybe before she was born: and her mother was concerned for *him*, her uncle had said that, too, what time she was not being scared of him for what he was.

Her mother had been dead. God! Did uncle truly mean that?

But Kavi was. She had known that for years—and it had never seemed entirely unreasonable that he was a ghost.

So there were grown-up secrets around him, tangled as grown-up secrets could be—but they looked not half so formidable or so forbidden as they had yesterday. Her uncle had talked with her as if she were grown-up. And if everybody could just be reasonable, her friend, whoever he was, might even hold some of the answers to what had happened to her mother, that her uncle and her father had no clue to. He might even help her mother, maybe talk to her, and show her he meant no harm, so her mother could stop being afraid and stop being so crazy about things. God, if she could just see him again—if she could just—

If she could just—

Her hoe beheaded a bean plant. Her mother would have a fit.

Uncle had always said that wishes could lie around doing nothing for years and then rise up and get you. Little things going wrong could be a sign of them. Wishes could last and last, even when you were dead, like that patch on the one old teacup, that uncle said her grandfather must have done; and if Kavi had been at their house before, if Kavi had known all of them when he was alive—then there very well could be a lot of old wishes hanging around and causing trouble for him and all of them.

Uncle said old wishes could make smart people forget things, or do little things that were not smart or stupid in themselves, but that just added up and pushed bigger things in a general direction—

You could never wish anything against nature, that was the first rule. You could wish a stone to fly, but it would not, as her uncle would say, do that of its own nature; an improbable wish just added to the general list of unlikely wishes always hanging about in the world waiting to happen when the conditions were right. And there must be a lot of them in the world, because other wizards had to be children once, and make stupid wishes—

So, one day maybe years later, along would come a whirlwind; or somebody to pick up that stone and throw it. Or a passing horse might kick it. And it would fly. But a storm or a person or a horse would have had to go out of the ordinary way to do that, which might cause something else and something else forever, to the end of the kingdoms of all the tsars in the world.

A lot of wizards had grown up around this house, it turned out, and terrible things had happened here, that could make even a grown wizard wish without thinking. Wishes attached to objects, wishes on the gates, the yard, her own room—

All the things uncle had told her began to come together of a sudden, and assume shapes that made her—on the one hand—feel better, because maybe there *was* an explanation for her mother acting the way she had: maybe her mother was not after all so awful as she seemed. Being killed could certainly make one anxious about the place where it happened. And maybe she could do something right for once, maybe one single wise wish would satisfy all the old wishes that might exist hereabouts: that was how to untangle a magical mess, as her uncle called it, just like looking through yarn for the master knot that snarled the little knots.

But—on the other hand—it was not all that simple: her parents certainly had never found that knot; and going down to the river tonight to ask the one other person who might have something important to say was not safe: *she* trusted her friend, but rusalki killed people, if she was mistaken; or even if she just said the wrong word to her uncle right now and he gave her the wrong answer and she believed it and made a wrong wish—something terrible could happen.

She was afraid to move when she thought that. She might be the only one in the house in a position to see the answer, the one person everyone ought to trust, and the very people she most wanted to protect could tell her no and wish her not to do things and *lie* to her, that was the scariest thought.

Her mother had been running things and wishing things in the house for a hundred years, her mother and Kavi both had, as seemed—not even mentioning her grandfather who had lived here before her uncle and her father had come. And her grandmother, who she supposed must have. And that was a lot of wishes—a *dangerous* lot of wishes that her uncle as well as her mother might not know about.

Not to mention her mother was the one her uncle said was

fighting that magical *thing*, whatever it was, that was so easy to use again.

If her mother had been dead a hundred years she could hardly have kept her book current. So her mother had broken one of the first rules she had ever learned: to write down exactly what she had done, in all its shapes. Kavi, who could not move the foam on the river, certainly had no means to write down his wishes—what was more, he had come back as a little boy: little boys hardly had good sense, rusalki could hardly help themselves; and if a rusalka could still do magic—god, what might a young one have wished?

"Uncle?"

Her uncle was squatting with the hoe against his shoulder, patting the earth along the radishes by hand. He looked up at her.

"If Chernevog's dead—what happened to his book?"

Her uncle went a shade of white against the flecks of mud on his face, but she felt nothing but her own careful thought. He was good: he truly was *very* good. "What put *that* question into your head, mouse?"

"I just realized . . . ghosts don't write things down. And wizard-ghosts could get in a lot of trouble that way, unless they remember things better than live people do. Couldn't they?"

"They don't. They're worse. God, mouse. Did you think of that all by yourself?"

"I think I did."

"I think you did, too. You're a very astute mouse. Yes. I've thought of that; and I assure you your mother has. It worries her."

"So where is his book?"

Her uncle got up and brushed his hands off on his trousers. "As happens, mouse, I have it."

"Have you read it?"

"Yes. I've read it very carefully. That, and your grandfather's book; and on one occasion, your mother's."

"Do you think she reads mine?"

That question seemed to give him pause. "I don't think so. I think I'd have known. And we agreed between us not to do that."

That was different than she had thought. Her mother might

lie to her: anybody might lie for good reasons; but her uncle wouldn't have that particular expression on his face when he did, or be as easy to overhear as he was at the moment.

He was thinking: 'Veshka might have. But she's curiously moral when you least think she will be.

Her uncle had not meant her to hear that. She felt herself blush; but she was also glad she had heard it: it made more sense of her mother in a handful of words than anything she had ever heard.

She said, "Would you let me read those books?"

Her uncle did not like that idea. No. He took a breath, and said, "I think they'd disturb you right now, to be honest. There are some few things left for you to learn before you're grown— things also more serious than the porch was; and I want to explain them to you the right way, before you read other people's mistakes."

"So explain them now."

"I don't know *how* to explain them."

"God!" She threw up her hands, her father's expression, she realized it even when she was doing it; and she looked at him the way her father would.

"I know, mouse, I know. I can say this much: some of Chernevog's reasons *and* your grandfather's . . . weren't right ones. You can learn from those books. But you have to realize where their mistakes were—and what they were, because the reasoning that led them to those mistakes looks very sound, if you don't see certain things a youngster might not know. And you can't learn them all at once, this afternoon."

That was at least the sanest no she had ever gotten. But it was a no. And it was still frustrating.

Her uncle said, "You're like your father. 'Why' is his word."

"To you?"

"To the whole world, mouse 'Why?' and 'Why Not?' He doesn't believe easily—not until he sees a thing happen. Which could be a very bad habit—except he doesn't believe a thing *can't* happen, either, including the chance that he could be wrong. He's stayed alive: he's kept me alive. And I was a very foolish young wizard." Her uncle took up his hoe again and gave the radish row a thumping down with the flat. "A very small dose of skepticism is a healthy thing in magic. And your father would add—a sense of humor is the most important sense. More precious than your eyes or ears."

She looked across the yard to where her father was sitting, planing down a board. She thought: How lonely he must feel, with mother and me both having tantrums.

She thought, I should have gone riding with him. I really should have.

She leaned her hoe on the garden fence, and went and hugged her father and told him that she was sorry, could they go riding in the morning?

"I suppose we can." He pursed his lips, peeled another curl from the board, and looked at her sideways from under his hair as if he was keeping just a little of his doubt back—in case she was up to something. That was not at all the effect she wanted.

She said, to cajole him out of that idea without magic: "Will you teach me how to jump Patches this afternoon?"

Eyebrows went up. "Your mother would—"

—kill me, he thought. She heard that completely by accident, saw him clamp his lips.

"I think I'd better teach you to ride by more than wishes, then, mouseling: staying on's not enough."

She's a great deal calmer, Sasha wanted Eveshka to know, before he opened his book that night. I've gone back up to my house, my own bed, you know. God, Pyetr's a restless sleeper.

He could feel the loneliness in her asking: How is he? and he answered her with all he knew—which he hoped was some measure of reassurance; about the talk he had had with her daughter, how Ilyana was not rebelling, was not going back to the river—

Be sure, Eveshka said, and almost—he felt it and wanted that thought *quiet*, quickly and thoroughly. Please, he said. She's sleeping. She's beginning to believe she can talk to you. Don't undo it all. She does love you. She will want you back—in not so long, I think.

Refraining from anything she had an opinion in was very hard for Eveshka. Refraining from her daughter was the hardest thing she could do—save one.

She said, Tell Pyetr I love him.

I will, he assured her, and wished her well.

It was quiet then, in his heart, in the house. Just the cluttered tables, the shelves, the little spot of light the candle made. He dared open his book then, separate of that troubling presence, and uncap the inkwell.

Damned lonely little house, never mind the bed was comfortable. The fire in the hearth, neglected last night, had gone out again, and the night chill reached his bones. He was alone up here. Eveshka was alone on the river. But he had laughed today, dammit, laughed so hard he had pulled a stitch in his side; Pyetr had—until the tears ran; and, god, yes, part of it was pain. They had been on the knife's edge for years with the child, Pyetr was desperately worried—and here were the two of them fooling about with that silly horse, playing games like the boys they had once been—

Because for that moment the years had not been there; and Pyetr had been himself; and he had. Not wise, not careful, considering all the things they had taught themselves to be, weighing every word and every wish—

They had laughed, and so had the mouse, thank the god— which gave him hope that, as much sense as the mouse was showing about what she was learning, there might be the day they could do that again, with Eveshka home.

That was the wish he wrote in his book.

That would make him happy—having his family back together, he was sure of that. A most definite wish—

The circle of light seemed very small tonight. Perhaps the wick had burned too fast for a bit, and drowned in wax. The untidy stacks seemed to close in on him—books and papers, books and papers, oddments that comprised his whole dammed life.

No more mouse to make toys for. No more little girl to come up to his house and make messes with his inkpot.

She was growing up, his mouse was. Not for him. The thought had indeed crossed his mind that they might be each other's answer—but he could not give up that little girl, could never change what had grown to be between them, or change her uncle Sasha in her eyes—they would both lose by that. Immeasurably. He could not think otherwise.

But he did think sometimes—of, as Pyetr had joked with

him once, not really joking—sailing downriver with marriage in mind, to find himself some beggar girl, Pyetr had said, who would think him a rescue.

When once they had joked about wanting tsarevnas, each of them.

But, fact was, he thought, making Ilyana's name carefully in his book, the fact was, while there had been one woman in the house down there, there were getting to be two, who had difficulties as it was—and somehow he did not think bringing some stranger into the household *and* dealing with an ordinary woman in the midst of magic was going to solve their problems this year or next.

Which meant that his own house just stacked up higher and higher, a pending calamity of stacks ready to crash down—and somehow he just could not care about the house he lived in: *that* was his house down there, dammit, that was his family, and up here was just where he spent his nights and kept his papers.

He closed his book, put away his pen, and rubbed his eyes—god, they were scratchy tonight; or maybe it was the sleep he had not gotten, with Pyetr tossing and turning all the rest of the night, after he had gotten him to bed at all.

He unstuck the candle from the desk—slopped hot wax onto his finger, and onto the floor. Damn it. Probably onto his trouser-leg. Candles were a mess—safer than oil-lamps in this clutter, but certainly hell on the furniture.

He set the candle on the bedside table, in a ring of previous wax spots, sat down to pull his boots off, thinking, A wife would be very nice. Someone to talk to would be nice. Someone to keep the damned fire in the fireplace lit, and the house warm, and echoing with voices.

That thought got completely out of hand. Completely. He thought, Why should I give up my whole life for everyone else?—which was not even reasonable: if not for Pyetr and his family he would be the sole occupant in that house down the hill, and within a year it would look like this one—or worse, stand neat and silent and full of unused furniture.

No, left on his own, he would have probably gone and courted some farmer's daughter downriver, and maybe had a little girl of his own by now, who did not exist, thanks to the years he had spent bringing Ilyana up; and who probably would never exist, considering the years he had already spent working and making notes and piling his house full of things he meant to take care of and still had to do. Somehow he had just gotten—

—damned lonely, in an overcrowded little house he did not quite know how had gotten this way. He wished for someone—

Oh, my god, he thought.

No. I *don't* want that.

He could not lie to himself. That never worked.

He thought— There's nothing for it; I've done it now. I've got to do something about this before it just happens—maybe go out and *find* somebody, if I can reason with 'Veshka and not have some poor girl turned into a toad on my account.

God, what have I done to myself? I haven't got time for this. I'm not sure I even want a wife. I'm not sure I want any stranger coming between me and my family. I'm not sure I want some strange woman who can't read straightening up my papers, or having another little girl to bring up, who *might* be a wizard, too—or, god help me, a little *boy*, or three or four of them—

It did not help that there was the sound of thunder in the distance: rainstorms were natural enough in the spring. But one *did not* like to make important wishes when nature was unsettled. Instabilities bred instabilities, and he certainly did not want distractions tonight, while he was chasing this unruly, unasked-for notion of a wife: distractions like Eveshka out on the river in a thunderstorm, or Pyetr worrying about her or Ilyana making wishes about the weather for her mother's sake—

Damn it all, miss us! Go north! We can do without the rain tonight!

But thunderstorms were damnably difficult to deter.

He blew out the light, slipped under a comfortable weight of covers and stared at the dark overhead, thinking—

I truly don't want this. I really, truly don't want this. I don't know why I do such contrary things—but I can't take it back, now. Something slipped, just then, I *felt* it go: old wishes, maybe—remembering the mouse was worried about me, something *she* wished for me.

Dammit all.

The wind rose. It was moving fast, that storm: hope that Eveshka was safely moored somewhere—but she had taught them all they knew of handling that boat, and she could certainly see and hear the storm coming. He had no doubts of her, so long as she had her wits about her.

Eveshka would kill him for what he had done—wishing for a wife. Maybe she even knew about it. Maybe *that* was the source of the storm. Or maybe what he had just wished was the answer to their present difficulties, maybe it was even good, what had happened: impossible to know until the air settled. They had brought Ilyana this far alive and well and nature had to take its course: he had no intention to do to the mouse what Uulamets had done to him—bequeathing him in one instant everything he knew: which itself might solve matters, but it was damnably hard on a fifteen-year-old, he knew that from experience; and besides, he was by no means sure a wizard who was not dying could do it.

Rumble. A spatter of rain.

Not a good time to think about Uulamets' death, or about lightning—god, he hated fires. He remembered Chernevog's house burning, and remembered, earliest of memories—his parents' screams, the neighbors flinching while he huddled behind a forest of grown-up legs, feeling the heat—

The neighbors had said, The boy's a witch, you know. Vasily beat the boy once too often—

Now a fire would not stay lit in his hearth.

He gazed into the dark above the rafters—hearing the thunder. He had a vision of himself directly beneath the sky, the roof seeming suddenly no shield from Uulamets' fate; or Chernevog's.

He felt the storm, felt the instability in the heavens. He thought—I should get up. I should go down the hill for safety tonight. I don't like this. Something's definitely fractured.

But to go outdoors under that lightning-pregnant cloud, perhaps to bring ill luck with him, to Pyetr's house, right where Ilyana—

No, that's foolishness. I should wish *not*, the lightning's up there right now, and I can't want it away from me—

Not if Pyetr's house is its other choice. Send it to the woods, burn the forest down? The leshys wouldn't understand that.

God!

4

✠ ✠ ✠ ✠ Bang! went the thunder, and Ilyana waked with her ears ringing and her heart in mid-leap. Rain on the roof. *That* one had shaken the house, as if a bolt had landed right in the yard.

Missy positively *hated* storms.

"Babi?" She rolled for the side of the bed, touched a straw to the night-wick with shaking hands and lit the lamp.

No Babi. Babi had been curled up on the covers at her feet, but he had probably gone for the stable the minute the storm started, that being his proper venue. She wished the horses well and calm, wished the lightnings not to hit that close again, please! while she pulled on the pair of trousers she wore for rough work, and the old pair of boots and the sloppy shirt, belt-less. She flew through the door to the kitchen and opened the front door on a rain-laden gust and a red glare. There was a fire on the hill, a huge fire.

Oh, god! *"Papa! Uncle's roof!"*

Her father's bedroom door banged open and he came running through the kitchen and past her—he had stopped to dress, too, pushing his arm into his shirt as he headed down the walk-up into the storm without a word what to do—whether to come help or stay out of the way. He ran faster than she had imagined anybody could run, banged through the outside gate while she was still clumping down the walk-up in too-large boots worn slick on the soles, and holding to the rail in quivery fright. She could wish there to be no more lightning bolts, and for her uncle to be all right and for his house not to burn—

Bang!

A horse screamed. Boards splintered. She thought of fire and

94

broken boards and panicked horses, and splashed around the corner to be sure the stable had not been hit. It was still safe; Volkhi and Missy were in the pen, but Patches was out, running around the yard in panic.

"Patches!" she cried, and wanted her to come to her; but Patches dashed in panic right through her mother's garden and charged right into the hedge—ran right through it, and the pickets, and fell outside.

"Patches!" she cried, running for the front gate, sure Patches had impaled herself on the pickets or the thorn-branches; but before she could even reach the fence Patches lurched up on her feet and bolted down the old road, toward the woods, where thickets and tangles could break her legs—*her* horse, her scared, stupid filly that papa had told her was absolutely her personal responsibility.

"Patches!" she cried, "stop, come back!" and, that working no more than the last, wanted her mother to know what was happening, wanted her to help papa and her uncle—wanted Missy—

No—*Volkhi*; Volkhi was the fastest. She ran back to the stableyard, unlatched the gate and climbed the rails, wanting Volkhi against the fence, wishing him to stand still just long enough for her to slide onto his wet back and grab fistfuls of mane. Then she wished him, "Catch Patches!" and Volkhi leapt into a run, right through the garden, right for—

Oh, my *god*!

She dared not wish him stop: she held on as Volkhi left the ground, and did not know the other side of the hedge how she was still on his back, except her lip tasted of blood and they were headed full-tilt into the trees. Branches raked her hair and splintered on her shoulders. Lightning flashed and confused her eyes. She hung on with both hands and went with Volkhi the way her father had taught her—impossible to see all the branches coming at her: it was Volkhi's sight she borrowed, different than hers, it was his body she felt moving, while she tried to remember where the bad spots were, to help him the best way she knew.

"Patches!" she yelled into the storm, what time she was not being Volkhi, insisting Patches come back; but if wishes were working right, Patches would have come to her in the first place, lightning would never have set her uncle's house on fire, and her father would not be back there where *she* should be right now, saving her uncle—god, god, she had done the wrong thing again. She should not be out here, listening too much to Volkhi and losing her wits . . .

But now she was too far along and she could only lose Patches and be in grown-ups' way where the fire was.

Be all right! she wished her father and her uncle; and wished her mother to do something—because her mother could, better than anyone.

Oh, god, mother, put out the fire, and everybody be all right!

"—Wake up, dammit! Wake up!"

Sasha's face was waxen against the firelit grass, spattered with rain, the both of them sprawled in the yard as Pyetr slapped and shook at him. Then Sasha got a breath and objected to being hit in the face. Sasha rolled over and started coughing.

Pyetr coughed, too, leaning on his hands and fighting for breath. A burning house was no way for Sasha to die, god, Sasha had such a terror of fire: he only just realized the fear he had felt, seeing Sasha's roof ablaze—when of a sudden Sasha scrambled up, headed back to the house.

"*No*, dammit!" He rolled and tripped Sasha by the ankle, then lost his hold as Sasha recovered his balance and dashed for the porch.

Flames were already gusting out the windows. "Stop!" Pyetr yelled, staggered up and ran after him, up to the smoke-seeping porch and through the door into a palpable wall of heat and light that seared the skin. Fire was already taking the stacks of papers, the air was thick with wind-borne cinders, too hot to breathe— but Sasha shoved two books at him and snatched an armload himself.

A timber crashed down. Shingles fell in a hail of embers. Pyetr held the book in one arm, grabbed Sasha and ran, knocked into the wall and found the door by accident or wishes. A blast of cold rain shocked his burns and Sasha slid and fell on the boards on the way down, but Pyetr dragged him clear all the same, pulled Sasha down and far out onto the slope before his legs gave out, and he sprawled into the wet, prickly weeds beside him.

"God," he moaned. His chest was burning. Rain stung like fire on his back and on his face as he rolled off the armful of books and let the water wash the smoke out of his eyes. "For a handful of damned books—"

"Our lives," Sasha gasped. "Ilyana's— Oh my god, Ilyana—"

Ilyana had been behind him a while back; he was onto his knees and intending another trip into the house before Sasha made him believe Ilyana had not gone inside after them—

Oh, god, no, Ilyana was safe from the fire: she was out in the woods on a runaway horse, and Eveshka had cast off to sail home, through the storm—

He had that from Sasha, or from 'Veshka herself, he did not stop to ask. He scrambled up and ran headlong downhill for a horse. Patches might almost be fast enough, but she was young and flitter-brained in a crisis—

Missy came trotting up out of the lightning-lit downpour before he reached the hedge: Sasha's horse, no question who had brought her or how he was going to track Ilyana: he caught Missy's mane and swung up to her broad, rain-drenched back.

Missy was the other side of too many years and too many apples, his sword was back in the house, he was soaked to the skin, blinded by rain, coatless and coughing so at times he could scarcely keep upright on Missy's back. Damned poor hope for a rescue, he thought, and hoped for Sasha to make the mouse use sense—burned and shocked and coughing his gut out back at the house, as Sasha was, with no horse at all and no way to follow him: Patches was what Ilyana and Volkhi were chasing. If his own wishes were worth anything, he threw them in: Wish Volkhi to use his head, if my daughter won't! What in hell's she doing out there?

He thought he heard, then, faintly and full of pain: Pyetr, I don't know, but I swear to you I'm trying!

There was Patches—Ilyana spied her through the brush, in the lightning flickers, with the roar of the rain-swollen brook in her ears. She was relieved to see Patches was on her feet, and terrified to see Patches had her hind feet almost in the flood: she had evidently fallen in, by the mud all down her side, and by luck or by a young lifetime of well-wishes, she must have gotten out again, if not all the way up the slippery bank. A heap of brush had partly dammed the brook there, and if Patches should step back and slip in now, Ilyana thought, that pile of brush could well trap her in the rush of water and drown her.

"Be calm," she wished Volkhi, trying not to frighten Patches as they eased their way through the lightning-lit undergrowth. "Be calm. Easy." She wanted Patches to pay sober attention to the water behind her, please, and use good sense and come on to them if she had the strength to climb the slippery bank. She had heard nothing from uncle Sasha or from her mother. The familiar woods had turned scary in the dark, with the water and the wind roaring and the lightning making the trees and Patches like ghosts of themselves. She would have hoped Babi at least would have come with her; but nothing was going right tonight, nothing she knew was working, her uncle must be hurt at the very least, and she wanted to get back to the house and know everybody had gotten out of the fire, please the god: the silence from her uncle was *wrong*, she could not understand what she had been thinking of, or understand why she was still out here chasing after a damned horse, any horse, to prove she was responsible, when her father and uncle Sasha were in danger. She had made a stupid choice, she had counted on hearing her uncle and knowing he was all right, and nothing was right, god—

But she was so close now—and Patches could still fall in and drown, right in front of her eyes, and if the damned horse would come on, it would only take a moment and she could ride back and leave the stupid filly in the woods until morning; she would be safe, just up the bank, just a few more steps up. "Come *on*. Patches, dammit! Oh, *god*—"

Lightning showed something caught in the brush pile, something the water had pushed there, not a log or even a dead animal. It looked like cloth. It looked like—

She made out a hand, a face profiled against the brush, above the white spray of the flood.

Oh, god, she thought, a *drowned* person, caught in the brush. She did not want to find someone dead—she *wanted* her uncle or her father, right now: grown-ups could deal with gruesome things—

But she was all there was, and if there was help she had to give it: she slid down from Volkhi's drenched back and wanted him and Patches to stand very still while she worked down the bank beside Patches and had a look at this person to see if he was alive. Patches gave a nervous little whicker and proved she could move by easing over for her, but she did not want Patches to do that: she grabbed a handful of Patches' black and white tail to help her footing on the mud. "Hey!" she yelled over the roar of the flood and the rain, hoping if the person was not dead he would hear and move and reach up a hand to her so she would not have to touch him to find out. But he did not move, so she leaned out over the rushing water, and grabbed a fistful of wet coat. "*Move*, Patches! Go on—dammit, no! *Up!*"

Patches gave a sudden jump and pulled so hard that both her arms were like to break. She held on until she had the body most of the way out of the water and that was all she could do: she let go of Patches' tail and fell on her knees in the mud, hauling on the coat and the arms and trying to get the body where it would not fall back in.

The lightning showed her a handsome young face—in which the eyes were partly open and the mouth was working to breathe. He coughed up water, choked, and she quickly rolled him over on his side so he could spit it out. Awful water, full of mud, he had been in; and carried the god only knew how far in it and under the flood. He coughed and coughed and finally caught a bubbling breath.

She shook at him then. "Come on, get your legs out of the water! My uncle's house is on fire and I've got to get home! Come on! Please, try!"

He tried: he got a knee under him, and slid immediately back toward the stream.

She grabbed him and pulled his limp body up against her, both of them sliding until she dug a heel into the mud. He weighed more than she did; he had fainted and she could pull him no further without chancing going in herself.

"Wake up!" She shook at him, he moved, and she shouted into his ear, "Get higher, get something to hold on to!"

Suddenly a Thing popped up right in their faces with a hiss and an appalling row of white teeth: the boy yelled and flinched back against her.

Babi, thank the god. Missy was beyond the screen of brush, her father was jumping down and running to reach her—

The breath went out of her. Her arms were numb, the leg that was bracing both of them began to tremble. She was soaked through, and cold, but all at once she could hear her uncle wanting her to answer him, and he could hear her, telling him she was safe, everybody was safe, her father was here with Missy and Babi, and she had found a half-drowned boy . . .

Her mother said, without warning, Oh, god—

Her mother—

—wanting this boy to slip back *in*—

"No!" she cried, wanting her mother *not*! *not*! to think of killing.

The feeling stopped. Her father had her arm, pulled her by that and the boy by the collar and said, in a voice as shaky as she felt, "It's all right, mouse, steady, I've got you both."

The boy certainly explained something, magic not working, Sasha's house burning, everything going wrong at once. Pyetr did *not* like this, he wanted Sasha to know, if Sasha was listening.

Sasha was not. Sasha was busy or Sasha was not doing well, or magic had failed again, for some reason, none of which possibilities made him feel any better at all.

"Your uncle's not answering me," he said to Ilyana, and Ilyana:

"He's probably holding mother off. She's—oh, *god*, papa, she wants—wants to kill him—"

He got the gist of that, grabbed her and hugged the breath out of the mouse, trusting Babi to go for the boy's throat if he made a single hostile move. Ilyana was soaked, cold, exhausted, he was no better; and getting her back to the house was all he cared about at the moment. A man could never count on winning with magic running wild like this—wishes stacked up like so much old pottery, Sasha described it, a whole place heavy with an unstable stack of wishes, all waiting for some reasonable thing to satisfy the impossible condition—

Like a girl desperately wanting a boy. A *wizard* desperately wanting someone—

Damned right Eveshka was upset. *He* was upset, and he could not feel magic happening around him.

Ilyana said, against his shoulder, "Did uncle's house all burn?"

"I'm afraid there's not much left of it. At least the sparks are all drowned." The rain was pouring down again, soaking them to the skin. "Who is he?"

"I don't know." She let go of him to kneel and look at the boy—handsome lad, Pyetr saw. Damn the luck. Older than Ilyana, maybe by several years. And that collar under the sodden coat glittered very expensively.

No farmer lad, that was sure. He dropped to one knee and gently slapped the boy's cold face. "Who are you, lad? Do you have a name?"

Eyes slitted open while he thought uncomfortably of shape-shifters.

Lips said, faintly, "Yvgenie. Yvgenie Pavlovitch."

"Where are you from?"

"Kiev."

"You're rather far from Kiev. The river washed you backwards, did it? Spat you out upriver. How did you get here?"

The eyes rolled, showed white. The boy had fainted away.

Didn't at all like that question, did it?

"We've got to build a fire," Ilyana said, through chattering teeth. "We've got to get him dry, he's freezing."

He thought—Hell if I want us alone out here with him. Get him to Sasha, is what we've got to do, and the faster, the better.

Aloud, he said, "In this rain, mouse? A horse's back is the warmest place we can put him; and your uncle needs our help. Let's just bundle him up and get him on a horse. You ride Missy back, you're lightest." He got his arms around whatever-it-was and pulled him up against him, the most dangerous position he could think of to be in with something magical, but he aimed him for Volkhi, as, after Missy, the most mannered horse they had.

In the small chance that this was truly the only shape young
Yvgenie Pavlovitch owned.

Eveshka shoved at the tiller and the boat's sail slatted and thundered above the rain. Way fell off immediately, and the boat
began to toss as she brought the bow on about, holding with
both arms and all her strength against the jolt as the sail came
over. The boat reeled at the deepest slack to a sudden, violent
gust, and only a wish and the ferry's good trim kept her from
rolling over in that instant before the wind slammed into the
sail on a new tack and the tiller bucked against her arms. She
hated the dark water, she hated the storm; she fought the river
and the weather for her life and safely damned what could feel
no possible danger from her.

She could not think now. She should not think now. Rain
and tears blurred the shoreline as old River tried to take her a
second time. The cold water wanted her back, and the deadliest
thought of all was that for everyone she loved it might be the
best answer.

Sasha insisted: The river's not the way, 'Veshka! You can't
leave us. You *couldn't* leave your daughter or Pyetr if you died,
and you know that—you know what you'd become!

Do you hear me, 'Veshka?

She had heard. She knew. They feared her: Sasha did, Ilyana
did—even Pyetr would not trust her help or her opinions.

She completed the turn and the wind sank. Having done its
best to capsize her, the storm settled down to a cold, drenching
rain.

Sasha shoved logs into the bathhouse furnace, slogged back out
in the rain to the woodpile and carried his next armload of wood
up to the porch and into the house, never minding the mud on
Eveshka's floors. Pyetr and Ilyana were coming in with the boy,
all of them half-frozen and covered with mud: he had water for
washing, he had a stack of towels, clean clothes, dry boots, blankets, water was boiling in the house and in the bathhouse—

He had hidden all the books in the cellar with the domovoi,
the safest and driest place he could think of under the circum-

stances, and he hoped to the god to be mistaken about what Pyetr and the mouse were bringing home.

Thorns. Thorns and golden leaves and blood—

Owl dying—

No magery. Memory. His mind conjured him that nightmare of Chernevog, the warning dreams—the dreadful stone—

Pyetr lying in the brush, in the dark, white shirt—dark branches—

He shuddered at that one. It *had* come true. Everything had come true, fifteen years ago. It was over with and he did not want to see those things again, or remember their so-thought bannik—

Not tonight.

Himself on a white horse, something clinging to his back—

But that had only been Missy. Missy had saved his life and saved all of them, thank the god. That dream had come true, and nothing but good had issued from it—

Patches had come of it. The mouse had. All these things. Chernevog was buried however restless his ghost. No bannik had ever come to the bathhouse to replace that strayed fragment of Chernevog's soul. And if all of it should have strayed back tonight—

—in whatever form—

But by the sounds of horses coming along the hedge outside, there was an answer forthcoming, very quickly now.

He changed to a dry coat at the door (one of Pyetr's old coats, as happened, a little long in the sleeves for him) figuring he was about to do a great deal more trekking about in the rain before he saw any rest tonight. He took down Ilyana's coat from the pegs, picked up a bundle of blankets and opened the door just as the front gate banged, and he spied Pyetr afoot, holding the yard gate open for three very tired, very sore horses.

"The stable gate's open," Sasha shouted, on his way down. "Just let them go."

Ilyana was riding Missy, and they had the boy slung over Volkhi's back, with Volkhi walking free. Patches broke into a jog for the stable, and Pyetr called out, "Stop Volkhi, for the god's sake, before he dumps the boy on his head."

Sasha wanted Volkhi to head sedately for the bathhouse while he was about it, and met them in the yard. "Warm water inside, mouse, once you've rubbed the horses down. Pyetr, here, two blankets. I've got Ilyana's coat. The bathhouse is fired up and ready for the boy."

"Good," Pyetr said, and trudged after Volkhi, wrapping one blanket about his shoulders as he went. He called back: "Ilyana, warm water for their legs, and a rubbing down. I'll help you as soon as I can. Don't over-water or over-feed, mind, a quarter measure of the grain, no more than that."

A very tired, very sore mouse slid down as Missy walked for the stableyard gate. Sasha caught her arms and steadied her, and flung her coat around her as Babi ran off after Missy. "Sorry," he said, then, on his own way to the bathhouse. "Help you when we can, there's a good girl."

"I'm all right," she panted, and overtook him, struggling in the mud, trying the while to put the coat on. "Is the house all gone, uncle?"

She desperately wanted him to be all right and not to be sad about his things. The truth was, and he let her know it, weak-kneed though he was from the scare and with his hands burned and his chest hurting from the smoke, his books were safe and the rest of it was actually a relief: there were *no* stacks of clutter in his house anymore. "Spring cleaning," he said, and coughed. "Finally got around to it."

The mouse grinned, the flash of a sidelong glance in the light from the shutters. He tousled her wet hair as their ways parted at the stable gate. "Brave mouse. Watch yourself. Magic's certainly loose tonight."

At the bathhouse, Pyetr had pulled the unconscious boy off Volkhi and hauled him in a trailing tangle of blankets for the door. "Go on," Sasha told Volkhi, slapping him on his side. "Good fellow, Volkhi. Warm rags and a rub in the stable." He followed Pyetr into warmth and light, in time to pull the door to behind them.

"She seems all right," he said to Pyetr, as he took the boy's feet and helped lay him on his back on the bench.

"Thank the god for that." Pyetr unfastened the boy's sodden coat. "Patches brought her right to this boy. I wish we had another place to put him."

Gold thread. Silk. Sasha whistled softly, helping Pyetr rid

the boy of the sleeves. "No farmer and no fisher, whoever he was."

"You think he's dead?"

"Not quite sure. He's certainly breathing." He picked up a chill white hand, and laid it on the boy's middle, put his hand on the side of the boy's neck and felt the beat. "Cold as last winter, though. There's hot water and towels over by the fire. He's already soaked to the skin. I'd say just pile them on him and let him and the towels and all dry in the heat. The fire's good till morning."

"Good enough." Pyetr went and soaked the towels while Sasha pulled the boy's boots off. He came back with an armful and began spreading them over the boy.

The boy opened his eyes, lifted his head and promptly fell back with a thump on the bench. Pyetr slipped a hand under his neck and shoved a hot towel under his hair. Dark hair, it was. Pale blue eyes that wandered this way and that in confusion. "This is a bathhouse."

"Our bathhouse," Pyetr said, setting his foot on the end of the bench and resting his arms against his knee. "As happens. He's Sasha, I'm Pyetr, and you're Yvgenie Pavlovitch, the last I heard, who swam all the way up from Kiev to drown in our woods."

"I rode a horse," the boy said, faintly, "from Kiev. I—"

There was a complete muddle in the boy's thoughts: running afoot through the woods, the rain coming down—

Someone or something chasing him, something to do with his father.

A fabulous palace, gold and gilt everywhere, a gray-haired, frowning man, not happy with him, no: his father would beat him, and kill the men who had lost him if they did not get him back.

Sasha put a hand on the boy's forehead, wished him calm, and the wish fluttered this way and that of an anxious heart. He looked through the boy's eyes and saw two sooted, wild-haired strangers hovering over him, who might intend to rob him or worse. His thoughts leapt around like a landed fish: death, and a demand for ransom, which his father might well pay—if only to have him in his hands.

Impossible to say whether he was what he seemed. A shape-shifter believed what it was and would not seem otherwise until one managed to find its single essential flaw.

He said, gently, "Yvgenie Pavlovitch, you're in safe hands if you're what you look to be. But this forest is full of tricks and tricksters. We don't dare ourselves trust everything to be what it seems."

Yvgenie said, "There was a girl—"

"My daughter," Pyetr said. "She pulled you out of the water. What were you doing in the woods?"

"I—don't—don't remember."

"Where did you come from?"

The boy thought (Sasha eavesdropped shamelessly): How *did* I get to this place? Aloud, he said, "Kiev." But there were black pits everywhere in his remembering.

"What's your father's name?"

"Pavel . . ." The father's features ran like wax, eluding the boy's recollection, and the thoughts began jumping again. Dark places multiplied.

"He doesn't remember," Sasha said, laying his hand on Yvgenie's chest, the better to gather up stray thoughts or hostile intentions. He wished the boy's body well, at least: wished it warmth and ease of the aches and bruises it had suffered.

"Is that better?" he asked.

Wizard, the boy thought in sudden fright, fearing what he felt happening to him, and not daring protest it.

"Yes," Sasha said, "I am what you're thinking—which is a good thing for you. Pyetr, put some water on the stones. He's cold through."

Pyetr dipped up water and flung in onto the hot stones. The water hissed, fire-shadows jumped, and wind whirled curtains of steam and shadow about the walls. The lad at least could not suffer chill in here—fainting now from the heat, perhaps. Sasha wiped the hair out of the boy's face and slapped his cheek gently to bring him back, but the boy's eyes kept going shut, and his breath was rattling.

Not good, not at all good.

"Come on, boy," he said, and put his hands on either side of the boy's face, wishing warmth and well-being and easy breath, thinking only about that, and not his doubts of the boy's nature.

"Listen to me, Yvgenie Pavlovitch, you're not to die, do you hear me?"

"No," Yvgenie Pavlovitch whispered, with his eyes shut, looking, Pyetr thought, very young, and very handsome, and very rich in his gold collar and his red silk shirt—which meant at least the opportunity to grow up a scoundrel, Pyetr knew it from his own youthful associations.

But a very ill and almost dead young scoundrel, for all that, and for the first time Pyetr found himself seriously wondering whether he might have been too rough with what might after all be an innocent boy. He listened to Sasha's mumbling over the lad, heard the breath rattling in the boy's chest in a most disturbing congestion, and truly, he did want the boy to live—

And be on his way to Kiev or wherever, without having the least to do with his daughter.

But Ilyana had already seen him, and the mouse was inevitably curious and most damnably, reprehensibly stubborn— which first trait was his and the latter one she had gotten fairly from both sides. Present the mouse a mystery, tell her no, and absolutely there was no stopping her.

And might this boy be, he wondered distractedly, the answer they had wished for, to win Ilyana's heart away from a most dangerous ghost?

Or might he be (as he most acutely feared) Chernevog's chosen way back from the grave?

Why should Sasha's house burn, except to keep Sasha busy while wishes came unhinged and this boy found his way to Ilyana's heart? Lightning had burned Chernevog's house to its foundations, and one could never say Kavi Chernevog lacked a sense of humor, even in his darker moments.

Their own looming shadows did occasional battle with clouds of steam, jumped as Sasha worked, with a good deal of muttering and an occasional puff of pungent smoke from the fire, firelight glistening gold on his frowning face. Sasha did not look happy, no; and the thought gnawed him the while Sasha did whatever he was doing, that somewhere in the outcome of this night, he might well be losing Ilyana from his life—not, he prayed the god, in the direction of Kavi Chernevog; but at least in her growing up and away from him, now that this boy had come into the question—this Yvgenie Pavlovitch, who, by that silk and gold he wore, might make his daughter very unhappy.

He prayed if there *was* a rich father and a palace somewhere involved, that neither should ever involve his daughter, who could have no patience for the scoundrels who went thick as flies about such places—and a young man who lived in such places could not help but entertain scoundrels among his associates, even granted his own impeccable good character.

—No, surely this can't be our answer. This *can't* be the boy our mouse will marry. He's something altogether other—thoroughly dead, by the look of him. Damned if it isn't Chernevog! Damn, damn, and damn the scoundrel!

He paced. He watched. He asked Sasha quietly, coming to lean over his shoulder, against one of the posts that held the roof: "If he is a boy, do you think you possibly wished him up? Or did the mouse?"

"I truly don't know," Sasha said, mopping sweat from his face. "I can say he's stronger now than he was, but whether that's good or bad for Yvgenie Pavlovitch I honestly don't know."

He did not like the sound of that at all. He muttered, "Where's Chernevog's heart right now, that's what I'd like to know."

And Sasha said: "I can't answer that. I do think we should take a very quick bath, get the mouse inside, and wish her a sound sleep tonight."

Yvgenie lay listening, watching sometimes from slitted eyes while water splashed and the wizard and the fair-haired man washed and talked in low voices that rang strangely through his ears. The heat made him dizzy. They spoke names that stirred no memory in him. He thought, What's my father's name? Pavel, of course. But what's the rest of it? What am I doing here and what do they want from me?

He stole glances at Pyetr, whose features recalled so strongly the girl who had rescued him—who had rescued him and held him when the river had tried to drag him away—she had protested, he remembered her voice, clear above the rain and the rush of water, Papa, please, not head down like that, he'll have a headache—

He had thought so too—but he had been too far gone to protest being slung over a horse's back like a bale of rags. And he was sure on those grounds he ought not to like or trust this Pyetr, but his heart wanted to—he desperately wanted Pyetr to trust him, and not to frown at him and wish him dead, and most of all, please the god, to stand between him and Sasha the wizard—who might have helped him so far; but whose ultimate intentions he dreaded more than he dreaded Pyetr's scowls.

What will he want of me? he wondered, recalling (so he did remember some things) an old woman saying that wizards drank from dead men's skulls and stirred their potions with children's finger-bones; wizards bargained very sharply, wizards could bind people helplessly to do their bidding, most probably lost young men who came into their debt, souls who became birds at night and flitted about the woods looking for their suppers.

Their shadows and their footsteps came toward him, making a cool space in the heat from the fire. He kept his eyes shut, while his heart pounded, trying not to let them know he felt the hand that rested first on his brow, and lightly then against his cheek and his shoulder.

"Rest easy," the wizard said, and it would have been very easy to slip right down then—they tried to take even his fear away, and that was the last defense he had. He fought that urge, held on to his doubts, and after a moment their shadows went away and left him in the light and the breathless heat. The door opened and closed with a single gust of chill from that direction, after which he dared open his eyes and look up at the shadows shifting among the rafters. He was at the first breath relieved that they had gone, and then not glad at all: he began to have the most terrible conviction that not everyone who had been with them had left the bathhouse, that there was someone standing just out of sight in the shadows behind the fire.

Perhaps Pyetr had stayed—perhaps they had only been trying to trick him into opening his eyes. But it did not feel at all like Pyetr's shadow—it had no feeling of a man at all. Perhaps he should call out to the wizard and his friend before they got too far to hear and beg their help—but like a child in the dark, he dreaded to cry out, first for fear they might not believe him, and might desert him here with an angrier, more wakeful spirit—

and then for fear he had already hesitated too long. They were surely out of hearing now.

It might be a bannik—surely that was it: he was in a bath-house, after all, a wizard's bathhouse, to boot, and an Old Man of the Bath was not necessarily a hostile or a baneful creature to strangers, just peevish and difficult and probably wondering what he was doing here, a prisoner in its domain.

He thought desperately—that if he could just gather the little strength that had come back to him, he would gladly oblige the bannik and make a fast run for the door, escape across the yard to the horses, wherever they were. He might ride out of this place, and reach—

But he had no idea where he had been going. Not home. Not back to his father, never, never—

A log fell, making his heart jump, with whatever-it-was creeping closer and closer. He *felt* it on his right, he felt it almost on him, and he leapt for his feet in a tangle of wet towels—fell and scrambled on his knees toward the door. He pushed it and pulled it and it no more than rattled to his efforts while the presence loomed over him. He flung himself around with his shoulders pressed to the door, his senses reeling with the heat and the light. The shadows of beams and posts and rafters gyrated in a gust of wind from the smoke hole.

Whatever-it-was cast no shadow itself, but he felt its chill between him and the fire. He reached back and gripped the solid wood of a beam, hauled himself up sitting against the door and waited for it.

A bannik? A Bath-thing, in a bad mood? They had long, long fingernails that they used when they were angry—always from behind you. He knew that from somewhere—they would always come at you from behind.

Which this one could not do, while he had his back against the door—so long as he could keep his eyes open, and keep from fainting in the heat.

Hot tea and blankets. Ilyana had never been so sore or so tired in her life. There were scratches all over her arms, her father and her uncle had had their baths, but that had only helped the mud and the soot: they both had deep burns and scratches she wanted *well*, dammit, right now: it was the one point on which her thoughts were not scattering tonight, and she wanted that fixed.

"Thank you, mouse," her uncle said, with that strange, distant feeling he had had since he started talking to her again, and she did not know how to fix that. She only nodded unhappily, having her mouth full, and wondered if her uncle were finally angry at her—not fair, if that was the case, though she had deserved it a hundred times before this, and supposed it was due on other accounts. Or on the other hand her uncle might be upset about the fire and just not trusting himself close to people. She did not want him to be upset, please the god: her mother being upset was enough to be wrong with the world. She *needed* her uncle to have his wits about him, please.

"Thank you for that, too, mouse—and, no, it's quite all right. There's just enough gone on today, and I'm very tired. Nothing's your fault."

"Everything's my fault. I didn't need to go after Patches, I could have wished her out, if—"

"None of us had choices," her uncle said. "That's why I tell you don't ever wish for generalities. You didn't chance to wish up a young man, did you?"

Her face went hot. "Certainly not to drown one!"

"Of course not," uncle said. "But if he *is* an ordinary young man, you above all mustn't make wishes about or at him. It wouldn't at all be fair."

"I want him to get well!"

"Of course you do." Her father, next to her on the bench, poured Babi's waiting mouth a dash of vodka, poured his own cup, and then poured a large dose into her tea. She had just taken another bite meanwhile, and she needed a drink even to protest her father's recklessness. She washed down her mouthful of bread with a gulp of the only liquid she had and gasped, her eyes watering.

"Father! That's more than I've *ever* had!"

"This once," her father said.

She took a more cautious sip. It was strong, but she could taste the tea this time, and the fumy vodka eased her throat and her eyes the way the tea had not. She sipped it slowly, thinking how her mother would say, Pyetr! Don't give her that much. But her mother was not here. Her father had the only say-so, and his rules were not so strict, about anything. The whole world seemed wider and more dangerous, with her father in charge, and he was treating her like a grown-up.

Her uncle said, "I think we should get some rest while we can. Our friend's asleep out there. I've seen to that."

"Sounds like a good idea," her father said. "Ilyana, your uncle's put the old tub in your bedroom; I'm afraid the bathhouse is rather well taken tonight."

"I don't know why you can't bring him up here tonight. The kitchen's more comfortable than the bathhouse. What if he needs help?"

"Your uncle's already sleeping here, remember? He's having to share a bed with me tonight, and I'm certainly not having any stranger bedded down next to the kitchen cutlery."

"He doesn't dress like a bandit. I think his father must be a boyar at least."

"That's no recommendation. I've dealt with boyars' sons, and there's not a one I'd trust outside your door."

Her face went warm a second time. She took a drink to cover what she was sure was a blush, forgetting about the vodka until she found herself with an entire mouthful of tea. There was nothing to do but swallow it. Her eyes watered and she felt hot all over—dizzy, too. "Father, I—"

"He stays in the bathhouse."

"I don't think he's any—" The room was stiflingly close of a sudden. Her head spun. She felt of her forehead to be sure where it was. Or where her fingers were. "Oh, dear, papa."

"Mmmm. Never mind the sheets, baby mouse. I think you'd better go straight on to bed."

"Papa—"

"Dirty trick. Yes." Her father stepped over the bench, took her arms and helped her step over. She caught her foot on the bench. He swept her right up in his arms like a baby and the whole room went around and around as she found the ceiling in front of her eyes. It had been years since he had carried her at all, and she grabbed at his neck for fear of falling. But he got her safely through her bedroom door and let her down gently on her bed.

"The mud," she objected.

"That's all right." He tugged at the covers under her. "Sheets will wash. You've had one near-drowning tonight. You don't need another, in the tub. Tuck your feet up."

Sleep settled around her, soft and deep as the covers her father pulled over her. He leaned down, kissed her on the forehead, and pulled a snag from her hair.

"Good night, mouse. Shut your eyes."

Silly wish: she already had.

The house was quiet, even the anxious domovoi having settled. Pyetr lay on his back in bed beside Sasha, with just the embers from the fireplace giving them light, wondering what 'Veshka was thinking tonight, and where she was, and whether she was warm and safe. Distracting Sasha with that question did not seem a good idea right now.

He asked Sasha instead, "What in hell are we going to do with the boy? We can't leave him in the bathhouse till the snow falls."

"I think we should get some sleep. In the morning we'll think of something."

"No guarantee we even have a guest at this point." The latch on the outside of the bathhouse door was new, Sasha's handiwork, the hour Sasha had learned they were bringing company this evening, but a latch might only keep a helpless boy inside. For other things the smoke hole was enough. So was the crack under the door quite enough for a shapeshifter, not mentioning that certain magical creatures could be anywhere they wanted to be without any cracks and crevices at all to slip through. Certain unpleasant things could pop into the room with them right now, except the domovoi's and Babi's watching.

"Babi hasn't objected to him," Sasha said, "and if it isn't a real boy, it certainly took a great deal of trouble getting here, only to leave now."

That much was true: Babi had curled up on the quilts at Ilyana's feet in quite his ordinary fashion, with no evident interest in the bathhouse. Babi hated shapeshifters: he would chase them so long as he could smell the least trace of them—once he could tell what they were.

"Go to sleep," Sasha wished him. So Sasha believed that

they were safe to do that now, no matter that Sasha's house was cinders and someone's wishes other than his had made havoc of this night.

"No," he tried to object—might have objected: an ordinary man could be more stubborn than a wish, but proximity made a difference with magic, and tired as he was, close as he was to Sasha, he had not a chance: he was already slipping down into dark.

—at the same moment he thought he heard 'Veshka say, out of the dark and the faint patter of rain on the roof: "Pyetr, take care of her. For the god's sake don't let that boy near her."

5

■ ■ ■ ■ ■ Uncle was awake, at the table in the kitchen—uncle was being as quiet as anyone could be, but Ilyana had heard the cellar door open and close a long while ago, and waked again hearing the scratch of uncle's pen, and the creak of her father's door, just now. "There's tea," her uncle whispered; then her father's voice said, very low: "How long have you been up?"

"Not that long." Ilyana strained to hear something she did lose, and heard her father walk across the kitchen. Pottery rattled. Tea cups, she thought.

Then she remembered the most remarkable event of a very remarkable yesterday and wondered if their guest was all right— whether he had slept last night, or whether he was feeling better this morning.

She thought, Yes, without a reason for knowing that.

And then she thought, He really can't stop me from hearing him. I think I just woke him up. —Please don't be scared, Yvgenie Pavlovitch.

He was more than scared. He was terrified, waking on the ground, against the door: she heard a pounding from far away and knew that was him trying to open the bathhouse door.

That's odd, she thought. Why doesn't he just lift the latch?

No. The door was barred from outside. But there never had been a latch outside. That was terribly dangerous, on a bathhouse. When had that happened?

How long have I been asleep?

She caught terrible fear, so strong it stopped her breath. —Please, she wanted Yvgenie to know, no one's going to hurt

115

you. They've only locked the door to keep you from wandering off last night. I'm sure that's the reason.

—Ilyana! Go to sleep!

Her uncle frightened her, he was so strong and so angry, surprising her like that. She heard, with her ears, him saying to her father: "She's fighting me."

Then her father's voice, sternly: "Mouse, go back to sleep."

That confused her. Her father was kind, her father would never hurt anyone, he was not on her mother's side. So why had they latched the bathhouse door? Why did the boy remember them threatening him?

She tried to tell her father, The boy won't hurt anything. You're scaring him!

And her uncle: Ilyana! Don't wish at your father. Go back to sleep.

She wanted not to. She was determined not to. Her father was saying, ". . . take him down the river, fast—if we had the damn boat."

Her uncle gave off terrible thoughts of a sudden, houses all crowded together, afire, and horses and men in metal, with swords.

Then uncle knew she was still listening: uncle was very angry at her and wanted her very sternly to mind him and go to sleep.

She said, making her lips work, too, so her uncle could not make her forget what she was saying, "Stop it, please stop doing this to me."

She felt cold and afraid. She was numb and cold in her right leg and bruised about the shoulder and her hand that she had used on the door—

"Ilyana!" her uncle said, and her door opened (but not that door) and she was lying warm and in bed with Babi at her feet.

"He's cold," she said. "He's cold and the fire's out and he's scared, uncle, please don't scare him any more."

Her uncle came and sat on the side of her bed and brushed her hair out of her eyes. Her uncle looked worried, and tired, and harder than she had ever seen him. Her uncle said, somberly, touching her under the chin, "Ilyana, you haven't been dreaming, have you?"

She shook her head.

"Nothing about Owl?"

Another shake of her head. God, she had not even thought about Owl last night. Or her friend. She had outright forgotten. Damn!

Her uncle said, "Ilyana, you can't take things as you want them to be. I very much fear your young man drowned last night."

"He didn't! There's nothing wrong with him, except the fire went out—" She had not meant to forget her friend, please the god he knew that—her father had made her sleep—

"Mouse, listen to me. Look at me. I don't want you to argue with me. It's very dangerous for you to argue with me, dangerous to your father and to you and to me. Don't think about Chernevog."

"Don't eavesdrop!" Thoughts of her friend went skirling away, like the mist. She could not hold them, could only feel the fear coming from the bathhouse—"Stop it, uncle!"

"Mouse, calm. Be calm. I'm not going to hurt anyone. Or frighten him unnecessarily. But you mustn't fight me. Go to sleep now."

"I don't want to go to sleep! I want to see him. I want you to let him out of the bathhouse! Please!"

"Don't be frightened, mouse." Her uncle touched beneath her chin, looking worried, but hard and distant, too. Like a stranger. "And don't listen to the boy. That's very dangerous. Do you hear me? —Do you hear me, Ilyana?"

"Yes," she said. She had to say yes. Her uncle put his hand on her eyes then, and wished her to sleep.

And she was not strong enough to stop him.

The door creaked and gave way abruptly: Yvgenie felt it go, too late, and sprawled in the dust at someone's feet—someone with a sword in his hand, who gathered him up by the arm while his eyes were confused by the sunlight. There were two of them— he could make that out; one of them was the dark-haired wizard.

"Come on," Pyetr's voice said: he was the one with the sword. But he could only take hold of Pyetr's sleeve and hold on to him, blinded as he was, and with his foot asleep. Pyetr tolerated it, put his other arm around him and helped him walk.

Pyetr took him as far as the first bench and let him down. The door was still open, the smoke hole let in light, and he could make out shapes again, through the watering of his eyes from the sun. Pottery clattered. He smelled hot tea, that Sasha was pouring, that Sasha then offered to him, and he held out both hands for the cup, not trusting one alone not to spill it.

It warmed his hands, it warmed his face, and he had not known till then how thirsty he was. It had a little vodka in it, besides the honey, and it soothed his throat of a pain he had not realized he was suffering.

He thought, They're not so bad, they don't mean me any harm after all.

Then Pyetr shut the door and latched it, and faced him with the sword crosswise in his hands. Yvgenie's heart went cold. He sat there with the empty cup in his hands, and Sasha asked him:

"More tea?"

"Please," he said, trying not to stammer, and looked away from Pyetr to hold out his cup, watching the teapot and the stream of tea and the swirl of bubbles, anything but the wizard's eyes. He drank the second cup more slowly, not chancing any glance at their faces. Then Pyetr left the door to stand behind him. Sasha poked at last night's ashes, and put on the last of the wood, provoking a few bright flames. Then he added herbs that sparked up like stars, and made a thick gray smoke.

"Did you sleep well, Yvgenie Pavlovitch?"

He could not make his tongue work right: "Well enough, sir."

"No dreams?"

He wanted not to recall those dreams: fire and shadow, and something touching him.

Sasha said, "Are you comfortable now, Yvgenie Pavlovitch?"

He still felt warm, felt, in fact, flushed with heat, but his fingers were growing numb again. He was going to lose the cup. He tried to hold on to it, but Sasha took it from his hands, and he sat stupidly trying to remember Sasha getting up—stared into Sasha's eyes when Sasha lifted his chin.

So he was caught. His heart pounded with fright, his head spun with the smoke. Sasha's whispered something to him, he had no idea of the words, until Sasha said, "Answer me, Chernevog," and he felt his lips move.

He said, not saying it, "My name is Yvgenie."

He thought, I've gone mad. And Sasha slapped his face, saying, "Kavi—"

It hurt. Not the slap. Something in his chest constricted about his heart, and he remembered that thing in the shadows last night, coming closer and closer to him, waiting for him to sleep or faint.

He had. He had been afraid when he waked this morning that it was too late, and now it answered for him, saying over and over again, in his voice, My name is Yvgenie Pavlovitch, I come from Kiev; while all the while he knew he had no home there, not now. His father had forbidden him to leave the house, and he had taken Bielitsa and run—

But he had forgotten why he had done a thing so desperate, except he had been running down little streets, going to a certain house.

He had been in love. But he was not now. He had found someone kind to him. But there was no one now. His father had ordered differently, and no one defied his father.

Pyetr and Sasha gave him honeyed tea, and spoke together— he could hear them, even when they thought not, saying that he was dead, that he had drowned last night, poor boy.

Sasha came and said to him that he should lie down on the bench, and sleep a while. He shook his head, hazily thinking of the blond girl of his dream warning him, pleading with him not to sleep, not to listen to them. He heard a frantic pounding at the bathhouse door, while his head was spinning and full of echoes. He leaned on his elbow and saw Pyetr go to that door and open it on blinding sun.

His rescuer was there, her hair like a flood of sunlight itself. She said, "I want to see him," and her father said, sternly, "Mouse, go do what your uncle told you. Not everything's right down here."

She leaned a little onto one foot, then, so he was looking right at her, and he took that vision of the girl and the sunlight like something holy, while her father shooed her outside and left, too—after more wood, he said to Sasha.

The door shut, the dark came back and he was alone with Sasha, whose face, lit from below with fire and above with sun filtering through from the smoke hole, became a vision, too, a hellish one. Sasha said, "Lie down, Yvgenie Pavlovitch. I wouldn't want you to fall and hurt yourself," and he had no choice: his arm began to shake under him. So he let himself face down on the smooth warm wood of the bench and watched Sasha feed bits of weed into the fire. He felt fevered, caught in a dream from which there was no hope of waking.

Sasha said, "How old are you, Yvgenie?"

He said, "Seventeen," but he knew at once that was not so, he was far older than that.

Sasha asked him, "Why did you come to this woods?"

And he said, or something said, "For—"

There *had* been a reason, something different than escape. Perhaps that would satisfy them. But he could not think of what. That reason fell away from him. It did not want to be there. And it was not.

The door banged, light flashed on the wall. It was Pyetr with the wood. And Sasha held up a hand, and said, very sternly, "Yvgenie Pavlovitch, what's his name?"

"Pyetr."

"And mine?"

"Sasha. Alexander Vas—"

"Tell me my *name*," the wizard commanded him, and something twisted next his heart, making him cold through and through.

He thought, Alexander Vasilyevitch. But he did not say so. He only knew that was the truth. He was in the bathhouse of a ferryman's cottage on a river that ran down to Kiev. The girl in the sunlight was a wizard, too, a young one, dangerous to everyone for that reason.

He knew then that he was going mad, or that something very scary had burrowed into his heart and made itself a nest it was not going to come out of. He let his head down against his hands and tried to remember who Yvgenie Pavlovitch was, or who his father was, or why he had no memory of a mother he thought he had loved, and vaguely knew was dead.

"I don't think I was mistaken," Sasha said at the edge of his hearing. "I very much fear not—but I can't lay hands on our visitor: he doesn't want to talk to us."

"I'll shake it out of him," Pyetr said, to Yvgenie's alarm, but Sasha said:

"No, I don't think you'll come at him that way. Be patient."
Sasha walked over and put his hand on Yvgenie's head, wanting
something, Yvgenie could not quite hear.

But Pyetr muttered something about rope and Sasha said that
they might let him out into the sunlight a bit instead and see
how he fared.

He did not understand. But Pyetr hauled him up by the arm
and walked him out the door into the light, and kept him walking despite the wobbling in his knees. The sun hurt his eyes.
Tears ran down his face, only from the light, at first, but then
they seemed to pour out of the confusion of his heart. He saw
the sun on a weathered rail, the light edging grass and flowers,
saw a black horse staring at him over the rail of a pen—a horse
he had—

—known somewhere. He knew this place. He knew this
house, and knew these two men wanted to keep him from Ilyana's sight. They intended to take him back into that dark
place very soon and by wizardry or by plain steel, take his life
away—because they could never trust him—he had deserved too
much ill of them, and done Pyetr too much hurt for Sasha ever
to trust him—

Yvgenie thought, Where have I met them? What did I do to
them?

They let him sit in the light a while, on the bottom rail of
the fence, where he could look at the house, and the woods
beyond the yard, and the horses that might have been a way of
escape if he had had the strength or the quickness to escape
them—but he did not, and he could not. The girl with the wonderful hair had it in braids when she came to say there was soup
ready, and they might bring him into the kitchen. He *knew* of
a sudden what that kitchen would look like; he knew the furniture inside—and the fireplace. He had sat there before—and
he was in love with this girl—

But her father said, "We'll have ours out here, mouse. Thank
you."

He listened to her voice, and watched his last hope of help
or even understanding walk away from him, head bowed—
watched her go, in the same way he looked at the sun or felt the
wind—storing every precious detail, against the dark waiting for
him inside—

Pyetr went into the house after her, and brought the soup back himself, in no good humor, and he told himself then he had had his last sight of the girl if her father had his way, or if Sasha had his.

"Have your lunch, boy," Pyetr said. "Or does turnip soup suit your appetites?"

"Be kind," Sasha said.

"Kind, hell," Pyetr said sullenly. "He needn't stare at her like that."

The soup held flavors too sharp to identify. The heat of it burned his mouth and left tears in his eyes and a lump in his throat.

A tear fell into the bowl, quite helplessly. It embarrassed him. He did not think he had been a coward. He tried not to be. He tried to think how to reason with them, or what he might say, but everything was confusion, everything scattered when he tried to think beyond this yard and the girl and the woods. He found nothing to say he had not said; he only tried to keep from shivering, so that he was hardly able to get up when they were finished, and when they wanted him to go back into the bathhouse. He tried to be braver. But the dark beyond the door seemed suddenly unbearable. He balked, spun about in the doorway to run, but Pyetr seized him and shoved him through.

He was blind, after, except the light from the smoke hole. He met a bench painfully with his shin and grabbed a post to save himself from falling. The door shut. The latch dropped.

God, he did not know why it had so offended Pyetr that he looked at his daughter, even that he had loved her, since he had never offered anything but a look, hardly spoken a word to her. He did not know why Pyetr should have brought him to his house, only for a wizard to lock him away in this place and ask him angry questions. Nothing made sense, not then, nor when Pyetr tied his hands behind him and Sasha made him kneel by the fire and breathe the bitter smoke—only that the thing inside him grew disturbed at that, and moved about his heart, tightening and tightening, like bands about his chest, and Pyetr stood by with the sword blade shining in the firelight, unsheathed, this time, to strike his head off, he supposed, when they had what they wanted—or if they did not, he had no idea.

He thought he heard Ilyana's voice, far and clear and cold, crying, No, papa, don't hurt him!

Then Sasha said:

"Eveshka's coming home, as fast as she can." And Pyetr said, "God, what can we do? If this Yvgenie lad is still alive—"

"We can get the mouse's help, perhaps."

"That's not damned likely, Sasha!"

Sasha then, with a ominous frown: "Or Chernevog could speak to us on his own. If he wanted to."

Yvgenie's heart was beating so it felt about to burst. He said, for no reason he could think of, "Go to hell."

"That's Chernevog," Pyetr said. "Or a boy with very bad manners."

Yvgenie began to shiver then, and he said, again without thinking, "She's her mother's image, Pyetr Ilitch. And her grandmother's."

Pyetr grabbed his collar. Yvgenie turned his face away, sure that Pyetr was going to hit him or cut off his head. But Pyetr did not. Pyetr held on to him a moment, then shook him as if to see if anything else would fall out of his mouth. Yvgenie murmured, in his own defense, "I didn't mean to say that, sir. I swear I didn't. I don't know what's the matter with me."

Pyetr said, "Damn." And hauled him close and held on to him, the way someone had once, he could not remember how long ago. Pyetr held the sword against his back and smoothed his hair gently, saying against his ear, "It's all right, boy. It's all right. The Snake's inside you, but he doesn't have all of you. We'll try to get him out."

"I think I'm d-dead," Yvgenie said, because something was telling him that. "I think I'm dead and he's alive, and pretty soon there won't be anything l-left of me."

"Damn him," Pyetr said. "Damn you, Snake, do you hear me? Kill the boy and I'll have a neck to wring with a clear conscience."

Something said, quite horridly, out of Yvgenie's mouth, "This one isn't to my account. I'd not have beaten him, or driven him to drown himself. But he's avenged for that, dear Owl, I do swear to you. His father's dead."

"Dammit!" Pyetr said, while Yvgenie listened to his own

mouth speaking, and heard, inside, a voice like his own, saying, Yvgenie, Yvgenie, the world won't miss him. Surely you don't. The men he'd have killed should be grateful. And he won't be coming here.

He wept against Pyetr's shoulder. He did not know why. It did not seem to him he had ever loved his father: he remembered the huge stairway and the gilt and the paintings; and his father holding him by the shirt and hitting him in the face—but he surely had loved someone—he had the strongest feeling he had loved the girl who had saved him, but his whole life was sliding away from him, all the things he might have loved, all the things he might have wanted, even his name, and his father's name.

He had Pyetr. He had the memory of Ilyana and the river. He had a wizard who believed someone inside him was his enemy, and who wanted to drive this thing out of him—or get answers from it—while Pyetr waited to cut his head off—and, god, he wanted to live, if only to find out who he was, or what he might have been, or whether he deserved to be treated like this.

"Poor lad," Pyetr said—he had hoped if he could once do right he might find kindness somewhere. But he heard his own voice whispering to him in his heart.

We're old friends, Pyetr and I. And his wife. A most remarkable man—friend of wizards, and magical things, and quite reliable. He wants us both to be ghosts. Be glad *he's* not the wizard.

Sasha was setting out herbs. Sasha said, quietly, "Just hold on to him, Pyetr."

"What are you doing?" Pyetr asked. "What do you hope to do?"

"I don't know what I'm doing," Sasha said. "If I knew I'd do it. I just don't want him wandering about tonight, in whatever form."

"Salt in a circle won't work. It never stopped my wife."

"I'd say keep the rope on him for his own protection." Sasha's voice again, quiet, as he tossed pinches of dust into the fire. "His and ours."

"We can't just talk about him," Pyetr said. "He's not a sack of turnips."

"Beware your heart," Sasha said. "If there's a shred of his own life left in him, we'll try to find it—" Sasha moved between

Yvgenie and the fire, a faceless shadow as he rested on Yvgenie's shoulder. "Go to *sleep!*" he said suddenly.

"I don't want to die," he protested; he had heard the anger, he saw it in Sasha's face, and said, while he was falling, "Pyetr, help me. Pyetr, dammit, listen to me—" as the shadow wrapped him in.

Not dead, Pyetr thought, with the boy's weight gone heavy in his arms. "What in hell was *that* about?" he asked, and held on to the boy as much to still his own shaking as for any good he could do. Something was grievously wrong, he was sure of it, but Sasha gave him no answer. Sasha had leapt to his feet, looking out toward the walls, toward nowhere—crying, "No! Stay out, stay away, you can't help us—"

Eveshka, Pyetr thought, and heard her like an ache in his heart. Eveshka had wanted the boy dead. She wanted him—

" 'Veshka," he muttered against the boy's hair, "listen to Sasha. It's a poor, drowned boy, 'Veshka, and it's Kavi's foolishness, don't do anything—"

Something happened. Sasha moved between him and that source; or wished a silence, or something of the like. Sasha cried aloud, "Eveshka, you're a fool. Do you understand me? Your husband won't forgive you that foolishness. Your daughter won't. Listen to me, dammit!"

It might have been a long while that passed. Pyetr's leg began to tremble under him, in its uncomfortable bend, the boy's weight grew heavier and heavier in his arms; he was sure something was going on, something both magical and desperate between his wife and his friend, and he ducked his head, pressed his brow against the boy's shoulder and made his own pleas for calm.

Eveshka said to him then, so clear it seemed to ring in winter air, Pyetr, I'm on my way home. I want you to let go of the boy, I want you not to touch him, not to think about him, I want you to go to the house immediately and take care of our daughter, do you hear me? Now!

So many wants. An ordinary man had no choice without a wizard's help. As it was, he had trouble letting the boy down gently and standing up.

He said, " 'Veshka—"

But she was not listening. She refused to hear him, and speech damned up in his throat. So he thought, instead, about the heart he had held for her, about its terrible selfishness, that weighed a lost boy's life so little against its wants and its opinions, and thought, I'm safer from him than from you, 'Veshka. He could only threaten what I love. You *are* what I love. What can I do against that?

He saw Sasha take a breath. He found one of his own.

"God," Sasha breathed then. And: "Mouse!"

The door banged open. His daughter was standing there in the sunlight. She looked at the boy on the floor, she looked at them, and said, faintly.

"Mother's coming home."

Pyetr crossed the floor to reach her, but she fled the doorway, out into the blinding sun, and ran across the yard before she so much as stopped to look back at him, not wanting them to touch her, no.

"Mouse, we need your help!"

"I don't *want* to help you!" she cried, and turned and bolted along the side of the house, braids flying, running like someone in pain.

"Oh, god," he said, and took out after her, fearing she might head for the river, or loose some foolish wish. He heard Volkhi protest something, a loud and clear challenge, he heard Ilyana running up to the porch before he rounded the corner of the house, and she looked down at him from that vantage. She was crying.

"Mouse, I've got quite enough with your mother right now. Are you going to wish me in the river? Or are you going to listen to me first?"

"No one ever listens! I told you he wasn't any harm!"

"But he is, mouse! He may be your friend, but he's killed that boy, mouse, he's wished your uncle's house burned, he nearly killed your uncle—do you call that no harm?"

She set her hands on the rail and bit her lip. Maybe she was listening. Or maybe his daughter was wishing him in the river, he had no idea. He heard the horses snorting and stamping about behind him, but he kept his eyes on his daughter and his jaw set as he advanced as far as the walk-up.

"Your mother is on her way back here," he said, setting his hand on the rail. "She's not in a good mood, mouse, and I'm trying to reason with her. But it's not easy."

"She'd better look out, then. She's not going to kill him, papa! Nobody's going to kill him!"

"I've talked to your friend. He's here to see you, mouse— mouse, dammit—"

But his daughter had gone inside, and the door slammed.

He started up to the porch. He lost his conviction halfway up, that he truly wanted to go into the house, or talk to his daughter. He looked aside in frustration and saw—god, a strange white horse with its nose across the hedge, a horse bridled and saddled, holding discussion with their three horses in the stableyard.

Damn! he thought. He did *not* like this. It took no wizardry for a lost horse to smell out the only other horses in these woods, and Yvgenie had lost one in the flood. It was the sudden accumulation of coincidences that set his nape hairs on end—that and the storm feeling hanging over the house.

That was from his daughter—who might or might not be responsible for the horse, which, *dammit*, was at least an indication that wizardry was lending them more trouble, and might have something to say about someone needing to get somewhere; or might mean only that Ilyana thought the boy should have his horse back. He set his jaw and doggedly did what he did not want at all to do, walked up to the porch, banged the door open and said, before he had realized it, in his own father's most angry voice:

"Mouse?"

She was in her room: the door was shut.

He knocked. He softened his voice. "Mouse, this is no time for tantrums. I *need* you, your uncle needs you and there's a visitor at the fence. Dry your eyes and come out here."

She said, through the door, "I don't know why anybody asks me when they never believe what I say. I'm sure the horse is my fault. Everything else is!"

"No one's saying anything's your fault, mouse, don't put words in my mouth. Come out here and be reasonable."

A long silence.

"Mouse?"

"I don't know what's happening," a small voice came back. "Papa, mother's going to do something awful to him. She's coming back and she's going to kill him."

"She's not going to kill him, mouse. She may even think she will, but she hasn't seen him. He seems a nice lad, other visitors aside—I'm sure he owns the horse out there, and it's not at all remarkable it came calling. Horses' noses work very well without magic. But Chernevog is involved in his being here, and you won't get your way slamming doors, mouse. Certainly not with your mother. We didn't hurt the boy, I swear to you we didn't. We need to talk about this."

Another long silence.

"Mouse, we're all very tired. Your uncle's at his wits' end and so am I, please don't cry."

"I won't let mother kill anybody and I won't let her make you do it!"

"Neither will I, mouse. That's a promise. But I want you to listen to me. Please. I want you to be ever so good and reasonable, and *please* don't scare your mother, for the god's sake, mouse."

"She wants you to kill that boy!"

"It's not her fault. It was a mistake and she knew it. And I'm not easy to wish. Do you mind if I open the door?"

"No! Don't!"

He dropped his hand from the latch without thinking about it. He said, patiently, reasonably, "Ilyana, we're going to help him."

"How? By wishing him dead? Why not? All my friends are dead. I don't have any living ones."

His own vinegar was in that remark.

"All right," he said to the door, "mouse, I suppose I'll have to do without your help. And I could truly use it right now."

"What do you want me to do?"

He pushed the door open. She was sitting in the middle of the bed. Babi was in her arms. Babi growled at him. Babi was not wont to do that. But he was not wont to fight with his daughter either.

He said, quietly, "There's a strange horse out there. That's one thing. And there's the house and the mud. I don't want your mother to have anything to complain about when she gets here."

"I did that, papa, you haven't even looked. I even scrubbed the floors."

He had not noticed. Not a bit. He looked at the floor, looked up at his daughter's reddened eyes.

"I'm terribly sorry, mouse. I really am."

"You're being awful to that boy, papa. You're scaring him, I can hear it!"

"Chernevog deserves it. The boy doesn't, not by anything I see. But in all truth, mouse, I'm afraid there's very little of the boy left. Rusalki do that kind of thing. Between Chernevog and your mother, I don't know where we stand—but the boy hasn't a chance in hell if certain people don't use their heads right now. If you and Sasha can agree about the boy, the two of you might have a chance of convincing your mother. I don't know about Chernevog—but if you do have any influence, reasoning with him wouldn't be a bad idea, either."

Ilyana looked terribly pale, terribly frightened. Babi went on growling, and the domovoi in the cellar caught the fit, so that all the house timbers creaked. "Uncle would side with mother," she said. "He thinks the boy is already dead, or good as, and there's no hope. He's no hope. He *can't* help me, he won't, he'll say he's being fair, but he wants him away from me, too. He's upset and he's *not* being very quiet about it."

"Try."

"*No*, papa!"

He started toward her, but he found the room spinning around him, and the floor and the edge of the bed came up at him.

He said, or thought he said, Mouse, stop! and thought that his daughter had tried to catch him, far beyond her strength to do, before he hit the bedstead and his head hit the floor.

Her shadow fell over him. He felt a somewhat damp kiss on the forehead, and the brush of her hand, and heard her say, Let her blame me for it, papa, not you. Please, *please*, papa, be all right. . . .

Sasha had fallen with no warning, and no reason so far as Yvgenie could see, and he was sure any moment now Pyetr would come back and conclude it was *his* fault his friend was lying unconscious on the floor, and not ask further questions. Yvgenie sat frozen in dread of the next insane event, hoping Sasha would move or give him some clue that he was even alive; but when Sasha did not wake up in the next moment, or the next, or still the next, Yvgenie bit his lip and cast an anxious glance toward the door, beginning to think he might make a break for it, now, this instant, never mind that his hands were tied, and only hope *not* to meet Pyetr coming in. He was a fool to have waited this long—if he had not waited too long already. And with a deep breath and a great effort he wobbled to his feet and looked to see if he might by some stretch of luck find a knife among Sasha's pots and herbs.

There was no such luck; and Sasha was most surely still breathing, though he was lying at a most uncomfortable angle, close to the hot stones. Yvgenie edged away, banged his knee on a bench in his retreat and stumbled into the door, sure that at the last moment Pyetr was going to arrive and cut his head off.

The door gave without resistance. Sun hit his eyes and tears welled up as he followed the side of the bathhouse toward the stable. That was where he reasoned he might find a knife, or some edge to free his hands; and a horse to carry him out of here before the wizard awoke and caught him.

He blinked his eyes clear, saw something white outside the hedge, and it was Bielitsa, it was *his* horse out there—

He staggered along the fence to the stable itself, up under the shadow of the woods. He bent and ducked through the rails—

And heard a door open somewhere up at the house.

He caught his balance in the corner of the fence and the stable wall and saw Ilyana looking at him from the side of the porch. He wished her, Please don't tell your father. Please just go inside and don't tell anyone—that's all you have to do—god, please, miss.

She left the porch railing: he thought she was going back inside. But she came down the walk-up instead, casting anxious glances his way. She ran across the yard toward him as he leaned helplessly against the wall, thinking—

Thinking how the sun shone on her hair as she ducked through the fence, and how beautiful she was as she crossed the stableyard, and how if her father would kill him for looking at her, he would flay him alive for involving her in his escape—

but seeing the distress on her face he wondered next if Sasha's malady might not have befallen her father; she looked as if she wanted help, and, oh, god, he could hardly stand on his feet, let alone rescue fathers who wanted to kill him, for beautiful wizard-daughters who equally threatened his life.

She said breathlessly, "You've got to get out of here." He agreed with that. He turned his back so she could get at the knots—to no avail, he felt after a moment of painful effort. She said, "Wait, I'll get a knife."

They were going to be caught, they were surely going to be caught and her father was going to cut him in pieces. He leaned his shoulders against the stable shed while she ducked into the shed—his head kept spinning and he could hardly hold his feet as it was, and somehow he had to get out of the yard, get on his horse and go fast enough and far enough—and he doubted he was going to get ten steps before the spell that had allowed his escape unraveled and he found himself with an indignant wizard and an irate father. More, he had no idea where he should go to escape: wizards he knew about sold curses and told fortunes. They did not crawl about inside one's heart and talk from other people's mouths and compel them do whatever they wanted.

The girl came out again and cut him free, sawing his thumb in the process—*her* hands were shaking, he realized, which said that she was scared too. "I'm sorry," she said, about his thumb, but he swore that he was all right, and turned about to thank her and take his leave.

She said, "There's a horse. It's his. I've my book and everything packed. We've got to get out of here."

Where? he wanted to know. What 'his'? A girl looked him in the eyes the way she looked at him and told him they were running away together—and the ghost inside him reached out his arm without his thinking about it and touched her arm with numbed, clumsy fingers, saying, "Ilyana, where are you going? What do you hope to do?"

"My mother wants you *dead*, she's already *wished* that, do you understand? It's too dangerous to talk to my father, he can't help what he might do—"

His hand fell, painful and half-dead from the rope, and he believed her: he remembered Pyetr and Sasha talking, remembered them saying something ominous about Pyetr's wife—

Who was not reasonable, not at all reasonable.

Eveshka was her name . . .

"Come *on*," she said, pulling at him. "My father's asleep, but *she* isn't, she's coming here right now on the boat. She'll be here before dark."

He found himself crossing the stableyard before he realized where he was heading, but it was where he *would* go. He ducked through the fence, breathless and staggering, clung to it to hold him up as far to the hedge and the gate.

It *was* Bielitsa. He stumbled his way toward her and held onto the hedge, longing to touch her again, to touch anything that was his, any shred of his life that he could get back again—

Bielitsa did come to him, by tentative steps, let him catch her reins and hug her about the neck. He hung there, dizzy and catching his breath; and slowly felt stronger, as if her warm, solid presence brought sanity back to the world, and breath back into his body.

He knew one thing for true. He loved this mare more than anything in his life and if he had left her behind his father would have killed her for spite—because no one got away from his father, no one defied his orders, not his servants and not his son—

His father dead? God, his father was incapable of dying. Other people did. His mother had. Her sister had, and her sister's son. He heard the thump of axes—heard the voices shouting into the winter air—

He fumbled after the reins, patted Bielitsa's chest and neck to steady her and managed to get his foot in the stirrup and himself into the saddle, courting dizziness to drive the memory out.

A face, and gilt, and paintings. He had seen the tsar—many times; and knew that if the tsar knew what he knew he would cut off his father's head. He could do that to his father with a handful of words. He had had that power for years, and he did not know what had held his tongue, whether it was fear or the remote hope of being loved—because the tsar would never love him, the tsar would have no reason to trust a traitor's son, and no one would trust him, then, no one in all the Russias would have him—

Ilyana led her horse up to the house, and left it to stand

while she ran up to the porch and inside—to get her belongings, he supposed, while his heart pounded against his ribs and he waited for disaster. He wished they might have reasoned with her father—not a wicked man, he thought, only someone with just reason now to kill him.

Something fell into place then with the ghost next his heart, an eerie familiarity with Pyetr, and that situation. I've been here before, he thought. I've fled this house before. God, why? It seems all the same reason. It seems all the same time—but I do it again and again, until somehow I get away—but where to, but worse than this? That seems where we're bound, and it's happened before, it happens over and over again, forever—oh, god, where's an escape for us?

6

✠ ✠ ✠ ✠ The weathered wood of the landing showed
pale gray in the evening light as the boat met
the buffers, with no Pyetr and no Sasha to help bring it to shore.
Eveshka leapt from the deck to the boards and managed to get
a line snubbed about the mooring post, while the boat, with a
reckless amount of way on it, scraped along the dock. It hit the
limit of the rope: the rope held and the post did, and that was
all she waited to see. She whirled and flew up the hill, skirts
clinging and binding about her boots, catching at the hedge as
she forced her way through. She ran across the yard and up to
the porch.

"Pyetr!"

The door was unlatched. The house was dark, except the
gray light from open shutters. Embers still smoldered in the
hearth. The House-thing in the cellar groaned mournfully and
the floor creaked with the peculiarly desolate sound of empty
houses.

"Pyetr?"

She looked around her, with the most terrible conviction of
wizardry still enveloping the house and the yard. She flung wide
the door to her daughter's bedroom, saw bedclothes in disarray,
tumbled on the floor—and Pyetr lying beside the bed, not in the
way of someone sleeping, but with a pillow under his head and
a blanket over him all the same. She knelt and brushed back his
hair, saw a trail of blood running back above his ear, from a
lump on his forehead.

She refused to be angry. She refused to think of anything in
the world but of Pyetr's well-being. She took his cold hand in
hers, saying, "Pyetr, wake up, Pyetr."

His eyes opened. He blinked at her, confused at the dim light, at her presence, at the memory of their daughter: she eavesdropped without a qualm, demanding precisely what he last remembered, what he had felt—

Such hurt and such self-accusation—

She did *not* think about Ilyana. She did not want to be angry. She wondered only where Sasha was, wanting him to be all right; and thought how she loved Pyetr more than she could love her own life: that was what had saved him all those years past. Perhaps it still saved him—even while she wished his head not to ache and the lump to go away.

"She's gone with him, isn't she?"

"I don't know where she is." She framed every word carefully, holding Pyetr's face at the center of her thoughts, reminding her who was hurt, not who had done the hurting. "North of here, with him, yes, I'm sure she is."

Pyetr lifted his head off the pillow, reached for the bedstead to get up, and she gave him room. Somewhere nearby—the bathhouse, she thought—Sasha had waked, and she wished him up, on his feet and out the door, never *mind* his aches and his bruises, which he damned well deserved for his carelessness.

You *knew* better, she wanted Sasha to know, while Pyetr was staggering from the bedstead to the wall to the door, with every intention of riding after Ilyana, immediately, this instant.

She followed Pyetr into the kitchen, watched him gather supplies in an achingly random, confused way, while the blood traced a thin trail down his cheek. He was not upset with Ilyana, that was the hurtful thing. He believed it was his fault: Ilyana was only an innocent misled by a scoundrel—maybe not even a thorough-going scoundrel, at that, only a most desperate and unhappy ghost. Pyetr's capacity for forgiveness outraged her sense of justice and was such gentle sanity when she borrowed from him—

But that borrowing was like the other borrowing, the killing one; and it reminded her that she could have the strength to stop her daughter. She could have it at any moment she wanted to take it. . . .

While in the same reckless way Pyetr forgave Ilyana and Kavi, Pyetr forgave her, too, for things that, dammit, were not even true; and never had been. But how could one possibly refuse forgiveness for sins one had not done, when there were so many worse she contemplated?

He said, glancing around at her in shock, "God—where's Sasha?"

"On his way." A tear spilled down her cheek, all unexpected. His innocent dread made a complete wreck of her calm constructions. She wished not. She wished the whole business *not*, but that was mortally dangerous, oh, god, it was—

He flung his arms about her, hugged the breath out of her and said, " 'Veshka, 'Veshka, they're just young fools. I scared her. It's all my fault. She thinks she's protecting the boy, that's all. Don't panic. We'll get her back."

"She's protecting *him*? Don't! Don't argue with me! You don't know what they're thinking, and I don't want to wonder. Please—*please*!"

He caught her face between his hands, wanting her to look at him. "Wife, *I* was a handful. I know what she's thinking. We locked her in and we locked her out, and she couldn't breathe, that's all. *I* would have run, in her place—and dumped my father on his head, too, if he was trying to stop me—but she didn't mean to hurt anybody, 'Veshka. You know she could have done much worse—"

"Pyetr, dammit, she's not all your daughter! *Wishes* are her mother and her father, and we even don't know whose! I never knew why I had her!"

"She wanted to be born, that's all, the same way she wanted the filly. Two fools like us hadn't a chance."

She caught his hands. "Don't joke, Pyetr! God, don't joke, you don't understand what you're saying, you never have understood me! She shouldn't have been born. . . . She shouldn't *exist*, Pyetr, I don't know how I ended up carrying her, to this day I don't know!"

"You don't mean that."

"Pyetr, you don't feel it, you don't *feel* the silence out there. She's pulled a curtain around her, she's invisible, she's the whole damned *woods*. Pyetr! God, I *love* her, but love's not enough! —I should never have left you with her!"

He took her wrong. She hurt him. He turned away to his packing, saying, "I'll get her back." And, god—she all but *wanted* to want him to understand her, but he already blamed himself for losing her, and she was too confused to know what was right to want of him—

Meanwhile Sasha was on his way up to the porch, a very sore and repentant Sasha, who opened the door and said, cheerfully, "Well, she certainly did it, didn't she?"

She restrained what she thought. She bit her lips on what she thought of Sasha's damnable levity and Sasha's choices thus far, until she tasted blood.

And thought of thorns.

Sasha said, "They've taken the filly, that's all. We can overtake them."

She said, "I'll take the boat. And I'm not a fool, Sasha. Let's have no arguments. You know my opinions. I'll allow you yours. But for the god's sake don't tell me nothing's wrong!"

Pyetr said, desperately, "Let's not for the god's sake quarrel. You pack. I'll get after her. There's more than one horse, Sasha. His showed up. —'Veshka, do you have any clear idea where she's going?"

"North. And you're not going after her alone. She has no idea what she's going to do. *I* have no idea. She's never fought us like this."

"Then she's damned scared, is all! Hell, 'Veshka, maybe we should all just let her alone, let her think! If we all take off after her—"

"With *him*, let her alone?"

"Hush," Sasha said. "No. I agree with both of you. We shouldn't press her, but we shouldn't let her go off on her own either. There's too much come loose the last few days—more wishes than hers are involved here, and she doesn't know what she's going to do: she doesn't even realize what she *can* do— that's the worst danger. She could have killed you, Pyetr, with a less specific wish."

"Then she's smarter than that. She *knows* what she's doing, she's doing exactly what you predicted she'd do—what anybody would do, who's cornered . . . For the god's sake, it's *Ilyana* we're talking about—"

"—in Kavi's company," Eveshka cried. "Is that what you want?"

He looked at her in distress and she was sorry she had shouted at him, she was sorry for wanting him to listen to her opinions. She put her arms about him, wanted him well, wanted him to understand her fears, at least. "Love's no defense," she whispered. "God, protect yourself."

He said, his chin against her hair, "Love's *not* a defense; that's the entire point, isn't it?"

He terrified her. He went at fear the way he went at fences, headlong. And if what he loved had no concern for him—

"Ilyana's being selfish," she said, as reasonably as she could. "She's scared, yes. We're so easily frightened. Everything's so unstable to us. When your feet are sliding—it's very hard to love anyone but yourself."

"She's your daughter," he said. "And you do."

"Don't trust me, dammit!" She pushed away from him, and realized Sasha's embarrassed presence. "God, you reason with him!"

She ran for the door, ran down from the porch and across the yard.

" 'Veshka!" she heard Pyetr shouting after her, afraid for her, angry at her, she did not want to know. She wished she had kissed him goodbye. She wanted to run back now and do that, which would only make leaving him harder, and lead to arguments. She wished instead to welcome him home, sometime yet to come, which was as close as she dared come to wishing for their lives and this house—

But even that wish might have a darker side. Anything might. Everything might. Don't trust me, was the safest wish for them: Don't love me, she had tried for years.

" 'Veshka!" Pyetr shouted furiously, and maybe it was a wish that anchored him to the porch, maybe it was his own knowledge that his effort was foredoomed—but he had a sure notion which when he felt Sasha's hand fall on his shoulder. Sasha said, "Let's get packed. She's had a good start."

He shook the hand off, and was sorry he had done that. Sasha knew more than he did about what had happened, probably knew more than he did about Eveshka's intentions at the moment and Sasha had made no attempt to stop her. "What's she up to? What's she going to do when she finds them? Reason with them? Not damned likely!"

Sasha said, "Come on. Let's get what we need in the house."

"*She's* the one we ought to chase down! Why aren't we stopping her? Is it your idea? Or mine? Or hers?" He slammed his hand onto the rail. "God, I'm going crazy!"

Sasha said, "I think it's because neither of us can keep her here. And she could be right. We don't know *who* wanted Ilyana to be born. It wasn't 'Veshka's idea."

Heat stung his face. Anger welled up. "Babies do happen without magic, Sasha, and once they're started, they do get born!"

"Not to wizards."

No damned time or place to argue *that* point. He muttered, "To wizards the same as anyone else, unless they wish not," and started into the house to get his coat, his sword, provisions—

"The point is," Sasha pursued him at the door, "she's surrounded herself with protections for her life and her way. It shouldn't have just happened—"

"Protections against what?" He turned around, stopping Sasha short in the doorway. "Against the fact we love each other? Is that *safe*, Sasha? Is that even sane? She loves the mouse!"

Sasha said faintly, "She knew the hazards, too."

"The mouse isn't a damned hazard! She's the best thing that's ever happened to us!"

"There were others who could have wanted it. That's the *point*, Pyetr. That's what she's scared of."

"All right, all right, let's say it, shall we? Her mother. Draga. Draga's influence is what she's afraid of. But Draga's dead!"

He saw it coming, knew he had been the fool before Sasha even said the obvious: "So is Chernevog."

Babi had come with them, trotting along with a slight disturbance of dead leaves, upset and growling all the way.

Which might tell you something, mouse, her uncle would say to her. She had wanted Babi to stay with her father to be sure he was safe until her mother got home (and afterward) but Babi had turned up by Patches' feet as she led Patches out the gate—and now at the edge of dusk Owl joined them, too, flying ahead of them through the dark, a gliding wisp of white with black barring.

"What's that?" Yvgenie asked anxiously.

"Only Owl."

"He's not a real owl," Yvgenie objected, meaning, she supposed, that he was not a live owl. She said, distractedly, wishing silence close about them: "He's real. Ghosts are real." Yvgenie made her think of her father, so deaf to wishes, and so patient and good-hearted despite his weariness. She wanted to help him, but worrying about him or her father was dangerously distracting to her right now, and she longed for Kavi to speak to her again, but that was not fair. It was even dangerous to Yvgenie—

She thought it and Yvgenie's head began to nod—perhaps that her wish had done it, perhaps that Yvgenie had grown too weak or too weary to care any longer about overhanging branches. "Stay on," she wished him, riding Patches close where there was room among the trees. She pushed at his shoulder. "Please don't fall off." She had had enough of bumps on undeserving heads for one day, please the god, when she dared not even wish her father well now, dared not reach back into the house where her mother's wishes hung so thick and so stiflingly strong.

Wishes in that house had been directing their lives from generations before she was even born or her father or Sasha had ever come to live there. Magic in that house was all about her, attached to the china, the doors, stitched into the clothes she wore—magic there must always be more convolute than she knew, different than she could possibly understand. She could feel it tonight reaching even into the woods—and most of it was her mother's, she knew that now. All her life her mother had told her not to use magic, but her mother had been doing it all along, so subtly no one could catch her. Her mother had expected evil of her; her mother was afraid of anybody who wanted something in the least different than she did, that was the trouble with her mother: her mother wanted every living thing in the world to do what *she* wanted forever, to live all their lives as *she* wanted—that was how her mother's presence felt in the house, now that she had felt its absence.

Her mother did not want to be known, uncle had admitted to her: her mother would never give her heart to a child, in any sense—because, for one thing, no one *ever* did anything good enough for her mother. No one could: her mother trusted no one. Her mother's magic would strangle her, snarl her in its tangled threads and smother her father and her uncle if they tried to protect her, unless she could find somewhere a place those wishes had never reached—

Don't trust her, papa, don't listen to her, she's so scared, and so strong, and she *wants*, papa, she *wants*, stronger than I can deal with—stronger even than uncle can deal with—

The mouse could never hurt anyone. But her mother had always believed she would hurt her father—and now, dammit, mostly thanks to her mother, she had done that, in every sense. Beliefs, she meant to write in her book, can come true like wishes, when you put them on people.

But her father and her uncle had refused to listen to a child. They had only worried about her mother's feelings, and her mother's hurt, and never, ever thought their fifteen-year-old daughter might understand a danger everybody older had failed to see.

The mouse was running away now, because she could not stay the mouse anymore, not after her mother had wanted her father to kill an innocent boy only for being near her. A wish like that could come true years from now, and they would never, never know when, or how, even if her father might *like* Yvgenie and never want to harm him: he could still, within that wish, be responsible for an accident.

She would find her Place, she would make a house of her own, the way her uncle had had his house on the hill (and even that had not proved safe). She had no idea whether her mother had had anything to do with that storm, but she had her suspicions and she meant to keep a further distance than her uncle had if it was only a lean-to in the woods. She would have this boy and Babi and Patches and the white mare, and once things were settled and she was sure her wishes were strong enough to protect them, then her father and her uncle could visit her house and say how well she was looking; and she would cook supper for them, yes, and ask how her mother was, and whether her mother was speaking to her yet—

Her mother was loosing the cable that bound the boat to the dock. Above the steady creak of saddles and the jingle of bridle rings came the sinister lapping of water and the groan of old timbers—

Ilyana, came out of the dark and the silence, Ilyana, you're wrong. *Listen* to me while you still *can* listen. You're making wrong choices. He's already led you to hurt your father.

She didn't *want* to hear. No! She made her silence back again, but anger was a flaw, wondering about her father was—

Your father trusted you, and now he can't believe you: that's the first thing you've done. You hurt him and you hurt your uncle, who could have been seriously hurt, young miss, and you're not thinking about anything right now but your own way. That's wrong. Look at what you're doing. Are you acting like the daughter we taught?

"No!" she screamed aloud to the dark, struggling to keep her wits about her, and not to hear the river or the reproach in her mother's voice. "You don't love anything! You don't care! You're the one that's selfish, mother, you're the one that's taking over everything and killing everything! I'd talk to you if I could, but I can't, I can't trust your promises! If I came back we'd fight, and that wouldn't be good, *would* it, mother, because *somebody* might stop you from having your own way, *somebody* might tell you how you've hurt my father and my uncle all my life! Papa can't laugh with you. But he can with me, mother! *Stop wishing at him! Don't tell me who's hurting him!*"

"God," Yvgenie whispered, as the wind skirled round them and caught at the horses' manes and sifted leaves down through the branches. Patches sidestepped and Ilyana held her in: her mother called that wind and wanted the horses to take fright and leave them. Her mother wanted harm to Yvgenie; but she wanted *not*. Patches was *hers*, Yvgenie was *hers*, the white mare was *his*, and her mother could keep her distance. —Dammit, just let us alone! Give me time! Give me *room*, mother! If you ever want to hear from me again, give me room!

Patches shivered under her. The smothering feeling went away, like a cloud passing the moon, and Owl glided close, making an entire turn about them.

"Yvgenie, it's all right. It's all right. Don't worry."

"I'm not afraid," he said, and added, with a stammer, "except of wizards. And ghosts. —Can your mother really hear you like that?"

"She can hear me," she said. "But she's not listening." She wished not to shed the tears she found in her eyes. "She never listens."

Yvgenie said, faintly, "Maybe we should go back and talk with your father. Even if he's not happy with me right now."

"No!" She shook her head and wiped her eyes and lifted her chin. "Someone's needed to tell my mother no for a long time. Papa can't. Uncle can't. But I have. And by the god I will."

"I don't get a sense of where they are at all," Sasha said as Pyetr came down from the porch with the baggage. Eveshka was already down at the shore—well away by now, Pyetr was sure.

"Fine," he said, handing up Sasha's baggage to him on Missy's back. "In the woods. That's where they are. Going north, with a long head start. —Where are the leshys? What's Misighi doing, for the god's sake? If she's holding a silence out there, haven't they noticed?"

"Not that I can tell. But I did hear her—just a moment ago, and I don't think she intended that. I don't really get the idea we're unwelcome to follow her, either. It's a very odd feeling. A spooky kind of feeling, to tell the truth."

"It's her mother she doesn't want to meet," Pyetr muttered. He flung two of their heavier bags up onto Volkhi's back and tied them down tight. "I can't say I blame her, all things considered. Sasha, if you get another chance, tell her *I'll* come ahead and talk to her, myself, alone, no magic, nothing of the sort—"

"That wouldn't be wise to do."

"Wise, hell! She's my *daughter*, Sasha, not some outlaw!"

"She's not alone, either."

"Fine, Chernevog's with her!" He finished the ties. "I'm sure that gives me *much* more peace of mind!"

"I'm *not* putting you in Chernevog's hands, not twice. We're only lucky he's on good behavior."

"Good behavior." He gathered up Volkhi's reins while Sasha was securing his own baggage to Missy's saddle. "It wasn't good behavior that brought him here in the first place, it wasn't good behavior that made trouble between my daughter and my wife, if you haven't reckoned that. It damned sure wasn't good behavior when he killed that boy!"

"Or kept him alive. I'm less and less certain he has killed the boy, in the strictest interpretation of things."

"Interpretation? A handsome young boyaryevitch from Kiev just happens to fall in our brook in a rainstorm that happens to burn your house down? His horse just happens to find our front hedge the very hour my daughter runs off with Chernevog? So what do we call it? An uncommon spate of accidents?"

"No. But wishes can ride right over a boy who happened to be in their way. Anyone's might have—even mine. Mine might still do him harm, I don't know. Maybe wishing us well, I've unintentionally wished this poor boy into the brook that night."

Dreadful thought. Paralyzing thought. A man couldn't move who thought such a thing. "Sasha, that's damned foolishness. You've never wanted anybody to die."

"Hush," Sasha said hoarsely. "Please, Pyetr."

"Well, hell, leave your thieving uncle Fedya out of it! Reasons count for something, don't they? And yours don't kill innocents. Let's not for the god's sake sit and wait till everyone's sure, shall we? Let's wish my daughter to use the sense she was born with, first! Let's wish she'd stop worrying about her mother and worry about herself—and talk sense into the young fool that's running away with her. Hell, wish her to talk sense into Chernevog, while we're about it!"

"I've done that."

"And tell her I'm not upset about her dropping me on my head. It's far too hard to hurt. Make her understand that!"

"I've tried."

" 'Veshka wouldn't hurt her or the boy. Not when it really comes down to it—I've proved that, more than once. Oh, hell, never mind explaining everything. Tell her stop and wait for me. Tell her I won't lay a hand on her or the boy."

A damned lot of baggage to slow them down—only reasonable, Pyetr told himself: wizards needed books and herbs, and Sasha had needed time to gather such things out of the cellar— all of which had put them further behind, while Eveshka took a lead on them, not mentioning Missy's slower pace giving the mouse that much more continual advantage over them.

Small blame he could pass to Sasha or 'Veshka for the mess. He had made the essential mistake: he had had his head bounced off the side of a substantial bedstead onto an uncompromising floor—not the first time in his life that had happened, the god knew, but certainly the most deserved. He had yelled at the mouse, he had scared his daughter like a fool, and the mouse had no more than protected herself. Absolutely it had been their mouse whose wish had dropped him on his head—he could think of no sane reason Kavi Chernevog would have delayed to put a pillow under his head and a blanket over him, or waited while Ilyana did it, if he were in charge.

Besides which the mouse was terribly upset at leaving him behind. A man associated with wizards learned to trust his most unreasonable convictions as wizardous in origin—

In which light he knew the mouse had felt that crack on the head far worse than he had. It was entirely like a young wizard not to realize that a man wished asleep on his feet might fall onto the furniture—and, a former scapegrace himself, he was even proud of the mouse for having the presence of mind afterward to take her book and her inkwell, to pack food and blankets, all very foresighted behavior for a youngster, never mind she had filched every last single sausage in the house, the pot of kitchen salt, and half the flour, but, by all they could figure, not a smidge of oil to mix it with.

That was absolutely a youngster in charge.

Then she must have caught Yvgenie Pavlovitch down by the stable fence, where he had found bits of severed rope and drops of blood in the dirt—appalling discovery, except that Chernevog directing matters would have taken all the horses—at very least opened the gate and run off Volkhi and Missy. The mouse had an unarguable naive honesty in her choices—and that gave them the chance they had.

He led Volkhi out of the yard and let Missy and Sasha pass the gate—latched it, out of habit, though there was no Babi to mind the yard while they were gone. Babi was probably frightened, Babi had probably gone to that Place Babi went to—

Which was well enough for Babi, but that place was trying to swallow up his daughter, too, in a place no living creature belonged, and he had his mind absolutely made up when he swung into the saddle.

"I'm going to ride ahead."

"Pyetr—"

"I'm not afraid of Chernevog. God knows, we're old acquaintances. We can talk. The two of us together can make more sense than some people I can—"

"No!"

"Sasha—" He shook his head to clear the cobwebs out, and rubbed his eyes. "Dammit, stop it. Tell her! Or just wish me to find her before trouble does."

"It's far too dangerous!"

"Tell me what's too dangerous, with my daughter headed off into hills in the dark with Chernevog!"

"You haven't any way to feel what's going on!"

"My daughter's in trouble out there! Let me go, dammit!"

"All right," Sasha said, "all right, but—"

Sasha yelled something after him, but he reckoned he would hear that while he was riding—or if the silence swallowed him up, he reckoned there was nothing to do but what he was doing.

Yvgenie said, quietly: "We're lost, aren't we?"

"No. Of course we aren't. I know where we are."

"So where are we going?"

"North."

"To what?"

"Where I want to go." She was far from lost in the woods; and she was far from alone even in the silence: things near at hand were always talking to her, telling her where they were, even though the whole woods felt quiet and scary and pricklish with silence. She knew where home was, she knew where her mother was, and she would know her Place when she got there.

But if being lost meant missing supper and wanting a warm fireside, and being scared the way Yvgenie was scared, and having everyone in the whole world upset with them, they certainly were.

Yvgenie asked, "Where is that?"

"We'll know, I said." It was Yvgenie asking, she was sure. It was getting dark, he was beyond exhausted, and she had no idea how to answer him in terms ordinary folk understood—she had no idea what he did understand or how to reassure him: she trusted her friend for that; but her friend's long silence worried her, as if—

He said, faintly, "I think we should stop and make a fire if we can."

Something was singing in the brush, a lonely, eerie sound. A wolf had howled a moment ago. If she were on foot she might have been anxious herself. Things did not feel entirely right, now that he distracted her. Which might be her mother's doing.

Some animal crashed away through the brush. Patches jumped, and Bielitsa did.

"It's just a squirrel or something."

"I really thing we should stop."

"Are you afraid?"

"No. Of course not."

Another wolf called, in the far distance.

"That's another one," he said. "There must be a whole pack out hunting."

"Wolves don't hurt you. They're very shy."

"Wolves aren't shy!"

"Have you ever seen a wolf?" She wanted not to be angry with him, but he kept worrying at her.

"I don't know, I don't *know* if I have and I don't even know what I'm doing here!" He was frightened, he was angry at her, and she wished not: she wished herself safe from him—

But that was stupid. He could never harm her with his wishes, and now she had stolen his anger away from him, which was wrong, terribly wrong—

Talk to me, her father would say, when people forgot and wished at him:

Say it in words, 'Veshka—

God!

Pyetr meant to be careful, with his neck and Volkhi's; but he put Volkhi to a far faster pace than old Missy could possibly sustain, down the hill behind Sasha's ruined house, and under trees and over the next rise, into thicker woods, where the night had already begun to settle.

North. Owl's grave was there—the leshys' ring, where Owl had died, days north of here: a rusalka might haunt such a place, and be drawn there, against all reason—and whether their destination was Ilyana's choice or Chernevog's, it was certain at least she would not follow the shoreline path, within reach of her mother.

So it was directly overland, by every advantage of ground he knew, so long as Volkhi could bear it, as fast as Volkhi could travel in this last of the twilight.

He personally hoped young Patches would do what a young horse would do and leave Ilyana stranded the first time a hare started from a thicket. That was the very likeliest way Sasha's wishes might work to stop them, magic tending to take the easiest course. Patches taking his daughter under a limb was another, not the way he would want, given a choice—but that, too, if it gave him a way to catch her tonight. The specific wish overrides the general, Sasha maintained. Things happen that can happen, things happen when they can happen—and always at the weakest point.

Well, then, dammit all—the mouse must have wished her father well a thousand thousand times. So had 'Veshka and Sasha—and if the mouse's father was very specifically risking his neck out here in the woods in the dark, then the hell with caution: the mouse's magic might have a hard time tonight, working against itself.

"Come on, lad," he urged Volkhi, and took the ways he knew through the woods—having ridden this land many more years than the mouse had. He had planted no few of the trees on these hills, he had seen the land when it was all dead and bare, and Volkhi knew the ground, even granted a deadfall or two: Volkhi footed it neatly through a maze of birch trees and mostly jumped the small brook that wound across their path.

Splash! and onto the far bank, up across the facing hill, along the ridge and down the other side through a maze of saplings.

Damned sure Ilyana and the boy could make no such time, except by wizardry—and by all evidences the mouse was being as quiet as she knew how to be, interested solely in putting distance between her and her mother.

Which he figured most definitely put the matter up to the fastest horse and the surest knowledge of the woods, and outright daring the mouse to drop her father on his head a second time.

—

The wind held fair for the north, in the slow unfoldings of the river, and the star-sheen on the water was light enough to steer by. Eveshka had the rush of water and the singing of the rigging for company, and all too much time for a wizard to think of possibilities, running along a shore she could not touch and a forest that refused to trust her.

Silence lay heavy there, even yet, not the silence of solitude, but her daughter's fear that excluded her; and there was evil hereabouts—evil as ordinary folk held it, meaning what threatened their lives. In that light, perhaps evil also described her: her understanding did not extend beyond the woods and the river and a handful of wizards, all of which could just as surely threaten the lives of ordinary folk.

But there were creatures who fed on others' suffering, there were those that relished others' pain: that was what she personally damned for wickedness. And just ahead now on the leeward shore, was a cave that smelled of such wickedness and fear. A willow there had resurrected itself, a tree the leshys abhorred, though they loved all others in the woods. It had its roots in the watery dark, that willow, in a den she had never seen while she was alive. She was anxious passing it and vastly relieved when it fell astern. She wished her husband well; and Sasha, forgiving for now all his failures and shortcomings, knowing her own all too keenly.

She judged people too harshly. Pyetr would tell her that. Pyetr would say, That's your father, 'Veshka; he would say, with his vast patience: 'Veshka, you ask too much. Of yourself and other people. You're doing what you hated your father doing.

It might be true—but true, too, that as much as she and her father had quarreled when she was alive, and passionately as she had hated him, he had judged her wilful heart accurately enough, said no when he should have said no, and *wished* her to stay out of trouble, until a young wizard she thought she loved had lured her onto the river shore and murdered her.

She could imagine laughter in that cave tonight. She could imagine doubt and conceit flowing out of it like poison:

Do you know what your own daughter's capable of, pretty bones? Does she scare you? She certainly should.

The willow fell further behind. But northward, on the other

shore of the river, was a hollow hill, on which, in her dreams, lightnings still crashed. Her mother had been so much like her, so very much like her: Draga, Malenkova's student, Kavi's tormentor and teacher.

She should have said to Ilyana, calmly, reasonably, while there had been time, and reason:

Ilyana, Kavi might be my half-brother. Did he tell you so? My mother hinted at it. It might have been malice. She knew we were almost lovers and she wanted to upset me. But it is remotely possible he's my father's son, of a wizard named Malenkova—*his* teacher.

Child, I only tried to make you strong and hard enough. I never wanted you to hate me.

Now it was too late to say that. It was too late to say other things like: Don't trust Kavi. Don't listen to him. He was my mother's lover, years before he knew me, but they were both, my mother more than he ever was, Malenkova's creatures. . . .

You don't *know* about Malenkova. I hadn't time to teach you. And Kavi doesn't remember. He can't. He didn't hear from my mother what I heard—I hope to the god he never did. I'd spare him that—much as he deserves to know what I know—

She put her hands over her ears and looked at the sky above the sail, as if that could shut out the thoughts.

Never think about the anger, never think about betrayals, but never, ever think about forgiveness either: every damned time one trusted Kavi, every *time* one in the least began to believe him—

She tried to make Ilyana listen. She went on trying. But the magic reached the forest edge and stopped. Nothing got in, nothing got out, and she began to fear it was no longer entirely her daughter's silence. Not this, not the slow, deep strength of it, that had increasingly the mark of leshys: wizard-magic was not working within its hold, except, perhaps, perhaps, very close at hand, on very familiar, long-associated objects.

It might protect the forest. But leshys had nothing of wizards' purposes. And leshys could be mistaken in their wider judgments. She wanted them to hear her. She wanted their help. They had served the woods, she had atoned for the killing with planting and with care—but she had no feeling that they heard her—nor any certainty that they had ever forgiven her, or that they had ever understood wizards in their midst. They were younger now, Sasha said. There were so many young ones about—

And Kavi—

God, she had not for years longed to shed the body she wore and go, lay insubstantial hands on what might truly answer to that touch. She had not felt this—*anger*—in years.

—You damnable *fool*, Kavi! Even if you love her, don't touch her, don't even think of touching her. You don't *want* her to want you, god help you if she wants you: you can't stop her, by your very nature you can't stop her—

For the god's sake, Kavi, tell her how you died!

Night made the forest a shifting confusion of gray and black. Branches raked and caught, trees floated past the eye like ghosts. The black furball was still with them and the ghostly owl flew ahead of them from tree to tree—guiding them, Yvgenie hoped.

To a place *I* know, Ilyana insisted, but he had no confidence in that. He had no confidence he would even get through this night and he desperately longed for the sun. The ghostly owl seemed more real now, so much so he feared if he nodded again he might never wake up. Pain could be more real than Owl was, pain could keep him awake—and he bit his lip and fought the lapses that made his eyelids fall and the sounds of their passage grow dim in his ears. He caught himself from time to time against the saddlebow, found his fingers growing numb. He thought of his father's house, he thought of running away—he knew he had done that, *he* had, *he* had tried to take his life in his hands and do something honest that did not involve killing his father, or telling anyone about his father and the tsarevitch—

But Bielitsa took a sudden shift of direction and he found himself slipping helplessly: a grip on the saddle checked his fall, but only that—he swung completely off Bielitsa's back, still clinging with both hands to the saddle leather as Bielitsa turned to keep herself from sliding downslope on the dead leaves. An embarrassing position, his horse about to fall downhill atop him, himself about to pull her down: he looked quite the fool in the wizard-girl's eyes, he was sure. But he would not have Bielitsa fall, so he let go.

—And found himself after a dark space on his back at the bottom of the slope with a fair-haired shadow between him and a tree-latticed moon.

"Are you all right?" Ilyana asked solemnly. And for some stupid reason he started to laugh. Was he all right? Was he all right? He was lying on his back, head downward on a hill with a dead wizard's ghost slithering about inside his heart, and the girl asked Was he all right?

But breath ran out, tears of pain welled up and his stomach ached, so that he had to double over on his side—and he found himself facing the black furball's glowing yellow eyes and hedge of teeth. It snarled, spat at him and snapped at his face.

Ilyana said, sternly, "Babi, behave."

He would never of his own will have taken his eyes off the furball. Of his own will he could not get another breath. But his chest moved, and took it, his arm moved and braced under him. The ghost turned his face toward her and said, "Wish us well, wish us well tonight, Ilyana. Us *and* this boy—something's on our trail—more than your father."

Leaning there, head downhill, with Babi breathing on his neck, he thought for no reason of an ominous stone overgrown with thorns—Owl had died there. Wolves gathered like tame dogs about Ilyana's skirts. Solemn yellow eyes gazed at him with no glimmer of sanity.

He blinked the night back around him, and shoved himself up frantically on his hands and knees, uphill, with a stab of pain across his stomach as the furball hissed and snapped at him. He fell back down, sitting. It seemed to him he had never fallen into the flood. Ilyana had been riding with him, just then warning him of ghosts and wizards that lived in this woods, and he had been answering her only a moment ago that there were things much worse than ghosts.

But he could not remember how he had answered her. Kiev and the gilt pillars of his father's house became a painted, shadowy porch, and the shadowed trunks of trees. Imaginings became wolves, wolves became Owl, and Ilyana drowned while he stood safe on the shore and *wanted* her to die.

God, no, that was wrong—he had been the one drowning and she had pulled him from the flood.

She said, trying to lift him by his shoulder, "We've got to go on. Please. Please get up."

He tried. He shoved himself to his feet a second time and staggered upslope to catch Bielitsa's trailing reins. He had tried a jump, in the fields near the city wall. He had fallen and hit his head—

His father, watching from horseback, leaned back in the saddle and called him a fool in front of his men.

He caught his breath, clung to Bielitsa's neck and pressed his face against her mane, back in the dark and the woods.

I left Kiev. I had to take Bielitsa—there was nowhere safe for her.

But where are we running to? Where's safe, anywhere, now?

He remembered leshys and madness at their hands, a woods of golden leaves—an endless succession of days, while suns and stars careered across the heavens, while autumns and springtimes sped past in torrents of leaves and windborne seeds. He remembered anger that shattered stones, Forest-things as great as trees and very like them, with feet that were indeed backwards. He knew their names: Misighi and Wiun and Isvis and Priochni, scores of others—while he held Bielitsa's mane to keep himself on his feet, and used Bielitsa's strength to sustain him, knowing even while he took what was not his, that Kavi was betraying them—

But, god, he was so afraid of dying—

It needed only a little strength. Please the god and the Forest-things, too, only enough and not too much . . . the wizard-girl was in terrible danger of some kind, and he had come back from the grave for her sake . . .

But from whose grave—he was for a moment confused.

Ilyana touched his sleeve. "Is something wrong? Are you all right? Yvgenie?"

He had a debt to pay. He had no choice. He turned his back to Bielitsa's shoulder, looked into her night-shadowed eyes. "He wants—" The damnable stammer came back. He never would have thought of taking her suddenly in his arms, or of kissing her on the lips, which with his present dizziness, made all breath fail.

He thought, while he was holding her, god, it isn't me doing this, it's him, it's Chernevog doing it—

But the whole night spun about them. He lost his breath, with all of life within his reach. The forest was full of it. Nothing could withstand them, nothing would be strong enough if he reached out and took it.

He wanted to warn her. He wanted to say—don't trust him, Ilyana—because he truly was Yvgenie Pavlovitch, no matter whose wish had brought him to this place. He remembered drowning Ilyana, he remembered dying by fire and by water, and nothing could make sense to him. He thought that he would faint, he grew so dizzy, but life came with it, her life, life from the trees and the woods—from something vastly powerful—

God, stop it. *Stop* it, don't do this, it's wrong to do this—

Even if—god, even if it was the source of his next breath.

Ilyana fainted in his arms. He wanted to let her go. He fought for the will to do that. And the thing within him whispered, faintly, "Death's so long, boy, and so damnably cold."

Down one hill and up another, with, Pyetr was sure, his daughter's wishes earnestly trying to mislead him and Eveshka's and Sasha's fighting to guide him. In that toss of the magical dice, the god only knew which would win, but distance did make a difference, every experience he had ever had with wizardry assured him that that was so, and as long as Volkhi could bear the pace he was narrowing that interval—

Mouse, he intended to say when he found her and the boy— mouse, if you're going to be a scoundrel, you shouldn't leave your pursuers a horse to come after you—if, that is, you didn't truly want to be caught.

But he believed she did in fact want that, in her heart, if only she could be assured he would not harm the boy. She would talk to him at safe distance, far from other wizardly interference. He had not heard a word or a stray thought from Sasha since they had parted company; and he hoped to come within Ilyana's influence before the night was out. But they were past Volkhi's first wind now, and he set a pace to hold as long as had to be.

But on the down side of a hill Volkhi began to shake his neck and object to the direction they were going, snorting and dancing about as if he had something entirely unpleasant in his nostrils.

"Whoa," he said. On a vagary of the breeze he caught a whiff of it himself: river water where none belonged—

And snake.

Something heavy moved in the brush. A voice hissed, "Well, well, well, what have we? Is it the man with the sword? How extremely nice. We're so *pleased* to find old friends."

It spoke so softly. And it struck so suddenly, out of the dark brush. Volkhi shied across the slope as Pyetr spied a glistening dark body coming at them across the leaves and signaled Volkhi to jump over it.

A snaky shadow whipped out of the trees, hit his shoulder a numbing blow—that was his only startled realization as his foot raked across Volkhi's back and he left the saddle.

Missy was doing her best, poor horse, and for far too long there had been no answer from Pyetr—not a wisp of an impression where Pyetr was now. Nothing had passed the smothering silence from the moment Pyetr had ridden away, exactly what Sasha had feared would be the case. Pyetr had salt and sulfur with him, against noxious and magical creatures: he had given Pyetr that before he left the house.

But what with their arguing, and Pyetr rushing off, not hearing his warning—the god only hope, Sasha thought, that it was Ilyana's doing and that Pyetr had in fact found her, because for all his wishing he got now a fleeting sense of fright—which gave him no ease either.

"Misighi!" he called from time to time—but there was nothing from their old friend—and from the young leshys no answer, unless the Forest-things were contributing to the uneasy feeling in the night. The creatures abhorred magic and wizards: they were never easy neighbors to sorcery, and it was certainly an uncomfortably unpredictable lot of wishes that had gotten loose in the woods tonight.

Worse, there was a distressing feeling of self-will about it all, an irrational lack of forethought, or thought at all, and it was all too easy for a young wizard to make that mistake: Chernevog *had* made that mistake in his own youth, and that the mouse had run away made him fear that Eveshka was right, that they were not dealing with the mouse in her right senses. That the mouse had left her father lying bleeding on the floor, never mind the pillow, gave him no confidence at all tonight.

In cold truth, he was scared, he was terrified of the mouse's inexperience and her quick assumptions of persecution where none existed: Think, mouse, he wished her. Is it reasonable that everyone who loves you has turned against you? I'm worried about your decisions, mouse. I want to talk to you. I promise I won't harm your young man.

But he feared his wishes died in the silence and he could not breach it. He was not the naive boy who had bespelled the vodka jug: the years had worn away his certainties; and now a day removed from the fire that had taken his house and so many of his notes, he could not shut his eyes without seeing the flames; and knowing the books were worth his life, knowing now that they had almost cost Pyetr's, the more he thought about it the more he was, stupidly, belatedly, panicked.

Dammit, Pyetr, doesn't the silence mean something to you?

Doesn't the fact that you aren't hearing from me—mean something?

Pyetr, dammit, *notice* that I'm not talking to you! Stop and wait! I don't like what I'm feeling right now.

Misighi, do you hear me? *Please* hear me.

Then a faint, far thought did come to him.

"Pyetr?" he asked softly, and did not like—*did* not like the uneasiness he felt in the air. He suddenly wondered what Volkhi was up to: that seemed the safest question—

Volkhi was angry, his saddle was empty and he was frightened, exhausted and lost, in a place where Volkhi was sure there were snakes—which was, emphatically, Not His Fault.

"Misighi, dammit! Wake up!"

He wanted, oh, *god*! Missy to hurry, please! because he could hear a very quiet voice now that he knew beyond a doubt what to listen for, a sibilant and mocking voice, wholly untrustworthy.

7

✠ ✠ ✠ ✠ "Does its head hurt?" the vodyanoi asked out of the dark. It slithered over Pyetr's leg, and back again, up against his cheek, wet and smelling of river water. Something unpleasant flickered lightly against his ear, inside it, and Pyetr could not move, not so much as to ease the arm that had gone numb under him.

It whispered within his ear, "Is it sorry now, is the man sorry now for his discourtesies?"

Get away from me, he wanted to say; but breath failed him. The vodyanoi's serpent shape loomed up and up across the visible sky, and lowered, to nudge his chin familiarly with its blunt nose.

Salt and sulfur, he thought desperately. Salt and sulfur—in my pocket if I could reach it—

Did Volkhi get away?

"The horse ran, oh, yes, off into the woods. Maybe we can find him." A coil fell across his chest, and grew heavier, crushing the breath out of him. "Or maybe not. You're so fond of him. Maybe I'd rather eat him later. And no, you can't reach it, nasty man."

Sasha! He shut his eyes, thinking as sanely as he could: I'm in deep trouble, friend. Can you possibly hear me? —'Veshka? Then, on another, calculating thought: —Mouse, your father's in a damned lot of difficulty. Could we have some help, mouse? You could make things up with your mother . . . so much easier if I wasn't this thing's supper—

'Veshka! God, do something!

Heavier and heavier. He felt his ribs bending, felt the world turning around and around, dark shot through with colored fire.

Hwiuur said, tongue flickering maddeningly against his ear, "No one's listening. Perhaps it would be polite if I let it breathe a moment?"

He would. Yes. Anything to get feeling into his hand and find the salt, or his sword—not clever of him to think of that in the vodyanoi's hearing, no. But Hwiuur's weight eased all the same, and he gasped after the promised breath, thinking, What does he want? Whose is he this time, if not Chernevog's?

—who's off in the woods with my daughter—

Oh, god, mouse, where are you?

The vodyanoi rose up and up, huge, darkening the night over him. "Is it polite now?"

"It's very polite," he whispered to that shadow, discovering he had a voice. "What do you want, Hwiuur?"

"Pretty bones is on the river tonight. And in my cave. What do you think about that?"

'Veshka. The god only knew what the snake meant about the cave. He risked another, deeper breath. "My wife's not so easy to catch."

The vodyanoi hissed and bent lower, sharp teeth looming above his face. "Very dangerous, very, very dangerous. Foolish man, to get a young one with pretty bones. Life in death. Death in life. Her bones are still in my cave, foolish man, and she hears the river every night in her dreams."

"What *about* my daughter?"

"Such pretty, pretty bones. Tell Sasha, tell my dear, my sweet Sasha, that he's been as much a fool as you have."

"I'll be happy to tell him. Make him hear me."

"Oh, *can't* he, now? Too, too bad. Then perhaps we can make a bargain without him, you and I."

"Maybe."

"Dangerous, dangerous man. What will you give me?"

"What are we dealing for?"

"Bonesss." The vodyanoi slithered across his chest, beneath a numb leg and over it, under his back and around and around his body and still he could not move, not so much as a finger. "Bones, of course. What will you offer for them? What have you got to trade?"

He felt pain in his shoulder, apart from the general ache in his limbs. Another in his right hand, thinking of which, he tried to move if only a single finger—thinking, The damned snake's bitten me—that's what it's done. Come on, dammit—god—

"Will you trade?" Hwiuur asked. "Nice, *fresh* bonesss, I wonder?"

He might have his sword by him, if starting with that ache in his shoulder, he could move at all. There was the salt—

The vodyanoi moved across him and weighted his arms. "Nasssty man. Don't do that. Your daughter's run off with the rusalka. With our old friend Chernevog. Aren't you interested?"

"Sasha!" he yelled. The vodyanoi chuckled softly and caressed his cheek with a scaly jaw.

"Oh, Sasha should have done something by now. So should pretty bones. So might your daughter—but *she's* sleeping with Chernevog tonight. Such a dutiful child you've made. You should be so very proud."

Coils went around and around him. He shut his eyes, trying to move that hand, or to make someone hear him, without magic, without anyone in earshot—

"Misighi!" he breathed, because there were things that *were* magical as the vodyanoi, that needed no spells to hear their names invoked—

Breath stopped. There was no room for it. Then something snarled and spat and rushed, hissing and spitting, across the dead leaves toward him. The vodyanoi reared up and hissed like water on hot iron, carrying him in its coils.

He had a view of the ground. Far below. Then came a sickening drop. Something attached to his leg—he thought, Hell— what *is* it?

Pain got through the numbness. The coils slipped away from him and let him go.

For what good that did.

Missy was exhausted. Missy trampled down the undergrowth in her path and simply plowed straight ahead, her breath coming hard—*far* too many apples and sweets from the kitchen over the years—she could not keep such a pace as she took now.

But she smelled something familiar and friendly. Her ears went up and she lifted her head for a look as she went, on a last reserve of strength. It was Volkhi she was thinking of, in Missy's way, nothing to do with names: but Sasha knew what she smelled, he had wished Volkhi to come to them, and thank the god, Volkhi, alone of everything in the forest, seemed to have heard—Missy, if not him.

But where was Pyetr, he wondered of Volkhi, where had he left him, how long ago?

It was a thoroughly upset, thoroughly tired Volkhi, who did not know where his rider was, and who was sure he was in trouble for it. He arrived out of the brush like a piece of night, distraught, angry, his thoughts scattering every which way—

But he was willing to stand while Sasha slid off Missy and climbed up on his back. Volkhi thought it was stupid to go back where he knew there were snakes, but he would go, if everybody else was going. Volkhi was going to kick hell out of anything that moved back there.

Sasha agreed with him. He wanted leshys, he wanted the mouse's attention, he wanted Pyetr's, if he could reach him; and most urgently, knowing the name Volkhi did not, he wanted the vodyanoi sliced and fried, if it harmed a hair on Pyetr's head—

Hwiuur, you're being a fool. Hurt him and I'll get you for it, I'll *get* you, Hwiuur, there'll never be a day I'll be off your track.

Then he was certain of a sudden where he was going—the slack of Missy's reins taking up all but pulled him off Volkhi's back as Volkhi pricked up his ears and jolted into a brisker pace. Volkhi shook his neck and protested with an I-know-you sound as Sasha reined him down to a pace Missy could keep. He wanted to go where Volkhi wanted to go, fast, and it was not helping hold Volkhi in at all.

Babi was the thought he began to sort out of Volkhi's thoughts. Babi was no easy creature to wish and Babi would not tolerate eavesdropping—but the horses both could hear him. The horses had an idea of Babi that a man had trouble holding; but Volkhi was definitely answering him, in Volkhi's way: Volkhi launched himself straight up a hill with a drive of his hindquarters, wanting more rein as Sasha tried to hold on to Missy and stay in the saddle, while if ever a horse could swear, Volkhi was swearing, fighting the reins all the way to the crest, into a thin growth of saplings.

Something shone pale in the dark thicket below, a white

scrap of cloth gleaming through interlaced branches—a body ly-ing on the ground.

"Oh, god—" He almost let go of Missy's reins, then recalled that all their medicines were on Missy's back, and held on to Volkhi's saddle and to her, begging her to hurry, please! while Volkhi fought him all the way down the hill.

He *wanted* Pyetr to be all right, he wanted the whole woods to know they were in trouble as he slid down from Volkhi's back and shoved his way through the interlaced twigs of saplings. Babi was curled at Pyetr's side, a very small, very upset black ball of fur that growled and hissed at him as he fell to his knees.

Pyetr was lying on his stomach, one arm beneath him, his white shirt stained dark on his right shoulder, and, god, he had bled enough for three men. He was still breathing—but only just.

His hands were shaking as he peeled Pyetr's collar down and discovered a wound a sword might have made: a vodyanoi's bite, he was sure of it. On both sides of the shoulder—and blood was still coming.

Nothing had been going right: nothing of his magic had worked, and he was never good at doctoring; he believed in pain more than he believed in his own magic, 'Veshka always said so. Uulamets might have dealt with a wound like this, 'Veshka could, little as she worked magic; even the mouse was better than he was—if it was baby birds or a wounded fox—

Stop shaking, fool. The old man's voice echoed out of mem-ory. *Fool*, master Uulamets had used to call him when he hesi-tated. —What's more important, feeling or doing? One or the other, *fool*! Use your wits! Think!

—Warmth. Light to see with, herbs and wishes and bandages to stop the blood, *do*, fool! Don't sit there! Wish while you're working!

He scrambled up and broke dead branches off lower limbs, the driest wood there was; he untied his baggage from Missy's back, got the medicines and the fire-pot—oily moss for tinder: he tucked a wad in beneath the twigs, struck a spark and wished it—*dammit*! to light straightaway, no messing about with might-be's.

Candles tipping, spilling wax. The fireplace would not hold a fire, because in his heart he was afraid of it—

161

Dammit!

Fire took, the least point of light, and faltered. God, he was going to lose it—

—Please, please be all right, Pyetr, don't do this to me. It's no time for jokes, Pyetr, please wake up and talk to me, I'm not doing well at this! Someone's wishes are winning, but not mine tonight—

The mouse is wishing us not to catch her and her generalities are killing us—

So wish the specific, fool! Decide and do! Specific always wins.

Second spark. No infinite number of chances. There was only so much blood in a body, and magic had to *want* the fire, believe in the fire, one spark at a time, not flinch at the flames, not set out to fail from the beginning.

River stench clung strong about this place. Fire gave smoke, smoke of birch and alder, smoke of moss and herbs—and water gave way to it.

No time for medicines. Blood was flowing too fast. He laid both hands on the wound while Babi's fire-glittering black eyes followed his every move. *Babi* was here, too, Babi was wanting things to work, no less than he was.

One did not need the smoke, one did not need the herbs, one needed only think of them—yarrow and willow, feverfew and sulfur—

Vodka. Babi's eyes glowed like moons. But Babi stayed quite, quite still. And licked his lips.

Think of health. Think of home, with the crooked chimney and all. Think of 'Veshka and the mouse being there, and Pyetr, and himself—one did not need to touch, one needed only think of touching—and not even that—

But the sky in that image grayed, and the house weathered, and lost shingles—

He brought back the sun again. He put the shingles back, and added the horses grazing on the open hillside and Babi in the front yard.

Clouds tried to gather. Weeds tried to grow. A board fell off the gate.

He bit his lip and made it go back. A rail fell off the fence.

But he set himself in the middle of that yard, with Pyetr as he was, and wanted the shoulder as it had been.

That was the answer. Shingles fell, thunder rumbled, and he built a small fire in front of him and fed it, while he fed the one in the dark of the woods, and breathed the smoke, pine and willow.

He set the vodka jug beside him in the yard—the unbreakable and inexhaustible jug: his one youthful magic, the once-in-a-lifetime spell old Uulamets had told him a wizard might cast: no effort at all it had been to want that jug rolling across the deck—not unbroken—but truly whole, so whole it could never afterward be less than it was at that moment.

Scarily easy, so easy that he had felt queasy about that spell ever after. He had doubted it could be good, and most of all feared what wishing at some*one* might do—

But he needed that absolute magic now, if only once for the rest of his life, and the jug was the key. He saw the yard, with the wind blowing and the sky going darker; he picked up the jug among falling leaves, locked it in his arms and wanted, with the same simplicity, Pyetr to be with him, the same—the same—as in that unthinking instant he had bespelled the jug—

No! Oh, god, that day had not been the best in their lives. Pyetr had not married 'Veshka, yet, had not *had* a daughter then.

God, what have I *done?*

But the shingles were on the roof again, the yard was raked and kept. The house was standing solid and intact; but he had no idea who was living in Pyetr's house . . . as it would someday stand. He *had* wished something. He had felt the shift in things-as-they-were and things-as-they-would-be. He wanted to go inside the house and find out who lived there; or failing that, only to go up on the porch and look in the unshuttered windows, please the god, to reassure himself what he had done would not change what was inside—

But he was sitting in front of a dying fire with the vodka jug in his arms, and Pyetr was lying on the ground in front of him, while Babi—Babi had his small arms locked about Pyetr's neck, his face buried in Pyetr's pale hair.

Pyetr swatted at Babi. The hand fell limp again, but Pyetr had moved, Pyetr was still alive. Sasha suddenly found himself shaking like a leaf, unable to stop. He tucked his foot up and hugged his knee and watched, fist against his mouth to keep his teeth from chattering, wanting nothing but Pyetr's welfare, not wishing any more proof that the magic had worked than to see Pyetr look at him, whenever Pyetr wanted to, please, sanely and remembering everything since that day on the river.

Babi got up and waddled over, leaned on his legs and reached for the vodka jug. Something had changed: Babi knew. Babi was willing to leave Pyetr: Babi wanted a drink and Sasha unstopped the jug and poured a good dose into Babi's waiting mouth, libation to all beneficent magic in the earth. "Good Babi," he said. "Good, *brave* Babi—"

Pyetr half-opened his eyes, blinking at him through a fringe of hair. "God—where did *you* come from?"

"I was supposed to follow you, remember?"

Please, Pyetr, remember. Keep on remembering.

Pyetr rolled onto his back and felt inside his shirt. Made a face and worked his fingers back and forth in the firelight.

"Does it hurt?"

"No," Pyetr said, sounding confused, and felt again. "Blood. It's not me, is it?"

"It was," Sasha said. "It shouldn't be now. How do you feel?"

Pyetr took a breath, wiped his hand on his ghastly shirt, making another dark smear, and managed to sit up, leaning on his hand, staring dazedly past the fire, to where the horses were. "Volkhi—"

"Volkhi's all right. Not a scratch on him, from the vodyanoi, a few scrapes else, that I can tell."

"God." Pyetr made a try at getting up and fell on his back before Sasha could catch him.

"You can't go anywhere."

"My daughter, dammit—"

He could not admit to Pyetr what a fool he had been, or warn him of the changes that might happen. He *wanted* to amend that wish of his—but he doubted he could, that was the stupid part. He could only wish Pyetr to remember his daughter by the time the spell had run its course—and it would not have, yet, it might not have completed itself for days and years, but there was no stopping it—and telling Pyetr about it—what could it do but frighten him, and make his life miserable?

God, stupid, Sasha Vasilyevitch, *damnably*, terribly stupid! You can't wish against nature, you can't wish against time—

But Pyetr, instead of dying, had breath in him tonight, and warmth, and was determined to ride on alone, right now, if he could. "Sasha—we can't sit here."

"Volkhi's exhausted, Missy can't take it, if you could stay on, which you can't: the spell isn't finished with you; and don't ask me to borrow."

"I'll ask you." Pyetr coughed, and held his shoulder. "It's not a time for good sense. Or scruples. The leshys will understand us. It's for them as much as—"

"Not a time to make mistakes, either."

"Dammit, he's with her, you understand me?"

"Do you know that?"

"I know more than I want to know. The old Snake has a filthy mouth. The young one, Chernevog, damn him—"

"I don't believe everything Hwiuur says. He's left and right and full of twists. And even if it were true, Chernevog's not in any substance any longer. The boy is—and substance deals with substance." He felt the heat in his face, but the dark gave him cover. "Yvgenie's an honest lad. She could do far worse, Pyetr."

Pyetr could have shouted at him that he was a fool and he had no intention in the world of leaving it at 'could do worse,' or 'substance': Sasha heard it all the same. But Pyetr had no strength to go on right now. Pyetr leaned his head against his arm and shook it slowly. "God, how, Sasha? How could she do worse?" And Pyetr thought, wounded to the heart: Why didn't she answer me?

Because the vodyanoi had taunted him with that.

"*I* couldn't answer you," Sasha said, laying a hand on Pyetr's shoulder. "Remember? We aren't hearing each other. And I'm less and less certain our mouse is all the reason for the silence. I think the leshys are aware of it, maybe contributing to it— they did this before, when Chernevog was alive—not helping us, but maybe keeping other things from breaking loose."

Pyetr was shivering. Trying not to. Trying to be sane. Pyetr said, as calmly as he could, "This isn't going at all right, is it?"

Sasha put his arms about him, felt the chill and the shivering. "Sleep, Pyetr. Go to sleep."

Pyetr said not a word. His head fell and his body immediately went heavy in Sasha's arms: he was that far gone. Sasha suddenly found himself trembling, from cold, from exhaustion, from terror. He wanted Pyetr to be all right, he wanted Pyetr's daughter to realize her father needed her, and he wanted things right in the woods—now, tonight, this moment.

But—perhaps it was the way his latest wish had gone askew; and perhaps the way all wizards' wishes went amiss, past childhood—he was not sure he wanted the mouse here. He was less sure he wanted Chernevog, knowing the mouse might have wished him to be with her: wishes held so many conditions, wishes contradicted each other, and tied themselves in knots on wizards' conditions.

Fool, 'Veshka would say, in her father's tone.

And she would be right.

Yvgenie became aware of breaking daylight at the same moment he discovered his legs were asleep, he was propped against a tree and he had his arms mostly around Ilyana. There seemed no polite way at the moment to move his legs, the stretch of which was making his back ache terribly, so he sat there in pain, trying to recall, god, what had happened last night, or what he had done last night.

He leaned his head back and looked about at the trees, at the first glimmer of light on the branches, at the horses making a breakfast off spring leaves, and tried not to recall that too vivid sense of life that had driven sense from him.

Fatal, ultimately, the ghost whispered to him. I lend you pleasure I daren't feel. I'd lose all sanity, else. You're all the protection we have, Ilyana and I. . . .

He bit his lip, looked desperately up at the branches and thought—

Sanity?

He shifted his legs without thinking, and Ilyana stirred in his arms, put her hands on his shoulders and pushed back from him, eyes wide.

"I'm sorry," he said, but Chernevog said, softly, "Good morning, Ilyana."

She looked alarmed and struggled against him to be free. He

wanted to let her go, but the ghost pulled her against him and kissed her long and passionately, wanting—

Oh, god, no!

The world went dizzy. He forgot to breathe, until she had to, and fought for breath and reason. He made a clumsy reach for the tree behind him and purchase on the leaf-strewn ground, wanting to straighten his legs. He felt—

—not angry, no—shaken inside and out, and tingling with a feeling he had never had. He did not want the ghost doing *that* again, or anything else it had in mind. He struggled to stand up, to little avail, and found himself trapped with Ilyana staring at him as if trying to decide which of them was responsible.

He whispered, "I'm terribly sorry," then thought that he could have said something more flattering. He tried to amend that—and it still came out, "Be careful, please be more careful, miss," or something as foolish, as she took his hand, which was filthy with bits of leaf and dirt, and tried to help him.

Strength came flooding back to his legs, numbness easing unnaturally quickly. He stood up, he disengaged his hand and wiped it clean as something cold whisked through him, something of more substance than a passing chill.

Owl, he thought.

"Are you all right?" Ilyana asked him.

He answered, "He's very well, thank you, miss." And added, with an effort, "Please—you oughtn't to trust him that far—"

He wanted to take her in his arms himself. Instead he shoved away from the tree and staggered off toward the horses, while the ghost inside him—he was sure it was the ghost—said, without words.

Yvgenie Pavlovitch, you're a fool.

The boat scraped something and shuddered aside. Eveshka waked with a start as the tiller bucked beneath her arm, saw trees in front of the sail, shoved over hard, and hauled on the sheets, heart pounding as the old ferry skimmed the shoreline, its hull rubbing its length along some barrier.

She had not intended to sleep. The wind had carried the boat the god only knew how far—she felt grinding scrapes that threatened to take the side out, and wished desperately for a breeze to touch the sail and give her way to steer away from the shore. None was at hand. The trees were too tall and too near, shadowing her from the wind.

The boat scraped rock, as the shore wound outward across the bow. She leaned on the tiller.

The hull glided over sand. Hard. And cleared.

A breeze. Any breeze, god—no matter the direction.

The boat glided into calm water, between the shore and the bar, where a small stream joined the river. She worked frantically to bring the bow around, to catch whatever breeze the stream course might let escape to bear on the sail, but the breeze there was scarcely stirred the canvas. Only rain and gale, she feared, might free the boat from this trap.

She struck the tiller bar with her hand.

Not an accident. Not by any means an accident.

Something different rubbed against the hull, then splashed to the surface and chuckled with a familiar sound. She left the tiller in its loop of rope and strode to the rail. "Damn you, Hwiuur!"

Another splash. The vodyanoi could not bear the rising sun. There was no chance it meant to put itself in her reach at the edge of daylight: it kept to the shadow of the boat, the deep water, and only soft laughter and a spreading ring of ripples told where it skimmed the sandbar on its way to the open river.

Something dark red floated in the shadow of the boat, scarcely visible in this change between dawn and day: a scrap of embroidered cloth.

She had stitched that design herself, sewn wishes into the cloth, to keep Pyetr safe and warm—his coat, that was what Hwiuur had brought her—

"Hwiuur!" she shouted. "Come back here!"

But it had the edge it wanted. It spread doubt like poison, it scattered her wishes like leaves on the water. And it laughed, somewhere out of wizardly reach, in that place she remembered how to enter—but dared not, living.

Sunrise in the deep woods brought scant relief from the clammy chill of earth and air which long since had dampened their clothing and their blankets. Sasha folded up his book, quietly searched their packs for food and stirred up breakfast.

Pyetr opened his eyes in the midst of this, felt of the blanket across his chest and looked in his direction.

"Pain?" Sasha asked him.

"No." Pyetr struggled up on his elbows, filthy, bloody and ghastly pale between the beginning dawn and the firelight. He pulled the stiffened cloth away from his shoulder, took a look and murmured, "God."

"No argument out of you. Breakfast is just about ready. Hot tea. You're not going off this time by yourself."

"Don't wish at me!" Pyetr sat upright too quickly and leaned his head into his hands. "I'm sorry. You're right. You were right in the first place. Everything I've done has cost us time."

So he *did* remember. Sasha poured a cup of tea, wishing his hands not to shake with cold and sleeplessness. "We do as much as we can do. Despair is never our friend. And we're not really behind Missy's pace, as happens, though I'd have had a bit more sleep. —Here."

Pyetr edged over and took the tea, held the cup in both hands to drink it. Sasha turned the cakes and poured his own cup.

Across the fire, Babi waited, black eyes glittering with thoughts of cakes, one could be sure. There was certainly one for Babi, yes, indeed there was, especially for him.

"Had the salt in my coat pocket," Pyetr said. "Lot of good that did. Damned snake's gotten clever. Where *is* my coat?"

"I don't know. Gone, I fear. I looked, but the god only knows how far it dragged you. Have mine: it's yours, anyway; and I can wish myself warm."

"We have blankets. A cloak's all I need." All I deserve—was the thought in Pyetr's mind. "—Have you *heard* anything since last night?"

Sasha slid a cake onto a leaf and set it down for Babi, all his own. "No." He slipped the other two onto plates and offered one to Pyetr. "But we're not going to go breakneck into this."

Pyetr scowled at his caution, then said, looking glumly to his breakfast, "If I hadn't been so damned stupid—"

"Don't—" he started to say—stopped himself; but thinking it was enough.

"It's my *f-fault*," Pyetr declared fiercely, piece by piece, with painful concentration against his wish. "If you could just for the god's sake t-tell her—"

"I *can't*. I can't make her hear me. So you listen to me, please, Pyetr."

"I've no damn ch-choice, have I?"

That cut deep. Pyetr's look did. But he said as coldly and rationally as he could: "I don't *like* you taking the blame for things. Give me time to think."

"That's *fine*, Sasha. But d-*do* something!"

He wanted Pyetr not to have to struggle like that. He had not meant that wish for silence, he simply wanted not to be argued with right now, which meant Pyetr had to fight him to talk at all. "Pyetr, believe me, the mouse doesn't hate us. She'd have come flying back here if she'd known you were in trouble. She isn't Draga and she's not her mother: I don't believe it, I never believed it, no matter what 'Veshka says—"

"The hell with what 'Veshka says! It isn't the mouse's fault what happened. She thinks she's doing right. I don't have to be a wizard to know that. She's not against us."

"It's not her fault, and if you want the plain truth, I don't think it was 'Veshka's either. She was in Draga's house before the mouse was born. I honestly believe Draga wanted something that made trouble for us."

Pyetr stopped with the cup halfway to his mouth. "Draga—" But the thought escaped him and escaped his eavesdropping as well. Something about Eveshka's mother, about the time Eveshka had spent in her mother's house under the hill, about Chernevog and Draga's wishes—

Wishes could make a man think all around a matter. Wishes could defend themselves, the same as the mouse wishing them off her track. They could well be missing something essential.

He said, fighting Pyetr for pieces of that thought, "Eveshka was up there with Draga when neither you nor 'Veshka knew the mouse existed—Draga wanted the baby, no question. That's how she got her there—she couldn't wish 'Veshka herself, 'Veshka's too strong; but she could wish the mouse there: nobody wished anything about the mouse, since none of us knew she existed—"

"Draga didn't have a damned thing to do with the mouse."

Some illusions one hated to challenge. "In fact Draga or

Uulamets either one might have wished Ilyana into existence, Pyetr, forgive me. But we *don't* know either of them got what they wanted. Wishes can pull other wishes off the mark, make them turn out differently than planned—certainly a young wizard is a scary handful; and unpredictable; and dangerous—but not, *not*, in my considered opinion, the creature Draga wanted from the beginning, and not under her grandmother's posthumous influence."

"Who said she was? Who *ever* said she was?"

" 'Veshka."

"Hell," Pyetr said in disgust. "She gets those damn moods."

"No. Sometimes she admits what's in her heart. And she's right to worry."

"Ilyana's not a sorcerer! She's *not* Chernevog's kind, Chernevog himself isn't what he was."

"Pyetr, 'Veshka died—and in her own thinking, she never won her struggle, no matter that her father brought her back to life. She lost. Nobody wins against sorcery—one either uses it or one ultimately loses to someone who does. That's what she believes. She didn't want the mouse badly enough to protect her from Draga—that's what haunts her: she was surprised to know she had a baby, she was under her mother's roof, beset with her mother's arguments and she only scarcely wanted the mouse enough for your sake to keep her alive. Something could have gotten to her—yes."

"That's not so, Sasha!"

"I agree with you. I don't think you can make anyone good or bad without his consent. I don't think it's being sixteen, or fifteen—I think it's whatever moment you decide what you need and decide what other people are worth to you. I was five when I made my terrible mistake; but I think we taught the mouse her lesson, and I don't for a moment believe she has to kill anyone to learn it. More than that, I think there was a time you should have been here and 'Veshka should have taken the trip to Kiev, if you want the truth; and a time last year we should have taken the mouse downriver to Anatoly's place and let her meet the household, damn the consequences."

"Why didn't you say that, for the god's sake? Why didn't you insist?"

"I did say it to 'Veshka, I said it to you more than once, if you'll remember, but no one listened. They were delicate years. It *wasn't* a time for quarrels in the house."

Pyetr ran a hand through his hair. "God."

"When 'Veshka wished you to Kiev, I knew you'd be back; I knew the mouse would want you back. What's more, I knew 'Veshka would. She can't turn anything loose. Not her daughter. Not her husband. Not an idea, once it takes hold of her—and she doesn't ask where she got all of them. *That's* her trouble, friend. She learned to fight from her father. Her young lessons were *all* that way. And in teaching the mouse what to do with magic—I had to hold Eveshka off."

Pyetr was quiet a moment, staring into the fire. Sasha bit his lip, hoping he had not gone too far, wanting—

No.

"I won't tell you what to think, Pyetr, only what I think. There always seemed too many quarrels for me to start another. All I could think was—just get her to the age of reason. Eveshka says she wasn't working magic—but she was, she was constantly, in every opinion she holds. How do you convince someone not to hold opinions?"

"How do you convince *Eveshka* not to hold opinions?"

"The god only knows, Pyetr. I'm afraid neither of us was that clever. The things we want do come true: we *make* them happen, we shape them with what we say and what we do. It's not the mouse's fault. Not even his, I think. We made the mouse lonely. She wanted a playmate. She wished one up and he wanted—perhaps to come home. I don't know. —But *you* taught her things. How to hold a baby bird. Do you remember?"

Pyetr frowned at him, upset and confused. "Not how to hold lives in her hands."

"How to hold a fox kit. You said, 'If he bites it's only fear. Be careful.' Do you remember that? That's a very important lesson."

"A bite isn't a betrayal. It isn't your whole damned family against you. Or your mother wanting someone dead."

"I wish her to remember what you taught her, Pyetr. That's the wish I make for her."

"God, don't put it down to me!"

"All those years she should have been with you, all the years we kept you apart—what you did teach her, in spite of that, the mouse sets most store by. You were the forbidden. You were the one out of reach. —What would you wish for her now?"

"To wait for me, dammit, that's what I've been saying—for her to talk to me. That's what I want."

Dangerous wish. Dangerous and indefinite and putting Pyetr at risk. But Pyetr was, he had had faith in it for years, wiser and braver about such things than he was. So he said, slowly, with the awareness of everything unhinged, and everything in doubt:

"I wish that, yes. And I wish you well, Pyetr . . . as well as I know how."

Pyetr looked at him as if he were mad, looked at him in the gray dawn, that time that ghosts began to fade, and said, so faintly he could hardly hear: "Wish *yourself* well, Sasha."

Because he had chosen the wish he had—foolish wizard that he was: he had deceived himself for so many years that he wished Pyetr's welfare completely unselfishly, for Pyetr's benefit, and not his: Let Pyetr be well, let nothing change—

He thought, not for the first time, All of us brought him back from Kiev. Who knows, maybe we wished him into trouble to do that, and he never would have played dice with the tsarevitch *or* crossed Kurov. As it was, it got him home, and it put him here, where he nearly died last night.

Babi turned up in his lap, Babi grabbed for his neck and hung on, fiercely, with his small hands.

—Babi knows something Babi doesn't like. I wonder where Babi was before he showed up last night. Things aren't going well, Pyetr's right.

"Have you done that?" Pyetr persisted. "Do you wish *yourself* well, Sasha? Or have you done something completely foolish?"

Pyetr could tell he was woolgathering. Pyetr knew his habits, and his expressions.

"I wish myself to keep you alive," Sasha said slowly. It was all he dared wish this morning. In their fear for the mouse's abilities, they had wished nothing about a wizard too old for a child's mistakes, a wizard who had done a child's naive magic twice now—unwisely in both instances.

He got to his feet. He picked up the vodka jug and deliberately let it fall.

Babi turned up below it, caught it in his arms and glared at him reproachfully.

But it had not broken. He could not harm it, even trying. In its way it was dangerous. Fall holding it—and the jug would survive.

It was Pyetr's coat, Eveshka had no doubt of it when she had fished it out of the river. "Pyetr!" she cried aloud to the forested shore, to the winds and the morning; she wanted Sasha to answer her; but no answer came, not from her husband, not from her daughter, not from Sasha, not even from the vodyanoi, who wanted to torment her. She knew its ways; oh, god, she knew them—knew that it lied, but one could never rely on that.

What she wanted now was a breeze—with the sail canted, the tiller set—just a very little breeze, please the god. Ever so slight a breeze—while she trembled with fear and wider wishes beckoned.

The sail flipped and filled halfway. The boat moved, ever so slowly.

And stuck fast again.

She did not wish a storm. She shut her eyes and wished—please, just a little more.

The boat groaned, the sail flapped and thumped.

The wind was there. It took so little for a stray puff of wind to come into this nook, skirl among the trees along the little stream, and come skimming across the water. . . .

Something wanted me toward this shore. Then want me closer, dammit! I've no intention to swim for it!

The boat heeled ever so slightly and slid free, bow facing the brushy water edge.

She lashed the tiller and ran forward, past the deckhouse, under the sail and along the low rail to the bow, with the snaggy wooden hook they used for an anchor. She swung it around and around her with all her might and loosed it for the trees.

It landed. She hauled on the rope and felt it hold, threw a loop about the bow post and hauled, not abruptly, but with patience.

Wizardry waited to swallow her up. The river did, while the vodyanoi taunted her with cruel laughter and told her lies. It was a big boat, a very big boat, but on the water the slightest breeze and the slightest of women could move it.

There were terrible holes in the coat she had fished out of the water, and stains, despite its soaking, that were surely blood.

Hwiuur could not *be* killed, that she knew, not in this world—but there were powers outside this world, in that place where magic lived.

Branches cracked against the hull. The old ferry jolted and scraped along the shore.

The forest that shut out her magic could not shut her out— kill her if it could—but not stop her short of killing her.

Sasha would talk about morality. Sasha would talk about the safety of people she had never met, and children she had never seen, and beg her to have pity on them, remembering that magic sought a way into the world—which wizards must never give. But *Pyetr* was her right and wrong. Pyetr was her world outside the woods, and the world inside her heart. Without him, if anything should have happened to him—

Sasha had warned her against killing and against dying. —You know what you'd become. . . .

Oh, absolutely she did.

8

✠ ✠ ✠ ✠ The horses had not the strength now for hard going. No more did Pyetr—small wonder that Pyetr seemed thinner and paler than yesterday: Sasha noticed it especially when they had come to a small stream and let the horses rest and drink. Pyetr stripped off the bloody shirt and splashed water over him, sending a trail of stained water curling away over the moss—but of the wound there remained nothing but a white scar on his back and another on his chest. Pyetr touched the one he could reach, examined it, awkwardly situated as it was, and looked up with worry in his eyes that Sasha did not want to read—realization how close he had come to dying last night, certainly; and perhaps of the magic it might have cost to call him back.

"I didn't borrow," Sasha said. "If that's what you're wondering. You're white as a ghost and some bit thinner to prove it. —That shirt's beyond washing. God, don't put it back on." He pulled Pyetr's spare one from Missy's baggage. Pyetr shook the water out of his hair, dried it with the dirty shirt and put the clean one on.

After which they took the chance to wash and shave, filled their water-flasks and left the brook behind at a pace both Missy and Volkhi could keep.

In the white sunlight, without dirt and stubble, Pyetr looked paler still, the fine lines on his face smoothed away. He seemed—

Drawn thin, the way he had been in the days master Uulamets had first snared them, and used Pyetr for bait for his ghostly daughter. The god help them, he had snatched after an image last night, that very moment a young fool had worked his best

176

magic—they had been young, they had been on an adventure that would end well—but time had glossed the fear and the weariness and Pyetr's sure attraction for what he knew would kill him—the very destruction Pyetr had been, one feared with the clarity of hindsight, courting all his young life—

Because Pyetr had *had* that inclination in his youth: Pyetr the gambler's son, who valued his life less than his freedom and his own way. Old Uulamets had wanted a wizard lad, had wished for one for a hundred years, till a certain stableboy had been shaken out of Vojvoda—to rescue Pyetr from an unpleasantness occasioned by a lady's window and an irate husband who had dropped dead in the street.

They rode a narrow space between the hills, with noon sun slanting through the leaves. Babi was off somewhere, but Babi would do that—sometimes there and sometimes not, as Babi pleased.

Sasha murmured, out of his own thoughts: "When we first came to this woods, Pyetr, do you remember, master Uulamets wanted *me* to meet 'Veshka. You were an accident. He wanted *me* out of Vojvoda."

"*I* wanted the hell out of town. There was a rope involved. I call that a reason. —What are you talking about?"

"He wanted *me*. He wanted a wizard to attract Eveshka back to him. And after a hundred years of his wanting someone like me—and after my being born and growing up, and all, just to satisfy his wish—what did Eveshka do but fall in love with you instead?"

"Love, hell! The old goat meant you to die, friend. You weren't supposed to survive the honor."

"But he didn't need a wizard for that. He certainly didn't need one fifteen years old—"

"She was sixteen a hundred years. She was still sixteen then. It wasn't that unreasonable."

"But—" The train of thought was getting more and more uncomfortable, now it had started. "She'd have been sixteen another year or so. I'd have been older. It might have worked better then."

"Thank the god not. By then, *I'd* have been hanged."

Chilling thought. "But his wish worked too soon, didn't it? Or didn't get me born soon enough. Maybe something pulled his wish off a year or so. Maybe it was mine for my own welfare. Or 'Veshka's for help. —Or maybe it wasn't ever me that was going to work: you were his answer, and he wouldn't see it. He had his mind made up how everything was going to be, just like 'Veshka: it was me he still wanted, after you were right under his nose; and why, with you at hand, did he still want a wizard, when we all know the doubly-born are so dangerous? Did *he* want Ilyana?"

Pyetr frowned at him, thinking thoughts he most definitely did not want to overhear. Then Pyetr said: "Does a rusalka want anything but its own way? Maybe 'Veshka did it. Maybe her father wanted you and she wished me up to spite him."

A ridge loomed in front of them. The horses took it at a brisker pace, and after that it was a climb down again, through thin new growth, past a fallen tree. Since the forest's regrowth, young trees had grown old and massive; and some had died.

He said, had been waiting to say, when they came side by side again, "But all along we've said wizards shouldn't marry wizards. You were ever so much—"

Pyetr arched an eyebrow.

—safer? Hardly flattering, to the rascal Pyetr had so studiously been. His face went hot and he mumbled instead, "I just don't know why he was furious that she went for you."

"What in hell are we really talking about?"

Impossible to explain. They were coming to another rough spot. "I don't know."

Their course took them apart again, around a tree, along a hillside, Missy dropping behind. He overtook Pyetr at the end of a stand of trees and a thorn thicket and Pyetr said, "By everything you say, 'Veshka herself being born was no accident. The old scoundrel must have loved Draga once, I'll suppose he did—why else marry her? Or maybe—"

Missy had to drop back again, and Sasha started to eavesdrop for the rest of it, but it felt too private, something about Eveshka; and when they were side by side again, Pyetr asked:

"What are you trying to say?"

"That Draga couldn't have carried 'Veshka without wanting her—or stayed near Uulamets if Uulamets hadn't been willing for her to—a baby's just too fragile. He *knew* his wife was trying to kill him. He knew his wife wanted that baby, but *he* wanted Eveshka, too—not just after she was born. He had to— if a wizard-wife can wish not to have a child—so can her husband, granted he's thinking in those terms."

"Not a sure thing," Pyetr muttered, "granted wizards are like the rest of us."

"Eveshka's told me she wasn't even thinking about having a child, herself, before she conceived Ilyana, which—" He was sure his face was red. "—considering you both, was incredibly forgetful on her part."

"She didn't exactly have a mother's kindly advice."

A hill intervened. He rode it, trying *not* to overhear Pyetr's thoughts, and Missy picked her way down at Volkhi's tail. Babi turned up again and left by the time he overtook Pyetr on flat ground.

Pyetr said: "She's getting more and more like her father, if you want my opinion: scared to death of magic and using as little as she can."

"But why did Uulamets want a wizard to marry his daughter?"

"Forget 'marry.' He wanted to kill us!"

"You were the one he specifically didn't want and it happened anyway."

"What are you saying? I was *Draga's* choice?"

"No," he said in consternation. "No, I don't believe that. I'm saying I don't know what he wanted me for. Unless he was sure I could attract his daughter into his reach, and that I could help him—"

"—Be his damn servant," Pyetr corrected him.

"But the point is, if it's so terrible to have a child that gifted—what in the world did he want with me?"

"Better not to ask."

"No, it's important to ask. Why was he so upset that she wanted you instead?"

"What are you getting at?"

"I don't know. I absolutely don't know. I wish I—"

He checked himself short of that precipice. He hit the saddlebow in frustration and looked at the trees, the leaves in the sunlight—anything but wish. God!

Pyetr said: "Nobody could know she was a wizard until she was born. We didn't know—"

"But Patches' spots were a good possibility—considering Missy. And if Uulamets didn't argue with having a grandchild— which I don't get the impression he did, he was for it."

"Get to a point, for the god's sake."

"That I don't believe all the danger is in Ilyana."

"Oh, god, that's comforting."

He said distractedly, staring ahead into the sunlit green: "We've been listening to very few advisors. And doing everything we've done on 'Veshka's say-so. 'Veshka's *not* the most level head in the household. You have to admit that."

"I'll admit it. She'll even admit it, once and twice a year. I'll also admit the mouse is fifteen. And Chernevog's *not* a moral guide, Sasha. I know him, god, I know him—"

"She's convinced her daughter is dangerous. That someday she'd do exactly what she's done, and go—where we know not everything's been all right, for a very long time. But so's 'Veshka dangerous. *I'm* dangerous. My misjudgments certainly are. I'm only hoping I haven't made one."

"In what?"

Maybe being thinner gave Pyetr that fey, remembered face. There was the tiny scar on his forehead, above the eye—he had gotten that one the year Chernevog had died. That seemed fainter today. Maybe it was the light. Maybe he was being foolish in his worry.

"Sasha?"

"I'm not sure Uulamets' wishes are out of this game. I'm not sure 'Veshka's right in her worries. I—"

Birds started up, ravens, rising out of the hollow ahead of them.

Death was there. That was not unusual. There was no reason to turn aside. It only cast a solemnity on them as they rode further, into a patch of younger trees, where sunlight sifted through bright leaves. Insects buzzed here.

A deer had died. Such things happened—there were wolves. The sick and the lame died.

But no four-footed creature had hacked it in pieces, leaving most.

—

So many things were amiss with the world. Babi turned up in Ilyana's lap as they rode, and vanished again—with a hiss.

"Why does he do that?" Yvgenie asked.

"He's upset," was all she could answer. So was she. The sun showed Yvgenie so pale, so dreadfully pale—but the kiss this morning had had nothing of chill about it. She caught a furtive, troubled glance as they rode, seeing how leaf-dappled sunlight glowed on his face and shoulders, how he cast her kind and shy looks when he thought she was not watching: if her uncle Sasha were in love, she thought, he would look at someone like that; god, she *wanted* to help him, and not to have any harm come to him. He was kind, he was shy and gentle, and thoughtful, for all her father's bad opinion of boyars' sons—and even if he had had a terrible father, somebody had taught him kindness. She caught sometimes the image of a fat, gentle-faced woman who had hugged him and held him and told him stories—

Not flattering stories, about wizards and magic birds; and bears that talked and wicked sorcerers who hid their hearts in acorns—she supposed one could, but acorns seemed a very dangerous place; and bears talked, but nothing like people. So she told him, now that the silence was easier, about the bear in the garden, about uncle Sasha and the bees, about—

About Owl and Kavi Chernevog, and how she had known him for years and years. It was hard to remember he could not hear her pictures, not as easily as her father could. She had to tell them in words, which she was not good at—

"How did he die?" he wanted to know—and that question echoed around and around in their heads, his fears, hers—

She did not, she had to admit, know that answer: he gave her a most vivid and grisly image of beasts and fangs and fire and she shivered and wanted not to have any more of it right now, please—

Because she had the most dreadful growing suspicion that papa was right and that Kavi had done something both wicked and desperate—though, not, she thought, by intent: surely if the boy had been drowning, he could be far worse off than having Kavi find him and hold him among the living—and Kavi would not have made him fall in the brook.

(Mouse, uncle would say, sternly—don't hope things are so. Be sure. Know the truth, even if you don't like it . . .)

But Yvgenie reached out his hand, then, across the space between Patches and Bielitsa. A touch of his fingers, that was all it needed for that wonderful tingling to run from her arm to her heart. She felt warm through, as if she no longer needed the sun.

Perhaps it was Kavi reassuring her *and* Yvgenie. Perhaps, in the way of ghosts, Kavi could not get their attention during the day, with all the distractions sunlight made. Night was the time for dreams, and things one had to see with the heart—and she was *sure* that kiss this morning had been Kavi's, the same as the one last night—that had been—

—terribly dangerous. Don't trust him that far, Yvgenie had said—and Yvgenie had been unfailingly, painfully honest with her. Yvgenie felt some sort of threat to her—

The warmth changed. The tingling became like needles of ice—scarily different, making her dizzy. She thought, I won't be afraid, no, I won't be afraid, dammit, Kavi's touched me before and he's never hurt me, it's only his borrowing—

And it's *not* harmful. Uncle said it was—but papa admitted he'd felt it—and he's still alive. My *mother* knew when to stop—and wouldn't Kavi? Kavi loves me, he's loved me for years.

He's not very strong—he wasn't on the river shore. The first time he kissed me, he borrowed enough to speak, that was all. He could hardly move the froth on the river: and Yvgenie being so tired, he borrows only a little, only a very little. He's *never* threatened me. He said he'd never hurt me, that he had to do whatever I told him—he said he had no choice.

He said that he wanted it to be in this season, while he was with me—or I'd be alone—

Wanted *what* to be in this season, Kavi? What do you want of me? Is it love? Is it something else?

Suddenly she had a vision of vines and thorns, a great flat stone, and Owl lying on the ground, a real Owl, white feathers dewed with blood—at her father's feet, her father with the sword sinking to his side. She looked up at her father, grieving for Owl—caring little at that moment if he cut her head off—

She trembled then, thinking, But Owl's already dead; and papa would never kill anything—he's never used his sword—

But memory scattered. There were gilt roofs. There were great pillars and people in fine clothing, and there was music and dancing while people whispered furtively in corners, about the Great Tsar, and murders—and betrayals she knew and could not, except by killing her own father, betray elsewhere.

Yvgenie cast a desperate look into the branches over them—

Seeking Owl, no matter that Owl had not a shred of love for him—only habit. And the hope of mice, that Kavi could lure close: small murders, to win Owl's affection—but what else did one do, who loved Owl?

The ground told its own story—horses, men, and the ashes of a fire.

Pyetr kicked at the cinders. "Damn."

Sasha said, from Missy's back: "Yvgenie's father's men."

"Looking for him, Yvgenie said." Pyetr untied his sword from Volkhi's baggage and slung it on. The horses assuredly had as soon be away, fretting at being held, switching their tails and twitching their skins at the mere sound of insects. "Where's Babi? Is he still with us?"

"A moment ago."

"Hope there wasn't a young one," Pyetr muttered. "A doe. In springtime. Damn them."

It was wizardry led his thought on Pyetr's track, a simple wondering that brought him to a sight of monsters, a dreadful smell that meant Be absolutely still.

It knew that much. The rest was muddled in its thoughts, with blood and fear.

"God," he muttered, and slid down from Missy's back. He needed walk only a half a dozen paces to see a dappled hide beneath low hanging branches. Pyetr led Volkhi up beside him and stopped.

"Damn," Pyetr said.

One wished—

A heaviness came down on them like sudden cloud, a feeling of menace in the sunlight that prickled the nape and constricted the breath. Missy fought the reins. Volkhi shied up and Pyetr grabbed for his bridle.

The brush shifted, and in a very slender trunk a moss-green eye opened.

Shout all one pleased, a leshy might be deaf to it. A leshy

might hear instead the softest voice, might hear the breaking of a branch. Or the sound of a bowstring, where none had sounded in a hundred years.

This leshy was, as leshys reckoned, young as what it sheltered—perhaps it was wild and speechless. There were such. It offered not a word, only threat and anger.

"Little cousin," Sasha said quietly, "my horse isn't an enemy. She's a very honest horse, and you're scaring her."

The twiggy fingers that sheltered the fawn could break rock and break bones—and the anger it cast at them was extreme. But breathing seemed easier, then.

"Where's Misighi?" Pyetr asked it. "Young leshy, we need him very desperately."

The brushy arms folded more tightly, screening the fawn from their eyes.

"There are good men downriver," Sasha said. "Take the young one there. They'll feed it. They'll know it belongs to the forest and they'll let it go again."

There were both eyes now.

"Tell Misighi," Sasha began.

One never believed a leshy's moving when one saw it. It blurred in the eye, or it seemed not to be moving at all. There were suddenly a score or more such young leshys on either hillside, and the feeling of smothering grew. Rocks rumbled. The hill might have been coming down. It was a leshy voice, speaking no words that he could hear.

Come on, he wished Pyetr silently, and led Missy and reached back for Pyetr's arm, walking with Pyetr past the leshy and its fellows, and on along the cleft of the hills.

The feeling lifted slowly. He looked back as Pyetr did, and patted Missy's neck.

"In no good mood," Pyetr breathed. "Dammit!"

"You shouldn't—"

"—swear around them. I know, but, dammit, Sasha, we need their help! What's wrong with them? Where are the ones we know? Where are Wiun and Misighi, and why won't they speak to us?"

—

*That no harm may come of my wishes—that's the first thing I
wish tonight: that my wishes be few and true, that second. And
third, I wish my daughter to trust those who love her before
she trusts those she loves.*

*Hearts are so breakable, Kavi used to say. He used to say,
They're safer where they can't be touched. And if I could lend
her mine tonight I would. But I'm not sorry enough for what I
did. I can't be. I'm not that changed from what I was. I've only
a strong reason not to want things. And that's not enough to
take to my daughter.*

*What do I wish for my daughter? To find the wisdom I
lack—because mine fails me. And to find—*

Eveshka bit her lip and decided the quill had dried in the
night wind. She did *not* want to finish that. She put the pen in
the case and capped the inkwell.

She sat before her small fire with her hands clasped before
her lips and listened to the laughter out of the dark.

She thought, Wishing is so dangerous. I've never, never since
the day I died, dared wish too much.

But tonight—

Kavi, if she can't hear me, then, dammit, *you* listen—

*Mouse, Eveshka, I don't know if there is a way back from what
I've done. Take your lesson from me, mouse, and forever be
careful of your choices.*

*Uulamets himself told me—a wizard's never more powerful
than when he's a child; I didn't understand why that should
be, but it seemed so, and now I know why: because it takes
patience to see your wishes come true, and if in waiting for
them you lose your belief, you can't believe in your present ones
the way you did the first.*

*And the day you make your first mistake—you doubt your-
self.*

*But master Uulamets told me wrong. It's not once in a life-
time that a wizard can work a spell like I worked on the jug.
It's any moment you think you can. I might wish you back
here. I think I could hold you—if I was sure it was right to do.
It seems true too that no wizard can wish time; or if he can*

wish time, he can't wish place; or if he can wish place he can't be sure of the event.

Only a child can be so absolute in all—

Sasha ripped a page, crumpled it and cast it into the fire, a short burst of fire and a curling sheet of ash. Babi hissed, Pyetr jerked back the cooking pan in startlement—

"What was that?" Pyetr asked.

Sasha looked as if something had hit him. Scared. Terrified. That was not Sasha's habit either.

"Sasha?" If there were ghosts or if there were more substantial things he knew how to deal with them. Babi did. But something to do with that book, that Sasha would risk his life for, writing which held things Sasha had to remember—and from which he had just cast a page into the fire—

"Sasha? What in hell happened?"

"I wrote something. I wrote something I shouldn't have written. Things *changed*."

"*What* changed?" The hair on his nape prickled. There was a smell of scorched oil and burned paper beneath the trees and he found the presence of mind to rescue the cakes and set the pan aside. "Sasha, make sense, dammit."

"You can tell when magic works. You can feel it."

"You told me nothing can change what's written. Can fire?"

Sasha shook his head and shut the book. "But it can keep another wizard from reading it."

"Reading *what*?"

Sasha looked at him—terrified, he thought. Distraught. Sasha said faintly, "I—" and stopped.

"*Don't* tell me," he said, seeing it came hard. And he added, in the case it was something to do with him, "Sasha, I trust you."

Sasha put his hand over his eyes and bowed against the book. It scared him more than anything Sasha had ever done—and he had no idea whether to move, to touch him, to say anything— he was used to 'Veshka's fits, he had learned the lessons they taught; but one from Sasha scared him. He sat dead still, not moving until a tremor started that had nothing to do with cold.

If he could wish anything, he wished for Sasha's peace of mind. If Sasha was hearing him he truly wanted that—

And he was deaf to whatever storms might be going on unless Sasha wanted him to hear, absolutely could not feel them—Sasha should remember that, too.

Sasha lifted his head, with a fear-struck expression. "I wished—wished us to find her, Pyetr. If I wish her to find us, we could do us all harm."

One asked—carefully—because it was useful to remember sometimes, such small things magic might make Sasha forget: "Is there that much difference? What *is* the difference?"

"It isn't strength. It's inevitability. It's sliding down the slope of what is. *She's* the one in motion. All things follow her."

Nonsense, it sounded to be; but Sasha saw things Sasha could not describe in words. Sasha called them currents. Or drifts. Or whirlwinds.

"What—?" One ought to question—but one ought not to jostle upset wizards—no. One should keep one's questions behind one's teeth and tend to supper or something ordinary that might let Sasha climb back up off that slope himself, before someone slipped.

He carefully poured two cups of vodka from the jug. Looked for Babi to give him his, but there was no Babi.

He took a sip and offered Sasha his cup.

Sasha took it gently, steadily from his fingers, and Pyetr avoided his glance, not to disturb him.

Sasha nudged his arm with the cup, said faintly, "Don't do that."

He looked up—met Sasha's eyes in the flickering of the firelight; honest brown, they were, dark, flickering on the surface with firelight, but one could not see past that surface—could not now, could not for years past see past it, to what Sasha did not want him to know. Sasha was not the stableboy any longer, not the boy who had looked to him for advice—

"But I do," Sasha said. "I still do. I rely on it."

"Then the god help us." He had not meant his voice to shake. "I got us into this. I don't know why in hell the leshys won't answer us—"

"There's reason." Sasha's eyes wandered to the firelit trees about them. "I've felt a change in the woods over the years. Misighi said—old wood and young. You rarely see the old ones now."

"Trees we planted—all up and down the damn riverside. Even the young ones should know we aren't any harm here."

"Will the fawn? Or should it? Its rules are different, that's all." He glanced above them. "They never quite trust us, Pyetr. Maybe they shouldn't."

"What's this, maybe they shouldn't?"

" 'Veshka's in the woods tonight."

"In the woods. Where in the woods? Does she know where Ilyana is? Can you talk to her?"

"I—don't know. I don't think I should right now."

"Why?"

"I could change things. Maybe that's not a good idea."

"God. —Maybe your house was afire! Maybe you should have run for the damn *door*, Sasha! Remember the world, remember your uncle, remember the town gate, for the god's sake! There are times you just make up your mind and do something!"

"This isn't Vojvoda, Pyetr."

Fool, he figured that meant. So he shut his mouth and shook his head, hoping—hoping his friend had some intention to move soon. Please.

"Pyetr—you're all of the ordinary world I can understand. You're not the only one I can hear. But you're the only one who can answer me. —And forgive me for eavesdropping just then. You're not a fool, you're absolutely not a fool."

"Only twice a day."

"Nor afraid of things. I envy that."

"Not afraid of things. Damned right I'm scared. I'm scared of sitting here too long. I'm scared what else is wrong."

"But not afraid of us. You never think I'd harm you."

"No, I *don't* think that. But the fact is, Sasha—I don't *care* if you do. —And you know how I mean that. Stop worrying."

Sasha's lips trembled. "Dammit, Pyetr."

"Don't do that on me. God." Wrong thing to have said. He knew nothing else to do. He grabbed Sasha the way he would 'Veshka and held him tight. Eventually Sasha held on to him.

He heard the horses give alarm, thought, For the god's sake, Sasha, be sensible, don't frighten Missy—

188

Then he heard the rising of a wind in the woods. Or not a wind.

He thought—Misighi?—because it might be leshys—*they* had a sound like that, when the great old ones were traveling.

One of the horses thundered away. The other followed.

His thoughts started scattering like the sparks from the fire, going out in the wind, one by one, and he fought it, thinking— I can't go out, I can't—dammit, no. . . .

9

✠ ✠ ✠ ✠ Wolves came on his trail, soft-footed, golden-eyed, and there was no escaping them or the memory of the house, and of Draga. There was no breath left to run, except in short, desperate bursts of failing strength, and the woods closed in among winding bramble hedges, high walls of leaves and hidden thorns.

The green maze branched. The left-hand corridor looked lightest and longest, and he took it, but it rapidly became more ominous than the last, shadowed and leafless and wild.

He thought, This is foolish. I should never have taken this path, I should go back now—it leads nowhere I want to go—I might get back before they find the entry to this path—

Shadow fell between him and the light, shadow of a face, and something touched his arm. Ilyana said he should wake, they should go on now, where they were, and that helped him to the light. He struggled up on his elbows and to his knees, in a world gray and faint, shadowed with cloud like his dream. He saw Ilyana gathering up Patches' saddle and felt for some reason that the dream was still going on, that it was a presentiment to do with where they were going, that he had always known where the chase must end.

A place of thorns. And wolves. He had run that corridor of thorns and they would find him there—or had run it, already. He longed for that meeting, and for the sight of Pyetr's face, no matter how dreadful the moment, because after that he would not be alone with his dreams. After that—

"Yvgenie," Ilyana said.

He thought, There's safety there. Somehow there's safety,

but not the sort I want to find, and not a place she belongs. She won't forgive me, she won't ever forgive me for it.

As Owl brushed his face with a wing tip.

Why do I feel that all my choices were long ago?

Why does it seem I'm remembering all of this? Yvgenie, Yvgenie, boy, don't sleep yet, it's not time to sleep that deeply. Wake up, saddle the horse and let's be moving.

Pyetr was my friend once, boy. You missed really knowing him. But he was in that place. Or he will be, again, and we might just die there. Maybe that's what all this is leading to. Or from.

He waked on his feet, with the saddle in mid-heft, aimed toward Bielitsa's back. It landed clumsily, and he straightened it and warmed his hands against her, knowing the risk in what he was doing, and the risk in where they were, and the dream he dreamed—but he did what he could. He saw Ilyana climb into the saddle. She had her hair in braids, the way it had been in the yard that day, when he was noticing edges of grass, and sunlight. He saw her that way now, as if he were slipping toward the dark and she were still standing in the light: the whole world was fragile, and poised to slip away—or he was already leaving it.

Sasha waked with his arm asleep, and with someone lying tangled on the cold earth with him—Pyetr, he was certain. Pyetr, now he remembered it, had been reasoning with a very foolish wizard who had had the safe ground fall from under his feet—

He could *feel* his old master's knowledge stirring at the depth of his memory once he thought sanely about it, a discovery Uulamets had made and hidden from him, writing the one Great Lie in his book—the one that obscured all the other truths.

God, I *know* what he used when he brought Eveshka back, I *know* what Uulamets did to reach back from the grave—all the questions I couldn't answer then I know; and it's too damned easy. One daren't even breathe, knowing it!

But breath did come—and with it, awareness of the whole world, brittle, prone to fracture at the very curiosity that discovered its substance. It was indeed Pyetr tangled with him—one *knew* Pyetr's presence, and one could hear the rough, raw echo

of the earth, feel the cold mustiness of dead leaves, the acrid
smoldering of embers, and the fragility of a sleeping and half-
dead—

—girl.

His eyes flew open. His hand jerked toward the ground and
pressed wet, gritty leaves. His waking vision was exactly the
same: a girl was sleeping peacefully beside them, a girl with long
blond braids, wearing gilt and blue silk embroidered with flowers. Mouse, he all but exclaimed at first glance, except she did
not *sound* like the mouse, not inside. She sounded—

Pyetr bruised his ribs and his leg sitting up, sharp, welcome
pain, that shoved the noisy world back, and convinced him most
welcomely that Pyetr saw the same thing.

"What in hell?" Pyetr breathed.

Whereupon the girl's eyes opened and she stared at them
both as if they had fallen out of the moon—or she had.

"Who is *she*?" Count on Pyetr to ask the critical question,
count on Pyetr to grab him by the shoulder at the brink of wondering too much too fast—as the girl thrust herself up on her
arms, staring at them, frozen, quite. Blue eyes, straw-colored
hair that trailed free about a frightened face—

A rich girl's gown all tattered and bedraggled, gilt threads
torn, scratches on her hands—

"Yvgenie," Pyetr muttered, in the same moment Sasha
thought, too, of a red silk shirt and gilt collar.

The girl asked—she could hardly ask, she was shivering so:
"Are you his f-father's men?"

"I assure you, no," Pyetr said fervently, and the girl:

"Do you know where he is?"

No, Sasha warned Pyetr without half-thinking, and was sure
on a second thought that he was right. Brave as this townbred
girl might be, it was more than embroidery was raveled, surely,
and it was more than young foolishness had brought her to them.
Absolutely, magic was loose.

"We should make a fire," he said, nudging Pyetr's arm, wishing him to understand and be careful what he said. "Have breakfast." The pan was lying next last night's fire, with last night's
overdone cakes in it. The vodka jug sat beside it. He picked up
the pan and offered it to the girl. "There are cakes if you'd like

a bite—they're cold, I'm afraid. We haven't time to cook this morning. But we can make tea—"

"We need to find the horses," Pyetr said sharply, giving his shoulder a shake. "We need to find Babi, dammit. The boy wasn't alone, we can figure that, but we can ask her questions while we're moving."

"She's not a shapeshifter," he assured Pyetr, in case Pyetr was in doubt. He was virtually certain of it. "One of that kind would have *been* the mouse to our eyes." He made another offer of their untouched supper, wishing the girl to trust them at least that far, quite ruthlessly: she was white as a ghost herself, and her trembling, he was sure, was not all from fright. The forest offered food to woodsmen, not to a girl in silk and gilt. "Go on. It's all right. Take them."

She took the pan, perforce, asking, "Please—where's Yvgenie?"

"With my daughter," Pyetr said harshly, and, leaning on Sasha's shoulder, got to his feet. "Somewhere in this woods. We're looking for them. We've been looking for them for two damned days now."

Pyetr had been a long time from his courtly youth and the idle flattering of young ladies—Pyetr was in a hurry, the mouse was in dire danger, and he both frightened the girl and reassured her of his ultimate intentions, Sasha caught it in the girl's thoughts and in the glance she gave Pyetr—the hope that they were not liars and that there *was* truly a lost daughter and a wife and a house and everything that could make two strange men reliable and respectable.

God, she was so beautiful.

"The horses," Pyetr reminded him, and shook at his shoulder. "Sasha."

The horses were out in the woods. Not far. Babi was with them, one of those occasional times one could feel Babi's presence, fierce and warm as a cat with kittens.

"Sasha."

"They're all right. They're coming." He watched the girl break off a bit of cake in fingers that surely had never seen rough use before this woods, and said to Pyetr, absently, out of the welter of thoughts absorbing him, "It was leshys last night. They

risked a fire bringing her to us, Pyetr. You know how they hate
fires. Let's not question a gift, shall we?"

"The leshys could damned well stay for tea if they'd an interest in co—"

A branch fell, breaking branches below it, over their heads.
"Move!" Sasha said—and Pyetr stepped aside just in time, scowl-
ing up into the branches.

There was anger from the woods too, deep and dangerous.
The leshys are upset at us, he thought. They've a surfeit of wizards on their hands. Young leshys. They don't know us, but
they're watching. . . . He said to Pyetr, never taking his eyes off
the girl, who had frozen: "Fire. Tea." And to the girl: "We've
odd friends. Don't be alarmed. Clearly they were the ones who
brought you here. We assume there was reason."

She only stared at him with wide, stricken eyes. Pyetr had
walked over to the deadfall and began breaking it up for fire—
be *careful*, he wished Pyetr, feeling the precariousness of the
situation, hoping the leshy watching from the treetops would
not take offense, and saw to his chagrin how he had left his book
last night, with the inkpot left open. He hastily began to put
that away, and to stow all the books out of reach—though there
seemed no danger to them from a single frightened girl, who
looked at them, between bites of cold cake, as if she and they
had collectively lost their wits.

She asked, swallowing a mouthful: "You're a wizard, aren't
you?"

He made as courteous a bow as one could, sitting on the
ground. "Sasha," he said, raked his hair back and, to his chagrin,
pulled a leaf from his hair. "Alexander." *So* like the mouse when
she frowned like that.

"I've heard of you," she said. (Of course. People did know
them downriver.) "I thought you were—"

What? he wondered helplessly.

"Older," she said, in a way that meant *much* older, and made
him feel like foolish fifteen again.

Wood landed beside him. Pyetr was annoyed, Pyetr thought
he was woolgathering and Pyetr wanted the horses right now,
dammit—he caught the edge of Pyetr's opinions, while Pyetr
took the tea-pan to the rock that poured a thin thread of water
into a boggy puddle of a pool in this place. Sasha decided he

should see to the fire, stuck a branch into last night's coals and wanted it to light. It did.

She said, "Why is Yvgenie off with his daughter some-where?"

He piled kindling onto the burning piece and answered her without quite looking her in the eye, "He thinks we're upset with him. So does she."

"Are you?"

"No. Not with him." God, he thought, she must see us as liars at the least—and how do we tell her the truth? Forgive me, but a dead wizard's possessed your young man, and he's con-fused about who he's with? —Because Yvgenie Pavlovitch, with so many dark spots in his memory, must be confused. The re-semblance was so clear from some angles it upset one's stom-ach.

He had the fire going. She had finished one of the cakes—no knowing when she had last eaten, although the leshys would surely have left her in better health than they had found her. He opened the tea packet as Pyetr set the water on the fire, Pyetr muttering under his breath, "She looks like Ilyana. At least the hair. And about the same age, give or take. I think Misighi must have heard us, and made a mistake. They *don't* tell one of us from the other very well."

The girl's eyes went from one to the other of them, doubting their sanity, Sasha was sure. He saw another tiny morsel of cake go down dry and wished her not to choke.

"There'll be tea in a moment," he promised her, while Pyetr unstopped the vodka jug, thinking shadowy thoughts. Pyetr poured a small dose of vodka, and said, "Here, Babi."

Babi turned up. The pan clanged to the ground, the rest of the cakes in the girl's lap.

She made not a sound. Or a move. Thank the god. Sasha said quickly, as she gulped down a bite of cake. "He's a dvorovoi. Don't be afraid. He might go after the cakes—"

She picked one out of her lap and offered it hastily—tossed it as Babi came her direction. Babi swallowed the whole cake at a gulp.

"Behave," Pyetr said sternly, and poured another dollop of vodka that never hit the leaves.

"It's not everyone he likes," Sasha said, fluttery about the stomach himself, considering Babi's other shapes, while the girl drew small anxious breaths. "I don't think he'd really hurt you. It's absolutely only the cakes he wants—and he thinks you're all right, or he'd let you know it." He reached after the tea and burned his hand on the pan. Sucked a finger. "Why don't you pour a bit of vodka in the tea, Pyetr? And some honey. I think honey would be nice, don't you?"

Volkhi and Missy made a leisurely appearance through the trees, interested in the spring. The girl looked worriedly at that, at Babi, at them—

He poured the tea, sloshing it badly. Pyetr added vodka, added honey and Sasha offered it to her. "There. We've only the two cups—Pyetr and I don't mind sharing."

"Pyetr," she echoed faintly, and looked at Pyetr with—as seemed—an unwarrantably troubled look.

Pyetr lifted a brow and took a sip of tea-and-vodka. "Pyetr Ilitch Kochevikov. Notorious in Kiev and various other places, I gather. I'm flattered if my reputation's gotten to such lovely ears."

That was the old Pyetr. Rain would not fall on him, aunt Ilenka had used to say —meaning he was far too slippery. And far too false and angry to deal with a frightened girl.—Stop it, Sasha wished him. Can't you see you're scaring her?

Pyetr shut up. Sasha said gently, "Drink your tea. It's getting cold. We need to be moving as soon as we can."

She sipped at it, holding the cup in both hands. Winced, swallowing, and blinked tears. Too much vodka for a young girl, Sasha thought, and took a sip of the cup Pyetr passed him. There certainly was. His own eyes watered. He thought of the mouse at the table, the last night she had been home, he looked at the girl and thought—

Something's wrong. Something's very wrong here— While Pyetr asked, in a dreadful hush, "Where are you from, miss? Kiev?"

A shake of her head. The tears had kept running. She was staring at Pyetr.

"Where?" Pyetr asked sharply.

"Pyetr," Sasha objected, suffocating in that silence. And stopped, because the girl had taken on a scowl that—god, he knew in a way that made his stomach turn over. The match for it was sitting beside him.

The girl said, with that hawk's look, through a film of tears, "You *are* my father, aren't you?"

Sasha drew in a breath, it seemed forever, and said, the instant he had wind enough, "More tea, actually—I think we could do with more tea, here. . . ."

Pyetr said faintly, "Who's your mother?"

"Who's my *mother*? You—"

Silence! Sasha wished, so abruptly the girl winced. He got up and hauled Pyetr to his feet. "We could *use* some more water, Pyetr."

Pyetr was damnably hard to move when he wanted otherwise. "What's your name?" Pyetr demanded, a question so absolute his own curiosity slipped, and the girl said, in a hard voice.

"Nadya Yurisheva."

Pyetr sank slowly to his heels, stared his firstborn daughter in the face while she stared at him, then stood up and without a word took the pan back to the spring—

In a silence thick as the leaves.

Sasha whispered—one could only whisper, "Excuse me, please," and went after Pyetr. Anything might happen. Leshys were involved. One was still watching them, he was sure of it.

Pyetr leaned against the rock, put the pan against it to let clean water trickle in, while Volkhi and Missy blithely destroyed the little green that grew in that spot of sun.

Pyetr said, "She's about eighteen, nineteen, do you think?"

Vojvoda, a stable, Pyetr run through and bleeding, Pyetr having left the Yurishev's second story window very precipitately not an hour before—

"—Did you and Irina—?"

"Sufficiently, I assure you. Not that night—but certainly others."

"God."

"The leshys have a damned dark sense of humor, friend."

"I—don't think they're altogether to blame—"

"I *know* who's to blame! It's quite *clear* who's to blame! Nothing's an accident, isn't that it? Nothing's ever an accident:

her being here is no accident, her looking for that boy is no accident—She's no damn substitute for the mouse, Sasha! I don't know what's going on, but she's *not* what I'm taking home, I don't care what the leshys intend!"

"Hush! She'll hear you!"

Pyetr sank down on his heels and dumped the water from the pan. "God, Sasha."

What did one say? What did one do? *Or* wish?

Pyetr said faintly, "I don't know this girl. The daughter I know's off in trouble somewhere, not being reasonable, and I honestly don't think this is going to help, Sasha!"

"We don't know that. We—"

"Magic strikes at the weakest point, doesn't it? Things go wrong at the weakest point, and our weakest point's my own damned—"

"You said yourself the mouse is no hazard."

"Yes, and you've been making wishes all these years to protect my daughter, haven't you, and something *certainly* has, clear from Vojvoda! You wanted the leshys to bring my daughter to us, and they certainly did! Something's satisfied all your wishes, *if it had to start eighteen damned years ago to do it!*"

Pyetr was uncannily good at magic for a man who had never believed in vodyaniye until one all but took his hand off. Sasha sank down on his heels by the water's edge, trying now Pyetr said it, to think exactly how he had framed his wishes for the mouse or how he had thought of her all these years—whether he had left a way for disaster. He could not pull order out of his ideas about the mouse, *could* not determine how he thought of her, and that was frightening.

He said to Pyetr. "I was getting too damned cocky. We're *not* giving up on the mouse. We're *not* letting her go. The world's protecting itself, that's all." He recollected last night, recollected how easy—how dreadfully easy magic could be—

"You're not making sense, the world protecting itself—"

"The world does. Nature's far harder to wish than you are. What you see makes you doubt what you know. For the god's sake don't make this girl hate you."

"Make her hate me? God, what's she got to thank me for? The same my father left to me? Gossip behind my back and doors slammed in my face? Why don't you *wish* her to be grateful, Sasha? It's a damned sight easier than waiting for it."

That bitterness went deep; but he knew Pyetr's heart, at moments too delicate to eavesdrop. "You don't mean that, any more than you *really* want me to send her away into the woods."

Pyetr shook his head, looking at the water, the rock, the god only knew. Not at him. Not at anything present.

Sasha said, "I think you'd better talk to her."

Pyetr whispered, furiously: "I *think* we'd better get moving. We're not stopping for any damn cup of tea, Sasha. Magic's switched the dice on us. I'm not sitting here. Not now."

"Pyetr, magic's brought her. Deal with her. Be fair with her. Always at the weakest point, you just said it. You can't make her your enemy!"

"What am I going to say, for the god's sake? All of Vojvoda thinks I *killed* Yurishev—and you and I both know who gained from it!"

Irina's relatives. No question. With Irina very likely in on the deed. He said to Pyetr, "I think you'd better find out what she does think."

"You."

He blinked, looked Pyetr straight in the eyes.

Pyetr whispered, "Dammit, are you wishing me?"

"I'm honestly trying not to. It's yourself pushing you. Or it's someone else's wish. One can never be absolutely certain at such moments. —When in doubt, do right. Harm has far too many consequences."

"Damn," Pyetr said, shook the remaining water from the pan and left him with the horses.

The woods might be thicker here, or the sky had faded. But when Yvgenie looked up he could see the sun through the branches, white and dim as a sun hazed with unseen cloud. He saw the lacy shadows of branches ripple over Ilyana and Patches, he knew by the sharpness of the edges that there were no clouds, and yet it seemed all the colors in the forest and sky were fading.

A cold touch swept past his shoulder: Owl. He put out his hand without thinking: Owl settled briefly on his arm, a faint icy prickle of claws. Then Owl took off again, as a gray-brown shape crossed the hillside ahead of them.

"A wolf," Yvgenie said.

"Where?" Ilyana asked, and it was gone. He could not swear now that it had been there, but his hands had grown so cold he could scarcely feel the reins. "Yvgenie?"

"My eyes are playing tricks," he murmured; but he feared he had been dreaming again, and he feared what those dreams might mean. He thought, I'm slipping. And saw his own hands reaching after branches in the dark, remembered the water pressing his body against the brush, the roar of the flood in his ears, and knowing he was going under—

—even while he was riding in the sunlight. He was dying, finally, he knew he was, and soon he would grasp after anything to save him, even those things he loved.

She was so like the mouse. So like her. Pyetr sank down on his heels, tucked the empty pan away in the pack.

Easier to look at the ground instead. He gave Babi's shoulder a scratch, looked up. There was the anger he expected. And hurt; and curiosity: all the mouse's expressions; Irina's nose and *his* mouth—that was the combination that made Nadya different.

He said, quietly, "No one told me either. I didn't keep any ties to Vojvoda. How did you find out?"

She opened her mouth to answer, angrily, he was sure; then seemed not to have the breath for it. She made a furious gesture with a trembling hand and looked away from him, at the ground, at the sky, at the fire—at him, finally, with her jaw set and fire in her eyes. But no answer.

He said, "Is your mother still alive?"

"What do you care?"

Himself—of a drunken father, in a dark street outside The Doe: What do you care?

She said, "I grew up as Nadya Yurisheva. My mother's family kept me safe. I never heard. I never did, not in all my life until the month I was going to be married, and I didn't believe it even then, until I laid eyes on you. It turns out I'm the daughter of a gambler and a murderer who had to ask me who my mother was! How many sisters do I *have* across the Russias?"

He thought, he could not help it: With your mother's dowry and Yurishev's money at stake, damned right your family kept their mouths shut, girl. And equally likely somebody profited getting the story to the bridegroom's family.

But it was not Irina's delicate petulance in front of him. It was an outraged daughter with a chin desperately set, eyes brimming with tears she was struggling for pride's sake not to shed.

He said, "I didn't kill Yurishev. I swear to you."

"No. Of course you didn't. Your friend did."

"Sasha was fifteen, mucking out stables and washing dishes in a tavern. He didn't even know me till after the fact. Did you grow up with the Yurishevs?"

"No. They mostly died." A tear escaped and slid down her cheek, but fury stayed in her eyes. "My father's whole *family* mostly died—ill-wished—in Vojvoda, in Balovatz, in Kiev. . . . The wizards wouldn't let them alone."

Old Yurishev dropping dead after running him through, with no mark on him—the whole town in hue and cry so quickly after wizards and Pyetr Kochevikov—

God, he had lived so long with the misdeeds of wizards he had forgotten ordinary greed, relatives, and poisons. Yurishev had come back home unexpectedly that night, Yurishev might even have had time to drink a cup of wine before the alarm upstairs—

"Wizardry, hell. *All* of them, you say."

"*What* are you saying?"

"Plain and ordinary murder, girl. How did they tell you it was?"

Color flushed her cheeks. "That you broke into the house—that you—as-saulted—my—m-"

God. He reached for her hand, but she snatched it out of reach. So he said, gently, lightly, "Girl, I do assure you—whatever you've heard of me, force was never my style." He settled back on his heels and met her cold stare with cool honesty. "It was an affair of some weeks. Someone told Yurishev, Yurishev chased me out of the house, ran me through when I tripped, and died in the street without my laying a hand on him. Leaving town seemed a good idea right then. As simple as that. I don't blame your mother—" A outright lie, the kindest he had in him. "She had to tell the watch something, didn't she?"

"Then why did all the other Yurishevs die?"

Not a silly girl, no. One close to an answer that could trouble her sleep at night. "Good question. Wizardry, perhaps—but not likely. Let me tell you: *real* wizardry's not what they tell you in Vojvoda and Sasha's not the kind of wizard you'll find selling dried toads and herbs in shops. His kind won't go to towns. They can't. Towns scare them, and if you'll believe me in the least, they don't give a damn about the Yurishevs and the Medrovs and their relatives. Not to say his wishes can't go that far—but not with any purpose against the Yurishevs. There's no malice in him. None. Watering the garden—whether it's going to take rain from other people—those are his worries. They keep him very busy."

She was listening. The anger was a little to the background, now. Curiosity was at work, one could see it in the flicker of her tear-filmed eyes.

She asked, scornfully, "So was it all accident?"

"Sasha says there aren't any accidents in magic. No accident in your being here, either. Your young man—I take it he's the same you were about to marry—"

A quick, black scowl.

"Nice lad," he said, "but in serious trouble. Let me tell you a name. Kavi Chernevog."

"I never heard of him."

"Not likely you would have. He's not dealt with folk down-river in years. But things happened in Kiev because of him. Things are still happening because of him—no matter he's dead. I don't know why the leshys brought you here or what you were doing in the woods with this boy, but you're haven't heard the worst trouble: Chernevog's gotten hold of him and run off with my daughter, who's not being outstandingly sensible right now."

"Gotten *hold*? Of Yvgenie?"

"Wizards can do that. Living or dead ones." He saw the shiver, saw her wits start to scatter and grabbed her hands and said, "Dead, in this case. Rusalka. Which means no good for your young lad, and no good for my daughter either. The way wizardry works, with three and four wizards involved, things may happen that *none* of the wizards precisely want, and ordinary folk like us can't do a damn thing about it. Like Sasha over there—whatever he wants, we'd do. Absolutely."

Her hands were clenched in his. She darted a fearful glance in Sasha's direction, back again. He said, "That's the way it works, girl. All he has to do is want something. No spells. Nothing. He has to be very careful what he *does* want. That's why he doesn't go into towns. No real wizard can. The world's far too noisy for him."

She was frightened. And still doubtful. She drew her hands away from him. "Can he stop this Chernevog?"

"He has before."

She believed that part. He was sure of it. She looked him in the eyes and said, "They tell stories about you. They say *you're* a wizard."

He shook his head solemnly. "Not a shred of one. Not the least ability."

"You're different than they said."

"Worse or better?"

A hesitation. And silence.

"Fair answer. —How *is* your mother?"

Her lips trembled. "She won't forgive me. None of them will forgive me."

"For running off with Yvgenie?"

Silence. But the eyes said it was.

"So why did you?"

The tremor grew worse. The jaw clamped. Fast. Damn you all, that look said. It might have been Irina's teaching. Or his temper. He had no idea, but he knew the hazard in it. He heard Sasha come walking over with the horses, he looked up as Sasha stopped and stood there, with the horses saddled.

Eavesdropping, he was certain of it.

Sasha blushed and looked at the ground and up again.

Which said he was right. But little enough he could blame Sasha. He got up, offered Nadya his hand, and thought she would refuse it.

She took it, at least, with grace he was not sure he would have had, with his father, who had, dammit, dropped out of his life and into it again only often enough to keep the pain constant.

He flung their packs over the saddlebow, climbed up and offered Nadya a hand and his foot to help her. She tried to settle sideways on Volkhi's rump.

"You'll fall," he said. "Not in this woods, girl. Tuck the skirts up and hold on."

They told stories in Vojvoda, how Pyetr Kochevikov and his sorcerer ally had shapechanged their way into birds after murdering her father in the street—Nadya had heard the dreadful stories long before she had ever heard the whispers about her parentage. Her mother had told her about all the murders, and her uncles had warned her how cruel and terrible the wizards hunting her were, and kept her close within walls.

For fear of spells, her mother had said, spells which might find her even in the safety of her own house, in her bed at night. Who knew what mistakes the other Yurishevs had made or what careless moment had killed them?

But one had only to look at Pyetr Kochevikov to know what her mother had really feared, the whisper that would mean she was not Yurishev's heir, the whisper that would simply say: *Kochevikov's* eyes, *Kochevikov's* face, *Kochevikov's* likeness. Her true father's hair was even paler than her mother's, of which she was so vain; he was incredibly handsome even years away from the event, and far, far younger than she would have ever expected, even so—all of which suggested an entirely different account of what had passed in her soon-to-be-widowed mother's bedroom that night.

Her mother *had* to have known the truth from the day she was born. Her uncles must have seen it: anyone in Vojvoda must have seen it, if they had ever laid eyes on her real father—and now she knew why her uncles had never allowed her outside her garden, never allowed her to meet any children except her nearly grown cousins, never let her see the world except secretly, over the garden walls, never let her speak to anyone but the trusted servants who lived within the house—and except Yvgenie and Yvgenie's father's men, for a few bewildering hours when they had made the betrothal, and drunk a great deal, and for those few hours made the whole house echo to voices and to strangers' laughter. She had spent her whole life afraid of spells in her drink and in her food, spells on her doorway and on the steps she walked. She had expected assassins and wizards every day of her life, and *dammit*, her uncles had surely known all along who she was and whose she was: *that* was what she could not stop thinking, clinging as she must to her father's waist, jolted and tossed on the way to finding a husband she had never had: They knew. They knew all along and they lied.

Her new-found father frightened her: she was sure he used the sword he wore on bandits and trespassers in this woods— she earnestly hoped, on no one else. But when he had seized her hands in his, looked her straight in the eye and told her his side of things, everything he had said made clearer sense to her than she had ever seen or heard out of her uncles or her mother; and as for Sasha—Sasha looked nothing like the dreadful wizards of her imagining, either, except the books he carried. She had seen no skulls, no dreadful ravenous creatures, unless one counted the sullen-looking furball that suddenly turned up beside the horses, or, when they stopped to catch their breaths and got down, popped up in one blink on the black horse's rump, tugging at the pack with hands like a man's, looking askance at her with eyes round and gold as the moon.

Pyetr said, "Vodka, yes," got the vodka jug and poured the creature a drink in mid-air.

One never expected to see a dvorovoi with one's own eyes, since she had never seen one in her garden. Sasha lived sequestered in the woods? She had no idea of the world except her nurse's tales about talking birds and lost tsarinas and horrid wizards with long white hair and long fingernails. She had never ridden a horse before, she had never spent a night under the stars, she had never waded a brook or clung desperately to a branch to save herself from drowning—and now she had done all of that, fallen asleep on the bare ground night after night and waked up one morning face to face with her true father—like the tsarevitch in her nurse's story. And of wizards—one never expected one who taking a pot of salve from his pack, spent his rest like her father, rubbing down his horse's legs and talking to the creature in fond and worried tones, more kindly than she generally heard people speak to other people. Sasha's hair was brown, his very nice nose was sunburned and she found herself recalling how, waking this morning he had looked as startled as she was. Besides, he had said please. Would a wizard who laid spells on people's doorways and winecups beg anyone's pardon? Her uncles scarcely would. Only Yvgenie—Yvgenie who had met her a moment by the stairs—

Yvgenie who had shyly met her behind the stairs while their elders were talking and promised her Kiev and all the world— Yvgenie who had said—

Her father nudged her arm, offering her a kind of grain-cake from their packs, all wrapped in sticky leaves. He had his own mouth full. He insisted with a second offering and she took the cake doubtfully and bit into it.

Honey. Grain and currants. It was the best sweet she had ever tasted in her life, with her hands all over dirt and the tart musty leaf sticking to the honey. Her father went on to hand one to Sasha, who after washing his hands in the spring was wiping them on his breeches. Sasha took it and made one mouthful of it while he was putting the salve back in the packs and preparing to get back on his horse, all of a rush as everything had gone. Her father took up the black horse's reins, swung up in one sudden move and reached down a hand for her, while all she could think, trying to swallow down the sweet in a mouthful to free her hands, was how dreadfully it was going to hurt.

He looked her in the face, looked over her head at Sasha and said, "God, she's sore as hell, Sasha, can you do something?"

Her face must have gone absolutely, devastatingly red, when something odd happened, and the soreness went away. Like that. She glanced at Sasha, who looked elsewhere, and looked her father in the face, her heart pounding.

"Magic," he said, and whisked her up by an arm and left her nothing to do but to catch hold of him and the saddle and him again, trying desperately to get her skirts arranged while the horse was starting to move.

Her whole life seemed suddenly caught up and sped along faster than she could sort out the images. Nothing was true but the things everyone had said were false, her father just had embarrassed her beyond bearing and yet known exactly what was wrong with her, and cared, more than that, cared for someone he had no time for, in his care for his other daughter—

In her life she had been nothing *but* convenient to everyone around her, when they had talked about Yvgenie's father, and her wedding, and how she was going to bring the whole family to court at Kiev, and she was to remember how to mention this uncle to Yvgenie's father, and that uncle—

She felt cold, thinking: *They* needed me, god, yes, they did.

She remembered one summer climbing up the stack of old boards by the garden shed, and up and up the last scary bit to the forbidden crest of the garden wall, where she could look out on the lane behind the house.

There was a girl who walked by sometimes, with heavy baskets. One supposed she was a servant. But she sang as she went. And the richest girl in Vojvoda had used to wish she were that girl, able to wander the town with no fear of wizards and murderers.

Fool! her mother had cried, when a cousin caught her at it and told. You fool! Don't you understand anything?

Now she did. God, now she most certainly did.

Bielitsa lagged further and further behind, and Ilyana reined Patches around and rode back along the hill, seeing Yvgenie had gotten down and walked away from Bielitsa—on private business, she supposed. She got down from Patches and waited for him, taking the chance to adjust the girth that had been slipping the last while.

But something was wrong. It might be her mother wishing at them. It was coldness, it was demand, and need, and all those things she had felt lifelong from her mother—

Then she thought, with a chill, No, not mother—it's him. It's *him*, the same as my mother feels, sometimes—

She wanted immediately to know where he was, got a worse and worse feeling, and walked after him, leaving Bielitsa and Patches to stand.

She found him sitting on the hillside, on a carpet of old leaves, looking out at a hillside no different than this one. She walked up to him and he said, still gazing elsewhere: "I need to rest. Please. Just let me rest a while."

She wished him well, then, but he made a furious gesture. "There's nothing left, Ilyana." He put a hand over his eyes and wanted something, but there seemed a wall between them, and a wall ahead, and a weakening of her own wishes that made her feel as if—as if her mother were wanting her again, calling her away from the river shore.

Ilyana, Ilyana, come home now—

And if she gave up and came home supper would be waiting on the table again and Babi would be there and Patches and Volkhi and Missy in the pen. Papa and uncle would be there safe and sound and no one would be angry with her.

She rubbed her eyes and thought *no*. It was a trick and a trap, and it would not be that way again, it never could be. She was not the child she had been and she could not go back and live as if nothing had happened. But she missed her father and her uncle, and worried about them, of a sudden; and caught a muddled unhappiness, a sense of secrets and things out of place in the world. . . .

That was definitely her uncle, she thought: uncle was upset and thinking about her: uncle could feel that secretive and confused at once. She wanted him not to be distressed about her, she had achieved that much of calm. She said to him, Uncle, don't follow me any further. Please argue with mother. I'm all right, Yvgenie and I are all right, if you'll only not push us any more. This isn't a good time. He's so tired, uncle. We're all so tired, please don't chase us any more—please don't let mother chase us.

—Uncle, I'm so scared. . . .

The mouse was *there* for a moment, clear as if she were standing next to him, and Sasha said, "Mouse?" without even thinking— and felt an exhaustion and an anxiousness that turned his blood cold.

What you're feeling is dangerous, mouse, it's terribly dangerous, please listen to me. Stop and wait for us. We won't hurt you or him. . . .

But she caught some hint of wrongness, and fled him, then, wary and elusive as her namesake. *Eveshka* was walking near the river, he knew of a sudden, Eveshka was vastly upset, thoughts darting this way toward them and that way toward the mouse, violent and demanding—

No! he wished her, as Pyetr, riding beside him, said, "Sasha? Can you hear her? Can you make her listen?"

He was shaking of a sudden. He remembered that feeling, he remembered all too clearly, nearly twenty years ago, a wanting so nearly absolute—

Rusalka. *That* was the way it felt.

Pyetr wanted an answer, desperately wanted good news. He realized he was staring into nothing, and said, "She just tried to tell me she was all right." But he could not lie to Pyetr, not in something going so desperately, persistently wrong. "I didn't get that impression."

"What? That she's all right? That she's not? What does she want?"

He looked at Pyetr, at Nadya behind him on Volkhi, two faces so like—both with reason to want an answer; and to dread it.

"We've been pushing them hard," he said: Pyetr might understand what he was saying, Pyetr if no one else alive. "They've been pushing themselves. The boy's exhausted—"

"Yvgenie?" Nadya asked faintly. "Do you know where he is?"

"Ahead of us, and going further now, as fast as they can. —Pyetr, I don't like this, I'm sorry, but I'm desperately worried—"

"You're worried. God. Did you ask her to wait?"

"She wouldn't. She's scared now. She knew I was holding something back from her."

"Nadya," Pyetr said heavily.

He knew now he should have told the mouse about Nadya. Immediately. He might have protected Nadya against the mouse's startlement, might have caught the mouse's curiosity and drawn her to them by that very means. But Eveshka had so overwhelmed him with that feeling of strength, and *need*—

I wanted Pyetr back to that moment eighteen years ago and other things were inevitably tied to it: what 'Veshka was then, what I was—god, a young fool, that's what I was then! *I've* sent Eveshka back and done the god only knows what to myself in the bargain—

I was fifteen, I couldn't read or write, I didn't know what to do with magic except to be scared of it—

"Sasha?" Pyetr said. "Sasha, you're white as a sheet. What's going on?"

He had to get down. He had to stop moving and stop things from changing around him. Missy stopped and he slid off, taking his bag of books and the bag of herb-pots with him.

He needed quiet. He needed to get hold of things. He went off looking for a place to sit down and catch his breath and heard Pyetr saying, faintly:

"Better get down." And Nadya's quiet, frightened voice: "What's wrong with him?"

"I don't know." Pyetr said. "Something. Hush, don't ask him questions right now."

"Is it magic? What's he going to do?"

"Hush!" Pyetr said. "Yes, and don't bother him."

He was grateful. Pyetr was upset, he knew it, but there was no reassurance to give him and he could not afford the distraction of lying. He was not sure what he had felt from the mouse and from Eveshka a moment ago, that was first trouble; he could not totally be sure which feeling he had gotten from which place north of them: he knew Yvgenie might be a source of that disturbance, the same as Eveshka; and he was not sure of the accuracy of his memory even moments ago: magic could be like that, escaping recollection as quickly as water from a sieve. When a wizard wanted not to think certain things, the wizard in question could very well get his wish, and forget the unpleasantness that could be happening and believe some false thing more palatable, if he was an utter, self-deluding fool . . .

He found a flat rock to sit on, he set his bags down on the leaves and pulled out a book at random. He opened it and knew it then for his own.

Draga destroyed Malenkova. But Malenkova was too much for her. The beast took her and Draga became its purpose . . . ultimately that's all Draga was in the world. . . .

Pages back from that: *Owl should not have died—*

A sword should not have been able to kill a wizard's creature. Pyetr's had done it, in spite of all the wishes that should have protected Owl: Pyetr had killed the creature that held Chernevog's heart, and Chernevog's heart had necessarily come back to him—

But how? Chernevog's wish? Chernevog had grieved for Owl,

if for nothing else in his life, Chernevog had not *wanted* his heart, and tried immediately to put it elsewhere . . .

Leshys all around us, watching as Owl died, and Chernevog got his heart back, watching to see what wizards in their midst might do.

And when and where did the threads of Owl begin? When Chernevog was a boy—Draga had wanted him to find Owl, and bestow his heart on Owl, because *she* had a hold on the creature—

"Damn!"

—Pyetr wanted to kill Chernevog and couldn't. So the leshys took him, held him asleep three long years before they let him wake—*if* they let him wake. Owl was Draga's before he was Chernevog's. And where *is* Owl, now, that's another important question.

Owl's with him, I much fear, with him and with—

Get *away* from that thought!

He made his eyes see the place he was in; and saw Pyetr trying to put a fire together nearby.

"Pyetr, I think I know something."

"What?"

"Who's sustaining Chernevog."

"Which 'him'? Who?"

"Chernevog. I very much think it's leshys. They brought us Nadya. They had Chernevog asleep for all those years. And I think *they* killed Owl."

Pyetr looked as confounded as Nadya did. He stood up. "They killed Owl. *Why?*"

"I don't think Owl's a safe place to have put a heart. I don't think he ever was. I think they destroyed Owl, because they wanted Chernevog to have his heart back. I think—" One became aware of the whisper of the leaves, of the forest all around them, alive, self-interested, listening to everything that moved. And caution seemed of utmost importance.

"So we shouldn't worry? I don't think so, Sasha!"

"I'm not saying that. I'm saying I don't know what kind of a game the leshys are playing. Or what kind they have played." God, they had *relied* on Misighi, they had trusted the old creature, who had held the mouse in his arms—

A nest of birds and a child are the same to them. And was

it ever certain what friendship means to them? I rarely saw Misighi after that. And not at all in recent years.

Dammit, Eveshka's worked so long and remade so much that she destroyed, she had almost made her peace with the leshys before the mouse was born, and since, since, she's not gone any time at all into the woods—too busy with housework, she said, since the baby came, too busy once there was a child to take care of—

God, 'Veshka, did I never see? I thought it must be motherhood or something, I thought it must be some natural change, with babies and all—but you loved the forest, you'd mended every damage you could set your hands to, you wished it life with all your heart—and you feared it so much you dreaded letting the mouse out of her own yard and into the woods?

Trust the leshys, I said. —The child knows their names, 'Veshka, of *course* she's safe. Would Misighi ever let her come to harm?

He bit his lip, saw the bright spark of the fire Pyetr had been making, thought, distractedly: The leshys hate fire. I can't wish it. Maybe that's why we've gotten along. And she hasn't.

—Eveshka, hear me—

But he thought instantly of Nadya, glanced at her and flinched, thinking, God, 'Veshka never did like surprises, and she's not being reasonable, no more than the mouse. There's no telling what either one of them might wish about this girl, or about us—

Burning papers. Stacks and stacks of papers and moldering birds' nests and feathers and old, outgrown clothes—

Breathe the smoke. Let the fire mingle the elements of the problem, pinecones and curious dried beetles, old nests, old clothes, old papers, and lonely, disordered years—breathe it in and let it work—

God, she's *my* doing. Most certainly she's my doing, this—girl, this lost daughter of Pyetr's, this—calamity—the leshys have dropped in our laps—

She can't be. She *can't* be what I wished up. She would have had to begin all those years ago, before I even left Vojvoda, before Pyetr and I even met—

Can we even choose? God, *where* are our choices, if I was Uulamets' wish and everything that got Pyetr in trouble and brought Yvgenie to this woods and put the mouse in danger was only for a stupid wish I was going to make on a rainy night eighteen years later—

I felt the whole world shift when I wished someone. And the lightning came and Yvgenie drowned. Was it all for her? Or is magic only riding the currents of what already will be—*has* to be?

Leaves on the water—

"Sasha?" he heard Pyetr asking him. But he could not move, could not get out of the current if that was the case—

No wizard could, if that was the case. There was no way back. He looked at Nadya and thought, The mouse won't accept her. Eveshka won't. How did things get so tangled? And what is the mouse doing out there in the woods, if this is all our doing? When did we ever wish it?

Or is it Uulamets' who did it to all of us? And what was the old man thinking of and what did he want in the world, but—

—but—

He drew a panicked breath. And wished the way he had taught the mouse to do when magic began to go amiss—

Sasha fell before Pyetr could reach him, just sprawled on his side, senseless or dead, Pyetr could not tell until he could get a hand inside his collar and feel life beating steadily.

Then he could breathe, himself; but not feel in the least safe, not for himself and not for Sasha or for anyone he loved. It was nothing a sword could get at or an ordinary man even hear going on.

"What's *happened* to him?" Nadya asked, and one could not even be sure of her, if Sasha had misjudged what shapeshifters could do. But one had to trust, one had to deal sanely, and not act in panic.

"He's fainted," he said. "But I don't know whether he wanted it or something else did."

His daughter looked at the forest about them—but there was nothing eyes could see. No Babi, either, which was *not* a good sign. The inkpot had turned over, the ink had run out and blotted a page of Sasha's book—and if that was any indication of how things were going, it was none he liked. He propped Sasha's head on his knee, put a hand on Sasha's brow and pleaded with him, "Wake up, can you? Come on. The ink's spilled, Babi's missing. I don't like this, Sasha. I truly don't."

Nadya came and sank down close to them, tucked down in a knot with her hands clenched white before her lips. Scared, decidedly, this daughter of his in gilt and tattered silk. Worried. With damned good reason.

10

✳ ✳ ✳ ✳ A wolf—it might be the same wolf—slipped in and out of view, threading a path through the brush, and one could easily feel more anxious not knowing where it was than knowing. It had come closer a moment ago— but Bielitsa had made no protest, not even a twitch of her ears, and Yvgenie rubbed his eyes with chilled fingers, wondering was the wolf a ghost itself, and whether the ghost inside him knew it.

He was convinced there was a place ahead of them where the wolf could not reach, a terrible place, but safe from that danger. He had no clear memory any longer where the boundaries were between himself and the ghost, it was all a struggle now, moment by moment, to keep awake. Perhaps it was bewitchment. Perhaps it was simple weariness. But his hold on the world was slipping, that was the only way he could think of it; and he did not want to alarm Ilyana—everything seemed so precarious and so fragile now, and he did not want to talk about ghosts, or dying.

They reached the bottom of the hill and Ilyana reined in a moment, where there was water. The horses drank, wading into the stream, heedless of danger.

They can't see it, he thought. They can't smell it. It's sure a ghost, like Owl.

It was there again, the wolf was, trotting across the slope in front of them.

"Do you see it?" he asked desperately.

"The wolf?"

"There," he said. But by the time she had looked where he pointed, it had gone.

She patted Patches' neck while Patches drank. Bielitsa gave a little twitch of her shoulders and lifted her head. "Probably he's a little crazy. Uncle says they'll kill one that's too different."

"Like people," he said, and found himself remembering, not knowing what he was going to say, "My father had other sons."

There had been another wife. His mother was dead. His father had had something to do with that, but he could not remember what, he could not remember his father's face, try as he would. He only recalled a silhouette against a window; remembered nothing of home, though it seemed to him a while ago he had known more than that. He saw a gray sky, above stark walls. He did not know why that image should terrify him, or why people shouting should be so ominous. A dreadful thump, then, shocked through his bones.

The ghost said, against his heart, The man deserved what he got. Can you possibly mourn him? He gave you nothing but pain.

He understood then that it had been his father's death he had just witnessed, and he was sure he had not been there—it had not happened when he had left. He thought, cold and sick at heart: The tsar must have found him out. The tsar must have learned he was plotting against him—but surely it wasn't my fault—please the god it wasn't my fault he's dead—

Fool, the ghost said. I give you justice and you're sorry? How can you forgive so much evil?

Memory of a gray sky. A feeling of justice done, but he could take no joy in it. The ghost's question seemed wistful and angry at once, as if it truly did not understand. His hands felt chill as he drew up on Bielitsa's reins, going on in the lead, he had forgotten where for the moment, and why, except he felt the wolf's presence closer now, and he wanted them quickly on their way.

How can you forgive him? the ghost insisted to know, determined to know, because he had tried very hard and very long to understand what justice was. He did harm to everyone around him. How can you forgive him? How *dare* you forgive evil like that?

But Ilyana said, riding beside him, "What did he get? Who are you talking about?"

Her question confused him. He knew too many things, knew

he had been hours ahead of his father's men when he had reached Vojvoda; and he had known then they would kill Ilyana, and all her house—for nothing that was her fault—

No. The ghost was adamant. No. There had been a river shore.

She had said once, behind the stairs, I don't know the town. I've never been outside the walls. My window only looks out on the garden. —And he had remembered that. And drowned her, for fear of what she was, or might become.

"Yvgenie?" she said.

He said, desperately scanning the branches and the sky, "Owl's gone."

"He'll be back. He comes and goes. —You're not worried about the wolf, are you?"

"Owl's gone. The black thing is." His heart was pounding in his chest, as if he were drowning. He knew that sunlight was still around him, he could see it everywhere, every detail of the branches and the leaves around them, every detail of her face and the sunlight on her hair. He kept remembering that day on the river, that he had known he loved her, quite, quite help-lessly, and far differently this year than the boy he had been, the lost boy the woods had sustained in innocence—

There was no more innocence, once awareness came, only a struggle to love, and not to kill—this moment, and the next, and the next—

He shut his eyes and rubbed them, with fingers gone quite chill, thinking, I can't remember what's mine any longer, god, whoever you were, Kavi Chernevog, whatever you did, give my memories back to me—or remember your own. I'm losing things. I'm trying to hold on, but I'm so tired. . . .

But he remembered the river too, ill-matching pieces coming together for a moment, and said, "He forgives too much, Ilyana. There is evil in the world. There truly is evil. And he's been too close to it. —So have I. And the wicked ones never tell you the truth. Do you know that?"

"Are you one of the wicked ones?"

"No." He said—and it was a great effort to say, against the need he had for her: "Ilyana, don't wish. Don't wish anymore. Don't expect things. You're stronger than you know. Let go and let me lead you."

She looked at him in dismay. She said, in a voice scarcely louder than the wind, "Who are you? Is it Kavi?"

He could not shape the words. He fought them out, not even understanding what the ghost made him say, "Ilyana, that place of yours— You're wishing for what doesn't exist. You don't imagine how dangerous that is. You don't know enough, Ilyana. You're getting yourself deeper and deeper into trouble."

"But can't it exist? What else is magic, but wishing what isn't yet? It *will* exist if I want it to—"

He saw the rooftops of Kiev, suns and moons careering above the golden domes, above the banners of the Great Tsar— remembered leaves and thorns, ominous as the echo of axes off snowy walls. He thought, in utter despair: I don't want to do what I'm doing; but he could not remember why he felt so afraid of the place he was going, or so apprehensive of what might befall her there. He looked to the reddening sky and began to think, It's because it's too late. We can't go back from here. There's only wanting—*his* wanting, now, and I'm so damned tired I can't keep them apart, even knowing what it's doing—god, I'm not even sure it's right—

"Wizards can do this to themselves," Pyetr said, while Sasha slept.

Nadya looked at Sasha distressedly, and darted a look at him as he fed a few twigs into the fire. "Why?"

"Hell if I know." But he did know. It was a way out of bad thoughts, dangerous thoughts, which were the straight path to unwise wishes. It was the powerful wizards that did it, so far as he knew of how things worked: small need the village toad-sellers had of such defenses—if they could do it at all. To his observation only Sasha and the mouse *could* do it; and Eveshka, he supposed—last resort before one burned down Kiev or something—

Bad thought. Very bad thought.

And do what now? Throw Sasha over Missy's back and keep going blind, completely unable to feel what was going on ahead of them, or what they might run into? He had no idea what had made Sasha do what he had done—or even whether Sasha had done it. Neither could he know whether his hesitation now was wisdom, cowardice, or someone else's or Sasha's wishes. It was only sure that Sasha was in no good way to defend them or himself if they ran into the least hazard in the dark.

"Just sit still," he said, started to settle himself, and saw a glint of metal among Nadya's skirts as she moved her foot. He made an unthought reach after it. "What is that?"

Nadya evaded his hand, tucked her skirts about her ankles and gave him an anxious stare, all offended modesty.

But that had been bright, hard metal, not gilt. And, having been a father for no few years, he looked her quite steadily in the eye, expecting an answer, until finally she ducked his gaze, moved her foot and the hem of her skirts and showed a knife-hilt in the side of a very costly and sadly out-at-the-seams boot.

"What in hell do you intend to do with that?"

She tucked the foot under her, clasped her arms about her ankles and scowled at him.

"Let's see it." He held out his hand with the same no-nonsense expectation. "—Come on. Let me see that thing."

She reluctantly drew it and laid it in his palm, an old bone-hilted kitchen knife, honed down to a sliver. He turned it to the light and felt a razor edge with his thumb. "You're full of surprises, aren't you? Who is this for? Bears? Bandits? Stray fathers?"

She set her jaw and looked embarrassed. He lifted an eyebrow. "Well?"

"You think I'm a fool," she said.

"I think I've seen better plans. I take it your young man had some idea in his head. He didn't just pick any girl in Vojvoda and say, Let's run away and drown ourselves in the woods."

"No."

"Did he give you this?"

A shake of the head.

"You always carry a knife in your boot."

"For wizards," she said, and clamped her jaw a breath and said, with a worried shift of her eyes toward Sasha and back again. "Not him."

"Not him. Why not?"

"He's not what they said."

"I see. Just in case a whole band of wizards came down on you. In Vojvoda."

"I never knew what might come. I never—" Tears started up, glittered in the firelight. "They told me people were trying to kill me. I wasn't just going to stand there. Ever."

God, he thought, and held out an arm to her. But she sat where she was, with her hands clenched between her knees and ducked her head.

He let his hand fall. "So you ran away with Yvgenie. Off into the woods with nothing to eat, no blankets, no shelter—"

"Because his family found out who my real father is, and his father was sending people to kill us!"

"Kill you, for the god's sake. *Why?*"

She got a breath, wiped beneath her eye with the back of her hand. "If anybody who knew you had ever seen me, they'd have known who my father is. But no one ever did, except the servants. And Yvgenie. He came and he was going to marry me because I was rich." Another pass of the finger beneath the lashes, in a face pale and angry. Justifiably angry, he thought, finding nothing to say for himself. "I was very rich. My uncles said I was going to marry someone close to the tsar and bring the whole family to Kiev. I thought I might have to marry Yvgenie's father. But the Yurishevs weren't noble enough. So he married somebody else and I ended up betrothed to his son." Breath came easier for her now. Thank the god. He wanted to stop her but he wanted to know, too; and he listened, while she looked at the fire and not at him.

"Yvgenie came to the house. He wasn't the oldest son. I wasn't that important. But he was the nicest person I'd ever met."

"Did you love him?"

A long, difficult pause. "I don't know. I tried to. I was going to marry him. I didn't think I was going to like him but I did. We slipped away and talked behind the stairs." A rapid flutter of the eyes in the firelight, the spill of a tear that ran gold down her cheek. "Before they caught us. —I thought we were going to be happy. I really did. I thought I was going to leave the house and go to Kiev and not have to live shut in and scared of wizards. But somebody—maybe one of the servants, maybe just someone who'd heard rumors—waited all this time and came to Yvgenie's father and told him I was a—"

She stopped and leaned her mouth on the heel of her hand.

The silence went on painfully long. He said, desperately, "So Yvgenie came to warn you?"

A nod. "His father was furious. He said I had to be one of the wizards who killed the Yurishevs. Most of all he didn't want any link with my family and he sent soldiers to kill us. But Yvgenie—Yvgenie rode ahead of them all the way from Kiev. He got through the gates at night—the guards knew who he was; they wouldn't give him any trouble. And he warned my family and he took me on his horse and said he couldn't go home again. He said he'd take me somewhere safe. My family—I don't know where they are now."

One could call the boy a fool. But not a scoundrel. He said, past a knot in his throat, "Where *was* he taking you?"

"To the river. He said he'd rather be a f-fisherman than his father's son."

"God." He looked at the little knife in his hands, turned it and flung it into the ground next the fire. "Damn!"

"So I have to find him."

"*I* have to find him." He thought of the mouse, and Chernevog, and a very desperate and maybe dying boy. "Hell and damnation! Sasha! Wake up!"

But Sasha did not stir.

We had to stop and rest. Bielitsa's failing, and I know he's borrowing from her and from Patches, but I can't say no. He's so pale now it scares me, and I try to wish him well, I try to wish both of us well, but it's like pulling a weight uphill. I think I could do what he does and I don't even want to think about that. I know now what uncle was saying about mother fighting on slanted ground. And Yvgenie's getting more and more confused. He used to have just dark spots, but now there's no dark, it's things that can't fit together, scary things, about thorns, that I don't know why they should be scary, but I feel it when I try to listen, and I don't think he or Kavi either knows which is which anymore. In the dark, the same way the dark is when you can see ghosts Kavi can talk to me, but only for a moment or two because after that we don't know what we're doing. I know I'm being a fool. I think we both know it. I'm scared and I'm so tired I can hardly think tonight, and the awful thing, I think from time to time this could be what being in love is, but then I keep remembering what uncle said about rusalki. It feels so real, it feels so good, and I know we're hurting ourselves, it hurts even when it's so good. We've got do something different soon but I'm scared of every wish that leads away from what we have and I'm scared even of wishing one of us well because if I do it with Yvgenie that's one wish; and if I do it without, that's another, and I don't know what's safe or what's right—

He was cold now in a way no fire could warm. He sat in front of it, held out his hands to it, but it had no life to give him. The dark behind him grew far more than the light that danced in front of him. Ilyana dipped her quill in the inkpot beside her and wrote something with a fierce concentration, ignoring Bielitsa's complaints—the horses, like him, had to stay. Her magic held them. Attraction did.

"Ilyana," he began.

"Hush," Ilyana said fiercely, without looking up: his next breath stopped in his throat, while the quill continued its furious course.

He had never thought he would long for Owl or the black Thing that had hissed at him—but no matter it had spat and hissed and bared its teeth every time it got close to him, so long as Babi had been there, they had been safe. And they were not, now. So long as Owl was with them, Chernevog loved—not Owl, precisely: Owl knew nothing about love, but Owl was saner than the wolf, he was sure of that.

Perhaps it was an answer to the wolf Ilyana sought—he saw how frightened she looked, how desperately she clutched the edge of the book and turned pages—looking for some spell, perhaps, some incantation to banish that drifting shadow from the brush, where it circled their fire.

He rested his elbows on his knees, his locked hands before his lips.

He saw it—passing at the very edge of the firelight, not so terrible as the wolf of his imaginings: thin, rather, lank and furtive—

"It's out there," he said. And Ilyana said nothing. He could hear the scratch of the quill above the wind in the leaves.

His father's hounds had killed a servant boy once—torn him in pieces. That night the same dogs had sat at the great fireplace beside his father's chair, great black beasts that feared his father, no less than the servants did—

Wolves in the woods—hunting him down an aisle of thorns.

Hate, and fear, and never help from anyone—until—

Trees moved like living things. Vines writhed like snakes and crept across gray, weathered stone—

A fair-haired little girl walked precariously along a stream-side, a little girl who would look up any instant and say, with a glance to fill up all the empty spots—

"Who are you?"

Threatening question. Important question. He had been hiding in the woods. A terrible lady would find him and take him to her house. She had Ilyana's face. Or Ilyana would have hers someday. But for now Ilyana was a little girl who walked balancing on the water's edge—lonely, too, he was sure, though lonely did not always mean harmless.

He was on a porch, at a door of a house he knew, and Ilyana opened it—of course: it was her house the lady had sent him to find and it was Ilyana's father the lady aimed at—a fierce, unforgiving wizard, who lectured him about honesty, and *wanted* things of him the way the lady did—

But he would not, *could* not give himself or his trust to anyone again. The lady held him. The lady made demands on him. He stole the old man's book and searched it for secrets that might free him or save him—before the old man caught him at it.

Ilyana wanted him back, Ilyana or Eveshka or Draga, the images tumbled over and over in his memory—fair-haired child or girl or woman, all alike. Ilyana wanted him to a meeting, wanted him to face her father, *trust* her father—

He had drowned Ilyana. Or was it Draga? He could not remember. The wolf was there again, in the brush—he saw it staring at them.

If Ilyana would scream, if she would move, he might move—if she would say, Yvgenie, help me—he might have strength enough. But nothing moved, except the wind among the leaves. His joints were locked, his jaw would not move to let out a sound—

He could only remember he had killed her, or would kill her, to save himself. He bit his lip until the pain could bring sense back and he could recall the bathhouse, and the way back to what he knew. He remembered the hunters, and Ilyana, and Vojvoda—

He remembered his mother, and his nurse—a fat, comfortable woman who had told him about wizards and wolves, and flying houses. But that did not agree with being lost in the woods, or living in that terrible house with Ilyana. His house had had tall pillars. Dogs, not wolves, slept at the door. And he had never met Ilyana until he had come to her house to be betrothed to her, but he had ridden to Vojvoda, because they were hunting her to kill her—for wizardry—and murders—

Both could not be true, god, he could not remember both at once. Draga's wolf circled their fire, while Ilyana wrote by firelight, the way Draga would. . . .

"You take this," her father told her, and put a packet of something in her hand. "Salt and sulfur. You put it in a ring about you and Sasha, and you stay inside that ring no matter what and don't trust anything you see, no matter if it looks like me, or Yvgenie, or anyone else you know."

"Why?" Nadya asked.

"Shapeshifters. Vodyaniye. Trust Babi. And take care of him." With a glance toward Sasha, and to her again: "Tell him where I'm going and tell him—" He hesitated, with a second worried glance and a shake of his head. "You don't have to tell him. He knows things like that. Just take care of him. He doesn't remember to do that himself."

He's a wizard, Nadya thought. What kind of a wizard is he that he needs people to take care of him?

Her father turned his back to her. Her father was going after his legitimate daughter and Yvgenie, alone, because somebody, he said, had to look after Sasha till he waked, and because the other horse was too old and too fat, and the black one could not make any speed carrying her. She knew that he was right, and that she was no help but here. But his saying tell Sasha this and tell Sasha that upset her stomach. He should tell Sasha when he had found Yvgenie and his daughter and come back—because she was not through talking to him, please the god. He knew the important things about her. She knew nothing about him.

She thought—I should at least tell him I want him to come back, I should at least hug him goodbye—it's not lucky, him saying those things. . . .

But he was in the saddle before she had quite made up her mind, and then it was too late. He looked down at her, said, "If everything else fails, there's a house south of here, on the river. No one comes there."

And while she was wondering what house, and what he meant, he turned the horse's head and rode away, fading quickly into the dark outside the fire.

A shadow fell across the page. Ilyana looked up at Yvgenie's dark shape between her and the fire, and he said quietly, kneeling and taking her hand:

"Ilyana, put the book away. Please. You're coming no closer to the truth."

"You're eavesdropping!"

A lowering of lashes—a glance up at her: Yvgenie's eyes, pale and deep and gentle. Kavi's unmistakable gesture. And the motion of Yvgenie's hand to lips and heart and to her. I love you. To brow and to heart, frowning. I'm worried. It was the old way of talking. Maybe it was the one he found easiest now. And he was as silent as only her uncle could be, not a whisper of his being there the moment she accused him.

"Sasha's very good," he said ever so softly. "And very strong. He scares himself. And that's good. A little fear will save you so much pain."

Sweat glistened on Yvgenie's face. A bead broke and ran. "Kavi—is that truly your name?"

A nod.

"Is it so hard to speak?"

A second nod. A gesture toward his heart, with a hand visibly trembling. "He can't last much longer. He has to rest. Just a little farther, Ilyana, and then we can all rest. . . ."

One did not like this idea of resting when a ghost said it. But looking into his eyes this close made her think how it felt to touch him and to be touched, and one wished—

—one wished, that was the trouble, when a wizard loved a ghost: one wanted, and one could have, and if it were not for Yvgenie's gentle, distressed look to warn her she would not even be thinking *no, this is wrong, this is dangerous.* He looked so dreadfully upset—

"Please don't," Yvgenie asked her, "please don't." And after that, taking her hand in his, on the open book that *nobody* was ever to touch but her, "He loves you. He loves you very much, Ilyana, and he's very scared, and something's dreadfully *w-wrong* tonight. We're going somewhere dangerous—and he's trying to t-tell you—I don't think he's ever loved anything in his life but Owl, and he loves you so much he doesn't want you to go on with this. He wants you just to go home to your father and not to try to help him anymore. Please. He can't—can't—go any farther with this—"

"With *what*?"

Yvgenie had no idea. And Kavi when she tried to wish him to speak to her was uncatchable, scattered in pieces, like Owl on the river shore. There were tears in Yvgenie's eyes, which he was not accustomed to shed in anyone's witness, he wished he could make her understand that—but he knew what Kavi was doing now, and he knew that for all the advice Kavi tried to give he was helpless to leave her, he could not stop following her or loving her or killing her the way he was doing—he loved her, *he* loved her whether it was Kavi's idea or his own, he had come to think more of her in these few days than he had ever loved his own confused existence—

He touched the back of her hand, where it rested on the book, and she felt that tingling she could never forget and never quite remember. He began to say something—

Then hurled himself to his feet and away from her, as far as the old tree that sheltered them both. He leaned against its trunk, holding to it like a living person, wanting—

—its life, because he refused to die, he could not want to die.

Not life, uncle had told her, and she had not heard him. Not life—but hell.

She folded her book and got up to go to him—wanting him— god, wanting to hold him and help both of them—wanting just that touch again—

The first leaves drifted free of dying branches, and need had become its own wish—little it could matter. She reached out to touch him.

But he shoved away and turned his back on her. *Yvgenie* wanted her not to touch him, not to make him touch her, please, no—and he stopped cold, if only because there was nothing in the world Yvgenie could do to stop her. Not *fair*, not *fair* to wish someone who could not even hear her doing it, not *fair* to insist on her own way with someone who could do no more to stop her or Kavi than he was doing now.

The mouse could never do that—never hurt her father— never hurt this boy. . . .

But *mother* thinks otherwise. And expecting something is a wish, isn't it? The mouse can't hurt anybody. The mouse can't. That's why I like her better.

Ilyana's not that good. Ilyana's her *mother's* daughter. But what's the mouse to be, uncle, grown-up and lonely for the rest of her life because she can't want anybody?

That's crazy, her father had used to shout at her mother. Because we both want something, you have to want not?

"Yvgenie," she said, in the mouse's voice, very soft, very quiet, and held her hand a little away from touching him, making herself *not* want him the way she wanted Kavi. "Yvgenie, I'm sorry. It's safe. Please look at me if you want to."

One had to be so careful with ordinary folk. And when he did look at her, one could never know whether it was wizardry or not or whether she was only deceiving herself.

She said, with as much honesty as she could find, "People have to love me if I want them to, even wizards, especially wizards, uncle says, because we hear magic—but ordinary people, too, if we want them to. They can't help it."

"A spell?" he asked her.

"I don't know what you call it. I don't. I just didn't want to be alone all my life and I wanted Kavi back—I never wanted anything bad to happen to anyone, I never did, I don't know what's gone wrong, or why it was, except it's wrong to want people to love you—"

He touched her cheek and looked her in the eyes. "If I'm bewitched, I don't care, so long as you love me back—that's what matters, isn't it? I love you, *I* do, the same as he does. And I don't care why—"

It hurt. God, it hurt.

He said, then, faintly, "Damn him." He shut his eyes, and she wished, aching, Don't *do* that to him, Kavi. Please. It's not fair.

Yvgenie sank down where he was, head on his arms, not looking at her. There was pain, that was all she could hear, pain and fear and not wanting her to die because of him, when he was already sure he would die, and follow her, and do anything he had to stay with her until someone put an end to him— because he would not leave her—not so long as he existed—

Nor touch her again, so long as he could help it, no matter what he killed—

"Please," he said without looking at her. "Please just leave me alone."

She wanted—but wanting stopped short of hurting him again. She went back to her book and sat down and wrote,

I wanted someone like my father. I didn't know what I was wanting. I didn't know what my father is with my mother, and what Kavi is and what she was. Now I know what it feels like. Now I know and I can't do anything. There's nothing I can wish that doesn't hurt and there's nowhere for me to go but with Yvgenie, because—

A leaf fell onto the paper. Other leaves were falling, some on the ground, a few into the fire, where they flared and burned and perished.

11

✠ ✠ ✠ ✠   A ring of salt, her father had said, and Nadya had done that as quickly as possible, around her, around Sasha, around the spotted horse, too. But she had not been thinking about firewood when she had been drawing the circle, and the fire was getting desperately low. She added leaves. She stood up and broke off overhanging twigs, and a branch and broke it up and saved it back as long as she could.

But the fire began to die. And the spotted horse made a soft, anxious sound. That made her think that she might have been fatally foolish, that with the fire grown so small, whatever was out there dared come closer and closer, and if the light did not even reach the bushes she would have to go out there totally in the dark.

She had to do it. She took the knife from her boot and went out of the circle, breaking branches with cracks that sounded frighteningly loud in the hush about her.

Something hissed at her, right at her feet. She jumped, clenching her knife, and all but fell over her own skirts, seeing two round gold eyes looking at her.

It was the Yard-thing. Babi. Babi stared at her and growled and she very carefully backed away, taking her armful of wood and her knife back into the circle.

Babi turned up there, too. Pop. Babi crouched down with his head on his paws and showed white, white teeth while she fed sticks into the fire and wished, please the god, that Sasha would wake up soon, and not be angry with her about being left—and that the Yard-thing would not decide she was a threat and bite her hand off.

Please.

Babi barked at her. And vanished. She sat there with her knife in her hand and her arms around her knees and waited, shivering despite the fire.

Sasha would not be angry with her. Sasha would *not* be angry with her. She had waited all her life for some ill-wish that would make her slip on the stairs or catch a fish-bone in her throat or even just take a fever—the silly knife was only because nobody took her seriously, the guards never took her orders, the guards and the servants would never listen to her if she was in danger, and at least if she had the knife she had something, if only against whoever might break into the house the way Pyetr Kochevikov had done.

Except he had *not* broken in, she believed that part. She believed everything else. Her uncles had snatched up the silver and the gold and her mother had gathered up her jewels and her best clothes and when she had come to say goodbye—because Yvgenie had said he would take her where people would forget who they were—her mother had said go where she liked. Go where she liked—and no truth even then.

She wiped her face with the heel of her hand, angry, dammit, for that, for all the years of lies, all the years of modest, *lying* virtue that had made her afraid of this and afraid of that, most of all afraid of—

Sasha's eyes had opened. He was looking at her. He went on looking at her and the breath froze in her throat.

Anything he wants, her father had said.

He moved his elbow, and pushed himself up to look around. "God. Pyetr?" He staggered to his feet to look about the fire-lit woods, and at her, with an accusation that made breathing difficult.

She remembered her father riding off into the dark, she remembered him telling her, Take care of Sasha. . . . *Tell him— you don't have to tell him. He knows things like that. Just take care of him. He doesn't remember to do that himself . . .*

"Oh, god," Sasha said, and she got up, she had no idea why, except he was in a hurry, and she could think of nothing but gathering things up and getting on the horse, whose name was Missy, and finding Pyetr before something found him, please the god—

Sasha was packing up his books. He said, "How long has he

been gone?" and she answered, "A while," shivering inside, because she realized then he was making her think of things, and he was sorry. He wanted her to forgive him and she did, she had no choice. Dammit!

"Please." He cast her a look of purest misery. "I think I wished you here, I could have wished you born and Pyetr into trouble for all I know, and please excuse me, I'm not used to being near ordinary people, except Pyetr."

Her father knew how to listen to him and answer him with just thinking, her father was a brave man with no fear of him, or of half the things else in the world he should be afraid of. Like vodyaniye. Like wizards and his other daughter and the rusalka who had taken Yvgenie. . . .

"Please," he said faintly, aloud, and she saw herself standing there with a knife in her hand, while he was standing there with his hands full of ropes and packs, and wanting her not to stand in his horse's way, please, so Missy could reach him, so they could be moving. Something might have wanted Pyetr to go alone. Pyetr had had that notion from the beginning. And Pyetr had so little defense against the people he loved. Please be out of the way—and do what he asked—right now. Please.

Day came creeping through the tangle of branches, with the distant muttering of thunder—decidedly not the sound a man wanted to hear, with wizards involved. Pyetr dipped his hands in cold water, splashed his face and wiped his hair back for the moment it would stay out of his eyes, rocked onto his knees and sat with his eyes shut a moment, while Volkhi drank.

Not the wisest thing to do, perhaps, going off the second time alone, but in coldest sanity he did not think that surprising the mouse or 'Veshka with Nadya in his company was the best idea right now. Jealousy, hurt feelings, he had seen enough, even between his wife and the daughter he had known all her life.

And if an unmagical man had gotten any wisdom about magic after all these years, or about the hearts of wizards, there seemed only one way to put a stop to craziness when wishes got out of hand, and that was to put himself squarely in their way.

Sasha, Eveshka, Ilyana. Do what you like. But I'm not on anyone's side. I won't be. Don't think it.

A second splash of water. The air was cold. But he and the old lad had been moving, and he had hurt his hand somewhere, add that to the account of an aching shoulder and aching bones. Nothing against nature, Sasha would say.

But, god, what else have we done in this woods?

Third splash of water. He shut his eyes and let the water run down his neck, numbing the fire in his shoulders and the ache behind his eyes. There was no constant pull and push here, no knowledge turning up unasked—it was quiet, truly quiet, except the wind in the leaves.

At this distance from aggrieved parties the man in the middle could draw a few sane breaths and try to think how many sides there were to this affair—

No one's side. Not even excluding Chernevog's. Or the boy's. Or my other daughter's. None of you and all of you are my side. And I'm all alone out here—any wish that's ever let loose about me has its chance. Even Chernevog's. Mouse, you chose him. If you want him and you want me, and he wants that boy—magic's got the best chance at me it's had yet.

I do hope you love your father—because he's going to put himself where he needs help, mouse, he's going to do it until you notice.

If you want things to be right, mouse, and you want your own way, you'd better want the right things. Can you possibly hear me?

No? Then I'd better be moving. Fast as I can, mouse. I was right in the first place. Maybe Sasha can't catch up with me this time. Maybe it'll be up to you. What do you think of that, mouse?

I do hope you think about that.

It was less and less effort to hold the silence: it seemed to be holding itself, now, and it had a lonelier and lonelier feeling since last night. They had waked this morning under a blanket of new-fallen leaves, and berry bushes, young trees and streamsides of bracken and silver birch gave way to shaded solitude, aged beeches and oaks far rougher and stouter than the trees to the south—perhaps, Ilyana thought, they had come to the end of the woods that they knew—at least, despite Yvgenie's warnings, they had gotten, if not further than others' wishes had ever been—at least well away from any place wizards who knew her had ever been. Perhaps that was the silence. But one hated to break a branch here. One felt fear—whether that it was something in the forest itself or whether it was only the unaccustomed stillness.

But when she wanted Patches to go a little more carefully Bielitsa brushed past her, finding a way through the thicket that her magic had not found. It was surely Kavi guiding them again, she thought, and set Patches to follow the gently winding course.

"Not a friendly place," she said when he stopped and gave her the chance to overtake him. She had pricked her finger moving a branch aside, and sucked at it. "Can you feel it?"

"It was never friendly. I *knew* we were close last night. I didn't know how close. We might have reached it. . . . But something's wrong."

Absolutely it was Kavi now. He slid down from Bielitsa's back, bade her follow and led the way afoot, a long, difficult passage in among aged, peeling trees. Not a wholesome place, she thought to herself: the further they went the more desolate the place seemed, until at last nothing near them was alive. Thorn-bushes broke with dry crackling, the moss went to powder underfoot, trees stood ghostly pale, bare-trunked.

"Kavi," she said, "Kavi, stop. There's nothing good here."

He looked back at her, so pale, so frighteningly pale and afraid.

"There's nothing alive here," he said distressedly. "It's *dead*."

She thought, Is *this* what he meant, that it was wrong to wish a place where wishes weren't? Is this that place?

It's as if wishes fail here, as if you can pour them into this place, and nothing gets out—

But Kavi was leaving her, going deeper into this place. She was sure it was Kavi now, sure it was Kavi who ignored her pleas and kept going—

It was surely Kavi who led Bielitsa into a ring of dead trees, to a stone slab that might have been nature's work—or not. She pushed her way past a fragile thorn-branch and led Patches through, as Owl came close and lit on the ground before the stone—the same place, god, her father and the sword: it was that stone, it was the place where Owl had died.

And standing all about them, huge trunks, peeling bark, white wood, like trees but not. Nor standing as trees would grow, wind-trained and orderly. There was disarray here. There was randomness.

"They're dead," he said, faintly, distressedly, "they're all dead, Ilyana."

She looked about them, seeing in the peeling trunks the likeness of empty eyes and the whiteness of bone. She wanted Babi with her, please. She wanted anything alive, besides herself and Yvgenie and the horses, because nothing else here was. She wanted anything magical and wholesome—because magic had gone from this place, magic had died here—not well, or peacefully.

Kavi sank down on the stone as if the strength had gone out of him, too—and she felt alarm, thinking: A rusalka's magical, isn't he? as Owl flew up to perch by him on the stone. He took Owl on his hand and said, faintly, "They wanted me to bring you here. But it's too late now."

"Bring me here? Why? Misighi's my uncle's friend. Misighi could come to the house—they don't need anyone to bring me to them. If they wanted me to come here, they could just have asked, couldn't they?"

He only shook his head in dismay, and for a moment, a very small moment, there seemed hazy edges about him, Kavi's shape and Yvgenie's.

"He's afraid," Yvgenie said. "He—" Yvgenie's blurred shape got up from the stone and looked into the woods, shaking his head slowly, once and twice. She tried to eavesdrop, and caught only images of Kiev, and Yvgenie's father, and a hallway at night where men gathered and talked of murders. He recalled a stairway, and towers and walls, and leading Bielitsa out into the dark, out the gates of Kiev—

Yvgenie said, looking around at the sky, the dead leshys. "The falling suns. The moons and the thorns. This is the place. He had to bring you here—to them. They wanted him to. He slept for years here. But he forgot and it was too long, it was much too long. He was only a boy—and leshys don't understand little boys. —God, it's all full of dark spots—"

"Don't say that—" Oh, god, a *stupid* wish, when he was desperately trying to warn her. She wanted out of this place, she felt the life going away from him and Owl as if he was bleeding it into the stone and the ground, the longer he stayed here. "Come on. We've got to leave this place. Yvgenie. Come away."

He shook his head, with the most dreadful memory of fear, and thorns, and a confusion of suns in the sky. Owl dying, struck by her father's sword.

She came and took his hand, wanting Patches and Bielitsa to stay with them: his fingers were cold as winter. "Don't argue with me, please, Kavi, it's not good here. It's not *safe*, Kavi, please listen. Something terrible happened in this place, and it's dead, and you can't be near it any longer, Kavi, please, let's get out of here, let's go on!"

He stood still, resisting her pulling, and gazed out among the trees. "It's there," he said faintly, and she looked, and saw nothing but dead leshys and dead brush.

"What's there?"

"Where I was buried. Where I died. Across the river . . ."

The cold was spreading from his hand to hers. She held on, she *wanted* him to leave this place, with all her mind she wanted it, and pulled at him, made him walk, that direction, any direction, if that was all he could want—as long as it was out of this place. Please the god it was out of this deadly grove.

She wished Bielitsa and Patches to follow them. They left the stone behind, they re-entered the maze of thorns. She was colder and colder—her fingers could not even feel his, now.

"Please, a little further, a little further—"

Thorns scratched her arms, caught at her skirts and at him and at the horses. Then something cold brushed against her. Something flitted through the brush ahead, and following it with her eye she saw it take a path she had not realized was there. She fought through the thorns and saw the way through, if only she could reach it. "There," she said. "There! There's a path, do you see?"

Babi turned up, at Missy's feet as they went, and Sasha was only half glad of that. "The dvorovoi," Nadya said, the instant he appeared, trotting beside them as they rode, and he said:

"I'd rather hoped he was with Pyetr."

Nadya held sometimes to his belt, sometimes to his waist—at the moment it was the former, but a fox darted from cover and Missy made a little toss of her head, and immediately it was the latter, tightly.

"Only a fox," he said. "Missy's never trusted them since—"

Since he had thought shapeshifters or the like might use that form, and most unfortunately told Missy.

Nadya's arms stayed where they were. She had never ridden a horse, she was thinking, she had never even left the walls of her house and her garden—

Nor seen a fox, nor a bear nor any wild creature. Considering that, she was very brave.

And reconciled to Pyetr, at least she knew certain things that made her understand him—Sasha most earnestly tried not to eavesdrop, and all the same caught embarrassed and embarrassing thoughts about *him* while they were riding, which, god! were no help at all to a wizard trying to think. One could hardly tell her not to have thoughts like that: the fault was the eavesdropper's, or his concentration: she was all unaware and innocent. She was thinking—how he felt so strong, although he was hardly taller than she was; how he *must* ride horses and do things other than magic; how just thinking about him—

—made her feel—so entirely different than poor Yvgenie, who was handsome and kind and brave and everything any reasonable girl could ever want—but no one had ever looked at her and made her shiver all the way to her toes the way he did when she had looked him in the eyes. She had no idea even when she had begun to feel that way, except last night she had finally believed her father was telling her the truth, and therefore that her father's friend must be everything he seemed to be—

It was not her idea, the god help her, *he* had done it with his stupid, selfish wishes that had nothing to do with what this girl—Pyetr's daughter, for the god's sake—had ever wanted for herself. He had done one damnably wrong thing after the other since they had left home, he had completely lost the train of his thoughts last night, blotted an entire page he could not recall in entirety, spilled all but a few pages' worth of ink, and now with Nadya's arms about him he could not even remember the straight and the whole of what he had been thinking when he

wished himself asleep. Something to do with the mouse—
something to do with Nadya, that simply would not come clear
to him, or that had not even been that urgent, only leading up
to some brink he dared not cross.

Dammit, he *knew* now how to do real magic, he had discovered the truth old Uulamets had hid and he could let fly a wish
that would surely make the mouse hear him—or bring rains
clear to Kiev.

But he could not believe in his own wisdom any longer, he
knew the scope of his mistakes already, and how did one wish
belief back, when belief was central to the wish?

The great magics were always easy—to someone in the right
moment, at the exact moment of need—and always impossible,
to someone who did not expect the result.

Make up your mind, Pyetr would shout at him. God, he
wanted to. But what was fair to wish, with Pyetr's daughter
involved? Leave me alone?

Go love Yvgenie Pavlovitch?

He had no idea where that might lead her either—to harm,
in this woods; to heartbreak and disaster, if Yvgenie was dead;
to disaster for all of them, if she provoked the mouse to jealousy
and foolishness. Everything wrong seemed possible, and the only
wish that made sense—was not fair, dammit, simply was not
fair to her. What in the god's name could he do with a girl who
had no idea of wizards or magic and no idea what she could
expect of him?

The ground dipped and rose again. Nadya caught hold of his
shirt, and of him, thinking of bears and wolves, of bandits and
dreadful walking houses, and thinking over all it was better than
the four walls of a garden in Vojvoda, if she was eaten by a bear
out here it was better than that—she would never go back, never,
never, never live like that. She feared for Pyetr, she wished she
had been worth enough to go with him, she was glad enough
they were going, and if she was any help she was willing to try—

("Tell me, what would you have done if your father had decided you shouldn't be on the streets, and locked you in The
Doe's basement?")

("I'd have—")

Damn, it was like listening to Volkhi.

She had a knife. She had stolen it. Her father had thought it was stupid, but all the same it was better than having nothing. She understood her father going off the way he had. She was glad Pyetr was her father and not some dead old man she had never met—all in one night she had a father who would take his sword and go off into the dark after to rescue a daughter and a young man he hardly knew from rusalki and ghosts, and would her uncles, would her uncles ever dare?

(Her uncles had gathered up the silver—knowing the killers were coming. Her mother had packed her jewels, and told her, when she had come upstairs to announce, with a lump in her throat, that she was going with Yvgenie, "Go where you please.")

Damn them, Sasha thought. And remembered something too painful, nights in the stable when something had gone amiss in the tavern and he had realized his aunt and uncle were talking about being rid of him. He had tried (because he had known then that wanting things was deadly dangerous) not to have an opinion about the matter. Even if he had nowhere to go. Even if he tried to love them. He only worked the harder the next day to please them—

And here he had the most beautiful girl he had ever seen with her arms close about him, thinking, the way Pyetr would jolt him into thinking that it was all right to want things like Pyetr's staying alive, that it was all right to want to get Pyetr's daughter back and Yvgenie back—

No!

Dangerous, that thought. But *she* thought it. She wanted it of him, she expected him to do it, for the sake of a brave young man she owed her life to—no matter he had spent the night lying senseless and no matter he could not find the thread of his thoughts—*she* believed he could do it, she wrapped her arms about him and believed the way she had believed in the world beyond her walls.

Dangerous for a wizard, dangerous as walking a roofline drunk, dangerous as a rusalka's kiss—

Don't be a fool, he told himself while they rode. But for a few drunken instants he had believed in it, too, and thought—Yvgenie. Life and death. Death in life. Yvgenie's the instability.

Yvgenie's the stone that moves the hillside. Wish him to our side while his life lasts. Is that wishing against nature?

—

Thorns stood like walls on either hand, braced by tall dead trees, and Yvgenie walked, following Ilyana, following Owl, who glided in bands of sunlight and shadow on gossamer white wings. Owl was back, since the leshy ring, and Yvgenie told himself that should be a hopeful sign, but his heart could not quite believe it: I dreamed this, he thought. Or I've been here before. And from time to time he glanced over his shoulder, expecting the wolves of his dream.

"This is wrong," he said. "Ilyana, this isn't the way to go. Ilyana, we're losing the horses—"

"They'll follow," she said. "Come on! They'll follow us once we get through."

"Through *where*?" he protested. But his voice came from faint and far away, and the daylight seemed colder and grayer with every step. "Ilyana, look ahead of us. There's nothing living."

"It's further to go back," she protested. "It can't be that much further through—I can *feel* something ahead of us—"

He reached for her hand, to compel her if there was no other way—take the strength she had and carry her back to the horses; but she evaded his touch, wishing *no* so strongly it stung. "Kavi, I can help you, there's a way back, I know there is, my mother died and she's alive again, she had *me*, didn't she?"

"At whose cost?" The ghost wrapped itself about him, cold, wary, and protective against her magic. "And what will we be then? Come back, don't go any further."

"Kavi, Kavi, come *on*!"

He flinched as a sudden cold spot swept through his middle. Another grazed his shoulder, and became a wolf and a second wolf, walking tamely ahead of them, creatures of gossamer and pallor, like Owl, wending their way through thorny hedges that parted, simply *moved*, to let them through. White wisps streamed and wove through the thorns of the hedge like serpents, and he began to hear a voice saying, Ahead is where you belong. Here's the rest you've deserved. Here are all the answers to all the questions you ever asked. . . .

Another cold wisp swept through him, and another, stealing

life and warmth. "Ilyana!" He caught a branch to hold the hedge apart, scarcely feeling the thorns. "Ilyana!"

But more branches closed between them as she turned to look at him.

"Kavi!" she cried, trying with bare hands and wishes to unweave the tangled thorn boughs. Ghosts streamed like snakes about them, thicker and thicker. He shoved his arm through the thorns to draw her back through, leaned against the branches, almost touching the tips of her fingers—but the cold spots shot through him more rapid than his heartbeats, and the weakness he felt now was its own warning that he dared not touch her if he could.

"Kavi!" she cried. But he clenched his hand just short of her fingers and drew his arm back. "Kavi, stay with me, we'll find a way through—"

"I can't," he cried, and tore and fought through the thicket away from her, blind and breathless. He would have killed her just then, the way he would kill the horses if he found them in this desolation: he would draw the last life from the ground, draw it from anything in his path. He drew it instead from the stubborn thorns, fended brittle branches away from his arms and ran, fainting from cold and weakness—heard the voices of wolves amid the wailing of the ghosts, and, glancing over his shoulder, saw them coursing after him, slow and pitiless as nightmare.

Something had shifted. Sasha felt that much: an essential pebble had moved, somewhere. But as to how things were falling now— he was blind and numb with terror, resolved *not* to let his fear reach beyond him, or do more harm than he might already have wrought with his wishes.

God, Pyetr, hear me. The boy's in trouble. Chernevog is. I did *something I don't understand—*

Nadya whispered, "What's wrong?" Missy had stopped, abruptly, standing with her ears pricked and a shiver going through her shoulders. Within his awareness, Nadya was trying not to be afraid: she had known the world outside her walls must be dangerous, but she had chosen her course, she was with a wizard she was sure could fight the invisible dangers and on a horse with strength to carry them through the tangible ones.

Dear fool, Sasha thought, feeling her arms about him, dear young fool, nothing of the sort—

But it made him sure all the same that he had imminently to do something. Pyetr would tell him so exactly that way. Though he did not have Pyetr and his sword and his good sense at his back, he had a lost boyarevna armed with a kitchen knife and a faith only the young could have, a faith he so desperately—

—O god!—wanted for himself.

Thickets gave way to green again, to scantly leaved trees struggling for life, and sunlight that blinded and did not warm. Yvgenie slid on a muddy edge, sat down hard on a bank of a cold spring-fed rill with his heart pounding for fright, as if a mouse could drown in that water that soaked his leg—but it seemed to him he had been on the verge of another fall, and drowning, and that the bank where he lay and the sunlight shining down on him were less real than the other shore.

He looked up the hill, thinking of wolves, not sure now that any had been there, not sure that they might not yet come over the wooded hill.

Get up, keep moving, the ghost insisted. He recalled that Ilyana was in some dreadful danger, that he had let her go and lost her and that he dared not go back, because he was dying, he much feared so, dying finally and forever, when he had died truly that night in the flood, in a woods in which the dead did not rest. He wanted not to steal strength; but he wanted not to die, either, or to wait for the wolves, and he hauled himself up on his arms and his hands to try to get his feet under him—with the sudden feeling—perhaps it was the ghost—that there was help to be had, that it was very close now—

An arrow hit the bank, among the dead leaves, beside his hand. He flung a look over his shoulder at riders coming down the opposite leaf-paved slope, and tried to run and sprawled again on the leaves in the weakness of his legs. He rolled over and looked at them as they came—god, they were the tsar's men, not his father's; and that made him hope—

Although why they should be here in this woods, he had no notion at all. He only stared at them as they came. He had no strength to flee them, not even to stand on his feet to face them.

They stopped, their captain's horse standing half astride the rill, the mustached captain looking down at him grimly from that vantage as two others rode across to dismount on either side of him. Their armor and their manner recalled Kiev, and streets, and sane places where the Great Tsar ruled, not wizards. They would kill. They would do anything they pleased, in the tsar's name. But they might be here on some other cause, they might even be here hunting his hunters.

"Yvgenie Kurov," their captain said, as the horse took a step closer, looming over him. "Where's the girl? Where did you leave her?"

"I don't know," he said, and the two men on either side of them came and hauled him up by the arms. Why should the tsar care? he wondered. Why should the tsar take a hand in my father's troubles, or want to find me or her?

The ghost said, Because your father is dead, poor young fool, with his servants, the second wife, and all his house, and they intend no traitor's heir survive—nor any question of an heir, born or unborn. The Kurovs are gone, the tsarevitch is scrambling for his life, and heads will roll if some pretender comes out of the woods: that's what I hear in them. I'd not fall afoul of Eveshka's ill will. But no one told the tsarevitch that, when he tried to switch dice on Ilyana's father. . . .

He was dazed. Their grip hurt his arms. He found no sense in what the ghost was saying, and the captain of the tsar's men leaned close to ask him and seized him by the hair, making him look up. "Where is Nadya Yurisheva?"

The name echoed strangely in his ears, recalling—recalling—

—a talk behind the stairs, vows exchanged besides the witnessed ones, with the bride they had contracted for him: they had conspired to try to love each other, his bride behind her walls, himself within his father's treacheries and the Medrovs' climb to influence. Until someone had whispered the fatal secret, a taint of wizardry—"Where is she?" the captain asked, shaking him, but he saw only forbidding thorns, and ghosts, and the fire and Ilyana writing in her book. He had no idea how he had become so lost, or where he had lost Nadya and fallen in love with a wizard who wanted him for a ghost's sake—

For Kavi Chernevog, who had sustained his life and who

with a confidence beyond courage was not afraid of these men, no. Kavi *wanted* them, he felt it coming—

"Let me go!" he pleaded with them. But the breath and strength that came flooding through his arms was theirs, all the arrogant violence they had brought to this woods. Two horses bolted, free through the woods. Go! he wished them, heard the captain cry, "Kill him!" and shut his eyes and wished not, wished all the horses free: it was his own morality, that, and the ghost did not fight him on that point. It was too well satisfied with the life it had in reach, and with every gasp of breath came anger at his victims. He had tried all his life not to hate, had kept his father's wicked secrets, poured his love into a man whose only passion was cleverness and strength, and fear in the eyes of his dogs and his servants and his sons. . . .

But that was over. They were gone now, his half-brothers were dead, his stepmother must be dead: everything he knew and understood was gone—he was drowning, and he caught at last at what he could. Branches, lives—it was all the same.

Finally he was sitting by the water with breath in his body, warmth where cold had been, and three dead men beside him. He had not intended it, god, he had not set out to do murder— it was the ghost. It was all the ghost—

—Well, well, well, something said, then, that was not harmless, either, that reeked of sunless cold and coils. —A boy. A boy with the smell of my old master all about him. My *kind*, dear master—is it help you want?

Fear washed over him—he had no notion of what, or why, only that the ghost knew its serpent shape, and that killing had drawn this creature here as surely as rot would draw ravens.

You've only to wish me, the creature said. *I* know what you need. I can supply everything you need.

It shivered up the streamside like a passing cloud. It brought cold where it passed. And stopped where a woman stood, a woman Ilyana's image.

A woman he had murdered once. And rescued from magic. And lost again forever through his jealousy.

He said, in sudden despair, "—Eveshka."

And the creature who smelled of dark and murder said, suddenly behind him, "The years do turn. Don't they turn, my old master?"

—

Something was ahead of them, *not* the mouse, Sasha thought, and said, quietly for Nadya, who was holding only to the saddle on this level ground:

"I'm hearing something. Someone. I don't know who."

"Is it my father?"

He shook his head, gazed through the sunlit forest, along the hills behind them. "It's—" It was something out of the ordinary, not like the thoughts of deer or the earth-smelling habits of bears. He stood up in the stirrups and looked over his shoulder.

"It's not near us. It's north of here. Too far to hear—it feels like some*one*. Several someones. Like voices you can't hear. I don't like this."

"The ones we're looking for? Could it be?"

He shook his head. "I want them to ignore us. I want them not to see us."

"I'm scared."

"We've Babi. Wherever he is." He reached back a hand without thinking, patted a bare knee with half-felt embarrassment. He did *not* like the feeling from the woods. "It's not safe. But I've nowhere safer to put you."

There was a little tremor in her voice. "My *father* said stay with you." And she added: "I have a knife in my boot."

"We don't want them that close." He had his own misgivings about putting her afoot and out of his sight—misfortune and magic tending to strike at the most vulnerable point. "Don't be afraid. Just think about the wind, think about green leaves, that's the sort of thing Missy thinks about."

She thought about walking houses and wolves and dreadful wizards. She tried to see the leaves instead, and admire the sunlight: everything was brighter in the woods, the whole world was more dangerous and sharper-edged than she had ever imagined. She thought, I shouldn't be alive, I shouldn't be thinking thoughts like this—

Yvgenie rode all the way from Kiev for me—and he's in trouble and we've got to save him; but I can't even think about what to say when I see him. I never felt with him the way I feel now—I never imagined anybody like Sasha and it's *stupid*! I can't tell

whether I'm shivering because I'm scared to death or only because he touched me. . . .

Dammit, he thought, we're fools, both of us are fools. I can't
afford to think of this girl, god, Pyetr's in deep trouble out there,
the mouse is—I *need* to talk to 'Veshka right now, and I can't,
I daren't, because of Nadya.

God, one clear wish—one clear wish and I could break the
silence. Two clear thoughts and we all might have a chance; and
the girl has me so upset I don't know my own name.

I brought her here. It's my fault. Yvgenie is my fault. Or have
I been assuming too much all along?

"Where is she?" Eveshka said, demanded everything, and ran
through those memories like a fire through dry leaves. He remembered countless faces, he remembered desperation, going
barehanded against Draga's creatures; he remembered dying—
and first meeting Eveshka's daughter by the brook where
Yvgenie would die.

He remembered Owl dying, and the precarious bridge above
the river; he remembered his heart lodged as a guest with
Pyetr's—and *knew* Eveshka the way Pyetr did, saw her the way
Pyetr did, in the sun and the wind, at the helm of the old ferry;
he forgave her the way Pyetr did—with the firelight on her face
and thoughts in her eyes he could never, ever speak to—

Thoughts like doubt of one's own life, one's own right to
walk the earth, doubts that echoed off his own wizard-bred despair.

She still remembered loving him. And she hated that. She
remembered him wishing harm on Pyetr with no reckoning of
Pyetr himself, only his own pleasure in pain and mischief—that
was always at the core of what he did and what he chose. He
enjoyed mischief. That was who he was. She believed it.

He did not dispute her—but the enjoyment of it he could not
now remember, could only recall that he had done it, and knew
that of men alive or dead, he regarded Pyetr as his friend: "I
never knew anyone who was good, but him, 'Veshka, allow me
that much and don't argue with me now—*listen* to me!" A pit
was at his back: he could recall all life behind them pouring like

a waterfall over an edge that gnawed its way closer and closer to the world and this place. He wanted her to see it, he wanted her to understand he had tried to stay with Ilyana.

" 'Veshka, I love her, I was never supposed to fall in love with her. They wanted me to bring her here, to them. But they're dead, and I couldn't stop her—"

"Damn you! You couldn't face me, you couldn't come to me with your 'bring her to them—' What were you going to do, Kavi? What did the leshys intend with my daughter?"

"To make her safe, that's all they wanted—"

"*Was* it? Was it now?" The sunlight dimmed before the dark and the anger in front of him. She would kill the boy, he was sure, kill Yvgenie and him and take the magic he had, she was that strong and that desperate to be stronger—rusalka no less than himself, a sink of life as deadly as that place beyond the hedge—

While life and magic poured over that rim and threatened to sweep her and him and everything they loved into itself.

"Eveshka," he said. "Eveshka, don't help it, don't—wish against them—"

"Bonesss," the vodyanoi said.

The whole world tottered for an instant. Breath failed. But she spun about and stalked away from him, and laid her hand on a bare white trunk.

Something whispered, slithering to the other bank: Don't trust him, pretty bones. He's not at all nice. But there is a place that wants him, there is a place that would certainly trade for him, trade for something very, very nice—

It was day. The vodyanoi could not abide the sun—except someone enabled him, except Eveshka was listening to the creature. And who was so foolish, god, who but him had ever been so foolish?

Eveshka rolled a glance at sky and woods, looked at him last, desperate, angry for all the long seasons of cold and dark he had damned her to. She hated him, for lying, for pain, for deception and his theft of her peace and her daughter—

She *wanted* the strength he held. She took it, in one dizzy rush, that left him on his knees; and wanted him from her sight, *now*, that was the single grace she gave him, because there was a wisp of life left in him and she would not kill—from moment to moment, so long as she could, she would not kill . . .

"*Run*, damn you, Kavi! *Run!*"

He found the strength somewhere. He fled the streamside, blind, raked by thorns—he stumbled and fell and ran again, mindless, until he found himself lying on dead leaves in the sunlight, watching an ant make anxious progress across a sandy, mold-eaten leaf among other leaves, and stop, and quite suddenly—

Shrivel and die.

His heart gave a painful thump. A leaf fell. Another followed. He wiped his mouth with a gritty hand and tried to get up.

Green, untimely leaves showered about him. His teeth chattered with winter cold as he gathered his feet under him and kept going, where, he did not know, except he felt powerless against what moved him—he, Kavi, Yvgenie: the distinction was no longer exact in his thoughts.

He wiped tears that ran on his face, revolted by the chill of his own hand, and slid as much as walked down the face of the hill, gathered himself at the bottom and stumbled further, thinking—the god help him—that if he could only find the horses—they could carry his failing body in more than one sense.

But there was no trace of them, and from Yvgenie nothing but terror and grief. Yvgenie loved the white mare. Ilyana loved the filly. So did he, for Ilyana's sake. And his living always required murder, it had before and did again, even of what trusted him.

The sun sank below the treetops. In a deeply shadowed passage Volkhi blew and shook his head, and Pyetr shivered for no reason that he could think of—a passing wish, perhaps, either good or ill, if any magic at all could reach him. Volkhi had his head up, smelling something of interest, that much was certain. Pyetr asked a little more speed of him and Volkhi picked up his pace, pricking up his ears and flattening them again, listening and worrying.

The mouse? One could only hope.

No, god, it was Patches, riderless, with Yvgenie's white horse behind, coming slowly down the wooded hillside. His heart said hurry; but he rode quietly so as not to startle them, and saw bloody scratches and countless welts on their hides, thorns snarled in manes . . .

Sasha could easily have asked them the questions he most wanted to ask. All an ordinary man could learn of them was the evidence of a panic flight through thorn thickets: dirt from falls, scratches all over them, and everything Ilyana and the boy owned still bound to the saddles—god, Ilyana's book was there along with the rest of her belongings. She would never have parted from that—willingly.

He slid down, slipped Patches' bridle, tied it to the saddle, and sent the filly off with a whack on the rump—home, he hoped, where young Patches understood home to be; or to Sasha, or whatever refuge she could find on their own. He held on to the white mare for a change of horses, swung up onto Volkhi's back, argued Volkhi and the mare into an uphill track, and rode along their backtrail, not breakneck, but slowly, observing an occasional print of a hoof on soft ground, a snag of white horse-hair in brush. The horses had both gotten away clear: life had escaped Chernevog's grasp, and if it was Chernevog's fault what had happened, the horses could not have gotten away without magic.

Which could most reasonably mean the mouse—who, being the mouse, might have driven them off for their own safety, if things were going wrong; but she would *not* have chosen to send them away with the book and their food and their blankets, not unless something had gone very wrong, very quickly, or she had had some destination in mind for them. Like her uncle. Like— the god knew. The book might have every answer he needed, which he might know now if Sasha were with him, which, dammit, Sasha was not—nor could possibly be, this fast.

So he was here—for what little he could do: at least whatever he could do was sooner than he could do it at Sasha's pace; and if the mouse's wish or Sasha's was indeed guiding the horses, Sasha might yet get his hands on the book and the answers in time, and ride to the mouse's rescue.

Or his, if he was on the right track—and by all evidence he was.

Only granting, please the god, Sasha had ever waked up.

"Babi's left," Nadya said, and Sasha looked about at her, saying, "What?" so distractedly she was sorry she had said anything. It was getting toward dark, he insisted on walking and letting the horse follow him, and if he was working magic she might just have ruined things.

"No," he said.

It was very disconcerting to have someone answer her thoughts.

"I'm sorry," he said, and patted Missy's neck as they walked. "Pyetr and I do it. I forget. I'm dreadfully sorry."

"I shouldn't bother you when you're thinking."

"You couldn't bother me."

It was an odd thing to say. She was not certain whether it was good or bad. Maybe she was too silly to bother him. Her uncles called her a damned nuisance when they thought she was out of earshot. They called her stupid girl—

"You're not," he said, and stopped a moment and looked up at her. "You *are* distracting me. I'm sorry. Please don't talk to me. I'm trying to think of something."

"What?"

"A wise wish."

"Wish us home," she said.

He had the most distressed look on his face. He stared at her and went on staring. He said, finally, "Home."

She said, "Mine's *not* in Vojvoda. I don't know where it is but it's not there."

He said, "Mine burned."

"I'm dreadfully sorry—"

"It *wasn't* mine, really. Or it was. It didn't matter. It was just full of papers and things."

She did not understand. She did not understand how she had troubled him, but she had. She frowned and wondered what she had said so dreadful.

He walked on, and Missy moved with his hand on her neck,

at her steady patient pace. She thought, I wouldn't hurt him. I truly wouldn't.

How can a wizard's house burn? Can't they stop the fire?

"Not always," he said. "I'm dreadful at fires. —God, don't— *bother* me. Please! God!"

Her breath seized up in her throat. And he shook his head furiously and laid a hand on her knee, saying, "I wanted you here. I wished you. I wanted—"

"What?"

"A wife. And it's not fair for us to want somebody. And you shouldn't think about me and you shouldn't want to—" He stopped, quite suddenly, then said: "I sound like 'Veshka."

She felt fluttery inside. She felt guilty for Yvgenie and guilty for being a wicked girl, her mother would call it, and guilty for upsetting Sasha—it was not fair for a boy to risk his life for her and her not to love him, but it was nothing like Sasha.

"It's a damned *wish*," he said. "It's magical. You can't help liking me!"

"I do," she said, feeling very strange inside. "I *do*, and maybe it *is* magical. It feels that way. I never felt like this. I never did. . . ."

He stood there staring at her. Missy had stopped quite still.

"What about Yvgenie?" he asked.

She said, hard as it was to say, "We never—" and stopped there, her face gone burning hot despite the evening chill. She said, "I didn't love him. I said I'd try to. He's very nice." The fact was, she had slept in his blanket and he had slept curled against a tree, because—

—because she had been so dreadfully afraid of strangers. Or of lasting mistakes.

"God," he said, and shook his head and started walking again.

She did not think he was upset with her. She thought quite the opposite. Maybe it was him hearing what she was thinking again.

He stopped Missy again. He looked so dreadfully upset with her. No, *not* with her. With himself. Because he was not thinking about the things he should be thinking about, he was thinking about himself, being selfish, and a fool—

She shook her head, refusing to believe that, upset because he was upset—

And not, again. Feelings came and went quickly as breezes. It scared her. Except it was magic, and she loved a wizard, and things like that seemed likely to happen in his company.

He said, "I can't wish you not. I can't wish you away. It's not safe. God, what do I do with you?"

She said, "I don't know." A nice girl would never think of looking a strange man in the eyes. But she did. She said, shakily, "I'm in the way, aren't I?" The woods was not where she belonged. Sasha was walking because the horse was tired. He was out of breath, he was sweating, he looked exasperated and worried, and she bit her lip, *not* going to add her tears to his problems. Which went away, anyway, the moment she felt her eyes sting.

She said, "I'm not scared of you." It felt as if every fear she had ever had had gone away from her. And anything the woods could hold was nothing to the fears she had lived with, expecting murder at any instant, every day of her life. She had found her mysterious wizard and he was the answer, not the danger. She said, feeling very strange, "I think you should think about getting my father out of trouble."

Because that was what he was trying so desperately to think about—and if she was an echo, she could at least do that to help him.

She said, "I'm scared of meeting Yvgenie, too, but I think you should help the people you need to help, and not worry about me meeting my half-sister, *or* my father's wife. . . ."

He was afraid of that idea. She saw it in his face. He gave a small shake of his head and of a sudden the back-and-forth in her thinking stopped, like a sudden silence, as he started Missy moving again.

She said, because she was stubborn, "They don't scare me." Which was a lie. But she was trying to make it true. She said, on a cold, dreadful thought, "If my father got killed or something because of me—"

He gave her a strange look and she felt colder and colder, thinking about that. Or maybe it was magic again.

He said, "Pyetr's damned hard to kill."

And walked ahead of Missy for a while, in a silence she had never heard in her life—not a lonely one. A cessation of his presence, even when he was right in front of the horse. She watched him, as distant from her as he had been close a moment ago, and thought: He's thinking about my father.

He's doing something. My father said—he *wants* things and they happen. Anything he wants—

God, one has to be so careful with him. Careful *of* him.

Take care of him, her father had charged her. She had thought—until he wakes. But she began to see what her father had trusted to her, and how very much Sasha needed someone he could trust—

Someone as brave as her father, someone not afraid of him—no matter what.

Desolation, ghosts, stones and peeling roots of broken trees, banks of thorns that went to powder in a grasping hand, that was the place Ilyana saw: Owl was still with her—but cast about as she would among the hedges she could not find a way out again, nor, it seemed, could Owl. Ghosts wove pale threads through the hedges and the branches of dead trees, cold to the touch and angry, one could feel it.

"Yvgenie!" she had shouted till she was hoarse, but only the faint wailing of ghosts answered. He was alone with Patches and Bielitsa in a place where life was fading and the result of that she did not want to imagine—Patches had never asked to be taken out into the woods and lost to a ghost. Her father was looking for her, beyond a doubt, and if she had feared her father harming Yvgenie, now it was Kavi harming her father she had to fear. She thought in despair. God, he couldn't keep up and I wouldn't listen. I've done everything wrong and now I can't get back again. Papa was right and I wouldn't listen to him, I thought I knew better—

Something moved in the tail of her eye. A wolf sat there, the one that they had followed into this place. It looked alive, yellow-eyed and with fur mostly white, but touched with gray and buff. Behind it, tongues lolling, sat others, milky-pale as Owl. Those were surely ghosts.

The living wolf got up and trotted away. The others followed it; and Owl glided after.

Dangerous to wish for what doesn't exist, Kavi had warned her. Now she was on the verge of wanting her uncle to rescue her and most dangerously on the edge of wanting her father, the god forbid she should be so selfishly stupid. Her mother might know what to do, if her mother would even listen to her situation now, of which she despaired entirely: her mother was not inclined to patience; but god, she was in trouble. The leshys were dead. No one had ever told her that such things could happen, let alone that the woods might suddenly change beyond her understanding.

But they had warned her about Kavi. And she had thought it was so simple—as if loyalty and wishes could sustain him. She thought, on the edge of tears: Uncle tried to tell me. Hope never seemed dangerous till this. Now I know what it can do to fools that won't listen.

Ghosts belong here. Yvgenie doesn't, not yet: he's not dead and he's not a wizard. That's why he could get away and get Kavi out of this place. God, I don't want to follow these creatures—it's stupid. But Owl's going. And if I lose Owl, what other tie have I got to the other side of the hedge?

Mother, I'm listening now. Uncle, I'm dreadfully sorry . . .

Papa, *please* don't come after me. Even wizards don't belong here. You couldn't—

A ghost poured out into the aisle ahead of her, and shaped itself into a great lumbering bear, white as snow. It looked at her over its shoulder, and its face showed a dreadful scar, as if something had burned it once.

She thought, It's not just a ghost of a bear, it was a real bear once. Something dreadful happened to it. And what does it have to do with me?

A ghost swept near her, saying, Ilyana, granddaughter, look at me.

She did look. She saw a man's misty face, fierce and young and very handsome.

It said, You're my wish, Ilyana. And your grandmother's. We never agreed, so least one of us has to be right. Your father was no one's choosing—or he was your mother's whim. I've no idea. I only know he's made you terribly dangerous.

She was stung by that. She said, There's nothing wrong with my father!

A raven had joined the ghost, shaped itself out of the mist and drifted with them, on gray wings. The ghost said, Your father is a gambler—but he's no one's fool. Your mother is a damned good wizard—and that's enough to know. —I wish you to make your own choices, granddaughter. Be what you are.

"But you say I'm dangerous!" she protested, seeing the ghost fade away. "Are you my grandfather Uulamets? You must be! Come back! I'm not through talking to you!"

But the ghost shredded apart and streamed away through the hedges. The scar-faced bear and the wolves and Owl went ahead of her, and sometimes the ghostly raven, until through a last screen of thorns she could see what shone so pale and strange, a beautiful palace of curious design, made all of white stones, on a hill girt about by thorn hedges laced with ghosts.

The evening light cast strange shadows on the white palace, making odd shadows, making its walls and its towers appear like lace. How beautiful, Ilyana thought, pulling aside a last few thorn boughs. How can anything so beautiful be wicked or dangerous? Kavi was wrong.

Something crunched beneath her foot. She looked down and saw a broken vault of bone—some old skull, buried in the earth. There were more such. Not stones, she thought, gazing up a hill where other such objects lay half-buried all up the hill to the foundation of the palace.

God, no, not stones that made such lacy walls and towers— but bleached and dreadful bones.

12

Birds took sudden flight from beyond the hill. Pyetr saw it and earnestly wished for Sasha, for the mouse—for his wife, if he could truly rely on her now. They were not the only venturers in the woods, the dead deer had proved that; and an ordinary man had no way to learn what had raised that alarm in the direction he had to go except to go and see. Slipping up and over the hill afoot was one choice; but that meant leaving Volkhi tied, and, risking him, chancing being surprised afoot.

So he drew his sword as quietly as he could and kept riding, watching the trees ahead. He rounded the shoulder of the hill at a walk, feeling something eerily familiar and untrustworthy and magical at once.

He thought: 'Veshka? Eveshka's presence had touched him first like that—years ago; when he thought of it, it felt frighteningly like her, not his wife the way she had been for the last eighteen years, not the way she had felt since she had returned to the living. It stirred old nightmares. And an infatuation with his own destruction that had moved him once, in his bitter youth—when now life was very precious. He thought, 'Veshka, god, *is* it you?

A patch of red showed on the hill, the red of blood; of flowers that never bloomed in woodland shade; or a silk shirt that was folly in the woods. Yvgenie.

But no sign of the mouse.

Volkhi had stopped unbidden, laid his ears back and swung half about. An ungodly feeling crawled up and down his spine while his own good sense and his experience of a rusalka's attraction said stay clear, get away, Ilyana was his first obligation. But the boy—

He reined Volkhi around and around again while he hesitated. He was not making clear choices. But, dammit, he had prayed for Chernevog in his reach. He had set himself deliberately in the way of chance and others' wishes. And the question now was whether he even had the power to ride past, or whether, trying, he would run head-on into fate.

Then he felt the likeness of an arm reach about him, like ice, and Chernevog whispered ever so faintly, at the very nape of his neck, "Pyetr. Dear Owl."

He made a wild sweep of his arm, but it met only deathly chill and fell numb at his side. His heart struggled, his head spun, and Chernevog said,

"Your daughter's in danger."

"I know she's in danger, damn you."

"The harm I could do is only death. Get down. Get down, now, Pyetr Ilitch."

He wanted *not* to, he wanted to swing around and lay hands on Chernevog, but that was not a choice; his hands and feet were growing numb and he found himself sliding down from the saddle and staggering his way to Yvgenie's side, where Chernevog wished him to go.

The boy lay like the dead, scratched and bleeding, the red shirt in snags and ruins. For a moment he pitied the boy, wanted to help him—

Then Yvgenie reached and seized his arm and the tingling crept up toward his heart, beyond his power to tear away, beyond his power even to want to escape, or to look away as Yvgenie's eyes opened and looked into his, as Yvgenie's lips said quietly, "Dear Owl. You came in time. And brought us horses. How foresighted of you."

Damn you, he tried to say. But words and sense were beyond him. There was only the feeling of suffocation, that once had had infatuation and desire and everything he loved wrapped with it, and now had only desperation and fear and the memory of his wife as a killer, no different than the men who had hunted him.

—

He waked lying helpless on the ground and Chernevog was bending over him, brushing his cheek with a gentle touch and saying, "Catch your breath, dear Owl."

His head hurt. His whole body was floating. The leaves against a darkening sky made a dizzying sound. "Where's my wife? Where's my daughter, damn you?"

"Where's Sasha? Following you?"

"You're the wizard. Figure it out."

A great breath then, a rapid blink of Yvgenie's eyes and a different touch, at his shoulder this time. "I had to leave her, sir, I was afraid—afraid he couldn't stop if he got near her—" Another breath. Another blink of the eyes as Chernevog caught up his shirt in his fist. "The boy's Kurov, do you understand me? Your wife's wishes have come home to roost. A great many dark birds have, do you hear me, Pyetr Ilitch?"

"Kurov!" Nothing made sense.

"Didn't he say?" Again the tingling ran through his bones. And stopped. "He must have forgotten that part."

"Damn you!"

"He brought your daughter here. Ill wishes have a way of burning the hand that looses them. Do you understand me now? Your *wife* wanted harm. And harm there is, Owl, harm in Kiev, harm in this woods, harm to you and Ilyana and the woods itself."

"Harm from you, you damned dog." He made a try at getting up, but his head spun and Chernevog slammed him back to the ground.

"Listen to me, Pyetr Ilitch."

One had to. One had no damned choice. And no breath left to protest. One recalled faces, years ago, a dice game in Kiev, with the tsarevitch, a man who had stood aside to whisper to others in a corner. And a lump on his head and a damnably uncomfortable night thereafter with certain men, until they had left him alone in the room with a very small window above a clothes press.

A reeling progress through the dark—

Pavel Kurov. Kurov's house—

"Out the window and along a rooftop—you certainly never lost your knack, dear Owl. Unfortunately neither has your wife; and your *wife* has driven your daughter to what she's done, your *wife* wished harm to me and harm to your enemies, and she's got that, now. That your enemy's son should bring your daughter to this woods is the tendency of wishes—they take the easiest course. Harm does, do you hear me?"

He stopped fighting. It sounded too much like the sort of thing Sasha would say. Had said, repeatedly. Always the easiest course. Always the course that satisfies most wishes at once. Like piles of old pottery, Sasha was wont to say, all stacked up and waiting the moment they all become possible. . . .

Things happen that can happen—

"Why in hell," he said when he had a breath, "why didn't you come to *me*, if you're so damned concerned about my wife?"

"I didn't know what she'd done. I do now. I talked with her. She took everything I'd gained. She wanted Kurov to suffer. She wanted everyone who ever harmed you to suffer. Do you half understand? She's looking for Ilyana right now and I can't stop her, Pyetr Ilitch."

"God." He rolled onto one arm and tried to get up, failed and found the boy's arm under his, the boy's face broken out in sweat. Kurov's son. Eye to eye with him.

He was sure it was Yvgenie who said, ever so faintly, "I love her. I know you hate me. But I swear to you, I truly do love her."

"Love her, boy? You're in the hands of wizards! Do you even know what you want any longer?"

The boy made a desperate shake of his head. "I don't care."

He thought, Fool, boy!

But that described more than Yvgenie Kurov.

He leaned on Yvgenie's arm, he put himself to his feet and staggered after Volkhi, saying, "If we're dealing with my wife, you'd better stay to my back."

A hand landed on his shoulder. He knew before he looked around and saw Yvgenie who he was facing.

Chernevog said, "I love her, too, Pyetr Ilitch. The god help us. I had nothing to do with it. I couldn't stop it. Misighi, damn him. . . ."

God, tears welled up. And spilled, in his old enemy's confusion. What did one say?

Fool for believing them, that was what.

"Pyetr, they wanted me to bring her to them. Misighi did— to be sure she wouldn't—go my way—"

"What do you mean, go your way? If they wanted to talk to her they could have come to the door any day. —*What did they want with her?*"

Chernevog shook his head. "I don't know. I can't do anything against them, I can't remember things, I'm not strong enough any longer— Being dead's a damned inconvenience, Pyetr."

"The hell!" He grabbed a fistful of silk shirt. "You're not a fool, Kavi Chernevog, never try to persuade me you are. What did the leshys intend?"

"To save her. Their way. But they're dead, Pyetr, they're all dead, and I couldn't stay with her in that place, I'd have killed her—"

"You're a liar, Chernevog. You've been a liar since you were whelped, a hundred and too damn many years ago—"

"I'm not lying now, I swear to you, there's something where she is, there's something in that place and I couldn't go any further—the boy's not dead, and I couldn't go—"

"The boy's not dead! My *daughter* isn't dead, Snake, don't talk to me about loving her after you ran off and left her somewhere—"

"Because I'd kill her. Because the boy was dying, and he had the sense to do it, that's the truth, Pyetr Ilitch. I'm not sure I did."

God, he thought. Chernevog admitting failure? One could almost believe the scoundrel.

If one did not feel at the moment as if something was crawling on one's skin, and know that even *thinking* about life, Chernevog was wanting it.

"Get on your horse," he said. "Damn you, we're going."

Wishes come true at a time they can. So here I am, damn you, too, Snake: you swore once you wanted my friendship. And isn't that wish of yours older than my daughter?

Yvgenie. Kurov's boy. God.

The shadows were getting longer, and the way more overgrown. Babi skipped ahead of them, stopped and stared at them as if he could not after all these years understand why they could not pass a thicket the way he could.

Babi was upset. Sasha could tell that in the aspect he took, in the fact that Babi did not sulk about supper. It was cheese and honey-lumps eaten on horseback, water when they could, vodka to ease the aches where magic was elsewhere occupied; and Nadya had not made one complaint of pain or weariness the day long. She looked so tired as he held up his hands and let her slide off Missy's rump for a little while. Missy took a step down to cool her feet in the brook that offered them a moment's comfort. Nadya knelt to drink and wash her face, a very pale face in the fading light. He began to do the same.

Brush cracked—something coming through the thicket, he thought, a bear or a deer, something large and strong. But Missy thought suddenly of moving trees and grabby-things, and he made a snatch after her bridle, waded into the stream to hold her, wanting her to be reasonable, please, stand still, no moving tree would catch her while he had hold of her.

Brush cracked, and he heard a voice like rolling rocks, saying from a thicket across the stream, "Young wizard."

He wanted Missy to stay calm. He was not. He was shaking as he led Missy across the stream, Missy strenuously refusing his assurances. No. It was a moving tree. She did not like them. They were not nice. They should all run away. Please.

He knew the leshys' names, at least two and three score of them, knew most by sight and some even by the sound of their voices—but this one was so ruined and changed, peeling and hung about with spiderweb and dry leaves and grown over with living vine—he was appalled.

The leshy lifted an arm and reached for him. "Don't be afraid!" he turned to call out to Nadya, as Missy jerked back and the reins burned through his grasp. But Nadya had followed him—much too close for safety. "Stay back!" he cried as leshy fingers wrapped about him and drew him inexorably away from her and upward. Like limber twigs, they were—like being enveloped by living brush—

But not harmed. Yet.

"Where's Misighi?" he demanded of it, angry, desperate, and all too aware of the strength in the fingers that wrapped about his waist; while from below: "Let him go!" Nadya cried, and pulled at his foot. "Let go!"

"Misighi is dead," a deep voice said, deep as bone. "So many are."

Dead, he thought, stunned. Misighi dead? No. He recalled Misighi's booming voice and the last time he had seen him—walking by the streamside—

Nadya cried, below him, with a dead branch in hand, "Sasha! What shall I do?" and twiggy fingers reached past him with a crackling and shattering of brush.

"Run!" he cried, but the creature had gathered up Nadya too, far too tightly. "She can't breathe! Dammit, be careful! You brought her, don't kill her!"

"Calm, calm," it said, and drew them both close to its trunk and smelled them over. "This is the same, yes. Pyetr's young one. Who else would attack us with sticks? And the young wizard. Yes, both. Don't you know me?"

He caught a breath. "Which are you?"

"Wiun. It's Wiun, young wizard."

"God." There was no resemblance, no likeness. Wiun. Their old friend. As mad as Misighi, wandering apart from other leshys, but younger than most, far younger. And—dying? This peeling wreckage? "Wiun, god—what's happened to you? The vodyanoi's loose, Chernevog—Chernevog's run off with Pyetr's daughter...."

"Chernevog. Yes. We know Chernevog." A deep rumbling then, as of rocks under a flood. "Death in life. Life in death. But he serves the forest."

"Chernevog is yours?"

"Death in life. Life in death. We sustained him. Go to the stone, young wizard."

"Wiun! Pyetr has *two* daughters! Ilyana's in danger—she needs your help!"

"Death in life. Life in death. Beyond our help. Beyond the old ones' strength. We tried. The last is yours. For all our young ones. Go to the stone, young wizard."

The voice grew very faint. Wiun let him to the ground with a gentle crackling of twigs. "The stone, the stone that fed Chernevog—the sword that gave back his heart—all of these, our working, young wizard. But all we did is failing. Chernevog failed us. We had not the strength—and she was too strong—"

"Eveshka?" Sasha asked, out of breath. "Is it Eveshka you're talking about?"

"The stone." Wiun let Nadya down to him, and shut his eyes and ceased to move.

"Wiun?" he asked, waiting. And: "Is he dead?" Nadya asked after a breath.

"I don't know." He wanted Missy back, and Babi, now, please, quickly. He was shaken himself, and Missy was not going to come near the place, for all his wishing. "Come on," he said to Nadya, and took her hand and drew her up and up the hill, where he wanted Missy to go now, quickly. One never forgot—never dared forget, in dealing with leshys, how strange they were—and how strong. "Hurry. There might be young ones, that don't know us."

Nadya grabbed her skirts aside and climbed with him, out of breath and with her hair trailing loose from its braids. He pulled her a steep part of the slope, holding on to a sapling, as Nadya panted:

"I'm all right, I'm all right," the way her father would when things were not in the least all right, or sane.

Misighi dead—god, Misighi could not die: Misighi should outlive all of them, like the woods itself—

But Eveshka had destroyed the old woods, down to one last, wicked tree. The whole heart of the woods had died, and if the leshys of that forest were dying . . . and dying only now—

God, what did Ilyana have to do with? And how did Chernevog fail them?

"What did it mean?" Nadya asked him. "What did it mean, Go to the stone?"

"It's a place." He felt Missy's presence—she had run along the hill and through thickets. But Missy was not alone. Missy had company she knew. He caught sight of Missy's spotted rump. And another set of markings.

Patches. God—

"It's another horse," Ilyana panted.

Wiun had wanted them here. Magic had. It was no chance meeting. And magic, mindless or mindful, went on attracting pieces that belonged together, the god only hope it would include Ilyana—but he feared not. He feared all sorts of things with scattered pieces falling together as they were.

"Everything that belongs together," he muttered, wanting Patches and Missy both, please, quickly now. "Stacks of pottery—"

"What?" Nadya breathed, struggling to stay up beside him, fighting her tattered skirts clear of brambles.

"Pottery. Old wishes. They just damned well hang about waiting. It's dangerous as hell when they start going—one after the other: impossible conditions all over the place and they make each other possible— It's Ilyana's horse. God, she's all over mud and scratches."

"Can you ask her where she's been?"

Pyetr had never believed in such things. Nadya came believing them.

All Ilyana's packs were still on Patches' saddle—for whatever dire reason.

He said, with a sinking heart: "I don't have to ask her."

Eveshka sat on the stone, hands blotting out the fading day, thinking deep, deep, into the earth and the stone, *wanting* the little life that might remain in this grove to wake and listen. She wanted the lifeless hulks to drag up their faded strength— once more—just once more—

But something else came up from the dark, all dripping with malice, saying, "Well, well, you let the boy go, and *where* would he go? Where do you think?"

Pyetr, she thought, trying not to think, and felt a deathly chill. God, no.

"Oh, they're marvelously agreed. They're very worried about you. Why, do you suppose?"

She wanted the creature away from her. But wanting—was so dangerous from this stone.

"I know a secret," Hwiuur said. "I've heard it in the streams. I've smelled it on the wind."

"To the black god with you! I don't want your secrets!"

"But you do, pretty bones. Was there ever a secret you could bear not to know?"

She put her hands over her ears. But that could never silence Hwiuur.

"Your husband has *two* daughters. Did you know that, pretty bones?"

She had not. She cursed the thorns, she cursed the hedges, she cursed the magic that shut her out in silence. She tried not to hear what the creature was saying. She refused to think. Or to wish.

"The leshys protected her all these years. *She* came along with Yvgenie. What do you think about that, pretty bones?"

Pyetr had gone to Kiev. She had wanted him to leave her. He had taken to his wild ways again—if only for the while. And there were women he remembered from long ago—she knew there were, even not wanting to know. He swore not to care for them. He had not then. But he still remembered them, and other people, and the inns full of voices—

"Did I say Kiev?"

"Damn you, Hwiuur!"

"Aren't you the least bit curious?"

No, she thought. No. And no.

"Maybe a boyar's daughter. Maybe very rich. So much gold. Golden hair, too. Pale, pale gold. Like his. I've heard she's very beautiful." The voice slid to the other side of her and said, close to her ear, "All the years Sasha wishes to protect Pyetr's daughter—and he's protecting *her* all along. Isn't that amusing? You know I don't lie, pretty bones. I never lie."

"And you can't tell the truth without a twist in it! Get away from me!"

"Maybe it wasn't Kiev. There are farms. Maybe she's a farmer's daughter. A goat-girl."

"Be silent!"

Hwiuur hissed and writhed aside. She clenched her hands in her lap and stared helplessly at the thorns that walled her out, at hedges shot through with ghosts that whispered now in her hearing, Eveshka, Eveshka, murderer—

She thought, Ilyana, you young *fool*, don't listen to them, come back, listen to *me*, Ilyana—your father is in danger. He's in dreadful danger—

From all of us. . . .

I wanted someone like my father. I didn't know what I was wanting. I didn't know what my father is with my mother, and what Kavi is and what she was. Now I know what it feels like.

Now I know and I can't do anything. There's nothing I can wish that doesn't hurt and there's nowhere for me to go but with Yvgenie, because—

Something cold shivered through the air while Sasha thumbed pages to the light of burning twigs, deeper in the woods, where Wiun would not be offended. A passing cold moment, he told himself, maybe the spookiness of the gathering night, maybe the thunder muttering in the distance. But it was a hell of a place to leave a page.

And to lose a book.

"I don't like this," he said, and met Nadya's worried eyes. "God, there's nothing in it to like, the book stops on a thought and she'd never leave it—Babi. Babi, there's a good fellow—" He unstopped the vodka jug and poured, and Babi swallowed.

"Find her, Babi. Can you find her?"

He was thinking of rusalki, and lovers, wolves—and Draga. And Babi—Babi turned up on Missy's rump again, eyes glowing balefully gold in the firelight.

Sasha said, "He can't. I wish to the god—"

No. Fool. One did not think about safe places or putting Nadya in them. Magic was too fickle and too much was loose. One scarcely dared breathe.

His old master would say, Then *do*. Use your hands, not your wishes.

He picked up the fire-pot and lidded it, leaving them in deep dusk, thinking: Wolves. And rusalki.

If the leshys are dying—it's not their silence. It's stopped feeling like the mouse at all. And it's not Eveshka. It's nothing, that's the dreadful thing. It's—

—nothing. Wishes just go nowhere against it.

The day was shadowing out of the east, hastening toward that time when ghosts could most easily get one's attention—no more real at night, Ilyana reminded herself, only that there were fewer distractions for the eye in the dark, and being alone was worst of all.

But she had no desire to go up to that awful doorway. She walked the whole circuit of the hill, hoping another path through the thorns might lead out.

God, but it only came back again, back to the hill and the palace of bone, and all the while the ghostly wolves lay about the door, the bear lazed near them, and Owl, faithless Owl, who should have guided her out of this, kept a watch from a white and dreadful ledge above the porch.

She did not have to see them. She could wish not to see any ghosts at all and they would be gone until her resolve weakened. But she believed in Owl too much to think he was not there, and she was too afraid of the wolves and the bear to ignore them for long. Besides, they tended to move above especially when one was not looking, and she did not trust them. It was not true that ghosts were harmless. Kavi was not, by day or night. If Kavi was here, Kavi would—

—Kavi would be a greater danger than any of them.

A cold lump rose in her throat. She thought, I should try again. I should wish something far cleverer than I have and get out of this place before dark. Uncle would. Mother would. Kavi would think of something if he were here, and uncle was telling the truth, he's ever so much older—

Owl can see over the maze. Couldn't Owl have shown him the way—couldn't he listen to Owl, if Owl is his?

I might. I could wish that. But Owl scares me. He always was a standoffish bird.

If other birds came here I might listen to them. If they did. But all I've seen are ghosts. . . .

Darker and darker. She was scratched and chilled by ghosts, and came to the end of the path again, back at the hill, with no more daylight left and countless aisles of the maze untried—but her legs ached, she was hungry and thirsty, and she sank down in a knot to warm herself and to think and to wait.

The dark grew. The doors and the windows of the palace began to glow with the slow movement of ghosts. She did not want even to look at it. But it kept drawing her eyes, the way the bear and the wolves did, and Owl at last left his perch and swept a turn about her, winging his way uphill.

Come back, she wished him, and expected no more obedience than she had ever had from Owl, but he glided about again to settle on her hand, a weightless chill, with baleful and too cognizant eyes.

The wolves and the bear appeared suddenly in front of her.

Away from me! she wished them, and the wolves showed their throats and the bear ducked his head and looked away as a bear would from a wish.

They did not leap on her. They did not threaten. She took courage from that and wanted them to lead her from the maze.

But Owl left her fist and flew back up the hill, and the wolves and the bear slunk after him.

—Is that the way out? she wondered, hugging herself against the sudden chill of that thought.

Is the way out to go into that place and deal with what lives there?

I'm not uncle Sasha. I'm not as strong as he is.

But he said I was.

If I dared listen to Owl—if I dared—

"Grandfather?" she asked the empty air.

A horrid thing burst into her view and gibbered at her and fled.

Grandfather, if that was you, behave! I *want* you. Right now. No nonsense!

"Disrespectful whelp," a shapeless thing said, a mere wisp in front of her.

If I can't wish someone who likes me, what chance have I with something that doesn't? Show me the way out of this place.

"Is that all?" The thing became an upright shape. "Magic brought you here, and you want to run away."

This isn't a nice place, grandfather!

"Isn't a nice place. Isn't a nice place. Ha. What a grandchild! Whose daughter are you?"

Papa's. And uncle's. . . .

"Ha," the ghost said. "You're *my* wish, girl. But so far I like your father better."

He was going again. She did not understand him. She did not understand what she had done to make him say that, or what he meant—

—Except . . . papa takes chances.

And this *isn't* a place without wishes—my grandfather's here, and he wished me, but that doesn't matter: there can't be a place there aren't wishes, Kavi was right. When I ran I only took them with me—because I took *me* where I ran to. . . .

And why would he say he liked my father? He didn't like

him. They didn't get along, mother always said that. She didn't get along with him. Nobody could.

Ghosts can't always tell you all the truth. No more than they can lay hands on you. They can get just so close. Because they can't do anything in the world—and their wishes aren't strong enough unless they're rusalki like—

—mother.

If I'm his wish he had to have made it before he died. And he died bringing mother back. Uncle said.

She looked up at the palace on the hill, at the doorways where ghosts moved.

Did he wish me here? He hated Kavi. Didn't he?

Is this whole place—my grandfather's wish? Is he what's waiting inside?

She drew a breath, thinking how nice breathing was, even here, and took a first step up the hill. Nothing told her right or wrong. Nothing would, she decided, and took several breaths.

Uncle would say, It's up to you, mouse.

Another handful of herbs. Firelight fractured in smoke-stung tears. Eveshka drew in a deep breath, deeper still—

Papa would say, The magic's not the smoke, the magic's not *in* the smoke—

She recalled an ember in her mother's hand, fire against unburned flesh—magic, against nature—but *not* wholly against nature. Easier to wish the air than the ember, and send the heat away as fast as it could come—

Draga tried her with such illusions, but a young wizard's eye had seen the means: not sorcery, but cleverness. Not magic: seeing to the nature of a thing. Draga's only great magic, her truly dangerous magic—was her own daughter's murder: was death, and a naive girl's wish for life.

The magic's in the thinking. The magic's in facing the *truth*, young fool!

I was the spell you cast, mother, wasn't I? Kavi only thought he betrayed you. But when you wish something as strong as I am dead—who can know how it might defend itself?

It was such a foolish act, mother. Kavi said you were a fool in all the important ways. Or perhaps you aren't through with your own wishes yet, and *you* wished Ilyana born—though I doubt that, one can never be sure. One can never be safe enough.

Time had been that she had resented her father's meddling, time had been his advice and his teachings had seemed foolish limits. But his daughter wished him back now, if it were possible—wished a ghost out of the earth and longed for even the whisper of his presence.

You never taught me forgiveness, papa, but I try, I do try, the way Pyetr said—and you never trusted him. Why?

Is there foresight? Is it something he would do? Or that I would, for him? Or is it the daughter we would make? Sasha says—the things that will be change with every change we make. Sasha says—that's why no bannik will stay with us.

So there's *no* predicting. Is there?

Pyetr's hands, fingers so long and agile with the dice—teaching Ilyana—

No, she had said. No. Pyetr, it's not a toy for a wizard. *Not for us*—

Why? he had asked. And had not understood her distress.

It disturbs me, she had written in her book that day. *I don't know why. Prediction—that's what it does. But every time you throw them, every time you hope for an outcome, every time you wish into uncertainty*—

Pyetr had said, Try it, 'Veshka. For the god's sake, it's just a *game*.

It's just a game. . . .

She squeezed her eyes shut, pressed her hands against her head, thinking: Is that why you feared him, papa?

You drove our bannik away, you wanted to pin the future down and you kept after it with questions and questions until it ran away.

Even looking at the future changes it. You have to walk blind or you're not walking where you would have—

I could wish things right. I'm stronger than my mother. Or my father.

If I knew beyond a doubt. If there were no uncertainty.

There was a sudden chill in the night, a shift in the wind that carried the smoke aside. And in her heart the old Snake whispered: "Well, well, pretty bones. Do you finally need my help?"

She felt the thoughts that went left and right of reason. Change? Hwiuur was on all sides of a question at once. Hwiuur *had* no sides. And no real shape, nothing, at least, permanent.

Like Pyetr's dice.

"Well, pretty bones, how does it fare tonight? Missing its young one? Its young one's gone where it daren't."

One *wanted* the creature. And so few ever would.

He lunged, he rolled and twisted. She remembered his touch, she remembered the water and the pain of his bite, blindingly sharp.

"Wouldn't you like to know where your husband is tonight, pretty bones?"

There was cold, there was dark. Time was that she had refused to die. Now there were conditions under which she would not live.

A heart's so fragile, Kavi had used to say.

But a heart's capable of more than breaking, snake.

Hwiuur twisted and slithered aside, blithely, powerfully bent on escape and mischief—on Pyetr, and Chernevog, and the boy. She thought of an aged willow, a muddy grave in a dank, watery den.

And thought of lightnings.

"It wouldn't!" Hwiuur hissed, whipping back about. "Its bones are there. It daren't!"

She said, as Pyetr would, "The hell."

She folded up her book and wished the fire *out*.

And it was.

Pyetr felt a sudden chill—maybe present company, maybe just the persistence of fear in this nightbound tangle. His hand ached with a bone-deep pain. The misery went all the way to his wrist now—he must have fallen on it a while ago. His right hand. His sword hand, if it came to that—though there was little a sword could do against foolishness or jealousy and he could find no enemy but those and weariness. Volkhi had been on the trail too long now; the god knew the white mare had little left, and he feared increasingly that they were lost: Chernevog swore he knew the way and that he had seen Eveshka not far from here, north and riverward, near the leshy ring—wherever that was, in the dark, and without landmarks.

They came to a thread of water between two hills. "Soon, now," Chernevog had been promising him for the last while. Now he said: "Not far."

Volkhi dipped his head to drink. Pyetr let him have his sip, and the white mare had hers, against a last effort, he told himself, if only the old lad had it left, not to break both their necks.

And when they found Eveshka, the god only hope Chernevog had not deceived him. If Chernevog *had* lied, and meant some harm to her through him . . .

He felt a sharp stab of pain from his hand. He looked down the dark stream course and thought of water—of dark coils, and pain, and the mud about willow-roots, and carried the hand against his mouth.

"My hand's hurting," he murmured. "It hasn't done that in years."

"My sympathies," Chernevog said acidly. "Is it a cure you want?"

"No, dammit, I mean it used to do this. Hwiuur's about."

"The creature was keeping company with Eveshka. Not surprising."

"What do you mean, Not surprising?"

"He wanted your daughter. But I wouldn't let him."

Chernevog was a shadow in the dark. A wizard might have told what that meant, whether fair or foul intentions, but he could not.

"So you aimed him at my wife?"

"You have the worst expectations of me. No. I said I wouldn't let him at your daughter. God! Give me once a moment's credence! It's that way—" A lift of his hand. "I could be there now if I wanted to. But I'll rather you deal with your wife, Pyetr Ilitch, thank you."

Chernevog started off down the stream, that ran as a sometimes glistening thread through this trough between the dark hills, a reedless, leaf-paved passage. Pyetr rode glumly beside him: Sasha had to appeal to him to deal with Eveshka, Ilyana did, and now Chernevog—there was nothing wrong with Eveshka, dammit, she was Eveshka, that was all—and there was more to her than old resentments and present pain. Even if he seemed himself somewhere to have forgotten that. He had not been able to help her. Or nothing that had happened would have happened.

"You amaze me," Chernevog said.

"Snake—"

An odd feeling came on him then, as if Eveshka had spoken to him. He stopped Volkhi and listened to the night-sounds and listened to his heart.

He did not *like* what he was feeling. The pain in his hand was quite acute. And he had the distinct impression that Eveshka's attention had brushed past him and fled him in fear.

Eveshka? he thought.

And felt Chernevog's cold touch on his arm, Chernevog's horse pressing hard against his leg, the darkened woods become a dizzied confusion to his eyes. He thought, He's killing me; and tried to free himself, but there was nothing hostile in what he was feeling, rather that the danger was elsewhere close, that Chernevog was holding on to him and finding something of magic about him that Chernevog did not, no more than the last time, understand or wholly trust or have words for—

But he wanted it, and the boy wanted it—

Rusalki both, he thought, and tried to get past that veil of dizziness and confusion to reach Eveshka, thought then of Sasha, and how he had continually been driven to come this way, into Chernevog's reach—

Things once associated are always associated—he could hear Sasha saying that. No coincidences in magic—

He could hear the whole woods, hear the passage of a deer, the midnight foraging of hares and the life in the trees around him; and under it, through it, a sense of balances gone amiss, and something—

He did not want to look at that. But he tried. And it made no sense to him. It just was, and Chernevog was there, telling him he did not have to understand, not even a wizard could, but that it was where the silence came from and where it went, and the leshys had kept it in check so long as they could—the stone and their ring and the heart of their magic, that this *thing* wanted to drink down—

The leshys were dead. The leshys had misjudged young foolishness, and the self-will of two wizards' hearts—he had not brought Ilyana to them in time. He had not wanted to. He had loved her too much. There had always been time—next year and next.

Misighi, holding Ilyana in his huge arms . . . Misighi, who could break stone with his fingers, returning her so carefully, and striding away from them, never to return to the garden fence, never again that close to them—

God, what did they want? What have they done? If they wanted her, could we have stopped them?

Eveshka—would have tried. Sasha would have—I would have—

Whatever a man could do, I'd do to get her away from that thing. . . .

Whatever all of them could do, they would do to get her back.

The world went hushed then, so abruptly it only gradually dawned on him he was hearing the wind in the leaves, and Chernevog's voice saying his name, bidding him not fall off, damn him—that he had no right to be alive, no more than they did, and that they were, him, and the boy and Chernevog together, and that they knew where they had to go—

"Come *on*, dammit, Eveshka's going after her."

He found the reins somehow, he found his seat and turned Volkhi uphill, as Chernevog was headed, not breakneck after the first ten strides. In the moonless dark and on this root-laddered ground, there was no hurrying—like a bad dream, in which haste could manage only a numbingly slow progress over one hill and another and onto a level stretch overgrown with trees and thorn brakes.

Bits of white horsehair hung from thorns here, and Bielitsa made one futile protest against a wizard's direction; but Volkhi went, panting now, into a barren starlit thicket with no trees to shut out the sky, with only peeling wreckage of dreadful aspect—leshys, Pyetr realized, all dead.

"Eveshka!" he called into that desolation. But no answer came. They rode among dead leshys as far as the stone that was the center and found smoking ashes beside it, where a fire had been.

That, and everything Eveshka owned, her book, her pack, and her abandoned cloak.

"God," he muttered in despair, but Chernevog wanted his attention toward a gap in the thorns, a broad pathway dark as midnight and more threatening.

Magic had made it. That was where Ilyana was, that was where, Chernevog made him believe, Eveshka had surely gone, and he had no question about following—only about his company.

Magic was slipping loose at every hand. Sasha felt it like pieces tumbling out of his hands and there was no way in the world to go faster. Missy was breathing like a bellows even with Nadya's lesser weight and the absence of the packs; young Patches, saddleless, with his weight and the books, Babi's vodka jug and a handful of herb-pots, was blowing lather. It was all confusion of trees and brush and dark hillsides—rough ground, and the god only knew how Nadya was managing, whether it was his distracted wishes for her safety, or her death-grip on the saddle and Missy's mane. Don't lose her, Sasha pleaded with Missy, and promised apples and carrots and every delicacy in the garden if she would only keep Nadya on her back and keep out of trouble.

Babi scrambled onto his shoulder. They were close, god, close enough to the mouse and Eveshka that he could feel presence through the silence. And a gulf dropping away into somewhere dark, deadly and deathly. He could not think of the mouse in that place. He could not think of Pyetr and Eveshka there. They would not be. No!

He thought, while Patches found her own way along a spring-fed thread of water, Mouse, listen to me. *Listen!*

For a moment then he had her, clear and true and very, very, very scared. There was open sky and the smell of the earth and river. He *knew* that place, he knew the feeling of it—the hollowness beneath—

God—

The mouse caught at him, the mouse was frightened, wanted him the way she had in the yard—and came around him, enfolded his wishes—

No, he had said then. Now he said yes. And did a more frightening thing, and wanted Eveshka to know he was there.

Now.

—

Beyond the doorway was starlight and river chill and a grassy edge along the shore—beyond the door was a dream, a very sinister one—as calm and as tranquil a place as the ghosts had been horrid, the water glistening beneath the stars and a fat old willow whispering in the dark. But the heart of this place was hollow and cold, one could feel the falseness of safety here. And one remembered that it was still the palace of bone, and that what one saw was not the truth—or the palace was not. The mouse was very scared, and very quiet, and very determined to have the way out—please the god. And grandfather might have wished her to be born and to be here, but she wished to do things her uncle would approve—that was the wisest thing she could think of.

Make up your own mind, a ghost said, and startled her when she saw it drift from the willow-shade. Mother, she thought, with a cold seizure of fear. But the ghost said:

Your grandmother, dear. Is the old fool telling you lies again? Or can't he tell you?

The bear came out of the shadow, and ambled to her grandmother's side, seeming far less fierce than she had thought. Her grandmother said:

Listen to me—

It was a wish. And it scared her. There was something in this place, something that *made* her want to listen, even knowing her grandmother had been wicked—

No such thing, the ghost said. Do you want Kavi alive again? From here it's easy. Everything is easy—

Uncle would say, Magic is always easy. But is it wise?

Don't you have any thoughts to yourself, child? What do *you* want?

She wanted—

Kavi. And knew it was foolish and selfish and wrong. She turned away, toward the dark rim of the woods at the end of the grass. She wanted to leave.

But something drew her to look back—and her grandmother was not there. There were wolves—and other things that spun in confusion, faces screaming, hands grasping—it wanted, and wanted and wanted, and she wanted it to stop changing! Now!

It did. It became a shriveled old woman and a pack of wolves, and it wanted her youth and her life and her heart. Come here, it bade her. *Listen* to me. . . . And the thing under the earth echoed it and echoed it until she was confused.

No, she said, and told it No again, and it said:

What do you want, wizard?

And she thought, I want—

—and stopped herself at the brink, thinking: You don't catch me twice, on. Go away!

It broke apart. The wolves did. The bits scattered in light and fire.

Not so dreadful, she thought, letting go a breath she had forgotten. I'm all right. I can wish them—

"Ilyana," a voice said behind her back. And she *had* to turn to it—had to—before the echoes of it died in the earth under her feet. It was her mother, white and tattered and dreadful, with shadowed eyes and bloody scratches on her arms, her mother wanting her with more strength than she had ever felt in her life.

No! she bade her mother, and took a step backward.

Look *out!* her mother wished her. Her mother wanted her to look behind her, and the hair prickled on her neck. She thought—it's a trick, it's a trick like the others. She's making that cold feeling. . . .

"No!" her mother said, and started for her, wanting her as she spun about to escape. Wanted her to stop, warned her of death under the willow's branches and for a moment the very earth underfoot seemed to tremble.

Another lie, she thought, and cast a look back at her mother. "Don't come close to me!"

"Ilyana!"

Look, her mother wished her. And wanted what was there into the starlight. Coils rolled out, glistening wet, a head as large as a horse's rose up and grinned at her with white, white teeth.

Something hit her breast and seized her about the neck, familiar arms, a desperate and frightened Babi: she hugged him without any thought but imminent destruction. She wanted Babi safe. That was all she could think of—could muster no conviction against that Thing her mother conjured—

Her *mother* wanted it here.

Her mother said, at her back, "Ilyana, Ilyana, come back, right now. You don't belong here."

She could not move. Perhaps it was wishes. Perhaps it was terror. Babi growled and shivered in her arms.

"Ilyana!" her mother cried, and fear and feeling that never had been, for her, not once, not ever, came flooding up, with anger, and desire that was shattering as Kavi's touch and tender as her father's. Her mother wanted her safe at home, her mother wanted her away from this dreadful place that *she* belonged to.

"Bonesss," the snake said. Hwiuur. She had no doubt. And Babi ducked his head beneath her chin and hissed. So did the vodyanoi, and the air shivered with river cold. "Your mother's bones are still mine. She wants you safe. But you never should have existed, little mouse. She can be my pretty bones again. And what will you be, I wonder? Supper?"

Hwiuur! her mother said, forbidding him.

Hwiuur said, "One or the other is mine. One or the other; and I *own* you, pretty pretty bones, I only haven't pressed matters—I only let the old man think he was clever, sending a mouse to catch a creature far, far cleverer than he was. And ever so patient." More coils poured out of the shadows, glistening wet and black. "On the other hand—you could give me the mouse. And I'd give you—oh, Kiev. Or whatever. Anything you like, pretty bones."

"No," her mother said. And of a sudden someone else was there, god, her *father* was there, and Kavi, and Yvgenie—

The vodyanoi hissed and lunged and Babi jumped from her arms, ran hissing and barking into Hwiuur's face. She wished at the creature—hurt and harm and pain—and only got its sudden attention. It reared up and lunged for her and she furiously wished it no! as thunder rolled down on her from behind and hit her in the back.

The world jolted. A arm was around her waist, she was wholly off her feet and against the side of a white horse.

And her father—oh, *god*—

Volkhi shied off and Pyetr left the saddle, not—not his best dismount, no. He landed on one foot and lost his balance, fell and saw the creature coming down on him, a vast shadow with breath like the grave and there was no time for aim—he shoved his arm at Hwiurr's face and dumped the whole damned herb-pot, salt and sulfur, in the jaws that closed on it—

—and opened again, with a hiss and a fetid breath that he knew in his nightmares. It hurt, god—it hurt, he all but dropped the sword in his good hand, and a coil whipped over him in its wounded frenzy. He hit it. He kept wondering where help was and got his feet under him and hit it again and kept hitting it, with everything he had, while Babi lunged at it and hissed and snarled.

It grew smaller, and smaller, and its struggles never ceased. Neither did his hitting it, until it was a shriveled black thing, with arms like a man, hiding its face with its hands and wailing, "No more, no more, man, oh, the bitter salt—"

"Let my wife and my daughter go! Let them alone! Do you hear me?" Another whack with the sword. "Do you swear?"

"Yes," it cried, "yes, yes, no more."

Eveshka was with him, Eveshka stayed his arm and hugged his shoulder, saying, "It won't die. It can't die. They don't."

"Ilyana—"

The pain stopped. The fear for the mouse did. The mouse was very well, give or take bruises, with the boy's arm about her, and she was safe right now, no matter the quality of her suitors—Yvgenie Kurov was a damned fine rider, thank the god: wizardry might keep a man on a horse—but never guide a catch like that.

Hwiuur made a move to slither away. Pyetr hit him. What Eveshka wished he could not tell, but the air felt heavy. And Hwiuur shrank and shrank until he was like a withered, glistening serpent again.

"Make him swear by the sun," the boy said—but that was Chernevog. "He's afraid of that, at least. Make him swear."

"I swear by the sun!" it cried in a faint, high voice. "I'll never, ever, ever do harm to you. I'll be your friend. You'll see, I'll bring you such nice gifts—I'll never harm anyone in your house—"

"Nor our children or their children," Eveshka said, "forever! Nor our friends or theirs!"

"I swear, I swear to everything you say!"

"Hit him," Chernevog said. Pyetr hit him, and Hwiuur added, "By the sun, by the terrible sun! I swear! Let me go."

"We have to be away ourselves," Chernevog said. "This place itself is a ghost. And it won't outlast the sun."

He had greatest misgivings. But he lifted his sword and stood back, and let the creature slither away toward the willow.

Babi was faster. Babi pounced, and swallowed, and sat up with his small hands folded across his belly.

And licked his lips.

The stars were gone. In a while more there would be sun, but Sasha refused to dwell on that thought. He said, aloud or not he did not clearly notice, More wood. And thought, Mouse. Pyetr. Eveshka. Time you were moving.

One did not know clearly that everything was well. But there had been a moment that he felt he could breathe again.

In a bit more Missy made a soft, worried sound, and horses arrived out of the dark. They trotted up to Missy and Patches, trailing reins, glad to find friends. There had been snakes. Volkhi's rider had ridden him straight at a snake and fallen off in front of it. Volkhi was never going near any snakes again, never, ever. Even if his favorite person wanted to be, he would not. No. And Bielitsa thought the same.

Worrisome. Exceedingly worrisome. He looked at Nadya across the fire they had made on this barren, windy hilltop, and she looked back at him, scared and staunchly not saying a word. For a moment he did not know what more he could do than he had done.

But he wanted his family back. He wanted them to meet Nadya. To have evenings together. By a nice fire. Hundreds and hundreds of thousands of evenings. One would not accept otherwise.

And of a sudden he felt very much better. *Very* much better.

He said, on a long sigh, "Bring them back, Babi, bring them here. Vodka, Babi."

He unstopped the jug. He poured. Babi was immediately there to catch it, a very satisfied Babi. One could tell.

Then he heard the mouse cry, "Uncle Sasha!" and saw the lostlings coming out of the dark, the mouse, hand in hand with young Yvgenie. Pyetr with Eveshka. He felt everything at once, too confused to defend himself from them until Nadya rose and stood beside him.

He put his arm about Nadya as she did and wished her well—wished 'Veshka not to be upset, please. Nor the mouse. Yvgenie said, "Nadya?" and came and took her hand, but to a wizard's hearing it was very clear where hearts were, and Yvgenie's was most honestly with the mouse.

"I *like* her," the mouse said, quite sure herself where Yvgenie's heart was. And Kavi Chernevog's as well, the god help them.

Then Eveshka wished something at Nadya quite strongly, not at him, Sasha thought, but about him—and Nadya said, hugging his arm the tighter, "Yes. I know he is," leaving him the most distinct impression Eveshka judged him extravagantly kindly, *far* too kindly, considering his recent succession of mistakes. . . .

Which he did not want to tell Eveshka yet. But he feared he had just let the worst one slip. God, they could *see* it for themselves: Pyetr was changed. Or the same again. Pyetr might always be the same, for all he knew, and it all was his fault, god—he wanted them not to hate him. He wanted them to love him. Nothing worse could happen to him than losing that. And wishing them not to was desperately, terribly wrong of him. So they should love each other. Not minding him and his wishes. Please.

There was a breathless hush then, in a piled-up calamity of possible wishes, wise and foolish, thick as the fallen leaves. But Pyetr said, "Sasha," strolled over, kissed his eldest daughter on the forehead, then set a heavy hand on his shoulder and looked him straight in the eye, thinking, as if he had only chanced upon the thought—You did something, friend. Didn't you? Like the damn teacup? The jug that won't empty? Eveshka thinks so.

"Pyetr, forgive me, I'm—"

"—sorry?" Pyetr shook him gently. He heard a laughter in Pyetr's voice this morning, a youthfulness that could have no patience with slow-moving wizards and their deliberations. "—Does the teacup care? It's lasted this long: it might last longer. Who knows? —Who ever knows? Dare we even mention my seeing grandchildren?"

ABOUT THE AUTHOR

C.J. Cherryh was born in St. Louis, Missouri, but has spent most of her life in Oklahoma. She now lives in Oklahoma City. She has a BA in Latin, an MA in Classics, plus additional language courses; she also qualified in field archeology, but never practiced. She was a professional translator in French, and has taught Latin, Greek, and Ancient History.

Her first novel, *Gate of Ivrel*, was published in 1976, and she quickly became a leading writer of both fantasy and science fiction. She received two Hugo Awards, one for her short story, *Cassandra*, and the second for her novel, *Downbelow Station*. Her novel *Rusalka* was published by Del Rey in 1989, and *Chernevog* in 1990.

In her own words:

"I write full time; I travel; I try things out. I've outrun a dog pack in the hills of Thebes and seen *Columbia* lift on her first flight. I've fallen down a cave, nearly drowned, broken an arm, been kicked by horses, fended off an amorous merchant in a tent bazaar, slept on deck in the Adriatic, and driven Picadilly Circus at rush hour. I've waded in two oceans and four of the seven seas, and I want to visit the Amazon, the Serengeti, and see the volcano in Antarctica. I can read history in a potsherd, observe time in a stream-bank, and function in a gadget ancient or modern—none of which has ever cured me of losing my car keys or putting things together before I read the instructions."